AN AWAKENED PASSION

Eve felt forbidden heat in her body again. She'd never kissed a man before.

Why would she? She was a nun. It was wrong. Right?

God forgive her, it didn't *feel* wrong. And she wanted to do it again.

She closed her eyes and leaned forward, opening her mouth in invitation.

Adam answered with a kiss so tender, she wondered if she imagined it. But nay. His touch was real. His breath was warm.

Fearing he'd pull away, she angled her head, deepening the kiss. But then she feared he *wouldn't* pull away, that she'd be swallowed, body and soul. She faltered, unable to decide whether to stop or go on.

He decided for her. He pulled her into his embrace.

This work is a work of fiction. Names, places, characters and incidents are the product of the author's imagination or are used fictitiously. Any resemblance to actual events, locales or persons, living or dead, is coincidental.

LAIRD OF SMOKE

Glynnis Campbell – Publisher
P.O. Box 341144
Arleta, California 91331
Contact: glynnis@glynnis.net

Cover design by Richard Campbell
Formatting by Author E.M.S.

ISBN-13: 978-1-63480-147-8

Published in the United States of America

LAIRD OF SMOKE

The Warrior Lairds of Rivenloch, Book 3

DEDICATION

For anyone
who feels invisible...
I see you.

OTHER BOOKS BY GLYNNIS CAMPBELL

THE WARRIOR MAIDS OF RIVENLOCH
The Shipwreck (novella)
A Yuletide Kiss (short story)
Lady Danger
Captive Heart
Knight's Prize

THE WARRIOR DAUGHTERS OF RIVENLOCH
The Storming (novella)
A Rivenloch Christmas (short story)
Bride of Fire
Bride of Ice
Bride of Mist

THE WARRIOR LAIRDS OF RIVENLOCH
Laird of Steel
Laird of Flint
Laird of Smoke

THE KNIGHTS OF DE WARE
The Handfasting (novella)
My Champion
My Warrior
My Hero

MEDIEVAL OUTLAWS
The Reiver (novella)
Danger's Kiss
Passion's Exile
Desire's Ransom

THE SCOTTISH LASSES
The Outcast (novella)
MacFarland's Lass
MacAdam's Lass
MacKenzie's Lass

THE CALIFORNIA LEGENDS
Native Gold
Native Wolf
Native Hawk

ACKNOWLEDGMENTS

My sincere gratitude to

Rich, Brynna, and Dylan,
who never hesitate to answer questions like
"How would you pick a handcuff lock?"
"Can I get away with a food fight in a medieval?" and
"Does this description sound like a roundhouse kick?"

Amy Atwell, Kirby, and Jill Glass,
whose talent, integrity, and reliability
keep my anxiety at bay

Becca Syme,
who helped me recover my JoieDeVotion
and blesses me with her brilliance

Glynnis Campbell's Readers Clan
for their love and loyalty

Peanut (RIP),
for being the best little writing buddy

Tom Holland and Tatiana Maslany
for their inspiration

CHAPTER 1

The best thing about being a nun was the invisibility.

Eve tucked a stray wisp of her chestnut hair under her plain white veil. She lowered her eyes to the damp sod, her manner dutiful, humble. With her tresses hidden, and her feminine curves obscured by a nondescript gray habit, she was completely unnoticeable. Dull. Ordinary. No more conspicuous than a dead autumn leaf blowing along the ground.

Now she could venture wherever she willed without drawing attention. Which was how she managed to steal her way into the middle of the angry throng gathered before Perth Castle.

No one gave her a second glance as she wove her way through camps of striped clan pavilions, sparring soldiers, and muttering lairds. She attracted no attention as she shuffled past them all. Men-at-arms sharpening their weapons. Horses in harness stamping the sod. Maids in greasy aprons cooking oatcakes over scattered fires.

She'd learned about the siege at Perth at the nunnery.

Her convent sisters might not be the most worldly women. But they had an ear for news and a penchant for gossip.

Word was King Malcolm had at last returned from abroad and was back home in Scotland.

Many of his lairds, however, were unhappy. They felt young Malcolm had made too many gestures of friendliness toward King Henry of England. At Toulouse, he'd even dared to side with Henry against Scotland's ancient ally, France.

Rumor had it Malcolm had courted Henry's affections simply for the honor of being knighted by the powerful king. If that had been the end of it, his moment of youthful vanity and hero worship might have been forgiven by the lairds. But to further appease Henry, Malcolm had offered to return to the English king some of the Scots lairds' hard-won clan lands.

Six of the malcontent lairds had therefore gathered troops to lay siege to Perth Castle, where the Scots king currently resided. They hoped to force Malcolm to renounce his alliance with Henry and to secure the return of their holdings.

It was a challenging situation. King Malcolm could hardly go back on his word and undermine his new friendship with Henry. But as Eve passed through the ranks of clansmen, she heard their bitterness, their animosity. They felt betrayed by their king. The king to whom they'd once sworn an oath of fealty.

As Eve saw it, there was just one thing that transcended loyalty to king and clan.

One force that could unite them all.

One entity capable of returning peace to the realm.

God.

A sennight ago, sitting in her humble cell, packing her things, Eve had felt sure she could be a much-needed agent of change. She could bring the Lord God to these negotiations. Certainly she had the diplomacy to broker peace between the king and the clans. To be the instrument of His will.

It was what she always hoped. Spreading the word of God was her duty as a nun, after all.

Unfortunately, the abbess at the convent didn't always agree with Eve's liberal interpretation of God's will. So Eve usually had to do the Lord's work on her own, without the abbess's knowledge.

Of course, Eve always confessed to whatever liberties she'd taken. Eventually. Then the abbess would furrow her brow, chew at her lip, and shake her head. But the large stipend Eve's father sent to the convent was usually enough to keep the abbess from protesting too much.

It wasn't that Eve was intentionally willful. She simply couldn't help her sense of conviction. She got bored with the everyday charity the sisters practiced. Collecting alms for the poor. Feeding the hungry. Praying for the sick.

Eve was meant for more. She could feel that, even though the abbess warned her that was only the sin of pride whispering in her ear.

Eve didn't believe that. She simply wanted to do good in the world. To right wrongs. To balance injustices. To take a stand for those who couldn't defend themselves.

It was the reason she'd agreed several days ago to help an old acquaintance, Sir Hew du Lac of Rivenloch. The poor lovelorn Sir Hew had been torn from the object of his affections, Lady Carenza. Due to a series of unfortunate circumstances, Carenza had been mistakenly betrothed to Hew's *cousin,* the illustrious Sir Gellir Cameliard. Natually, Hew was devastated.

As for Eve, she'd been more than happy to help untangle the star-crossed hearts. Praying for God's blessing on her good deed, she'd stolen the bride-to-be right from under the bridegroom Gellir's nose and spirited her away to the convent to marry Sir Hew in a clandestine wedding.

Had her intervention been a wee bit daring? Aye.

Had abducting the bride of a Rivenloch warrior come with risk? No doubt.

But Eve didn't mind danger when it came to steering the course of fate. Especially when it was clearly God's intention and in the best interests of everyone. When it came to the Lord's good works, Eve felt it was her calling to help Him carry them out.

As was this.

After all, God couldn't possibly intend for King Malcolm to be welcomed home from France by six irate lairds with drawn swords.

Obviously what was needed here was divine intervention. Proving to both parties that there were more important things at stake than who owned what or who was friends with whom.

They just needed to be convinced that God favored the Scots and smiled on King Malcolm.

That all parties wished for the same thing—peace in the land and harmony among the clans.

That God meant to bless the Scots with health and wealth and prosperity.

It wasn't exactly *untrue*, though Eve suspected God left men largely to their own devices. He was too busy moving heaven and earth to care much whether men warred among themselves.

Still, it was certainly true that a people at peace were more productive and happy. So she was certain God would approve.

Before she could make her way toward the gathering lairds, however, a skirmish broke out. Caught up in the clamor, Eve was elbowed aside as warriors rushed forward with their weapons drawn.

Peering between the crush of bodies, Eve was astonished to glimpse a familiar figure. It was the groom she'd disappointed by stealing his bride. The magnificent Sir Gellir of Rivenloch. What was the great knight doing here?

He appeared to be wielding his mighty sword. In defense of the king. And against the lairds.

All six of them.

Singlehandedly.

Her breath caught. One man against six? The Rivenloch warriors certainly got embroiled in some perilous undertakings.

Then she noticed Sir Gellir wasn't quite alone. An odd-looking monk battled at his side with surprising expertise.

Eve could tell, long before the monk's hood fell back, spilling free a waterfall of fiery curls, that the fierce fighter was a woman. She supposed she shouldn't be surprised. After all, the Rivenloch clan was known for its fighting females.

Still, she was no Rivenloch lass that Eve recognized.

There seemed to be a bond between the two fighters. Gellir was resolute in his efforts to protect the woman from their foes. And the lass battled like a vixen defending her mate.

A smile curved the corner of Eve's lip. It appeared the spurned bridegroom had wasted no time finding a new ladylove. This was further proof Eve *had* done the right thing in absconding with Gellir's betrothed. Lady Carenza was never meant to be his. *This* was obviously the woman with whom Gellir belonged. A happy ending like this pleased Eve and made the messy details unimportant.

At least she *hoped* they would have a happy ending. They were still two against six.

But soon, incredibly, it appeared the pair of sparring sweethearts were beginning to win the upper hand.

Suddenly a bold shout rang out from the crowd. *"Audite!"*

The combatants began to lower their weapons. The skirmish dwindled and slowly came to a halt.

"Audite!"

All eyes were drawn to the tall monk inviting them to listen.

He peeled back his cowl, revealing his face.

Eve took in a sharp breath. And suddenly she couldn't take another.

She'd never seen a man so perfectly made.

So handsome.

So heavenly.

So heart-melting.

This must be the man God had fashioned in His image.

He was broad-shouldered. Imposing. Confident, with an air of calm authority.

Dark curls framed his flawless face. His square jaw, cleanly shaved, was resolute. His chin lifted proudly, and yet he seemed to look down his nose at no one.

His expressive brows lowered fervently above eyes that glittered with the spark of passion and life. Eyes that could melt a woman's heart. Or penetrate a woman's soul. Or convince a woman to forget all about her religious calling.

Only then did Eve remember to breathe.

In the silence, he spoke in a low, rich, rolling voice colored by a soft foreign accent. A voice that made her think of the delicious wassail Sister Eithne served at Christmas. The concoction that warmed Eve to her bones and left her delightfully dizzy.

"I have brought word from *Roma*," he announced, "from His Holiness."

The crowd gasped. Eve's heart skipped a beat.

Was it true? Had the man come from Rome?

No wonder he looked so divine. He was a messenger from the Pope.

He lifted a rolled parchment in one hand. His sleeve slipped up a few inches, exposing a well-muscled forearm.

With his free hand, he solemnly made the sign of the cross.

Reflexively, Eve mirrored the gesture.

All at once, King Malcolm called down to him from the tower of Perth Castle. "You there! Did you say His Holiness?"

"*Si! Il Papa* Alexander III!" the monk called back. "You are *Rex Scotiae?*"

"We are," the king confirmed.

"Then, *Signore,* the missive is for your ears as well."

A message from the Pope to the king? Could he intend to broker peace?

Her mind reeled. Then, as soon as she could think straight, a reprehensible idea slipped into Eve's brain.

Never mind that the holy monk was handsome and compelling and persuasive.

He was about to undermine her ambitions and foil her plans to save the day.

Of course that thought was beneath her. Prideful. Ridiculous. Did it matter who handled the negotiations? As long as the results were beneficial, what difference did it make who initiated them?

If the Pope wished to claim credit for solving the conflict, so be it. After all, she'd said it herself. A happy ending made the details unimportant.

Yet the thought kept biting at her like a determined flea.

For months, she'd longed to do something important.

More important than rescuing pups from abusive owners.

More significant than praying over sick children.

More heroic than helping a knight elope with his true love.

And now, when she finally had an opportunity to prove her worth, who had shown up to ruin her plans? None other than the esteemed representative of the Pope himself.

She sighed.

It was an unspeakably selfish thought. She knew that. Selfish and unworthy of her station as a nun. The abbess had even told her so. But she'd always had a hard time controlling her wayward thoughts.

Like the wayward thoughts she was having now as she let her gaze course down the monk's impressive form.

His cassock, belted below his waist, clung to his narrow hips and trim buttocks. The powerful gestures he made as he spoke to the lairds belied the sedentary life of a monk. His hands were muscular, closing into fists and then opening with strength and grace. He held one commanding finger aloft to make a point. Then he clasped his hands together like a warrior celebrating his victory.

She could imagine those manly fingers running through her hair...caressing her cheek...brushing her lips...

She started as he turned to follow the lairds, across the bridge from the bailey to the motte. Of course. King Malcolm wasn't coming to *them*. He'd naturally conduct negotiations privately, in the comfort of his keep. A place a mere nun couldn't follow. No matter how invisible she was.

Shite.

She'd hoped to make the acquaintance of the Pope's representative. After all, he was an important man in the church.

She frowned.

Then she straightened with determination. She could fix this.

She'd simply wait for him to emerge, she decided, and strike up a conversation with him. Inquire about some biblical interpretation or request moral direction. Before they parted, she'd whisper her name in his ear and ask him to pass it along to the Pope. Perhaps, with holy guidance from on high, Eve could find her Greater Purpose.

It was a worthy notion.

However, her plans to wait patiently among the pavilions were foiled when a contingent of Rivenlochs suddenly arrived.

Sweet Saints! Had they followed her?

Eve dared not let them see her. Any of the Rivenloch clanfolk might recognize her. She was the nun who'd been at Darragh Castle for the clan wedding, after all—right before Sir Gellir's betrothed had mysteriously disappeared.

Nuns might be invisible, but the Rivenlochs were clever and discerning. With the exception of Sir Hew, of course. Hew, not realizing Eve was a nun, had once tried to court her.

In any event, she needed to slip out of sight and watch from afar.

The worst thing about being a Rivenloch, Adam decided, was the visibility.

The clan was so well-known, it was nigh impossible for a Rivenloch man to blink an eye without someone reporting it to the town crier.

Yet, despite being the nephew of the laird, Adam la Nuit had somehow escaped the curse of Rivenloch fame. His cousins and even his sister were renown for their words and deeds. But no one really saw or remembered Adam. Which was how he was able to pose as the emissary of the Pope.

He supposed any other man would have been shaking in his boots to commit such sacrilege.

But Adam wasn't afraid. Situations like this seldom frightened him. Indeed, his unflappable nature made his Rivenloch kin assume he was fearless.

That wasn't quite true.

There were things Adam feared. Rabid wolves. Debilitating sickness. Being permanently marked by a scar that would make him forever identifiable.

But feigning to be the messenger of the Pope? That didn't scare him.

After all, he reasoned, no one in Scotland knew what the Pope's emissaries looked like. If indeed the Pope even *had* such emissaries.

Adam spoke passable Latin, and he could feign a respectable Roman accent.

Besides, he'd played lofty roles before. The French artist Godefroid de Claire. The German Minnesänger Meinloh von Sevelingen. The mystic Hildegard of Bingen. To obtain free lodging, he'd once posed as the right hand man of young King Malcolm himself, while his cousin Brand pretended to be the king.

Adam was confident of his skills. He was a good mimic. He had a forgettable face. And it didn't hurt that he was the son of spies. No doubt Lady Miriel and Sir Rand had passed on to him their natural talents for stealth and secrecy.

Of course, he'd met King Malcolm before—as himself, Sir Adam la Nuit of Rivenloch. The Rivenlochs were some of the king's most loyal and valuable vassals. They'd protected Scotland's southern border for centuries.

But garbed as a monk in holy robes? The king failed to recognize Adam, even in the close quarters of his great hall.

Adam had originally come here on a rescue mission. After his cousin Gellir was abandoned at the altar by his betrothed, the despondent bridegroom had headed to Perth, determined to fight for the king's honor. Or die trying.

It was that second part that had spurred Adam to follow Gellir.

Adam had worked hard all his life to measure up to the standards of the Rivenloch clan. To be as dedicated as Brand. As fierce as Hew. As magnificent as Gellir.

In the end, he'd had to come to terms with the truth. He would never be as noteworthy or celebrated as his cousins. He would always stand in their shadows.

Eventually he realized the truth. By keeping to the shadows, he could better protect them. His weapon was his anonymity. A weapon he wielded with great skill.

This time he'd used it to keep Gellir from making a foolish sacrifice.

He'd brought along Merraid the maidservant, also disguised as a monk. He knew the lass had feelings for Gellir. Perhaps she'd help persuade Gellir to abandon his self-destructive fight.

Instead, Merraid proved her affections by joining the battle at Gellir's side. Thankfully, she could hold her own. Trained by Adam's sister, Feiyan, Merraid had considerable warrior skills.

As it turned out, she also had an impressive gift for words. She managed to scribble out for Adam a diplomatic missive, ostensibly from the Pope, meant to forge peace between the lairds and the king.

And it had worked.

Adam had delivered the message. The king was content. The lairds were mollified. And Gellir was out of danger.

All Adam needed to do now was destroy the evidence and tie up the loose ends.

Passing by a small campfire, he discreetly dropped the scrawled missive into the flames, where it was quickly consumed.

As far as witnesses, Gellir and Merraid were the only ones who could identify Adam.

He knew Merraid wouldn't breathe a word.

And his cousin Gellir would never disclose his identity. Indeed, Gellir had aided him, taking Adam's satchel for safekeeping while the "Pope's messenger" handled the negotiations in the keep.

But as Adam brushed past his cousin to surreptitiously retrieve the satchel, he spotted an entire company of familiar faces.

Shite.

His whole clan was here.

Seizing the satchel and pulling his hood low over his eyes, he reversed direction and turned back toward the castle.

Damn.

A pair of puffing, red-faced monks were swiftly waddling his way. No doubt they wished to speak with the esteemed emissary of the Pope, hoping His holiness would rub off on them.

Adam angled again, striding off toward the forest so abruptly that he knocked someone aside.

A swift glance told him it was a wee figure in gray.

A second glance revealed it was a lass. A lass whose breathtaking face was instantly engraved on his mind.

He hesitated, intending to apologize, but unable to form words.

A third glance revealed she was a nun.

She opened her mouth to speak, and panic widened his eyes.

He whirled to make a hasty escape.

The naive King Malcolm had been easy to impress. A pair of awestruck monks he could handle. But a nun?

Nuns were notoriously well-educated. A nun might ask him questions he couldn't answer. Questions about scripture. Or Rome. Or what the Pope ate for supper.

He needed to get to a place of concealment and divest from his vestments before anyone grew the wiser.

Eve arched a brow as the Pope's emissary fled in terror.

How rude, she thought. He'd bumped into her. Made no apology. And then set off again as if pursued by demons.

She frowned in disappointment. Perhaps that was the way of those close to the Pope. Perhaps they had no time for ordinary folk.

Or perhaps Roman law forbade men of the cloth to speak with women.

Or maybe he thought the collision was *her* fault, that she'd planted herself in his holy way.

At any rate, his stride was too long for her to attempt to chase after him. She feared the effort would have been useless anyway. Gazing at him at such close range had left her utterly tongue-tied.

She wondered if all Romans were so handsome. His sun-kissed skin had glowed from the shadow of his hood. His dark eyes had gleamed with divining interest. His mouth had softened and then tensed as he turned to go. It was a face she'd never forget.

Then she blew out a dissatisfied breath. She supposed she'd come to Perth for nothing. She was no closer to performing a great act of service than before. She'd been unable to even send along her best wishes to the Holy Father.

As for the Pope's man, he'd apparently achieved what he'd come for. The king and the lairds were all smiles when they emerged from the castle. Spying from the back of the crowd, she learned King Malcolm had even granted Sir Gellir and his loyal maidservant Merraid permission to be wed.

At least someone was enjoying a happily-ever-after ending.

Lingering a bit longer, she overheard the soldiers talking about an upcoming tournament in a fortnight. The king had insisted Sir Gellir's nuptials take place at Perth. And because it was a Rivenloch affair, a tournament would naturally follow.

Eve smiled to herself as a new plan formed in her head. Perhaps all was not lost after all.

CHAPTER 2

Adam squinted through the slit of his jousting helm. A fortnight had passed since he'd shown up at Perth as the Pope's emissary. Long enough for the king to forget his face. Still, it was wise to keep his identity secret. Particularly since most of his clan was here to celebrate Gellir's marriage with a royal tournament.

He eyed up his opponent across the list.

It was his cousin Brand, mounted on his destrier, impatient for battle. Even with a great helm covering his face and his lance at rest, Brand had an ominous presence that made him look ready to kill.

But Adam wasn't afraid. Brand's growl was worse than his bite. Besides, Brand had recently discovered that ladies preferred knights who were merciful over those who were ruthless. Adam was confident Brand would cause him no intentional harm. Not at a friendly wedding tournament.

There was a good chance Brand *would* knock him off his horse. Adam had had to purchase an inferior beast he'd never jousted on before. And jousting wasn't his best event. He preferred contests that required dexterity and speed rather than brute force.

He also preferred to fight under an assumed name. Which was why today he'd been introduced only as *Le Goupil,* the Fox, of Paris. He had donned weathered leather and pitted armor, a helm swathed in russet silk, and a dark blue surcoat featuring a snarling fox.

Competing anonymously allowed him to engage in the challenge of combat without the risk of bringing dishonor to the Rivenloch name.

He'd already come to terms with the fact that he would never be the warrior his cousins were. He would probably never even best his older sister, Feiyan, who had trained with their mother's master from the Orient, Sung Li.

Adam certainly had no wish to disappoint his parents at a public tournament, especially one overseen by the king. If he competed as Adam la Nuit, he'd be judged by Rivenloch standards. But fighting as an unknown, he might be praised for his talents.

Adam did have considerable combat skills. He was observant. He learned by studying. By mimicking the battle techniques of his kin—Gellir's fine swordsmanship, Feiyan's dexterity, Hew's skill with an axe, Jenefer's archery—he had come close to mastering them. So it was a rewarding challenge to do battle with his cousins.

He had to admit he also derived a certain satisfaction from deceiving his clan with his many costumes.

"Sir Brand Cameliard o' Rivenloch," the herald announced.

An enormous cheer went up from the clan as Brand lifted a hand in acknowledgment.

"Ridin' against *Le Goupil* o' Paris."

Adam lifted his hand. There were a few polite shouts of encouragement.

Then both riders watched for the herald to drop the silk that would begin the joust.

The scarf drifted down, and Adam spurred his horse forward.

It was over in one pass.

All Adam could remember afterward, lying in the dust on his back with the wind knocked out of him, was a brief thunder of hooves, a jarring blow to his chest, and the sensation of flying over his horse's arse.

Brand leaped from his horse, tore off his helm, and rushed over, offering him a hand.

Adam took it gladly. Wrenched upright again, he was able to cough and catch his breath.

Brand clapped him companionably on the back, then waved his hand to accept the men's cheers and the ladies' impressed sighs at his honorable behavior.

It was customary for a man who unhorsed his opponent to claim the horse as his prize. But Brand had access to dozens of horses in the Rivenloch stables. They were far finer than the one Adam had purchased. So Brand made another virtuous gesture.

"I wish to give the animal I've won to the newly made bride and knight, Lady Merraid."

The women erupted in another round of jubilant cries.

That was clever, Adam decided. Clever and amusing. Growing up, his cousin had taken no interest in the fairer sex. Brand had deemed lasses inferior, useless, and troublesome. It was only in the past few months he'd decided they might be worth his time and attention.

The gift was perfect. Merraid was delighted to own her first horse. And Gellir was pleased with his brother's gesture.

Seeing their faces shining with joy, Adam was truly glad he'd been able to play a part in bringing them together.

They came forward to claim her prize. Neither of them recognized Adam in his helm. But Merraid took the horse's reins and placed a hand on Adam's arm.

"Thank ye, sir. I shall treat her with kindness."

Adam bowed his head.

Gellir came near enough to murmur, "You rode well, sir. Not many can stand against my brother's lance."

Adam, who never ceased to be amazed when his own

kin couldn't recognize him, watched them lead the horse away. Then he limped from the lists, wondering if he'd ever find a love like Merraid and Gellir shared. If he'd ever have a grand wedding with a tournament like this.

He grimaced as a sharp pain cut across his ribs.

It might have been from the impact of Brand's lance.

Or it might have been his heart flinching in response at the painful truth.

Adam would never find a bride.

No woman would ever fall in love with him.

Not only was he forgettable. He wasn't the same man from day to day.

How could a woman want a man when she'd never know who he truly was?

"Jehan from Rouen!" the herald announced.

Beneath her hood of forest green, Eve adjusted the brown linen cloth over her face so only her eyes were showing. Then she strode forward with the bold steps and outthrust chest of a cocky lad, waving at the crowd with her free hand. Her woolen cloak covered a nut brown tunic and hose. A leather bracer protected her left forearm. A pair of worn boots two inches too big completed her garb. Slung over one shoulder was a yew longbow and a quiver of arrows.

To all appearances, she was who she claimed to be. Jehan from Rouen. A young French archer.

Today she didn't intend to be invisible.

Today she planned to win an archery prize.

Since this was a Rivenloch tournament, and since King Malcolm himself was hosting, the prizes had been quite generous. The winner of this competition would receive a gold medallion engraved with a longbow. The second place would win a similar medallion of silver.

Thus far, Eve had advanced through the ranks of archers. Now she was left with one final opponent. Jenefer mac Giric of Rivenloch.

Eve didn't stand a chance of winning. Jenefer of Rivenloch was legendary for her skills. But Eve was a fairly good shot. She would be content to come in second.

Stopping at the limit line, she swung the bow off her shoulder, eyeing the straw target.

In boring stretches at the convent, to the abbess's dismay, Eve often made a habit of practicing with a bow, shooting at rotten wine barrels, carcasses left over from supper, and once, at a straw effigy she'd made of a local priest who had ruthlessly impregnated a number of novices.

For his transgressions, the priest had paid no penance. At least not in *this* life. For her sin of crafting the effigy, however, Eve had been commanded to make a pilgrimage to St. Andrews. A pilgrimage that had turned out to be more enjoyable than punitive.

What the abbess didn't know about Eve's archery practice was that she perfected her skills in order to hunt deer in the forest for the hungry crofters. The king's law would have called it poaching. But Eve saw the surplus of deer and her talent with a bow as God's way of providing for his faithful servants.

Eve plucked an arrow from her quiver and nocked it into the bowstring. Due to her size, she couldn't wield a heavy warrior's bow. But what she lacked in power, she made up for in accuracy. She hoped to prove that now. She inhaled, then held her breath.

In one smooth motion, she lifted the bow, pulled back the bowstring, and let loose the arrow.

It landed a scant inch from the center.

The crowd applauded.

"Jenefer mac Giric o' Rivenloch," the herald announced.

Because Jenefer was a battlefield archer, she was accustomed to hitting targets on the run. With almost no preparation, she stepped to the line and shot. The arrow sailed straight and hit dead center.

Her clanfolk cheered.

Eve hoped she'd never meet Jenefer in battle. She stepped up to take her second shot, reminding herself of her motivation for winning.

She meant to deliver her prize to Prior Isaac at nearby Scone Priory. She'd made a visit to the priory last year, hoping to meet with the prior regarding funds for the convent's library. While she was waiting for an audience, she happened to note the coldness of the nave and the lack of peat on the hearth. In her efforts to correct the situation, Eve started a fire that quickly escaped the hearth and burned out of control. A fire which ended up destroying several tomes and documents, including the original foundation charter of the priory.

She'd naturally fled. Not for her own sake. But for that of her convent. She wouldn't dream of bringing that kind of shame upon them.

Still, she carried the weight of that debt on her shoulders. So today, if she won a silver or—even better—a gold medallion, she intended to compensate the prior for his losses in the form of a donation from an anonymous wealthy patron.

With holy purpose in her heart, she drew back her bow. This time the arrow arced and dropped, striking so close to Jenefer's that the fletching quivered.

The crowd oohed. Now the match was afoot.

Undaunted, Jenefer stepped to the line, scowling at the target, and nocked her arrow.

What she didn't realize—and what Eve could see clearly—was a bee had landed on her shooting arm and was crawling its way toward her hand.

Eve wanted to call out, to warn her. But it was too late. Jenefer had already planted her feet and was raising the bow to her cheek.

The bee hopped onto her face just as Jenefer loosed her arrow. Smashed between her cheek and her hand, it stung her thumb. It wasn't enough to completely ruin her aim. But after Jenefer cursed and brushed away the pesky beast, she saw the shaft had missed the center by an inch.

Now they were tied.

But Eve thought perhaps it hadn't been a fair contest.

"Madame," she said in the low, hoarse voice of a French youth, "the Devil sent that bee. You may shoot again, if you wish."

But Jenefer, normally renown for her fiery temper, simply shook her head. "If I can be distracted by a wee bee, I don't deserve to win."

Eve thought that was a very Rivenloch thing to say. The clan was known for their sense of honor. So she nodded and stepped up to the line for her final attempt.

Sending up a prayer that God would keep His wee bees at bay for one moment, Eve drew an arrow from her quiver.

Then she happened to glance off to the side of the field, where the crowd stood watching. Her eyes paused on a knight in a dark blue surcoat emblazoned with the figure of a fox. He held a jousting helm in the crook of his arm. His head was coifed in padded linen which was tied to cover the lower part of his face as well. Only his eyes showed above the coif. Staring at her. But she would have recognized them anywhere.

Adam narrowed his gaze.

It couldn't be.

And yet he was so sure those were the eyes imprinted

on his brain. The lovely, wide, beautiful brown orbs of the nun he'd nearly trampled in this very place a fortnight ago.

Surely he was wrong.

This was no nun. This was a young lad. An archer. French, if the calls of "Jehan!" were meant for him.

The lass he'd run into had most definitely been a nun. And though she'd said not a word, she'd had a wild Scottish look about her. Fair skin with a smattering of freckles. Fine, dark brows that had arched in judgment. An unruly lock of chestnut hair that had escaped her veil to curl upon her delicate cheek.

If it wasn't the nun, perhaps it was a relative of hers. He furrowed his brow and watched.

Though he hadn't been following the archery, a quick glance at the target showed it was a close match. The lad must be good if he was keeping up with Jenefer.

It certainly wasn't apparent from the lad's manner now. He dropped his arrow. And when he went to pick it up, the whole quiver slipped down over his arm.

Flustered, ducking his head, the lad retrieved the arrows and slid the quiver back onto his shoulder. Then he blew out a forceful breath and approached the shooting line again.

He nocked the arrow and drew. But he seemed to have trouble steadying the bow. And the longer he hesitated, the more his muscles trembled. And the more his aim strayed.

When he finally let loose the shaft, it sailed far wide of the mark, lodging outside the target in the margins of the straw. The crowd ahhed in disappointment.

Jenefer had the final shot. As usual, she spent no time in preparation. She swiftly and easily added another arrow to the cluster in the center to win the match.

"Hey, *Goupil!*" someone called out from the crowd, distracting Adam. "Are ye fightin' in the melee?"

The melee was the last event of the tournament. It was

the most dangerous. It was also the most fun. A free-for-all mock battle with blunted weapons that could nonetheless do damage in the right hands.

Adam's ribs were already aching from the joust. Even a light tap would mean a few days of coddling his injuries.

Still, he had enough Rivenloch spirit to accept the challenge. *"Mais oui!"*

The melee was also risky for another reason. In close combat, *Le Goupil* was much more likely to be recognized. He'd therefore continue to wear his padded linen coif to conceal his face and replace his jousting helm with a coif of chain mail.

He needed to return to his pavilion to prepare. The melee was next.

He turned back to the archery field in time to see the second place winner accepting a silver medallion from the king. Adam shook his head. He must be imagining things. That was no nun. The king stood a yard away from the archer. Surely he could tell the difference between a lad and a lass.

It was only that the face of that nun had haunted Adam for a fortnight now. And he didn't know why.

Did he know her?

He didn't think so.

But he knew her angelic face was going to plague him until he figured out who she was.

There was no way Eve was going to take part in the melee. She did many brave things, but the idea of willingly entering a field of combat to be pummeled half to death was not her idea of courage. It was foolhardy.

Besides, she'd achieved what she'd come to achieve. She'd won the silver medallion. Now she could repay Prior Isaac.

Peering down at her chest where the medallion hung, she rubbed her thumb over the engraving of a longbow. She'd have to have a silversmith melt the piece down into something more religious. Perhaps a decorative cross with the popular Latin saying which advocated a life of poverty, *Nudus nudum Christum sequi*, though the irony of engraving that on a silver cross wasn't lost on her.

She smirked. Since the cross was recompense for the fire she'd started, perhaps it would be more fitting to engrave it with *Quid pro quo.*

She patted the medallion. The sooner she had the work done, the sooner she could return to the convent. For that, she'd need to visit the silversmith in Scone. And she'd have to change her identity again. She'd travel in the guise of the Irish noblewoman, Lady Aillenn Bhallach.

That was just as well. Despite fooling Jenefer of Rivenloch and King Malcolm, Eve had the uneasy feeling she'd been discovered. That knight in the crowd—the one who looked so much like the Pope's emissary that it had unnerved her and ruined her shot—had been staring at her. Not so much staring as piercing through her disguise into her very soul.

It couldn't have been the same man. She knew that. The emissary was likely on his way to Rome already. And this man was a weathered fighter with a jousting helm. Besides, his face had been shrouded in a linen coif. Only his eyes had been visible.

But the way he'd looked at her, as if in recognition, had rattled her to her core.

Perhaps he'd only realized she was a lass, not a lad. Perhaps that was what had made him gape.

Either way, it was time for her to change into another guise and flee. She hadn't survived this long by being careless.

A hue and cry went up from the field. Suddenly, dozens

of combatants surged forward, colliding with a bone-jarring crash. Now was her moment to escape.

As she made her way past the spectators who clung to the wattle fence, cheering on their favorites, her eye was caught by the flash of a blue surcoat in the midst of the fighting.

It was him again. The knight. The one who looked like the emissary.

This time he wore a chain mail coif and carried a blunted broadsword. He was hacking away at one of the Rivenloch warrior maids. She was dodging every blow.

Unable to tear herself away, Eve watched him thrust and block, whirl and lunge, desperate for any sign that would dispel the notion he was the man she'd seen before.

His fighting was superb. He battled with great insight, as if he knew what his opponent's next move would be. He was obviously a seasoned warrior.

The idea that he might be the same man, that he might have been the messenger from the Pope, was absurd. There was a similarity perhaps. But no dedicated man of God could possess such combat skills.

So she convinced herself. And so she believed. Until, in the middle of a lunge, he turned his head toward her, and she saw those piercing eyes again.

She gasped.

He looked as startled as she felt.

He paid for his instant of inattention. The warrior maid he was battling took advantage of his distraction to push aside his shield. Then she planted her boot in the middle of his chest and gave him a great shove.

He folded in half with an "oof" and fell back onto his arse.

Eve's eyes widened.

She had to get out of there. She didn't know what was happening. Who he was. Why he looked so much like the man she'd seen a fortnight ago. How he seemed to recognize *her,* even with her face completely covered.

She definitely didn't want to be anywhere near the battlefield when he recovered, sword in hand, and started looking for the one to blame for his defeat.

Once she got to her pavilion and transformed into Lady Aillenn, she'd be safe.

At least, she *hoped* she'd be safe. An expensive crimson velvet gown, gold jewelry, and her loose tresses adorned with pearls would surely hide the fact that, mere moments ago, she'd been the young archer Jehan of Rouen, and a fortnight ago, a humble nun.

CHAPTER 3

Adam didn't care that the melee wasn't finished. He didn't even care that his ribs were throbbing where his cousin Hallie had booted him to the ground.

He had to know who that archer was.

He'd almost convinced himself that he'd imagined the resemblance between the lad Jehan and the nun. That at most they might be brother and sister.

But the shocked recognition he'd glimpsed in those familiar brown eyes staring at him in mid-melee was not a figment of his imagination. It had been real enough to cost him the battle.

He'd seen something else in those eyes as well. Alarm.

Why?

By the time Adam struggled to his feet, dodging the mayhem around him, the archer was gone.

Suddenly the melee lost its appeal. Adam used his sword and shield to pummel his way through the combatants to the outside of the main battle. Then he leaped over the wattle fence bounding the tournament field just in time to glimpse the archer hurrying toward the pavilions.

The lad was definitely fleeing. No doubt he'd gather his things from his pavilion, pack up, and make his way out the palisade gate.

Adam dared not follow in his battle gear. He'd be too conspicuous. The pavilions were deserted. Everyone who wasn't sorely wounded was attending the melee, watching or fighting.

But once the lad emerged from his pavilion, Adam could be waiting for him at the gate.

Since the archer would be expecting *Le Goupil* of Paris, Adam would don another disguise.

Thankfully, his satchel contained everything he needed. Indeed, its capacity was the subject of much teasing in the clan. His youngest sister Merewen thought the satchel was magic. His aunt Deirdre claimed he could carry a full retinue of knights in it. His cousin Ian said it defied geometry.

None of that was true. But he did manage to stuff a substantial number of useful items in it. In his line of work, it was essential to be prepared for anything.

So when he emerged from the pavilion moments later, he'd packed his chain mail away and put on the tattered rags of a beggar. One eye was covered with a patch. His chin sported a fake, gray, ratty beard. His hair he covered with a grimy coif. And he limped along on a low wooden crutch, bent under the weight of his enormous satchel.

Near the gate, he dropped his satchel beside the wooden palisade and reclined against it, feigning sleep. He watched the exit through the lowered lashes of his uncovered eye.

He almost overlooked the archer making his escape. Because it wasn't an archer.

Nor was it a nun.

Sweeping toward the gate with the grace of a wind-blown rose was a vision in scarlet. Her sumptuous velvet skirts hugged her legs as she strode forward at a rapid clip, her pendant and a girdle of gold links lashing her surcoat. An oversized satchel bounced on her hip with every hurried step. Her dark hair, bedecked at the crown in pearls, streamed out behind her in curls that rippled like a rain-swollen stream as she rushed to freedom.

Adam almost let her pass. He hadn't seen the noblewoman at the tournament. She must be some lord's wife, uninterested in the fighting, who'd remained behind in their pavilion. Or some knight's noble courtesan, fleeing home before his wife could catch her. Indeed, she may have well been the *king's* mistress, so beautiful and richly-appointed was she.

She spared him not a glance. Which wasn't surprising. He looked more like a pile of rags than a human. But even though he saw her only through his one uncovered eye, when she drew near, his breath caught.

She was the one he sought. The archer. And the nun.

How was that possible?

She scurried through the palisade gate and out of sight.

Adam unfurled, coming to his feet, and shouldered his satchel. He shuffled forward on his crutch with a limp that was only half feigned after falling to Brand's lance and Hallie's boot. Then he passed through the gate and eyed the road in both directions.

There she was on the northward path, racing like a hare pursued by hounds.

Still, he hung back. There was no need to alarm her. Unless she took a turn, the road ran directly to the ancient bridge across the Tay.

She probably meant to cross the river. But he doubted she'd go far after that. It was already late in the day. It would be unwise for a woman so richly appointed to journey alone after dark. Indeed, it was unwise enough for a woman so eye-catching to travel alone by day.

Even if he hadn't been tracking her, Adam would have likely followed the foolish lady for her own protection. Outlaws lurked around every corner.

He was well-versed in handling outlaws. He knew all their tricks. Indeed, he was the son of such an outlaw. A mysterious woodland thief who robbed from the rich and gave to the poor. He occasionally enjoyed such pursuits himself.

The lady slowed as she crossed the bridge. He likewise slackened his pace.

On the other side she continued on the north road.

Adam was careful to hobble harmlessly along the path, keeping his head bowed. He didn't want to arouse her suspicions.

Still, every now and then she turned nervously, as if she sensed she was being followed.

Eve couldn't shake her suspicion that the old, crippled beggar doddering along behind her was following her.

Honestly, it was absurd. Why should she fret? This was a public road. He was simply a traveler.

Besides, why would an old, crippled beggar be following her?

Clearly, encountering that knight who had the same eyes as the Pope's emissary had unsettled her. She needed to pull herself together before she started jumping at shadows.

The poor old man walked with a crutch, for heaven's sake. By his raggedy clothes and his raggedy beard, she guessed the satchel he carried contained all his worldly possessions. The load bent his back into a severe hunch. Under other circumstances, Sister Eve would have offered to carry it for him at least a mile or two.

But she wasn't Sister Eve now. She was Lady Aillenn. A refined Irish noblewoman of wealth who was accustomed to getting what she wanted. And she wanted to get to Scone before the silversmith closed his shop.

So she satisfied herself by maintaining a safe distance. Surely in his condition, he wasn't planning on traveling to Scone anyway. It was a three-mile journey.

He must have been fitter than he looked. Against all odds, he did indeed manage to shadow her all the way to Scone.

Now she definitely had to lose him. He could be a thief. If he wasn't considering robbing her already, he'd be inclined to do so if he saw her visiting a silversmith. And she absolutely couldn't have him following her to her place of lodging.

So once she entered the village, she intentionally dawdled, stopping in at several shops to make small unnecessary purchases. A ribbon here. A pair of gloves there. Herbs for the bath.

But always when she exited a shop, he was there.

He no doubt imagined himself inconspicuous among the crowd of villagers. Lounging against a wall. Sorting through his satchel. Examining the wares at a craftsman's counter.

But his ubiquitous presence was too coincidental. He must have marked her for theft. She needed to shake him once and for all.

Walking briskly, she turned left down a narrow street between shops and then made an immediate right. She pressed herself against the plaster wall, waiting to see if he would follow.

She heard the clop of his crutch and the scrape of his boots as he came down the street. She held her breath, waiting for him to arrive.

She would do him no harm. She only meant to scare him. To make sure he learned she was not a lady to be victimized.

So when he stepped past her place of hiding, she sprang out, shouting, "Off with ye!"

To her astonishment, he wasn't all that surprised. He blinked a few times. But he wasn't frightened off at all.

Perhaps he was simpleminded. Perhaps he'd only followed her the way a duckling follows its mother.

Still, she didn't want him tagging along behind her. She led a clandestine life. She couldn't afford to interact with strangers.

To make her point clear, she furrowed her brows and in her best Irish accent, bit out, "Leave me be, sirrah."

He only stared, seeming not to understand.

Then she noticed his beard was drooping oddly from his chin on one side.

It wasn't real, she realized.

The knave was wearing a disguise.

She'd worn such fake beards twice before. Once when she'd posed as Mahmud the Arab spice trader. And once as King Arthur of Tintagel's bastard son.

With a gleam of revelation in her eyes, she reached up and gave it a sharp yank.

The man cried out in pain and surprise as the beard tore off his chin, plopping onto the palm of her hand like a fat, furry squirrel.

She beamed at him in triumph, anticipating his look of outrage.

But it was she who was astonished.

"Ye," she breathed, searching his vibrant brown eyes. It was him. He was the Pope's emissary. *And* the knight. "'Tis ye."

Adam paled.

His skin stung where she'd ripped the beard away. And now she knew his secret.

But how had she recognized him? His disguises were

unparalleled. He'd never been unmasked before. Never. Not even by his own kin.

"How did you...?" he began. But he remembered he had a more pressing matter to address. "You're that archer."

Her face betrayed no emotion. "Archer? What archer?"

He narrowed his eyes, searching hers for a glimmer of deception. There was none.

Was he wrong? Did she only look similar to the archer? The archer had been from Rouen. This lass had a distinctly Irish lilt to her voice.

Then he remembered. "And the nun."

She held his gaze. "Me? A nun? Ye must have me confused with someone else."

Adam frowned. He could usually tell when a woman was telling a lie. They glanced away. Or licked their lips. Or fussed with their sleeve.

This woman did nothing. She looked at him directly, without artifice, as if she were telling him God's truth.

"So ye didn't win second place in the archery contest?" he asked, crossing his arms in challenge. "And ye weren't at Perth durin' the siege?"

"I don't know what ye're talkin' about."

She seemed sincere. She hadn't even lowered her gaze.

It was true, now that he thought about it, the nun had been much plainer than this elegant noblewoman.

And no archer lad could look so beautiful. The king, at least, had believed he was a lad.

Why then was Adam's memory insisting they were all the same person? Were his powers of observation dwindling?

"But what about ye?" she challenged, holding up his fake beard between a thumb and finger. "Can ye explain this?"

He held out his hand. She dropped the beard into his palm.

To his chagrin, lies always came readily to mind. "Verily, I was hired by the king to follow ye."

"Follow me? Why?"

"He was concerned for your safety."

"The king? Concerned for *me?*" A furrow creased her brow. Apparently, the woman didn't believe that. Perhaps she had a strained relationship with the king.

He continued. "Aye. King Malcolm posted us at the gate with instructions to see any unaccompanied ladies to their destination."

"Is that so?" The subtle arch in her brow indicated her skepticism. "Then why the disguise? Why not send a knight in full battle dress bearin' the king's arms?"

That *did* make more sense. Damn, the lady was clever. He liked that. Even if it made his deception more challenging.

"'Tis less threatenin'." He shrugged. "And most people don't even notice old crippled beggars. They're—"

"Invisible."

"Right."

"But *I* saw ye."

"Aye, ye did." That was remarkable. He'd grown so accustomed to disappearing into the shadows, melting into the crowd, moving unseen through the world, it was strange to be noticed.

"Well, ye've done your duty," she decided. "Ye may return to the king and tell him I arrived safely."

She was sending him away. Which was a pity. Despite her having him at a disadvantage by uncovering his disguise, he would have liked to get to know her better.

She was not only beautiful. She was bright. She was also bold, tugging on a stranger's beard like that.

He rubbed his chin. For that offense, the least she could do was tell him her name. Then he wouldn't make the same mistake again and confuse her with another.

"From whom shall I send word to the king?" he inquired.

She straightened proudly. "Lady Aillenn Bhallach." It was a good Irish name. He was rolling it around in his mind when she added, "And ye are?"

He took a breath to reply. Then, to his alarm, he hesitated. Who was he? Was he William the beggar? *Le Goupil* of Paris? "Adam..."

Ballocks! He'd given her his real name. Why had he done that? He never gave strangers his real name. It was like handing a dagger to a thief.

"Adam...?"

"Greenwood. Adam Greenwood," he improvised.

"Farewell then, Adam Greenwood," she cooed. Then she gave him a nod, picked up her satchel, and swept past him back to the main road.

"Farewell, Lady Aillenn."

He watched her depart, admiring the subtle sway of her scarlet skirts and the gentle bounce of her chestnut locks. Then he glanced at the large satchel she carried.

He scowled.

A piece of cloth protruded from the top and flapped against the satchel with each step. A woolen hood of dark green. Just like the one the archer had been wearing.

Eve felt his eyes on her all the way back to the main road.

She thanked God for her ability to look at ease in the face of danger. She walked with a practiced nonchalance, though inside she was shaking like a fall leaf clinging to a winter branch. Half from fright. Half from anger.

Adam Greenwood, her arse. He was no more Adam Greenwood than he was the Pope's emissary or a knight from Paris. Nor did she believe he'd followed her on the orders of the king.

Outrage and disquiet warred within her as she strode onto the street.

She was vexed with him for perpetrating such deception. And vexed at herself for nearly exposing her own.

For the moment, she wouldn't think about the hypocrisy of one pretender harboring such resentment against another. She needed to focus on her survival.

First, before she ventured on to the silversmith's shop, she had to settle her nerves.

Lady Aillenn would never show up to an appointment with flushed cheeks and darting eyes. Lady Aillenn was calm. Cool. Elegant. A wealthy Irish noblewoman with a discriminating eye for craftsmanship and design.

If Eve wanted excellent service, she'd have to look like a person who deserved it.

She saw what seemed to be a reputable inn, The Grey Goose. Perhaps a pint would help restore her sense of tranquility.

As usual, Eve earned abundant stares. Lady Aillenn was the opposite of invisible. One didn't often see a lady going into an inn by herself. But she'd dealt with that before. The key was to exude confidence. To walk in as if she owned the place.

She strode directly to the hearth. A man sitting on a wooden stool immediately vacated it for her. She seated herself with an entitled nod and set her satchel down beside her. Then she summoned the innkeeper with a lift of her finger, indicating she wished to be served.

A serving lass rushed over. "What may I fetch ye, m'lady?"

"A pint o' your best."

In the end, it took *two* pints to calm her rattled nerves. But by then, she'd lingered long enough to be sure Adam Greenwood—or whatever his name was—had left for good.

She smoothed her skirts, hefted up her satchel, and made her way out of the inn. As she exited, she looked both ways to be sure the crippled old impostor was gone.

She saw only a half dozen young men chatting, a woman carrying a babe on her hip, a pair of giggling lasses, a sour-faced monk, a lad herding a flock of geese, and a knight guiding his horse down the road.

Merging with the villagers, she continued toward the silversmith's shop.

By the time she rang the bell at his door, and the silversmith unlocked and opened it to her, she'd all but forgotten about the man in disguise who'd almost exposed her.

Now she was fully Lady Aillenn. Self-assured. Cultivated. And willing to pay for services well done and in a timely manner. She retrieved the silver medallion from her satchel and explained what she wanted.

When the mysterious lass emerged from The Grey Goose, her gaze glossed over Adam completely. Adam, standing at his regular height, capped and cloaked, and missing his beard, coif, eye patch, and crutch, was unremarkable. He easily dissolved into a group of chatting young men. She took no notice.

She'd lingered in the inn for nearly half an hour. Adam couldn't have followed her inside, of course. In the cramped quarters, she would have noticed him immediately.

Now she seemed less wary of her surroundings. She straightened with determination, heading north. He followed, keeping his cloak closed and his cap pulled low over his brow.

When she stopped at the silversmith's shop, his suspicions were confirmed.

She *had* to be the French archer, as wildly improbable as it seemed. *Le Goupil* had won second place in the archery tournament. He...*She* had been awarded a silver medallion.

But Lady Aillenn Bhalloch, an Irish noblewoman, likely had no use for such a trinket. No doubt she planned to sell it to the silversmith and pocket the coin.

He had to admit, it was a clever scheme. Especially since her disguise had been convincing enough to fool the king.

Was this a habitual pastime for her? Was she some sort of female archer-errant? Did she travel from tournament to tournament, winning prizes and cashing them in for their value?

He couldn't help but grin in appreciation. It was just the sort of spirited, rebellious, cocky thing his intrepid Rivenloch aunts might do. But they wouldn't bother with the disguise.

Now he was intrigued. He had to find out what this elusive pretender was up to. Even if it took all day.

But as the sun sank lower and lower in the sky, and she still didn't emerge from the shop, he began to think he'd been wrong about all of it.

Perhaps the green hood hanging out of her satchel was only a coincidence.

Perhaps she hadn't been the archer after all.

Perhaps she was the silversmith's wife and had simply gone home.

He was almost ready to shuffle back to Perth when the silversmith's door rattled open again. Adam drew back into the narrow space between shops and peered at her from beneath his cap.

She eyed the sky with a furrowed brow, as if noting the lateness of the day. Then she shouldered her satchel and pressed onward down the road, turning west toward the woods.

As he watched her walk away, Adam noticed he wasn't the only one with an eye on her. From behind the last building, two rough-looking men eased out onto the road behind her. They too must have been monitoring the silversmith's shop. Waiting for her to exit. Sure she'd have silver in her satchel.

Now Adam was *definitely* going to follow her. He was a Rivenloch at heart. He wasn't about to walk away and let a lady become the victim of thieves.

They wouldn't immediately accost her. Not this close to the village. Not where she could put up a hue and cry and bring the law down upon them.

Nay, they would track her until she was isolated in the dark middle of the wood and then demand their due.

So Adam would track *them*.

Eve could hear the travelers on the path behind her. There was a good chance they were thieves. It was a rare journey when she *didn't* cross paths with thieves. Times were difficult, and not every beggar had a charitable convent nearby.

They probably thought they were being inconspicuous. Which meant they weren't very experienced. Their boots scuffed through the leaves. One of them stepped on a twig and broke it with a loud snap.

It sounded like there were two of them. Maybe three.

Outlaws were always a risk in the woods. But she wasn't afraid of them.

In truth, she felt sorry for them. Most of them were simply poor folk in a desperate situation. They had no coin. And no skills to make a living.

Or they were outcasts and exiles.

Or they had been raised by thieves and knew no other way.

But Jesus had forgiven a thief, even from the Cross. He'd promised the thief He would see him in Paradise.

Who was Eve to be less forgiving?

Of course, she would have felt safer in her nun's habit. But it was foolish to assume bad intentions where there were none. She would do nothing unless they accosted her. Still, it seemed they would have made their presence known if they meant to be companionable.

She still hadn't reached the village of Scone, which was a quarter mile from the convent near Scone Priory, where she intended to stay for the night. But now she was heading toward the deepest, darkest part of the woods. The trees blotted out most of what sun remained. Only narrow spears of light shot down upon the path to show the way.

She hoped she wouldn't have to confront them in the shadows.

After several yards, her eyes grew more accustomed to the lack of light. She began to breathe easier. Perhaps she'd misjudged her pursuers.

No sooner did she have that thought than they suddenly rushed up behind her.

"Hold there, lassie," one of them growled.

"Where do ye think ye're goin'?" the other sneered.

She stopped with a resigned sigh and slowly turned to face them.

The light was too dim to identify them. With their hoods pulled forward over their faces, it was hard to see their features. But one of them was quite stout with a heavy black beard that sat on his chest like an overfed cat. His fellow was as thin and tall as a lance. Both were wielding daggers.

Still, there was no need to panic. All she had to do was channel a wee bit of her convent courtesy.

"Gentlemen," she said with a welcoming smile, "I'm so glad ye've joined me. I heard ye followin', and I wondered if ye meant to accompany me. As I'm sure ye know, the woods are full o' danger, and I'd be quite grateful for your protection. I'm Lady Aillenn Bhallach," she said, holding out a hand, "and ye are?"

The thin one was charmed and befuddled at once. "Tom, m'lady. Tom—"

His companion cuffed him. "Don't tell her your name. We're not here to make friends."

Properly chided, the thin man shrunk back.

Black-beard snarled, "We're here for somethin' a wee bit more serious."

"More serious?" She eyed them with innocent puzzlement. "Oh, are ye...?" She let her voice trail off, then lowered it to a whisper. "Don't fret. If ye're poachin' or gatherin' wood in the king's forest, I won't breathe a word."

"Gatherin' wood in the forest?" the black-beard mocked. Then he sobered. "Nay, wench. 'Tis your silver we're gatherin'."

"Oh!" she exclaimed. "Well, that's a shame." She clucked her tongue in disappointment. "Ye see, the silver I have is bound for Scone Priory."

"Not anymore," the thin one scoffed, hoping to get back into his fellow's good graces.

"We don't care where 'tis bound," the black-beard said.

"Right," said the thin one.

"What I mean to say," she gently explained, "is the silver isn't mine to give ye. It belongs to God."

"What?" the black-beard barked.

The thin one's shoulders drooped. "God?" He lowered his dagger.

"I'm afraid so," she said. "If ye take this silver, ye'll be stealin' from God Himself."

"That's shite," the black-beard muttered.

She shook her head. "'Tis one thing to steal a *man's* silver. 'Tis quite another to abscond with wealth intended for the Holy Church."

The thin one gasped.

"Don't listen to her," the black-beard ordered.

"But what if she's—"

"Silver is silver," he groused. "It all spends the same. Besides, what use do ye think God has for coin?"

Eve had to admit he had a point. According to Scripture, money was the root of all evil.

"The Prior will do God's work," she explained, "and deliver alms to the poor."

"Or stash it in his own coffers," the black-beard spat.

"And piss on the poor," the thin one added.

Eve could see these men had had bad experiences with the clergy. And sadly, she knew their cynicism wasn't unfounded. There were indeed corrupt and greedy men in the church, like the one she'd shot in effigy. Still, she wondered if she might restore the thieves' hope and change their path.

"There are some wayward priests, to be sure," she admitted. "But Prior Isaac is decent enough. If ye abandon your sinful ways and come with me to Scone, I'll introduce ye to the prior. I'm sure ye'll find salva—"

Where the third man came from, Eve couldn't guess. Suddenly a figure sprang out of the trees and bowled over the black-bearded thief. Then, with startling efficiency, he tore the dagger from the man's hand and threw it, embedding it in the trunk of a pine several yards down the road.

Stunned, the black-beard struggled to his feet. With a whimpered curse, he limped along the path to try to retrieve his dagger, abandoning his partner without a backward glance.

The thin man's eyes widened. His hand faltered on his weapon as the third man drew closer. Finally, he let out a fearful squeak, dropped the dagger, and lit out after his friend.

As Eve watched them escape, a bolt of disappointment streaked through her. She felt she'd been making progress with the two thieves. Offered them redemption. Given them a wee glimpse of hope. In another moment, she might have convinced them to come along to the priory. If they had, she might have been able to change their lives. Helped them to mend their wicked ways.

Now they were back on the road to ruin. Worse, this new outlaw didn't appear to believe in redemption.

"Haven't ye read the Scripture," he purred in a Highland brogue, "a leopard cannot change its spots?"

"Jeremiah," she replied out of habit.

She narrowed her eyes at him. It was too dark to see beneath the floppy cap he wore. But she could feel his mild derision. This thief she'd never persuade with promises of salvation. She'd have to use another tactic.

He bent down to scoop up the discarded dagger.

She had to think fast before he decided to use it.

"Here," she said, lifting her hands to her hair. "Take my pearls. They'll be easier for ye to sell."

She figured he'd do one of three things.

Settle for the pearls and be on his way.

Refuse the pearls and demand the silver.

Or take the pearls *and* demand the silver.

Instead, using the point of the dagger, he tipped up the front of his cap to study her, revealing a pair of all-too-familiar glittering and puzzled eyes. "God's blood, m'lady. Who the devil *are* ye?"

CHAPTER 4

Adam hadn't meant to reveal himself. And he hadn't meant to blurt the question out like that. He usually had a more conversational manner. A smoother tongue. He could tease information out of people without asking direct questions.

But this woman—with her impressive disguises and her changeable beauty and those eyes that looked deep into his soul—drained all the subtlety out of him.

"Adam?" she choked out.

The word jarred him. For one terrible instant, he thought she recognized him as a Rivenloch. Then he remembered he'd slipped and told her his real first name. But—damn his memory—he couldn't recall what last name he'd given her.

"M'lady," he said with a tip of his cap. He immediately regretted calling her that. In light of her penchant for disguises, it seemed more likely she was not a true lady, but an outlaw.

"Ye followed me," she accused.

He wondered if her Irish accent was as fake as his Highland one.

"I did," he said.

"Ye meant to rob me then," she decided, releasing a disappointed sigh. "So ye're just a common thief after all."

"Now hold on. I'm not a—"

"I should have known."

"Known what? I'm tellin' ye I'm not a—"

"No better than the men ye chased off."

"What the...?"

Why was she putting the screws to him? He'd just saved her from those thieves.

"Ye saw me leave the silversmith shop," she said, "and ye figured ye'd rob me o' my fortune." She blew out a disgusted breath. "At least the other two outlaws didn't feign to be sent by the king for my protection."

This was getting out of hand. He seized her forearm, hoping to silence her long enough to make her listen.

Her sharp intake of breath made him instantly regret grabbing her. But he needed to make his point.

"I don't want your silver," he said. *"Or* your pearls."

He thought that would placate her.

Instead, her eyes went round. "Then what *do* ye want?"

Unbidden, a dangerous idea flashed across his brain. An idea involving his hungry mouth and those cherry-plump lips of hers.

But he was no rake. After a prolonged moment, he released her.

"I want only to keep ye safe," he said.

"I don't need ye to keep me safe." Her voice came out on a rough whisper, and she absently rubbed her arm where he'd gripped it. "I can take care o' myself."

He rolled his eyes. She sounded like his sister. But Feiyan actually *could* take care of herself. She was a master of martial arts. "Ye mean the way ye took care o' those thieves?"

She bristled. "I'll have ye know they were almost convinced to come with me to the priory. To mend their ways. To seek redemption. If ye hadn't interfered—"

"If I hadn't interfered, m'lady," he said, losing patience

with her thankless stubbornness, "ye might well be lyin' by the side o' the road with a dagger through your heart."

She blushed at that. She couldn't deny the truth. Perhaps she finally realized the weight of the situation.

After an awkward silence, she mumbled, "I don't mean to seem ungrateful. O' course I appreciate your efforts."

He straightened. Now she was showing the proper gratitude.

Until she added, "'Tis only that I would have preferred ye use more brain and less brawn."

His jaw dropped. More brain? Did she not understand he was outnumbered two to one? Did she not know the intellect it had required to perfectly time his attack? The strategy it took to subdue them both?

Before he could sputter out a reply, she shouldered her satchel. That incriminating wool hood was peeping out of it again. Which reminded him...

"Ye still haven't told me who ye—"

"Ye'll have to forgive me," she said with a disarming smile, "but I really should be goin'. 'Tis nigh dark, and I've a wee bit farther to travel." She turned and, with a dismissive wave of her hand, headed down the road. "Farewell."

He watched her with narrowed eyes. She was a clever one. She'd managed to avoid his question. Again.

But Adam wasn't about to give up.

Besides, those thieves were probably lying in wait ahead. They were desperate men. They would resort to desperate measures, no matter how confident their intended victim was in the power of redemption. Their brief altercation with Adam wasn't enough to dissuade them from making another attempt at a lucrative haul.

It was a matter of common chivalry to follow her.

Eve was trembling. Hopefully not so much that the man who was still—unbelievably, stubbornly—following her could tell.

She wasn't trembling from the fact he was following her. She couldn't realistically expect him to turn around and go back into the woods when Scone Priory was so near.

She wasn't trembling from her encounter with the thieves. She'd faced down outlaws before.

She wasn't even trembling from the fact that Adam—or whoever he was—was prying into her identity. It happened so often when she was disguised as Lady Aillenn, she'd gotten very good at evading questions.

She was trembling because her arm was still warm where he'd enclosed it in his fist.

Her heart was still racing from the way he'd gazed into her eyes.

Her body was flushed with heat from the wicked thoughts that had flown through her mind when she'd asked the handsome rogue what he intended. Thoughts like what his mouth would taste like. How his strong arms would feel around her. What it would be like to have his powerful body pressed to hers.

She'd never felt like this before. Not when—posing as Lady Aillenn—elegant noblemen had flirted with her. Not when—dressed as the milkmaid Maggie Gall—she'd been wooed by stable lads and gardeners. Not even when handsome Sir Hew of Rivenloch had sworn his undying love to her.

What was wrong with her?

She'd always been able to keep her base urges in check. It had annoyed her how much the abbess had impressed upon the convent sisters the need for chastity. The abbess had advised, when earthly desires proved too much of the Devil's allure, the nuns pray doubly hard for willpower.

But Eve had never been tempted. The men she'd met had never turned her head, warmed the cockles of her heart, or, as the abbess liked to say, kindled the fires of her womanhood. Indeed, she always thought the abbess devoted far too much attention to the issue of carnal temptation.

Now she had to wonder.

It wasn't that Eve had disavowed pleasure. She wasn't made of ice. There were plenty of earthly indulgences that excited her.

The soft summer breeze brushing her bare cheek.

The delicious aroma of Sister Eithne's leek pottage.

The magical music of minstrels echoing in a great hall.

Snow sparkling in winter trees.

But this was different. This feeling was quite unsettling. It threw her off-balance. Confused her thoughts. Destroyed her good intentions, in the same way the bee had destroyed Jenefer of Rivenloch's aim in the archery contest.

She had to be rid of this man. This giddiness was dangerous, considering the vulnerability of her identity and her very serious purpose.

Without turning, she called out, "I know ye're followin' me."

"I'm not followin' ye," he called back.

The *hell* he wasn't, she thought. Instead she said, "I beg to differ."

"'Tis a public thoroughfare."

She bit her lip. She couldn't argue with him. All she could do was walk faster.

So she did.

So did he. And with his longer legs, he easily made up the distance between them. By the time the trees had begun to thin, and the full moon rose to light the path, he drew level with her. Then, without her permission, he seized her satchel and added it to his already burdened shoulder.

She gasped at his nerve. But she didn't snatch the satchel back. It was admittedly a relief not to have to carry the heavy thing.

"So which one are ye truly?" he asked. "The Irish noblewoman? The French archer? Or the nun?"

"I don't know what ye're talkin' about," she lied.

To her annoyance, he began to guess anyway. "I doubt ye're Lady Aillenn Bhallach. I can't believe an Irish nobleman would let his daughter roam the Scots countryside on her own."

"My da doesn't know."

He pressed on. "I can see ye're not the young archer lad."

He let his eyes graze her briefly from head to toe. To her dismay, even that fleeting glance was enough to heat her blood.

"That leaves the nun," he said. "And though ye do speak o' redemption for thieves, ye've told so many lies, if ye were a nun, ye'd have to spend years in contrition."

That was true. It was how she planned to fill her days in her old age.

"Perhaps I'm none o' them," she said.

"Perhaps," he said, but she could see he didn't believe that.

"What about ye?" she asked, eager to get the attention off of her identity. "Are ye an emissary o' the Pope? A French knight? An old lame beggar? Or a hunter o' thieves?"

"All o' them," he said.

"I don't believe ye're godly enough to serve the Pope," she decided.

He scoffed, pretending offense.

"A French knight?" she mused. Then she shook her head. "Nay. I saw ye laid low by a lass."

He bridled at that. "That lass was... I was distracted."

She felt a grin tugging at her lips. He was rather satisfying to tease. "And the beggar? Ye may be poor and old," she considered, "but ye're not lame."

"I'm not *old,*" he said with a frown of outrage, rising to the bait.

"Well," she said with a smile, "I suppose Adam isn't old. If that's who ye are."

He neither confirmed nor denied it. Instead he gave her a small chuckle. "'Twould seem we're birds of a feather, ye and me. Masters o' disguise, aye?"

She supposed there was little point in denying it. At least he still didn't know which one was her true identity. And she was fairly sure he'd given her a false name as well. She didn't necessarily believe the maxim about honor among thieves. But there was no reason for either of them to expose the other.

Eve still had her pride. She didn't want him to get the wrong idea.

"I'm not an outlaw," she said.

"Neither am I."

"Ye were posin' as a beggar."

"But I wasn't beggin'," he pointed out. "What about ye? Ye took that silver medallion at the tourney."

Her eyes widened. "I *earned* that silver medallion." Too late, she realized he'd trapped her into confessing she was the archer.

He grinned. "Fair enough."

Then she realized he was teasing her as well. That amused her. The man might well be an outlaw. He might be a spy. He might be an exile. A mercenary. Or an agent of the Devil. But he had a ready wit and a good sense of humor.

"So," he asked, clearly digging for information again, "where did ye learn to shoot like that?"

She wasn't going to fall for his tactics. "Where did ye learn to wield a sword?"

His low laughter resonated in her ears like the soft, soothing bells of Mass.

A contented smile tugged at the corners of her lips as they continued down the road. As long as she could keep from losing herself in his enthralling eyes, the "master of disguise" was proving to be good company. He was carrying her satchel, for one thing. He was also bright. Entertaining. And friendly. With a streak of mischief. She was still fairly certain he was an outlaw of some kind. But she almost believed he *had* followed her to offer his protection. Almost.

"Ye're quite good, ye know," he told her. "Ye have a talent for disguises. O' course, ye couldn't fool me. I'd recognize ye anywhere."

Taken aback, she frowned. "Ye would?"

"Och aye. Who could not?"

She stopped in her tracks. "Everyone. No one sees me. I'm practically invisible."

"Invisible?" he exclaimed. "Surely ye jest. I mean, your costumes are well-crafted. But the maid behind the mask? Unforgettable."

Her heart fluttered. Against her better judgment, she searched his eyes. She realized he was telling the truth. "Ye saw me," she said in wonder. "No one's e'er *seen* me before."

His gaze softened in the moonlight, warming her to her toes. "I find that hard to believe."

"'Tis true." Her words came out on a breathless whisper.

Then she got that dizzy sensation again. That dangerous feeling. As if she'd drunk too much ale and her knees might collapse beneath her.

She gulped and tore her gaze away, vowing not to look at him again. Then she continued down the road.

As he walked beside her, he asked, "The real question is, how did ye recognize *me?*"

Despite averting her gaze, visions of his features flashed through her mind's eye. Where could she begin? Because he was the most beautiful man she'd ever seen? Striking? Magnificent? Breathtaking? Because he had a smile that was charming and disarming? Because he had deep, penetrating, soul-searing eyes?

She wasn't going to tell him that. She'd only get herself into trouble.

"Your features are..." What was a neutral word? "Distinctive. Unique. Memorable."

"Memorable?" Adam echoed.

No one had ever told him he was memorable. Indeed, the reason he'd embarked upon a life of subterfuge was because he was so *un*memorable. Now, for the first time in years, he felt... What word had she used? *Seen.*

"Oh aye," she assured him. "Ye see, when ye're like me—ordinary, pale, brown-haired, brown-eyed, plain o' face—'tis far easier to slip through a crowd unseen and—"

He rounded on her, incredulous. "Plain o' face?"

Surely she was jesting with him. Or maybe fishing for praise.

But when he looked into her lovely face—at her tempting lips, the delightful sprinkle of freckles across the bridge of her nose, the tendrils of her lush hair curling upon her cheek, the dark, inviting pools of her eyes—he saw only sincerity.

"How can ye think ye're plain o' face?" he asked.

She lowered her gaze, obviously embarrassed. "Prithee, sir, do not mock me."

"Mock ye?"

"I'm all too well aware o' my flaws."

He blinked. Flaws? As far as he could tell, she had none.

"So ye're missin' a toe, are ye?" he asked with a smirk.

"Nay."

"Ye've got a tail?"

"A tail!" she exclaimed.

"Perhaps your knees are on backwards?"

He wasn't prepared for the chiding punch she gave his shoulder.

Apparently, neither was she. Caught up in the moment, she'd reacted instinctively. And scared herself.

"Oh dear," she said. "I apologize."

He laughed. "I deserved that." He rubbed his offended shoulder. "But the strength o' that wallop proves ye *were* that archer."

She only shook her head.

Through the stand of trees, he glimpsed a double row of thatch-roofed cottages with pale golden light flickering through their horn windows.

It was the last tiny village before Scone Priory.

To his surprise, his heart sank. He was enjoying the wayward lass's company. He wanted their journey to go on longer.

He knew once he saw her to her destination, his responsibilities would end. She'd be safe from the thieves. He should bid her farewell. It was the gentlemanly thing to do.

But he wasn't feeling like a gentleman. Not in the attire of outlaw-thwarting Adam Greenwood. And he didn't want to bid her farewell.

Not only because he was beginning to feel a kinship for her.

Not only because he knew a woman living a life of deception would never truly be safe.

But because, for the first time in his life, he'd met someone who considered him worthy of remembering.

Eve spotted the signs of civilization through the pines. She was equally relieved and disheartened.

She didn't want to part ways with the attractive, brilliant, charming stranger. It was rare to find a person with whom she could exchange lively conversation. Her sister nuns, bless their hearts, were mostly dull and predictable. Speaking with Adam had been as refreshing as taking a bracing dip in a cold loch.

Perhaps it was because it was the first time she'd been able to reveal her secret.

Of course, she hadn't truly revealed much. He still didn't know who she was. But he knew *what* she was. And he approved.

More than approved. He didn't think she was plain. Or invisible. He thought she was talented.

The abbess's dire warnings suddenly tolled like bells in her head. Now, as her heart melted and her veins filled with molten need, she understood the irresistible temptation.

But it wasn't just the call of lust. It was more.

An attraction as powerful as iron to a lodestone.

A profound longing for human connection.

A connection she would never be allowed to forge.

This easy camaraderie could lead nowhere.

She was a nun.

Living in a convent had always been her destiny.

As the fifth daughter of a wealthy merchant, she had no other choice. Her father had no sons, just an apprentice. Her sisters had all married well. It was up to Eve as the least useful daughter to secure her clan's place in heaven by devoting herself to God.

She'd never questioned that duty. Indeed, she found life at the nunnery rather freeing. Her father's generous donations to the convent ensured she could come and go as she pleased.

She didn't mind the small sacrifices. The boring sermons.

The long days. The manual labor. Waking up at all hours to pray. She was making her father and her clan proud. She was on her way to achieving a Greater Purpose.

But now she was beginning to have doubts. This encounter was testing her faith.

"Where were ye plannin' to stay tonight?" he asked, jarring her from her thoughts.

She opened her mouth, preparing to say "the convent." Then she remembered she'd had no opportunity to change into her habit. Rich Lady Aillenn certainly wouldn't seek lodging at a convent.

And for some reason, she suddenly didn't want to admit to him she was only a nun. She wanted to keep pretending she was an entitled Irish noblewoman. She wanted to wear her scarlet gown and gold jewels and pearls in her hair.

"I...haven't decided," she said.

"There's a decent place just up ahead. Anne Campbell's. 'Tis where I plan to stay. 'Tis a simple inn. But I can show ye the way."

Her breath caught.

Did she dare stay at the same inn? Wasn't that inviting Satan to work his wiles?

What if there was only a common room for sleeping?

Or what if there was a chamber, but the two of them were forced to share it?

And what if that chamber had only one bed?

She was grateful for the dark of night. Her face reddened with such shame at the direction of her thoughts, it felt like flame upon her cheeks.

Adam supposed it was too much to hope there was just one room left at Anne Campbell's. That they'd be obliged to share it. And there would be but one bed. Still, he couldn't help wishing it.

He'd never felt so drawn to a woman before. So enchanted. So fascinated, not just by her beguiling beauty, but by her nimble mind and her saucy tongue.

He'd had sweethearts before. Fleeting and frivolous affairs with giggling maids and sighing lasses. They had been entertaining. Delightful. Thrilling.

But in Aillenn, he felt as if he'd met his match. A woman with whom he could exchange jests. Have adventures. Share experiences. A woman who understood him. Who appreciated the challenges of a vagabond life and enjoyed, as he did, the freedom of anonymity.

The fact that she was also lovely enough to rouse the beast in his trews only made her more irresistible.

When they arrived at Anne Campbell's, however, their circumstances were made all too clear.

As soon as the humble proprietor beheld the lady in scarlet step into her inn, dripping with valuable gold and pearls, she fussed over Aillenn as if she were a queen. And when Aillenn pressed a silver coin into her palm, Anne became her loyal servant.

He couldn't blame Anne. Lady Aillenn did look regal. She held her head high, and her mouth bore a vague suggestion of a well-bred smile.

Indeed, he began to wonder if she was telling the truth about being the daughter of Irish nobility, perhaps even royalty. Maybe she'd run away to Scotland out of boredom. Or fleeing the law. Was her father looking for her? It was hard to tell when the lass flitted so seamlessly from lies to truth and from identity to identity.

"Ye're in luck, m'lady," Anne confided to Aillenn. "I have one room left, and 'tis my finest."

For a moment, Adam thought luck was on his side. They'd have to share a chamber after all.

His devious heart gave a silent cheer. After all, many a happy marriage had been made of such inconveniences.

But his hopes were dashed when Anne went on to assure her, "O' course your servant can have a place by the hearth with the others."

Was that a flash of disappointment he detected in Lady Aillenn's eyes? Or just his wishful imagination?

Of *course* the proprietor would assume he was the lady's servant. She was so blinded by Aillenn's brilliance, she hadn't given Adam a second glance.

But even when she *did* meet his gaze, she didn't recognize him.

It wasn't surprising. It was typical.

Still, he'd stayed at Anne Campbell's inn before. Twice. Once as Lugo the spice merchant from Castile and once as himself, Adam la Nuit. But as he'd explained to Aillenn, his face was forgettable.

"Adam," Lady Aillenn said, jarring him from his thoughts, "will ye bring my things upstairs?"

It was foolish to hope that was a conspiratorial glimmer in her gaze.

"Aye, m'lady."

Anne showed them to a chamber even more splendid than the one she'd given to Adam la Nuit of Rivenloch on his last visit. He frowned as he followed Aillenn into the room and dropped the satchels beside the curtained bed.

"I hope 'twill do, m'lady," Anne said.

"'Tis lovely." Aillenn's voice was considerate. But he had the sense she was not overly impressed. She must be accustomed to such opulence.

"I'll move a pallet near the hearth downstairs for your man," Anne said, then took her leave.

For an instant, Adam wished he'd donned a different disguise. Perhaps Margaret the maidservant. Margaret would have been expected to sleep here with the lady.

With a sigh, he went to the hearth to poke the coals of the banked fire to life.

"Ye don't have to do that," Aillenn said.

"If I'm to be *your man*," he told her, winking as he said the words, "'tis what's expected."

She blushed and moved toward the bed. Pushing the curtains aside, she peeked under the coverlet, looking for fleas. Apparently satisfied, she turned, plopping down to sit on the mattress and immediately emitting an indelicate gasp.

"'Tis goose-down!" she cried out in pleasure.

At her words, a wave of heat hit Adam full in the face. A wave that had nothing to do with the blossoming fire.

"Is it?" he managed to squeak out.

It took all his strength of will to keep his eyes trained on the fire as he added more peat.

Goose-down. There was nothing better than a goose-down pallet when it came to swiving.

Sinking into a woman while she sank into the mattress.

Feeling the embrace of feathery softness as they climbed together to a blissful ecstasy.

And afterward, floating in each other's arms on a downy cushion like a heavenly cloud.

"Aye," she replied. "I mean... 'Tis what we have back at the castle, o' course."

"O' course."

It was then he began to suspect she might *not* be Lady Aillenn after all.

Had she slipped up, exclaiming over the goose-down with such naive enthusiasm?

Was she unaccustomed to such extravagance?

Was she not the noble she claimed to be?

How curious that would be.

And how astonished she'd be if she knew that while she luxuriated tonight in her own chamber, in her own goose-down bed, the man waiting on her and bedding down by the communal hearth was a noble warrior of the Rivenloch clan.

Eve had made a grave error. Almost revealed her humble roots.

He didn't seem to notice her slip. But he could have. And she couldn't afford that kind of sloppiness. Not when her life depended upon it.

She dared not let down her guard again. Not for an instant. If anyone knew who she truly was—a runaway nun—they'd oust her from this royal chamber in a heartbeat.

She'd let childish delight, unbridled desire, and misplaced trust in a stranger interfere with her common sense.

When Adam finished with the fire, she'd thank him politely and say farewell.

And she would absolutely *not* look him in the eye. That would only cause trouble.

It seemed an eternity before he was at last satisfied with his fire-building efforts. Meanwhile, she pretended to sort through the things in her satchel.

Finally he replaced the poker and dusted the ash from his hands.

"I'll be but a shout away," he said, "if ye need anythin' in the night."

Staring into her satchel without seeing, she immediately thought about a dozen things she might need in the night. A hug. A kiss. A cuddle.

"I'll be fine," she said, stuffing the green hood farther into the bag.

"I'll be sleepin' with one eye open anyway," he said with a touch of sarcasm, "huddlin' by the fire with my other bedmates."

Guilt washed over her. It seemed silly for her to commandeer an entire bedchamber while men slept shoulder to shoulder in the main room below. She had never liked the idea of class distinction and social ostracism. One of the comforts of a convent were that the nuns might be daughters of nobles or orphans of harlots. But all were equal in the eyes of the Lord.

So believed Sister Eve.

To Lady Aillenn, however, such a thing would never occur. She'd been raised to believe she deserved preferential treatment. And at the moment, to behave otherwise would reveal Eve's secret.

Still, she couldn't let Adam leave without expressing her gratitude.

Keeping her gaze fixed on the floor, she said, "Ye've been a kind and chivalrous companion, sir, and I cannot thank ye enough."

She was holding her breath when he abruptly reached for her hand.

It was a simple reflex for her gaze to flit to his face. And once she fell into the deep, dark pools of his eyes, she was helpless to look away.

CHAPTER 5

For an instant, Eve felt like Lot's wife. Unable to resist temptation, she'd peeked at him and been turned into a petrified pillar of salt. Unable to speak. Unable to breathe.

With a brief smile, he lifted her hand in his with care, as if he cradled a baby dove. Where their skin met, she felt a warm tingling, like the healing rays of the sun.

Then he lowered his eyes and his head. He pressed soft lips against her knuckles. His breath curled between her fingers, stirring her spirit.

"Sleep well, m'lady," he whispered.

He was gone before she could even draw breath.

But she feared his image—his penetrating eyes, his determined jaw, his gentle smile—would be with her forever.

The touch of his hand and his lips were branded on her flesh as permanently as the marks on cattle.

And the thoughts that swirled through her head would not fade any time soon.

Indeed, it took her a long while to fall asleep. When she did, her dreams featured Adam in all his various manifestations. As a half-blind beggar. As a man of the cloth. As a noble knight. As a hunter of outlaws.

She was drawn to them all in her dream. But whenever

she'd get too close to one of them, the abbess would block Eve with a scowl and a stern warning.

By the time Eve awoke the next morn, she was exhausted from battling both the abbess and her own carnal urges.

It wasn't quite dawn when she slipped from the lovely goose-down bed and into her scarlet gown. Leaving early was a good way to avoid having to bid another fraught farewell to Adam. And arriving early at the priory was the best way to secure an audience with Prior Isaac.

She stole downstairs before the proprietor was awake and crept past the men dozing by the banked fire. One of them was Adam, she knew. But she didn't dare peer close to see which one.

She let herself out the door of the inn with practiced stealth and proceeded along the road to the priory. The morn was yet young. But the arriving sunlight already softened the black night to pale gray. The air was chill, but her brisk pace would keep her warm until she reached her destination.

When she finally arrived outside Scone Priory, she extracted a small silk purse from her satchel, tucked the silver cross inside it, and hid the satchel behind a boulder at the edge of the wood, covering it with leaves.

Just like nuns, monks kept early hours. When she emerged from the forest, the priory was already buzzing with activity. Monastery security was not what it was for a convent of nuns. Though there were guards, monks freely entered and exited the gates. And aside from a few unruly young oblates who ogled Eve with open awe, she was allowed to pass with little notice. After all, it would have been unseemly for a monk to let his gaze dwell on a woman.

As she expected, Prior Isaac, upon hearing her title and glimpsing her jewels, was quite willing to set aside his other business and answer her request for an audience.

Fortunately, he didn't recall her as the nun who had burned down half the priory the previous year.

"Your generosity is most welcome, m'lady," Prior Isaac said, gazing down at the silver cross.

By the gleam in his eye, she half wondered if he meant to melt the cross down and keep the silver for himself.

But his sins weren't hers to govern. She'd done her part. She'd repaid the priory for the damages.

Still, as long as she was here, and as long as he didn't remember her face, it wouldn't hurt to put in a request for the nunnery. It was a risky move. But she'd learned without risk, there was no reward.

"Ye know, Prior, there's a wee convent to the west near Mauchline. My cousin is the abbess there. If ye have half-burned books ye no longer need, I know she'd be grateful for one or two."

"Books? Indeed, if ye don't mind blackened chapters and ashes betwixt the pages. I'll send them forthwith."

Eve didn't have to feign her smile of gratitude. For a long while she'd bemoaned the lack of interesting books at the convent. The other sisters seemed to be content with one Bible and a few histories of the Saints. But how much more exciting were the kinds of books Scone Priory had—bestiaries and treatises on medicine and agriculture.

Eve could hardly keep the spring out of her step as she crossed the cloister to leave. This was what she loved. Her Greater Purpose. Not only had she repaid the priory. But she'd achieved what she'd failed to do at her last visit. Procured books for the convent. Books that would enlighten her dear sisters.

Indeed, so self-involved with delight was she, she almost didn't notice the monk lingering near the fountain in the midst of the cloister yard.

His head was covered by a brown hood. His shoulders were draped by a brown scapula. His belted cassock was brown and nondescript. To any other eye, he was simply one of a dozen faceless monks inhabiting the cloister.

But she knew instantly it was Adam.

Her heart jumped into her throat.

What was he doing here? Why was he dressed like a monk? Was he spying on her? How had he gotten here so fast? Had he followed her?

Her joy soured into anxiety.

On her own, she felt confident, sure of herself, able to take control even when things went awry.

But with Adam here...

He could easily undermine her efforts. Reveal her duality. Add peril to her mission. And endanger himself in the process.

She had to get him out of here.

"Ssss!" she hissed sharply, keeping her eyes trained ahead, but slowing her step as she passed. "Adam!"

Adam frowned in disbelief.

How the Devil had she recognized him?

He was completely concealed from head to toe. Not an inch of his face was visible. Not even his own mother would have known him.

"What are ye...?" she rasped out between her teeth, stopping and pretending to admire the fountain, but too vexed to even finish her sentence. "Begone. Now."

"How did ye know 'twas me?" he asked in wonder.

He lifted his hand to peel back his hood. After all, there was no need to hide now.

Her eyes widened as she whispered, "Nay! Don't!" Her fingers tightened on the stone edge of the fountain.

He froze. What was wrong with her?

Staring into the water intensely enough to boil it, she muttered, "Why did ye follow me?"

He answered with the truth. "I didn't want to say goodbye."

Following her had seemed a good idea at the time. Now he wasn't so sure. She seemed very upset.

After a split-second of indecision, she said, "Follow me," and turned on her heel toward the gates.

He gave his head a shake, wishing she would make up her mind. Then he started off after her.

"Not so close!" she hissed over her shoulder.

This was ridiculous. He reached for her arm to halt her. "Will ye explain to me what's goin' on?"

Her brow creased with worry. "Ye wouldn't understand."

She tried to pull her arm out of his grasp, but he held tight. If something was troubling her, he wanted to help.

"Try me," he said.

"There's no time," she bit out. "Just...shoo." This time she managed to pull away.

He snatched the back of her gold girdle, hauling her up short.

"I can help ye," he explained.

"Ye can help me," she mumbled, straining against the girdle, "by lettin' go o' me."

He did.

She would have fallen forward, so hard was she pulling against his grip. But he quickly caught her about the waist to steady her.

"Hold there!" bellowed a voice behind him. "Unhand the lady!"

Adam released her and turned to face Aillenn's champion.

His heart plunged to the pit of his stomach.

It was the prior himself.

And this looked very bad.

Before he could explain, the prior shouted, "Guards!" to summon two strapping monks posted at the gates.

He tried to explain. "I meant no—"

"Seize him!" the prior ordered.

Adam could have fought his way free. He was fast and agile. He could have run past them all and left them in the dust. But he didn't want to abandon Aillenn, who was clearly upset about something.

Besides, there was no point in resisting or trying to explain. In the prior's eyes, Adam was a monk who'd laid hands upon a lady. A lady who, if he'd guessed correctly, had just made a very generous donation to the priory. If Adam had been in the prior's place, he would have made the same assumption.

Eventually, Adam would straighten things out. Meanwhile, it would serve no purpose to antagonize the guards or the prior. So he allowed them to seize him.

"Take him to an empty cell," the prior growled.

As they lugged him away, behind him, he heard the prior speaking to Aillenn. "I must apologize, m'lady, for my monk's inexcusable behavior. I assure ye 'twill be punished. But ye're shakin' like a leaf. Did he harm ye?"

"'Tis only shock," she said.

"O' course," he said. "Well, make no mistake. I'll be sure the sinner pays for what he's done."

Just before Adam was dragged out of range, he overheard the lady's parting words. Her cold dismissal soured his stomach and sank his heart.

"My thanks, prior," she said. "I trust your judgment."

It took every bit of Eve's willpower to put one foot in front of the other and abandon Adam at the priory.

She knew he'd meant nothing by his actions. He was only concerned for her welfare and didn't realize he was becoming so physical. She'd done similar things herself, trying to make a point.

But to the uninformed eye, Adam appeared to be an errant monk accosting a lady. And she could think of no alternative explanation for what the prior had witnessed. Not one that he'd believe.

Could she say the monk's hands had somehow become innocently tangled in her girdle?

That he'd been practicing for an upcoming mystery play?

Or demonstrating a wrestling match he'd seen at the fair?

It all sounded absurd. Nay, she had to walk away. She had to come up with an alternative plan to get him out of this. And an alternative persona to pull it off.

It was mostly her fault. She shouldn't have acknowledged Adam in the first place. She should have ignored him.

He could have gone on pretending he was a monk. She would have maintained her composure and continued on her way.

But she'd been so surprised to see him. Almost as surprised as he was to be recognized. And once she'd gazed into his enthralling eyes, her mind had gone blank. Panic set in. She forgot for a moment who she was supposed to be.

As for who *he* was, she honestly didn't know. Maybe he *was* a monk from Scone Priory. If that were true, there wasn't much she could do to save him from the prior's wrath.

But something told her that wasn't his real identity. And since she'd gotten him into this mess, it was up to her to get him out of it.

Hopefully, he'd be safe enough until the morrow. Most monastic punishments weren't too severe. They commonly involved things like confinement in one's cell for a day or going to bed without supper.

Meanwhile, she'd change into her habit and seek lodging at the nearby convent as Sister Eve.

She dug her satchel out of the leaves and opened it to do an inventory of the contents. She had an idea for a costume that would take the rest of the day to complete. But with any luck, when she returned to Scone Priory in the morn, no one would recognize her.

As it turned out, Eve got a late start the next day. At breakfast, the abbess at the convent was eager for news from the traveling sister. Eve had scarcely buttered her bread when the nuns began peppering her with questions about the nunnery in the west.

Eventually she was able to excuse herself. She thanked them for their charity, though some of it they weren't aware of yet. But she left ample coin in the cell where she'd slept to pay for the things she'd procured without permission—the bedsheets, a wax tablet and stylus, a wooden candlestick, and most of the tail hair from the convent's old mule.

By the time she bid them farewell, the sun was already halfway on its morning journey toward midday.

In the woods, she changed into the disguise she'd stitched out of the pale linen bedsheets—a rough cassock with a braided belt. She stuffed the top with rags to thicken her torso. Tying back her hair, she covered her head with an oversized gray cowl. Then she rolled on the forest floor to dirty the garments. To disguise her hands and bare feet, she wrapped them with scraps of mud-stained linen. She'd wanted to stain them with blood and perhaps animal dung. But there were limits to her commitment to the role.

Using pine pitch, she artfully affixed the mule hair to her face, creating an unkempt, grizzled beard that hung halfway down her chest. She added the cross she'd roughly carved out of the wooden candlestick, as well as the tablet and stylus, hung around her neck by strips of braided linen. As a finishing touch, she smeared her face and fingers with charred peat. Along the way, she found a fallen oak branch that was just the right size for a staff.

It was midday when she entered the gates of Scone Priory with a slow and measured gait, leaning heavily on the staff, as if she'd been walking for months. Anyone who saw her would recognize her as an ascetic and a pilgrim.

Despite her unclean appearance, she would be welcome among the monks, of course. They would offer her food at their table. And unless part of Adam's punishment was going hungry, he would be among those supping.

She stopped at the fountain, ostensibly to get a drink. But she was actually perusing the cloister, looking for signs of Adam or the prior. And finding nothing.

Suddenly someone tugged on the back of her cassock.

She turned round with a scowl. It was a pair of oblates. They looked to be about seven years old, with brown cassocks, wide eyes, and inquisitive faces.

"Are ye a pilgrim?" one of them asked.

Eve gave them a slow nod.

"Where are ye goin'?" demanded the other.

She narrowed her eyes. Then she picked up the tablet and scrawled into it with the stylus, turning it toward them.

The first one squinted at the letters. "CAN...YOU... READ?" he read. "Aye, I can." He wagged a thumb at the other lad. "Timothy can't though."

"Edward!" Timothy frowned and stuck out his tongue at Edward.

She scraped the tablet clean and scrawled into it again.

"What's wrong?" Timothy asked. "Can't ye talk?"

She shook her head.

"Why?" He wrinkled his nose in disgust. "Did ye get your tongue cut out?"

Edward gave him a light shove. "Dolt! He's probably

under a vow o' silence." Then he glanced at her. "Are ye under a vow o' silence?"

She nodded. Then she showed him the letters on the tablet.

Edward read it for Timothy. "SAINT...ANDREWS. Ye're on pilgrimage to Saint Andrews?"

She nodded.

"*I'm* goin' to Saint Andrews," Timothy boasted.

"Nay, ye're not," Edward said.

"One day."

"Maybe one day. But we're stuck at the priory until we take our vows."

"When's that?" Timothy asked.

He shrugged. "My cousin John was fourteen."

Timothy's brows shot up. "Fourteen? That's..." He screwed up his forehead to think.

"He can't do sums either," Edward confided.

"I can do sums," Timothy protested. He proceeded to count on his fingers, finally giving up. "'Tis a long time, isn't it?"

"Seven years."

Timothy sighed. Then he gazed up at her. "How old were ye when ye took your vows?"

She scraped the board and picked up the stylus, considering what age to carve into the wax.

"Look!" Timothy hissed, elbowing his friend and pointing across the cloister.

She followed his gaze. The breath froze in her throat. Her fingers fumbled on the stylus and dropped it.

Two monks, led by Prior Isaac, were hauling Adam across the cloister.

"Gather, brethren!" the prior called. "In the chapter house."

Other monks began to follow them.

"Us too?" Timothy murmured.

Edward nodded.

Timothy narrowed his gaze. "What are they goin' to do?"

"That's the monk who accosted a lady yesterday," Edward said.

"What's accosted?"

Eve's heart was pounding. It was probably nothing. They were probably going to the chapter house to hear Prior Isaac lecture everyone on the sin of accosting ladies.

"Come on," Edward said, grabbing Timothy's hand and joining the mob.

It was a risk, following them. A traveling ascetic wasn't necessarily welcome in a priory's inner sanctum. But Eve could make herself invisible. She retrieved the stylus and managed to slip in to the chapter house with the last of the dozens of monks.

"Brethren," the prior intoned when everyone had grown quiet, "ye are here to witness the penance of a fellow monk."

Speculative whispers blew like an ill wind through the arched chamber.

Eve bit the corner of her lip. She'd been punished once for running away. The abbess had made her recite the Ten Commandments a dozen times in front of all the other nuns. The abbess had intended it as a humiliation. But it hadn't been so bad.

Maybe that was what the prior intended.

"Carnal temptation," the prior began, making Eve's eyes roll, "must be resisted if ye are to be faithful servants o' God. If ye do not resist, if ye succumb to the desires o' the flesh, ye become servants o' the Devil."

He beckoned to the guards, who dragged Adam forward.

"This monk, this servant o' God, fell to the Devil's wiles. He weakened in his faith and shamed himself with a woman."

Several gasps erupted.

Eve frowned. He hadn't "shamed himself." He'd only touched her about the waist.

"He shall be punished accordingly," the prior announced, "to silence the voice o' lust within him, and so ye may learn what happens to those who yield to the temptations of Eve."

Eve sucked in a quick breath at the mention of her name.

Then she remembered. Genesis. *That* Eve.

The prior gestured to the guards. They turned their prisoner round. With a rough yank, they wrenched the top half of his cassock down, baring his back.

Eve shuddered.

Surely the prior couldn't mean to... Not that beautiful, smooth, perfectly sculpted...

The prior picked up a thick wooden rod, testing it with a slap across his palm.

The breath froze in Eve's chest.

God's bones!

She had to do something.

Starting another fire occurred to her.

But there was no time.

Adam braced himself.

It wouldn't be the first time he'd taken a beating. Not as Adam of Rivenloch, of course. But once when he'd disguised himself as Black Conall, the sea reiver, he'd been beaten for fighting with a fellow crewman. And once as the beggar Tom, he'd been whipped for winking at a woman.

Neither had been severe. He'd been left with no scars, which was fortunate. The more identifying marks he bore on his body, the more recognizable he'd become. And becoming recognizable would end his livelihood as a spy.

He supposed his fate today depended upon how much religious fervor the prior intended to use wielding the rod.

He wondered if this was what Lady Aillenn had in mind when she said she trusted the prior's judgment. It certainly seemed an extreme price to pay for "carnal desire."

"Hold him still," the prior told the guards.

Adam held his breath.

Before the prior could begin, the expectant hush was broken by a growing disturbance from the back of the chapter house.

As the unrest increased, the prior demanded, "What is it? What's goin' on?"

The guards were holding Adam so tightly, he couldn't crane his head around to see what was happening. But any delay was good. Perhaps it was a fire. One could always pray for fire.

"Who is it?" the prior said. "Come forward."

There was no answer except for grunting as the assembly shifted to make way for someone.

"Who are ye?" the prior asked.

A youthful voice piped up from the assembly to address the prior. "Beggin' your pardon, Father?"

"Aye, Edward?"

"He said he's a pilgrim, goin' to Saint Andrews. He's under a vow o' silence."

"Is that so?" the prior asked. "Then how did he tell ye that?"

"He's got a wax tablet," Edward replied.

The prior cleared his voice, disgruntled. "Write on your tablet then. What do ye want?" After a brief silence, the prior read the pilgrim's message aloud. "MY...BROTHER." He paused. "Who? This man? He's your brother?"

Adam scowled. His brother? How could that be? Both of his brothers were at Rivenloch.

The prior continued, chastising the pilgrim. "Ye should

have kept a closer watch on him then. Did the Lord not admonish Cain when he claimed he was not his brother's guardian?"

Guardian? Adam's brothers were younger than him. Alexander wouldn't be knighted for another year. And Gavand wasn't old enough to grow a beard.

The prior read the next message. "HE...RAN...AWAY. So ye lost him?"

Who the Devil was pretending to be his brother? Was it one of his cousins? He tried to turn his head, but the guards still held him fast.

"Ah," the prior said with a sigh. "I see. MAD. So your brother is feeble o' mind?"

Adam felt the gears in his brain shift. He didn't know who this savior posing as his brother was, but that was a brilliant ploy. If Adam feigned to be mad, he naturally couldn't be held responsible for his actions.

All he had to do was act mad.

He let out a wordless bark, pleased when his captors jerked in surprise. Then he began humming to himself.

"Is that why ye're makin' a pilgrimage to Saint Andrews? To pray for healin'?" the prior asked. After a pause, he said, "I see." Then he cleared his throat and announced, "Very well. In light o' these new circumstances, I shall forego the man's penance. 'Tis clear he's sufferin' enough. Instead, let this be an example o' God's mercy. And we shall pray for his lost soul."

The guards released him then and draped the cassock back over his shoulders.

Careful to keep his eyes slightly unfocused as if he were dimwitted, he scanned the crowd until he saw the monk with the tablet. His alleged "brother."

His eyes went wide with recognition. But he said nothing. He didn't want to endanger them both.

Whatever he did next, he had to do it quickly. The

"pilgrim" was obviously a beautiful woman under that filthy beard. She'd be discovered any moment.

Quickly he cried, "Bruh!" careening toward the pilgrim. "Bruh!"

He wrapped her in a smothering embrace, hoping to keep her face hidden as they staggered toward the door.

She couldn't reprimand him verbally. She was supposed to be under a vow of silence. But she fought against his grip as they exited the chapter house and started across the cloister.

Finally breaking free, she muttered, "Your satchel?"

"In the woods."

She nodded in approval, and they strode toward the gates. Arm in arm. Like brothers.

The silent walk back to the woods gave Adam time to consider what had just happened.

His emotions were as varied and volatile as a spring storm. He was terrified on her behalf. Grateful for her rescue. Irritated that she'd abandoned him. Awed that she'd carried off such a complex disguise.

The woman was daft. And yet she was marvelous. Inspired. Ingenious. Daring.

Once they reached the cover of the forest, he stopped and turned her toward him. Bracing his hands on her shoulders, he grinned at her horrible costume and gazed into her sparkling eyes.

"I didn't think ye meant to come back."

She furrowed her brows. "How could I not?"

His heart swelled. "That was brilliant. I don't know how ye managed it. But ye're a godsend."

"And ye," she gushed. "Ye were quick to join the ruse. Ye sounded so moonsick, I almost believed ye."

"Maybe I *am* moonsick."

Then he pulled her forward and kissed her soundly on the mouth, beard and all.

He expected, after an instant of shock, she might share in his relief and return the kiss with equal enthusiasm.

She did not.

But Adam was no fool. He was not a seducer of unwilling maids. So he ended the kiss, searching her eyes with a frown of concern.

There was no conspiratorial joy in her expression. No clever mischief. No smug victory.

She looked positively stunned.

Then her gaze lowered to his lips, and her eyes filled with something else. Something he recognized at once.

Smoky longing.

CHAPTER 6

ve felt forbidden heat in her body again. Blood rushing through her veins. A heavenly hum in her ears. Drowsy desire in her eyes.

Despite years of wearing the garments of others—ladies, servants, archers, monks, even courtesans—she'd never kissed a man before.

Why would she? She was a nun. It was wrong. Right?

God forgive her, it didn't *feel* wrong.

And she wanted to do it again.

She closed her eyes and leaned forward, opening her mouth in invitation.

He answered with a kiss so tender, she wondered if she imagined it. But nay. His touch was real. His breath was warm.

Even that light brush caused a ripple of yearning to reverberate through her. Her heart quickened. Her skin tingled. Her breasts swelled. A delicious throbbing began betwixt her thighs.

Fearing he'd pull away, she angled her head, deepening the kiss. But then she feared he *wouldn't* pull away, that she'd be swallowed, body and soul. She faltered, unable to decide whether to stop or go on.

He decided for her.

He pulled her into his embrace.

Then he lowered his lips to hers again, firmer this time. Moving his mouth over hers. Nuzzling her cheek. Tasting her as if she were an irresistible, ripe peach.

His hand drifted up and his fingers left a trail of shivers along her bare throat. He reached beneath her hood and caressed the flesh at the side of her neck.

She made a sound she'd never made before. A soft moan.

It frightened her. Who was this woman making such sounds?

Yet his touch simultaneously excited and comforted her.

He groaned in answer, giving the lobe of her ear a gentle squeeze.

When she gasped, he parted her lips farther with his tongue, making cautious explorations.

Her pulse began to race. Was she afraid? Or excited?

She lifted her hands and placed them on his chest. Whether to push him away or haul him closer, she wasn't sure. She rested them upon the firm muscle there, remembering the similar enticing contours of his bare back.

Her head swam in a sea of confusion. Was she coursing through the waves like a spirited dolphin? Or about to drown in the depths of an unforgiving ocean?

She wanted more. Her body craved...something.

Just as she was about to press closer to discover what it was, she felt him chuckle against her mouth.

Jarred out of her lusty languor, she pulled back.

For one awful instant, glancing at the amusement in his eyes, she thought he was laughing at her.

What had she done wrong? Had she been too aggressive? Was she supposed to be still? She knew nothing about kissing.

Then he cupped her chin, tilted his head, and explained, "I've ne'er kissed anyone with a beard before."

Relief melted into a smile. "I've ne'er kissed *anyone* be—" The words were out before she could stop them.

His brow creased. "What?"

She hadn't meant to confess that. She was supposed to be a lady. Surely *Lady Aillenn* would have had many suitors.

"I mean," she amended with a blush, "the *pilgrim* has ne'er kissed anyone."

"Ah," he said. But he didn't look like he believed her explanation. "Shall we change out o' this holy garb ere someone thinks a pair o' errant monks are indulgin' in carnal temptation?"

She knew he was jesting. But those two words had never sounded so tempting as they did now on his lips.

He was right. They needed to change their identities to throw off any possible pursuers. Besides, the mule-hair beard was not only unsavory. It was getting itchy. Perhaps the painstaking process of removing it would erase any sensual, intrusive thoughts.

She gulped. "Aye. My satchel is in the copse ahead." Then she remembered. "But I'll need to find verjuice to remove the beard." The acid would help dissolve the pine pitch she'd used to adhere it.

"I've got verjuice."

"Ye do?" Who carried verjuice with them? She always had to seek out a kitchen to procure the stuff.

"In my satchel." Then he gave her a sly glance. "'Tis how I usually remove *my* fake beard, when 'tisn't bein' torn off by a vexed lass."

Thankfully, the mule hair hid her blush. She supposed she should be grateful he hadn't decided to tear her beard off in revenge.

"Come sit," he said, patting a moss-covered boulder.

Then he reached behind the boulder and pulled out his satchel.

He uncorked a clay vessel and wet a linen rag with its pungent contents. Then he began dabbing the liquid carefully along the edge of her beard. The odor was sour, sharp, and strong, but the verjuice effectively dissolved the sticky pine pitch.

As he worked, leaning so close to her face, she couldn't help but study him.

How no one could recognize him in his various disguises, she didn't know. True, it could be said he had no particularly distinguishing features. His hair and eyes, like hers, were a neutral brown. Unremarkable. Nondescript. He wasn't especially tall or short. Heavy or thin. Neither strong as an ox nor weak as a kitten.

She supposed he could be called ordinary.

But to her, he was singular. Exceptional. Unforgettable.

His skin was lightly tinted by the sun to a warm hue. His brows were refined and expressive. His thick lashes shadowed alert eyes that missed nothing. His nose was straight and noble. His jaw could be resolute or yielding. His mouth was generous and quick to smile. His lips were kind. And tender. And delicious.

He was gently tugging the mule hair free from beneath her nose when he lifted his gaze and caught her staring. He stopped his ministrations and gave her a knowing grin.

Unfortunately, the acrid odor of the verjuice-soaked linen tickled her nose at that moment. She squinched up her eyes. Gave a little gasp. And sneezed.

He recoiled with a laugh.

After that, she tried very hard not to meet his gaze. But it wasn't easy. When she tired of staring through the pines over his shoulder, she tried closing her eyes.

That only heightened her other senses. She felt his light breath upon her face. The soft touch of his fingers.

The heat emanating off of him as he crouched close.

She inhaled the scent of him. Worn leather. Clean sweat. And a faint, spicy incense that lingered in the fabric of his cassock.

"There," he murmured as he loosened the last bit of beard from her chin.

She made the mistake of opening her eyes.

Then she made the mistake of gazing into his.

His fingers still rested lightly upon her jaw, and he lifted her chin slightly.

Her eyes lowered. One corner of his lip rose in a welcoming, bemused smile.

She couldn't help herself. She wanted another kiss. This one without the beard. She leaned forward, pressing her thirsty lips against his in invitation.

At first, she simply enjoyed the pliant warmth of his flesh as she tasted his succulent mouth. Then her breath came in hungry gulps as she began to feast upon him, angling her head to consume more and more.

He responded with equal fervor, moving his hand to cradle her cheek. The other hand came round to press at the nape of her neck, drawing her closer.

The world spun around her as powerful sensations tumbled her thoughts and dazed her emotions. She let herself be tossed about like a feather on the wind, even as the currents increased in strength, threatening to take away all of her control.

A whirlwind swept through her. Filled her lungs with life. Flooded her veins with lust. She lifted her arms around his neck.

Then there was a loud rustle in the brush.

The noise startled them apart.

Panic scattered her senses.

What was that?

Who was it?

Curse her inattention. How could she have left herself so vulnerable?

But he quickly chuckled, muttering, "Damned squirrel."

No danger then. Still, the enchantment was broken. Her relieved sigh was shaky. And she was mortified by how unguarded she'd allowed herself to become.

She wiped a trembling hand across her lips. Whether to erase his kiss or to calm her hunger, she wasn't sure.

"We should go," she decided hoarsely.

He nodded in agreement. "Or at least change our disguises."

Eve was too upset by her own lack of awareness to appreciate his gentle humor.

What was wrong with her? She'd always managed to stay out of trouble by exercising caution. She was always aware of her surroundings. Attuned to sights and sounds and instincts that warned her of danger.

But this man—this beguiling man who could enthrall her with a kiss—left her devoid of sense.

She dared not let it happen again.

It was more than a matter of sinful longing.

It was a matter of survival.

Adam tightened his jaw as he stuffed the vessel of verjuice and the mule-hair beard into his satchel.

He had to be careful.

This woman was bringing out something dangerous in him. Something that made him act foolish. Take risks he shouldn't. And left him woefully oblivious to the outside world.

That squirrel could have been the prior. Or an outlaw. Or a lawman.

Anyone stumbling upon two monks in each other's arms could have meant death for them. At the very least, their true identities might have been revealed, and that would have been the end of Adam's livelihood.

The kiss was his fault.

She'd just been so damned irresistible.

And once he'd removed that ridiculous mule-hair beard, he hadn't been able to keep from leaning in toward her delicate chin, silky cheek, and yielding lips.

He hadn't expected to have such a strong reaction.

It wasn't as if he was inexperienced when it came to kissing. After all, he was a Rivenloch. Though his need for anonymity meant he tended to distance himself from others, sometimes he did exist as Sir Adam la Nuit. And as an unmarried warrior from a respected clan, he attracted a certain amount of female attention. Most of it from unclaimed lasses drooling over the wealth and status that would accompany marriage to a knight of Rivenloch.

He'd done his share of flirting and fondling. He'd swived more than a few maids in the course of his journey to manhood.

Still, he'd never had his blood simmer so quickly. Never been left so breathless with desire. Never had his body rouse so hastily to the point of near pain.

Most critically, he'd never had his mind emptied so completely of rational thought.

It was irresponsible. Perilous. Life-threatening.

Adam had to refocus his brain.

The lady needed to get out of her monk's attire. And it would be best if he did as well.

"Perhaps ye should change back to yourself," he suggested.

"Myself?"

"Lady Aillenn?"

"Oh. Aye."

She headed for the copse of trees where her satchel was stashed.

Meanwhile, Adam dug through his things. He supposed he could dress as the lady's noble father. Or her servant. Or an elderly lady's maid.

None of them appealed to him. What he truly desired was to be himself. To let Lady Aillenn know he was her peer. To reveal to her the real man behind the disguise.

But it was too much of a risk. People knew Adam la Nuit. For him to be seen traveling alone with a lady would set tongues to wagging. Which would be bad for both of them.

Perhaps he would come up with a new character.

He was already dressed in his white leine and dark blue surcoat, his velvet cap and fine leather boots, when she emerged in her scarlet gown.

"Ye look..." she said, stopping abruptly and searching for the right word as she perused him from head to toe with obvious approval. "Suitable."

Her attraction pleased him.

"And who are ye now?" she asked.

He felt much better about kissing her, now that she looked like a woman and not a monk.

"I'm Ronan Bhallach."

"Bhallach?" she squeaked. "My...my...husband?"

"Your brother," he said, though now that he thought about it, husband *did* sound better.

"Ah, o' course."

Was it relief or regret he saw in her face? It didn't matter. They needed to put distance between themselves and the priory.

"We should probably travel *away* from Saint Andrews."

"I was headed south anyway."

"Good. We can probably make it to Dunnin' ere nightfall," he said, shouldering both of their bags.

"I can carry my..." she said, making a grab for her satchel.

"Don't be barmy," he chided in his best Irish accent. "Our da would wallop the piss out o' me if I laded my wee sister like a mule."

She giggled at that. It was a sweet sound. "Fine, *brother*."

"So tell me about our kin," he said as they set out toward Dunning.

Eve narrowed her eyes. If he thought he was going to unearth all her secrets, he was mistaken. The Bhallach history was completely fictional, and she'd invented it years ago.

"Our da, Tiarna Fursa, is a chieftain. We grew up near Kilkenny," she told him. "When our ma died five years ago, he ne'er remarried. We have two younger sisters."

"Whose names are?"

He *was* thorough. She wondered how he'd remember it all. It had taken her days to memorize Aillenn's bloodlines. "Blinne and Caitilin." A. B. C. She kept things alphabetical for easy recollection.

"Blinne and Caitilin, right, and our da is Tiarna Fursa. And why have the two of us come to Scotland?"

"Da tried to wed me to a withered old soldier, so I ran away. I won't go back unless 'tis with a husband o' my own choosin'."

He nodded. "'Tis reasonable."

It might be reasonable, but it was completely made up. She would be saying Hail Marys for weeks after this pack of lies.

"So I came to choose a suitable bridegroom for ye?" he said with the smugness of an older brother.

"Nay. Ye came to guard my honor."

He gave her a look so sour it made her laugh. After a moment, he asked, "So now that Lady Aillenn is in Scotland, what kind o' bridegroom is she lookin' for?"

She knew he was baiting her. But two could play at that game.

She pretended to consider. "I prefer short men," she decided. "Aye, short. And pale. Fair-haired. Soft around the edges. And agreeable."

He gave her a disgruntled glare. "So womenly men."

A snort of laughter came out of her. She supposed her description *did* sound like a woman. Not *her,* of course, but the kind of woman most men seemed to desire.

"What about ye, *brother?*" she asked. "What kind o' wife do ye see for yourself?"

"Me?"

She didn't realize she was holding her breath, waiting for his reply, until he finally spoke again.

"I haven't thought much on it. But I think I may be developin' a taste for women with mule-hair beards."

That made her laugh again. It also sent a secret thrill through her, remembering his kiss.

But they wouldn't be doing that again. Not if he was supposed to be her brother.

As they walked along, the path opened into a grassy glade between copses of trees. The green expanse was dotted with meadowsweet and buttercups.

Adam nudged her and nodded across the lea toward a coney nibbling on a daisy. They paused to watch until it scampered off into the woods.

"What's our home like?" he asked as they passed through the glen and entered the forest again.

Their home? For a moment, she was still thinking about what he wanted in a wife. Had he already wedded her in his mind?

Then she realized he was speaking of their family home, as her brother Ronan.

"Have ye ne'er been to Ireland?" she asked.

"Nay."

She hadn't either. But never having seen a place didn't stop her from pretending she'd grown up there.

"Though I've heard 'tis like Scotland," he said. "Just greener, with rollin' hills."

"That's right." She'd heard the same.

"Do ye get along with our sisters?" he asked.

She'd never considered that. The Bhallachs were fictional sisters, after all. "I suppose I do."

"Tell me a story about them."

Her mind went blank. Then she remembered an incident from her own real childhood and her four older sisters.

"When I was a lass," she recounted, "my sisters were playin' with an orphaned lamb on the Sabbath. They accidentally chased the wee beast into a bog. It was bleatin' for dear life. But my sisters were afraid to go after it, for they were wearin' their fine Sabbath clothes. Well, I couldn't stand by and let the poor thing drown. So I lumbered into the bog and pried the beast out o' the mud. It thrashed and spattered me with muck, but I managed to save it. When my da saw me, he said I wasn't fit to go to church. He shut me in the sheep pen with the rest o' the beasts until they returned from Mass."

To Eve, it was a funny story.

Adam, however, didn't see the humor at all.

"Did your sisters not defend ye?"

"For what? 'Twas my own unwise choice."

"'Twasn't unwise. 'Twas merciful. The lamb might have died otherwise."

He was right. She'd never thought of it like that before. And a small part of her heart warmed at the idea that he was defending her.

But he wasn't done. He stared at the path, shaking his head and muttering. "What kind o' father shuts his daughter in a filthy sheep pen?"

It hadn't been so bad. Not really. She loved the sheep. And her da's impatience was partly due to raising a family on his own after her ma died. As far as missing church, she knew God didn't care if a person prayed in a chapel or a sheep pen. Still, for the first time in her life, Adam was forcing her to question her father's rigid sense of discipline.

"If I'd been there, as your brother Ronan," he said, "I would have stayed behind and helped ye clean up."

Her heart melted at his earnest declaration. His words made her wish she *had* had a brother around to protect her. Then she began to imagine Adam helping her clean up. Stripping off her muddy clothes. Easing her into the warm bathwater. Running a wet linen cloth gently over every filthy inch of her.

Her face grew hot. She had to change the subject before he noticed.

"What about ye?" she choked out. "Do ye have any tales o' childhood misdeeds?"

"Misdeeds?" he scoffed. "Nay, Ronan was an angel."

"Ronan was hardly an angel," she decided. "As I recall, he tied the steward's boot laces together while he was sleepin'. Put frogs in our sisters' beds. And regularly fed the hounds under the table."

"All that?"

"Aye, and more."

"I fear the truth o' my childhood is far less interestin'."

"What is the truth then?"

"No one paid much heed to me," he admitted. "I was quiet. Well-behaved. I broke few rules. Ruffled no feathers."

"Indeed?" Eve supposed she was a holy terror in contrast. She wasn't exactly ill-behaved. Just wayward and curious, adventurous and enterprising. And she had definitely done her share of ruffling feathers. "Then how did you become the sort o' man who dares to impersonate the emissary o' the Pope?"

"How do ye know I'm *not* the emissary o' the Pope?"

He was jesting with her, of course. Still, she wasn't exactly sure who he was. And she really wanted to know.

"Do ye have any brothers or sisters?" she asked.

"Just ye and our two younger sisters, Blinne and Caitilin, aye?"

"Not Ronan," she chided. *"Ye."*

"Me? A few," he said evasively.

"Older or younger?"

"Both."

She had imagined he was the youngest, like her. She was sure that was part of the reason she felt unseen. Perhaps being in the middle made him feel invisible as well.

It was no secret that Eve had been a disappointment to her parents, simply by virtue of her birth. The last thing a clan with no sons wanted was a fifth daughter.

But what was his story?

"Why disguise yourself?" she asked. "Are ye in trouble with the law?"

"Me? I told ye, I'm not a feather ruffler."

She wasn't sure she believed that. Anyone who dared to confront the king dressed as the Pope's emissary surely caused trouble once in a while. And he'd almost been beaten for carnal temptation at the priory. If that wasn't ruffling feathers, she didn't know what was.

"What about ye?" he asked. "Are ye a lawbreaker?"

"I told ye, I'm a runaway bride."

"Ah, so ye said, but are ye truly Lady Aillenn?" He didn't wait for her to answer. "'Tis yet to be determined. I'm not certain I've met the real woman yet."

She didn't reply.

He grinned.

As they walked on, her mind coiled around possibilities.

"Ye might be a mummer," she considered. Troupes of mummers traveled from manor house to village square, performing raucous plays for coin.

He voiced no opinion on that, simply gazing down the road with a half smile on his face.

"Or maybe ye're a tailor. That would explain how ye acquired all the clothin'."

He acknowledged her guess with a nod, but neither confirmed or denied it.

"Though some o' your clothin' is so bedraggled, perhaps ye're a rag-picker."

"My clothin' is not bedraggled," he protested, spreading his arms to show her the cut of his dark blue surcoat.

It *was* very high quality. His cap was rich velvet. His leine made of the finest linen. And the way his clothing hugged his masculine form...

She wouldn't think of that. But if he hadn't stolen the garments—and she still wasn't completely convinced he wasn't a thief—they must have cost a wee fortune.

Eve continued to mull over possibilities, including the most unlikely—that he was like her, devoted to the church, performing good deeds in God's name.

But she quickly had to dismiss that idea. No man of the cloth would pose as the Pope's emissary. Or lay hands on a woman the way he had at the priory. Or kiss her with the practiced passion of a man accustomed to...

She gasped in sudden revelation. "Ye're a spy, aren't ye? An agent o' the Scots king, sent to spy upon his subjects?"

He lifted one amused brow. "A spy?"

"Or maybe..." She considered another chilling possibility. "Ye're an agent o' the *English* king, infiltratin' the enemy."

He lifted the second brow. "An *English* spy?"

She glanced around the woods to ensure they were alone and whispered, "*Are* ye?"

"Well, if I were," he whispered back, "I certainly wouldn't tell ye, would I?"

She narrowed her eyes and bit the inside of her cheek.

What a frustration he was.

Eve had made an art of being oblique. Elusive. Dissembling. Like a leaf on the breeze, she could drift along on a current of deceit and—if a man came too close to her truth—dance out of his reach with words of distraction.

She was accustomed to being the deceiver. The one in control of things. An omniscient observer who could clearly see all the players while maintaining her anonymity.

So far she'd been able to remain anonymous. But she didn't like being the deceived. It made her feel off-balance and uneasy.

Adam—if that was indeed his name—was as slippery as a salmon.

To be honest, part of her was intrigued by that. He was clever. And mysterious. And enticing. In some ways, she felt as if she'd met her counterpart.

But she also felt threatened by his secrecy. And frustrated that she couldn't see through it.

Still, on such a beautiful day, it was hard to stay irritated.

Around them, the calm silence of the trees was broken by the chirrups of sparrows and wrens. Startled lizards skittered beneath rocks. A mouse scampered through last year's leaf fall while butterflies floated through glades of sun-drenched cowslip. A pair of red squirrels made chase up the trunk of an oak.

Spring was a time for fresh beginnings, and the forest was alive with the gift of resurrection. The sun dappled the path with light. Bright green leaves sprouted from winter-black limbs. Blossoms of yellow and violet popped up through the verdant glen.

Eve took a deep breath. The earthy scents of moss and

lichen mingled with the heady fragrance of woodbine. The breeze was warm. And ripe. And inviting. Whispering through the pines like a man summoning a lover to his bed.

She'd just begun to drift toward sinfully sensuous musings when she heard a sudden, loud rustle from the meadow beyond the trees.

She froze.

Adam stopped beside her.

Was it more thieves? A pack of wolves? A boar?

The rustling continued, and she peered between the trees to see a tumbling ball of brown fur in the midst of the grass.

"Hares," Adam decreed.

She saw them now. A pair of hares rolled and wrestled and romped in the grass. But they weren't young leverets playing with their siblings. These were grown animals. Which, since it was spring and mating season, meant they were likely two males fighting over a female.

While she watched, they reared up on their hind legs and began to pommel each other with their front paws. It was both comical and vicious.

She clucked her tongue at the fierce fighting. "Such a pitiful waste, two lads quarrelin' o'er a lass."

"I don't think—"

"But alas, it seems to be the nature o' the male animal of *all* species." She winced as she watched a tuft of fur fly free. "'Tis self-destructive and pointless. Yet they'd rather suffer bites and breaks and bruises than settle for not gettin' what they want, whether 'tis a hare or a dog...or a man."

"Is that so?"

"Aye. Like those two Rivenloch men at Perth who nigh started a clan feud o'er love o' the same lady."

"Rivenloch men?" he said.

She blanched. She'd said too much.

"What do ye know about Rivenloch men?" he asked.

She shrugged. "Just somethin' I heard at the tourney. A Rivenloch man will draw his sword o'er who gets the last oatcake, am I right?" Then she turned her attention to the battling hares once again. "'Tis foolish. 'Tisn't as if there's a dearth o' oatcakes. Or females."

"Right. As I started to say—"

"Oh. They've stopped." She looked over at him, pleased. "Perhaps they've listened to my sage advice and seen the error o' their ways."

Before she could fully enjoy her smug satisfaction, he cleared his throat and nodded toward the hares.

One of the hares had leaped onto the back of the other and was now rapidly pumping away in what was clearly fornication.

"Oh." Her jaw dropped. Her face flamed.

The idea that the second hare was a female had never occurred to her. But it had to Adam.

She heard him snicker beside her, which made her blush even more.

Gathering what dignity she could, she tore her gaze away from the mortifying spectacle, spun with a disgusted swish of her skirts, and paced down the path.

His repressed laughter followed her, but he thankfully spoke no more of it.

CHAPTER 7

Adam wasn't about to break the silence.

Not only because it was clear she didn't want to discuss the incident with the hares. But also because her mention of Rivenloch had chilled him to the bone.

No one had ever uncovered his identity. No one. He couldn't afford to be revealed now.

Later, when he was old and feeble, perhaps he'd retire from his life of disguise. But for now, he had too many services to perform, too much protection to render, too many cousins to look after to give up his gift of invisibility and his useful occupation.

He'd already made the mistake of giving her his real first name. The fact she'd mentioned his clan meant she was growing too close for comfort.

She'd been at the Perth tournament, of course. But it had never occurred to him she might be acquainted with his family. He'd certainly never heard of *her.*

Was it true she'd only overheard the gossip of others? Or did she have some personal connection to his clan? He needed to find out. Somehow he needed to pry into her past without sharing his own.

The morn was more than half gone when Adam heard

the burbling rush of water, indicating a burn close to the road.

"Shall we stop for a bit?" he said, breaking the silence.

She nodded.

They descended the bank to a place where the stream hurried over rocks and then slowed and narrowed and deepened. He wasted no time, crouching streamside and scooping up handfuls of refreshing, cold water to wash the dust from his face.

Aillenn cautiously washed her hands. Then she dipped a small scrap of linen from her satchel into the water and wrung it out. She patted her neck and face with exaggerated care, as if she feared she might dislodge a freckle.

Meanwhile, Adam spread a linen cloth on the ground and began pulling out the provender he always carried. A chunk of hard cheese. A sack of oats. Strips of salted beef. Dried apples.

She too dug in her satchel for foodstuffs to add to the offering. She had hard cheese and a sack of oats as well. A crock of butter. A neep. An onion. And a loaf of bread she must have procured this morn.

"Well, at least we won't starve," she said. "Too bad we don't have a cauldron. We might make a decent pottage."

"If ye wanted pottage, ye should have told me," he said, stifling a grin. "I could have butchered the pair o' hares we saw back—"

He hadn't even finished the sentence when she gave his arm a chiding punch.

He cried out, gripping the injured limb with feigned pain.

"A gentleman," she muttered, "wouldn't have brought that up."

"I ne'er said I was a gentleman."

"Ye're wearin' the garb of a gentleman."

"Guilty," he said, clapping his hand to his chest. "In future, m'lady, I shall try to remain true to my disguise."

She knelt gracefully on the linen and tore off a chunk of bread, slathering it with butter and offering it to him.

He sat cross-legged, unwrapped the cheese, and used his dagger to slice two thick slabs. He gave her one of them and added a dried apple.

No one spoke. They were too busy feasting. He was hungrier than he thought. He ate half of the salted beef and the last hunk of bread.

"We'll have to replenish our supplies soon, aye?" she said after they were finished, licking a crumb off her thumb.

That innocent gesture—the coy lowering of her lashes, the parting of her lips, the glimpse of her tongue—sent a bolt of desire through him. For an instant, he couldn't think.

Then, quickly replaying her question in his mind, he replied, "Aye, supplies, though we should get enough off o' Pitcairn tonight to last a day or two."

"Pitcairn?"

He instantly realized his blunder. He should never have named the clan at whose keep he planned to seek lodging. The less she knew about his acquaintances, the better. So he feigned uncertainty.

"Is that his name? Pitcairn? Pitfield? Somethin' like that. I o'erheard a traveler speakin' of a noble o' that name with a place south o' Dunnin'. Do ye know him?"

She shook her head.

That was fortunate. It would be challenging enough for a Rivenloch to sneak in under Pitcairn's nose, disguised as an Irish noble. If she didn't know the man, Adam could count on his beautiful Irish "sister" as a distraction.

She *was* distracting. As she packed up what little food remained, he couldn't help but steal glances at her vibrant skin, her lightly freckled face, her finely arched brows, her sweet bow of a mouth. He wondered if all Irish noblewomen were so lovely. Then he lowered his gaze, and his brow creased as he glimpsed her worn nails.

Curious, he reached out for her wrist.

Startled, she gasped.

Turning her hand palm up, he frowned. "These aren't the hands of a noblewoman."

Eve had to think fast. No one had ever studied her closely enough to discern that fact. They were usually too distracted by her coy looks and honeyed words to pay any heed to her calluses.

She grew instantly indignant, snatching her hand back.

"I've had to make my way as best I can on my own," she said defensively, adding a note of hurt to her voice. "If my beauty has been dimmed by my efforts to survive, it cannot be helped. 'Tis a price worth payin' for my freedom."

Her ploy seemed to work.

"I apologize," he said, looking sincerely contrite. "I'm a fool. And ye... Nothin' could dim your beauty, m'lady."

His words took her breath away. Flustered and blushing, she stood and busied herself with the satchel, rearranging things that didn't need to be rearranged, while she tried to regain her composure.

"I should have realized ye were a true noblewoman," he said, coming to his feet. He shook the stray leaves from the linen square and tucked it back into his satchel. "How else would ye know the Rivenlochs?"

Another bolt of alarm shot through her. She didn't dare meet his eyes. "Aye. Right."

"So ye *do* know the Rivenlochs?"

"Me?" she squeaked. "Nay, not personally." She licked her lips and hefted up the satchel, staggering back a step under its weight.

He reached out to steady her.

She danced back out of his reach, trying desperately to recall what she'd said before about the Rivenlochs. "I've only heard tell o' the clan."

"All the way in Ireland?"

"Aye?" she said, wondering if that could even be true. After all, no one in Scotland seemed to know any of the Irish nobles. If they had, they certainly wouldn't recall the Bhallach clan, which was a creation of her own. "They've got quite a reputation."

"Is that so?"

His eyes twinkled then with a curious sort of triumph. He knew something. Or he'd tripped her up. But how?

Suddenly she remembered. Shite. She'd told him she'd heard about the Rivenlochs at Perth. Not in Ireland. She took another evasive step backward.

"Careful," he said with a chiding smile, curving one arm around her waist.

Eve bristled. She hated to be outwitted, especially by a man who found amusement at her expense. And she'd always had a problem with authority. Careful, indeed. She backed out of his embrace. "Don't tell me what to—"

"M'lady!" he shouted, reaching for her again.

Incensed, she shoved her satchel between them and took another step back. Her heel caught on uneven ground, and she began to fall backward. When she tried to catch herself on her other foot, her boot slipped on wet, mossy rock.

Adam loomed in front of her. His eyes were wide. His brow was determined.

With haphazard grace, he snagged a fistful of her gown and catapulted her aside with brute strength.

She was tossed onto the grass on her hands and knees.

He was not so lucky.

She heard a great splash behind her. Apparently, the

force required to save her from falling into the water had propelled him into the burn in her stead.

She turned in horror to see him rising from the stream like a disgruntled Neptune.

"Why did ye not heed my warnin'?" he sputtered, finding his footing.

He took off his velvet cap and squeezed the water from it.

As he slogged forward in his drenched clothes, she began to see the humor of the situation. She fell back onto her bottom, stifling her laughter as she regarded him over her knees.

"Oh, ye think 'tis amusin', do ye?" he asked.

She *did* find it amusing. He'd gone to such efforts to preserve her balance that he'd utterly upset his own. Now he looked like a peevish cat retrieved from a well.

Still, she was grateful. If she'd stumbled into the burn, she would have ruined her best gown. It was a noble sacrifice on his part. She was about to tell him that when he tossed his cap onto the bank and hauled his wet surcoat off over his head. He wrung it out as he waded toward the shore, finally draping it over the limb of a streamside rowan.

He might as well have removed his leine, for all the modesty it afforded him. Soaking wet, the knee-length transparent linen clung to every sculpted muscle, leaving little to her imagination.

He pulled off his boots, holding them upside down to drain out the water before setting them down on a mossy rock. Then, with no regard for propriety, he reached under his leine and began to unfasten his trews.

She meant to tear her gaze away. Sister Eve knew it was improper to look upon a man in a state of undress.

But Lady Aillenn was fascinated by his boldness—and the muscular thighs he revealed as he peeled off the trews.

So entranced was she, she couldn't remember what she'd intended to say to him.

He plucked the leine away from his body, rippling it to try to dry the linen.

"This may add an hour to our journey," he warned. "I can't very well show up lookin' like a wet selkie."

She nodded, though she thought if he *were* a selkie, she would have gladly followed the fae creature into the water to drown. He was compelling and irresistible, even when the power of his gaze was diminished by strings of dark, dripping hair covering his face.

He strode near. For a moment, huddled on the ground, she froze. Another step, and she'd be able to see whether he was wearing braies beneath his leine.

But then he reached out his hand. She took it, and he pulled her upright.

"We should find a sunny spot to dry these," he said, collecting his boots and cap and surcoat.

She looked away then to pick up her satchel.

Finally finding her wits, she said, "Thank ye."

"For what?"

A wicked answer flew into her head. For letting me feast my eyes upon your body.

But that wouldn't do.

Instead she replied, "For savin' me."

He gave her a dramatic sweep of a bow. "O' course." Then he winked. "Anythin' for my sister."

She could not have felt less like his sister. Nonetheless, she gave him a nod of gratitude before they embarked on their search for sunlight.

He found a glade not far from the road with a hawthorn where he could hang his wet clothing to dry and a fallen, mossy log where they could sit in reasonable comfort.

"So tell me about your search for a husband," he bid her.

"Oh, I'm not searchin' for a husband."

He smiled. "I suppose a lady as lovely as ye doesn't need to *search* for a husband."

Lovely. He'd called her lovely.

"Nay," she said, blushing. "I mean I'm not...that is..." What did she mean? Sister Eve wasn't searching for a husband. But Lady Aillenn surely must wish to have children one day. "I suppose I'm...in no hurry."

"Ah. I imagine findin' just the right short, pale, fair-haired, soft-around-the-edges, agreeable gentleman may take a while."

She grinned. He'd remembered her silly description.

"And o' course," he continued, "'twould be hard to give up the thrill of our profession."

The thrill. She'd never thought of it that way. She'd always considered her disguises simply a necessity for doing God's work.

But he was right. It was thrilling, slipping into the identity of another person, altering her carriage and her speech. Fooling observers. Carrying off risky plots.

"I suppose if ye were to marry," he said, "'twould be the end o' your adventures."

She'd never had to consider that. After all, she was a nun. She'd already come to terms with not becoming a wife or mother.

"I suppose," she said. "But what about ye? Would ye give up your life o' deception for a bride?"

"'Tis the only skill I have," he admitted. "So unless I find a rich heiress to wed..."

"Perhaps *Ronan* can find himself a rich heiress."

He chuckled. "Perhaps."

"But certainly ye have other skills," she said. "I saw ye in the melee. Ye can handle a blade. And ye chased off the thieves. Ye could work for the king as a man-at-arms."

"A man-at-arms?" He stroked his chin, as if considering the notion. But there was a mischievous gleam in his eyes that told her he found the idea amusing.

"Or perhaps ye could take your vows," she suggested. "That way ye'd live a life o' chastity and be relieved o' the burden o' findin' a wife."

She half expected he'd react to that idea with distaste, indicating he wasn't a man of the church. That would help narrow down his true identity.

Instead he answered with a noncommittal, "True."

Still hoping to unmask him, she asked, "What other disguises have ye donned?"

He gave her a sly glance. "I'll tell if ye will."

"Fine." She supposed it would do no harm. Besides, there was something exciting about being able to share her life's passion. "I sometimes dress as a milkmaid named Maggie Gall."

"Maggie the milkmaid? To what end?"

"For the milk, o' course."

He grinned. "O' course."

"And sometimes I hear a bit o' useful tattle about a household."

"What kind o' useful tattle?"

"Who's ill. Who's soused. Who's stealin' from the kitchens. Who's sneakin' off in the middle o' the night."

"So ye're employed as a spy?"

"Nay."

"Then why do ye do it?"

She shrugged. "To right wrongs."

"Hmm."

"Your turn."

"Let's see... I once posed as the mystic Hildegard o' Bingen."

She gasped. "What?"

His brows shot up. "Ye've heard o' her?"

She realized he'd startled another piece of information out of her—that she was knowledgeable. Of course she'd heard of Hildegard of Bingen. Among the educated, Hildegard was a renowned abbess, a visionary versed in natural philosophy, medicine, writing, and music.

"Everyone has heard o' Hildegard o' Bingen. But how...?" She couldn't imagine Adam disguising himself as a woman, especially such a famous woman.

"Everyone has *heard* o' her," he said. "But has anyone *seen* her?"

He had a point. If he comported himself with enough confidence, she supposed he could fool anyone into believing he was the elusive abbess. That was how he'd convinced everyone he was the emissary of the Pope. Still...

"Ye can't pass for a woman," she decided.

"I can. And have. Granted, my Hildegard is a rather large woman with a husky voice, but..."

That made her laugh. This she had to hear. "Do the voice."

"Now?"

She nodded.

He cleared his throat, then spoke in a ragged voice with a thick German accent. "Zere is ze music uff heav'n in all tings."

Her eyes widened. Adam did sound like a wizened woman.

She skewered him with a glittering gaze that was half admiration, half scolding. "Ye know ye're wicked, feignin' to be Hildegard. Why would ye do such a thing?"

"To gain access to a library. My cousin needed a copy o' Aristotle's treatise on Physics."

"So ye stole it?"

"Not exactly. The laird was delighted to give it to Hildegard."

She shook her head in wonder.

"Besides," he added, "that tome was covered in dust. I'm not certain it had e'er been read."

Still, such an audacious undertaking was unthinkable to Eve.

"Your turn," he said.

"I'm afraid I'm not so bold as ye."

"I'd say a pilgrim with a mule-hair beard confrontin' the Prior o' Scone is fairly bold."

She had to smile at that. "That *was* a wee bit risky."

"So tell me about Jehan o' Rouen."

"Who?"

He chided her with a look. "I know 'twas ye. I saw the green hood in your satchel."

She sighed. She supposed there was no point in hiding it anymore. Even if he did know about Jehan, there was still much he *didn't* know about her. Including her real name and profession.

"Jehan is the oldest o' ten. His da died last year, so he goes from tourney to tourney, earnin' coin to support his brothers and sisters in Rouen."

"I see. And I suppose these brothers and sisters have names?"

"O' course." Eve was nothing if not thorough. "Alain, Beatriz, Caterine, Denis, Elaine, Florie, Guillaume, Heloise, and Isabeau."

His eyes were dancing with amusement and, perhaps, admiration. "And how did Jehan perfect his skills with a bow?"

"Huntin' hare in the forest. Indeed, he had to flee Rouen, bein' wanted as a poacher."

Adam's laughter rolled over her like a warm breeze and did something curious to her heart. It had been a long while since she'd heard such a carefree sound. She thought she could sit here forever, swapping tales with her fellow impostor.

"Now ye," she said.

"Have ye heard o' Godefroid de Claire?"

She had. The abbess at her convent had seen some of the artist's reliquaries on her travels. But Eve didn't want to reveal too much, so she shook her head.

"He's a jeweler. He makes enamels and reliquaries."

"And ye've posed as this jeweler?"

"Aye."

"Do ye know how to make jewelry then?"

"Nay. But it didn't get that far."

She lifted a brow for him to continue. "Tell me everythin'."

"My younger brother was leavin' an alehouse late at night when he tripped o'er the alewife's cat and landed in the lap of a drunken nobleman," he said vaguely. "The man, furious at bein' accosted, challenged my brother to combat the followin' day. He couldn't see my brother was too young for battle, and the proud lad wouldn't refuse the challenge."

She clasped a hand to her breast.

"So I ordered him to stay at home. Early the next morn, Godefroid de Claire," he said with a wink, "made a visit to the nobleman. Godefroid pulled out a quill and parchment and told the man that as a gesture o' thanks for his loyalty, the king had commissioned an enamel to be made in his honor. The nobleman was delighted. Naturally, drawin' up the design for the piece took most o' the day."

"Naturally."

"By the time Godefroid left, the man had completely forgotten about the battle."

"And the enamel?"

"The nobleman's friends agreed the man must have drunk himself into a stupor to imagine the esteemed artist Godefroid de Claire would make an enamel for him."

It was Eve's turn to laugh. Who *was* this hero in disguise who risked life and limb for his family? She desperately wanted to know.

She suddenly asked him, "Have ye e'er been unmasked?"

"Me? Nay. Ye?"

She thought about the time Hew du Lac of Rivenloch had tried to court her. "Not exactly, but 'twas close."

"What happened?"

"Someone fell in love with me," she recalled, gazing out at the sunny meadow. "He didn't realize I was—" She broke off. She'd almost said *a nun.* "I wasn't who I said I was."

"And who was that?"

She had to think fast. "A...a courtesan."

Shite. Why had she said that? She *had* on occasion disguised herself as a woman of easy virtue simply for access to men's secrets. But she'd never indulged in any immoral activity. When Hew confessed his love, she'd been dressed just like this, as Lady Aillenn. In the end, she'd taken pity on his bruised heart and admitted to being a nun.

She glanced at Adam. Suspicion was etched on his brow.

"I'm *not,* o' course," she said, reading his thoughts. "I'm not a courtesan. I told ye, I've ne'er e'en kissed..."

She *hadn't* told him that, though. She'd *almost* told him that.

"I knew it," he said in triumph. "I knew I was your first."

She blushed, more from the indignity of having trapped herself with her own words than his smug delight at being her first kiss.

Then he leaned in to murmur, "If it makes ye feel better, 'twas my first as well."

"Nay. Is that true?"

"Aye. I've ne'er kissed a bearded pilgrim before in my—"

She gave him a hard shove that almost pushed him off the end of the log, as he deserved. But the sight of his eyes widening in panic was so comical that she couldn't help but break into giggles.

He couldn't maintain his expression of outrage for long. Soon he was shaking his head and chuckling right along with her.

When decorum was restored, she asked him, "Why do ye do it?"

"Do what?"

"The subterfuge. The costumes. The deception." She wasn't sure she wasn't asking *herself* that question. "If ye're not hidin' from the law, why wear a disguise?"

He shrugged. "'Tis...amusin'."

Eve didn't believe him. "'Tis more than that. No one risks the wrath o' the king for his own amusement."

The lass was right. And though Adam knew it was folly to confide in a woman he barely knew—a woman who had too many secrets of her own—he didn't really want her to believe his disguises were all just an amusing entertainment to him. Because they weren't.

"The truth?" he said with a sigh.

"Aye."

"I do it to protect the ones I care about."

Her eyes were full of doubt. "Is that so?"

"Aye. I do what I can to keep them safe."

"So when ye said ye followed me for my safety..." She looked into his eyes, as if seeking the truth.

Her dark honey gaze melted his resolve. "'Twas true."

"And when ye came to the priory..."

"I wanted to be sure ye were unharmed."

Her voice was little more than a whisper. "But ye said ye protected those ye *care* about."

"Aye."

"So ye care...about me?"

He swallowed. In another moment, if she kept gazing at him like that, with her eyes all dewy and her face all hopeful, he'd close the space between them and show her just how much he cared about her.

But that would be a mistake. She'd already confessed to being untried in the ways of love. And sitting here in his damp leine, he might as well be naked. The last thing an innocent lass needed to witness was the rousing effect she was having on the beast in his braies.

Instead, he acted in her interests once more, protecting her. From himself. With a one-sided smile and a great deal of regret, he said, "O' course I care about ye. Ye're my sister, aye?"

Her brow creased.

Before she could shove him off the log again, he stood up and carefully turned away. "We should be movin' on, m'lady. We've a ways to go."

He donned his clothes, which were still uncomfortably damp, and tried to hide his disappointment as they returned to the road. She was disappointed as well. He could see that. They'd spent the day in a beautiful spring glade, whiling away the time in pleasant conversation, like two old warriors swapping battle stories. And now he'd put a cork in the bottle of their discussion.

He felt bad about it. But if they were to carry on this fiction of being brother and sister, they couldn't afford to ruin the deception with any show of romantic affection. Even now, with his unruly cock stuffed into damp wool, his show of romantic affection was undeterred.

After about a hundred yards, she spoke.

"So if ye disguise yourself to keep others safe," she asked, "who was the emissary o' the Pope keepin' safe?"

Adam hadn't been prepared for such a pointed question.

He should have been. The woman had a way of burrowing into him like a tick and sucking out the truth.

She already knew his real first name. She knew of the Rivenlochs. He'd been a whisper away from telling her about his real brothers and sisters. He'd shared some of his real exploits, divulging some of the characters he'd played. He didn't dare expose any more of his secrets. Some of his work was on behalf of some very important people.

"I'm not at liberty to say," he told her.

She emitted a frustrated sigh.

"What about ye?" he asked. "What were ye doin' at Perth that day?"

She was saved from having to answer him when they spotted two travelers approaching on horseback.

He fell silent as well.

In their profession, minimizing interactions was always best. The less memorable they could be, the better.

But as the horsemen neared, he studied their appearance with a critical eye.

The men were well-dressed. Their clothing was made of high-quality wool, beautifully dyed and trimmed. But it was stained and ill-fitting.

The horses too were decent rounceys. But they looked as if they hadn't been groomed in weeks.

"Outlaws," Aillenn whispered.

Exactly what he'd thought. He was impressed she'd figured that out as well.

"Or scouts," he whispered back. "Stay close."

If they rode past, they might be spotters who ranged the woods, eyeing prospects for robbery. In that case, their cohorts were likely hiding in the trees, waiting for a signal.

He guided Aillenn to the side of the path to let them pass, giving them a nod.

"Mornin'," the one in front said.

After they rode past, she held out her hand and murmured to him, "Give me my satchel."

Adam knew better than to argue with her. She was savvy enough to recognize them as outlaws. Perhaps she was savvy enough to carry a weapon among her things.

The riders were twenty yards past when one of them let out a high whistle.

"'Tis a signal," she whispered. "There are more o' them."

"Aye."

They were likely up ahead in the densest part of the woods. He slipped his hand into his satchel and stealthily pulled out his dagger. They might be outnumbered. But he had surprise on his side.

"And so I said to him," Aillenn said loudly, "I said, 'What do ye mean, ye don't have the rose silk? I was told 'twould be in by spring'."

His eyes widened in horror. What was she doing? He'd planned to steal up on the outlaws. She might as well be blowing a buisine to herald their arrival.

She glanced at him, taking no notice of his furrowed brows and glare of disapproval, and continued to blather on.

"What was I to do?" she continued. "I couldn't very well wear the same blue velvet I wore at Yuletide. And I told the merchant so. He insisted 'twas the fault o' the supplier in Byzantium. 'Byzantium?' I said. 'I asked for silk from Lucca!'"

He glared even harder, biting out between his teeth, "What are ye doin'?"

Her gaze slipped aside just for an instant, but he began to understand. She'd spotted the outlaws, and she was carrying on as if she had not. It was a clever ruse. And it would take the thieves completely by surprise.

"Everyone knows Lucca silk is far superior," she continued. "And the colors..." She paused for a dramatic gasp. "The yellow is as bright as the sun. The red as rich as strawberries. But the rose, I had my heart set on the rose. Ye know how much I love rose."

"I do."

He saw them now. On both sides. Hiding in the shadows of the trees.

"I asked for *three* ells o' the rose," she said, waving an arm to the left. "And *three* ells o' the blue." She gestured to the right.

The clever lass was using code to tell him how many outlaws she'd seen. He prayed she didn't mean to try to save their souls again.

"So *six* ells in all?" he replied. He could fight six men. "That doesn't seem unreasonable."

"Indeed," she said, glancing at his dagger. "If one has a sharp pair of *scissors,* I should think—"

The outlaws emerged with a cry that was likely supposed to startle their victims.

But Adam was prepared. So was Aillenn.

She swung her satchel about, knocking the first outlaw off his feet.

Adam dropped his satchel and thrust his dagger forward at a man wielding a cudgel, wounding him just inside his shoulder, which forced him to release his weapon and stagger off.

The next outlaw swung out with a knife blade, leaving a shallow slice in Adam's arm where he couldn't dodge fast enough.

He sucked a quick breath of pain between his teeth and returned with his dagger, slashing across the man's wrist. The man screamed, and his knife clattered to the forest floor. He clenched his wrist to stop the bleeding as he sought the haven of the trees.

Out of the corner of his eye, he saw Aillenn swinging her satchel forward again. This time, the outlaw leaped out of the way. And already the first man she'd knocked down was getting back up. He'd have to finish off the third outlaw on his side and come to her assistance.

The third man gave Adam a black-toothed, menacing grin as he advanced, twirling a staff before him.

Adam caught the staff mid-twirl and violently shook off the man's grip. Commandeering the staff, he shoved the man backwards with the butt of it, hard enough to make his head collide with a pine. He slithered unconscious to the ground.

When Adam turned back to Aillenn, she had somehow managed to knock one of the outlaws senseless. But the other two were on the attack. One of them had a makeshift club. One of them had a dagger.

Before he could reach her, she dropped her satchel, hiked up her skirts, and dove in front of the man with the club, bowling him off his feet. Then she hopped back up as if she did such acrobatics every day.

Who *was* this lass?

There was no time to wonder. While the man on the ground scrambled to right himself, the outlaw with the dagger charged at her with bloodlust in his eyes.

Adam only killed when it was necessary. And he hated to surrender a weapon. But he had no choice. The outlaw was too close to Aillenn.

Flipping his dagger around to pinch the blade between his thumb and fingers, he hurled it forward. It lodged in the man's throat. The outlaw dropped his weapon and clutched at the wound, gurgling as he dropped to the ground.

Now Adam was defenseless. And the second man had the same thought as the two of them raced to claim the dropped dagger.

But the outlaw was closer. He dove for the weapon, wrapping his fingers around the haft just as Adam skidded toward him.

CHAPTER 8

Eve had to do something.

Unfortunately, she had limited resources. Out of desperation, she attacked the outlaw clutching the dagger. She kicked him repeatedly in the arse, so hard she bruised her toes.

But it worked. Distracted by her pesky jabs, he rolled over to snap at her. In that instant, Adam was able to seize his wrist and wrench the dagger free.

She wondered if Adam meant to stab this outlaw in the throat as well. The idea sickened her.

But for now, he seemed content to take ownership of the dagger. The man was no threat.

For a moment, victory filled her veins. They'd done it. They'd defeated the six outlaws. She didn't even feel the least bit of remorse. After all, it had hardly been a fair fight.

Then the man bellowed, "Tom! John! Help!"

The riders. She'd forgotten about the riders.

Adam wrenched the man around, choking off his cries, and set the dagger at his throat. But it was too late. The horses were already thundering back.

Now they'd lost the element of surprise. And the only leverage they had was one man. She only hoped he wasn't the least favorite member of their band.

"What the Devil?" the first rider said, perusing the carnage around them.

"Dick!" the second man cried. "What did ye do to Dick?"

He dismounted and would have run to the dead man, but the first rider thrust out a boot to stop him. "Nay! He's got Roger."

Apparently Roger *was* important enough to warrant a hostage negotiation.

"That's right," Adam said. "I've got Roger. So don't make any fast moves unless ye want to see him join Dick in hell."

The first rider worked his mouth, taking time to consider his options.

The second rider looked aghast at the first. "Ye're not goin' to let him have Roger."

"How much have they got?" the first rider asked Roger, nodding to the satchels.

Eve blinked. Were they actually weighing the worth of the man's life?

Roger squealed in his throat, as appalled as she was.

"I'll make a bargain with ye," Adam said.

The first rider's eyes glittered. "What kind o' bargain?"

"Give us your horses, and I won't kill the three o' ye."

The rider smirked. "Kill us? By yourself?"

"Ye can see what I did with your other five," he said. "Oh, and by the way, this wasn't all my doin'. The lady here's the one who sent Dick to the Devil."

Eve froze in disbelief at the lie, as astonished as the second rider, whose eyes rounded in horror.

Adam's hostage knew it wasn't true. But he certainly wasn't going to argue with Adam's version of the story, not with a blade at his throat.

Which meant she had to play along with whatever tale Adam invented. So as gruesome as it was, she swallowed hard, marched over to the deceased outlaw, and pulled the dagger from his throat with a bravado she didn't feel.

The sound of the blade leaving his flesh would haunt her forever, and the trickle of blood made her stomach roil. But in the moment, she had to steel herself and feign to be Lady Aillenn, ruthless murderer.

"So what'll it be?" Adam asked.

The first rider scowled at her, as if measuring her ability to kill him. "One horse."

"Both," he countered. "I don't want ye followin' us."

She could see hesitation in the rider's eyes. He wouldn't agree to that. If they took his horses, his outlaw operation would be crippled. He'd have no scouting ability. No fast escape in the event things went badly.

"Leave us both horses," she offered, much to everyone's surprise, "and I'll give ye coin enough to buy two more."

"What!" Adam clearly disapproved.

"'Tis the least we can do," she explained, adding pointedly, "after I killed poor Dick."

"Fine. Done," the first rider said, dismounting before Adam could alter the terms.

While the men worked out the exchange, Eve dug in her satchel and plucked out five silvery coins.

When she tossed the coins onto the path, the outlaws' eyes widened. Adam made a strangling sound in his throat, but said nothing, releasing Roger.

Adam helped her to mount the horse. Then he hauled himself up, and they headed down the road at a gallop.

When they'd gained enough distance to slow their mounts, Eve could feel waves of anger boiling off of Adam. But he said not a word. For a long while they didn't speak at all.

Finally she could stand it no longer. When the road widened, she reined in beside him.

"They're not all evil, ye know. Outlaws."

He uttered a disgruntled growl.

"Some o' them are just misguided," she explained.

"Maybe they had bad parents. Or no parents. Maybe they were raised by thieves and know no other way. Maybe they've ne'er heard the word o' God and don't know stealin's a sin. Maybe they were robbin' from the rich to give to—"

"*Those* outlaws?" he said. "The ones who weren't willin' to trade two horses for their fellow outlaw?"

"But they did in the end."

"Only after ye threw in enough silver to buy two new horses. And three new Rogers."

She furrowed her brow. She doubted they'd be able to buy anything. Not with those coins. Still, that wasn't the point.

"I gave them the coins in order to spare a man's life," she said. "'Twas the only thing I could think to do after..." She didn't bother finishing. There was no need to remind him of what he'd done.

Adam knew what came after that "after."

After...you brutally murdered Dick.

He wasn't proud of that. It had been an unavoidable sacrifice. But the fact that Aillenn had rewarded their robbers felt like a double condemnation of his actions. That was the last thing he needed. He'd already condemned himself enough.

Killing had always been difficult for Adam. Maybe that was why he'd never been a celebrated warrior like his cousins. He was more likely to defend rather than attack. To pull back at the last instant. To withhold the full measure of his strength in battle unless it was absolutely crucial to disable his opponent.

This time he'd had no choice. The man had threatened Aillenn's life.

Still he was haunted by the sounds of the outlaw's dying.

By the dimming of the light in his eyes. By the horrible truth that he'd held the man's life in his hands and willfully extinguished it.

As they rode along in silence, he tortured himself, wondering if there might have been a way to avoid slaying the robber.

As if she could read his thoughts, Aillenn said, "'Twas unavoidable, ye know."

"What?"

"That outlaw. Dick. 'Twasn't your fault. Ye didn't have a choice."

Was that true? He wasn't certain.

"If ye hadn't done...what ye did..." She shook her head, unable to finish. "We had to resist them. I know that. If we hadn't, they'd ne'er have been content with five pieces o' silver. They'd have stolen our weapons, our clothin', our food, the rest o' my coin. And they might have..." She lowered her head and blushed. "Taken other liberties."

He closed his eyes to slits and bit out, "I'd have killed them all ere I'd let them lay so much as a finger on ye."

Her eyes filled with gratitude at his vehement chivalry. "I had a sense ye might. So ye see? 'Twas all for the best. Instead o' them sacrificin' all their men or us sacrificin' all our silver, they lost just one man, and we lost just five coins."

He smirked. How did she always manage to shine a ray of sunlight into the darkest gloom? Five pounds was a fortune to some people. "Just how much silver do ye have in that satchel?"

She shrugged. "Enough. Why?" She narrowed her eyes. "How much do *ye* have in *yours?*"

"Me?" he said with a chuckle.

The truth was, despite his wealth as a member of the Rivenloch clan and the rumors about his bottomless satchel, he traveled light. He could easily earn coin by doing common labor or, when the situation demanded it, impressing his way into free food and lodging. After all, who wouldn't offer Hildegard of Bingen a hot meal and a place to rest her revered head?

"Ye said it yourself," he added. "I'm just a master o' disguise, not a titled lady who can afford to lose five pounds in silver."

"Oh." She stopped her horse to address him. "Could ye not tell? The coins weren't *real* silver."

"What?" He reined to a shocked halt beside her. "What were they?"

"Lead."

"Lead?"

She nodded. "I always carry lead coins with the silver. 'Tis the easiest way to appease outlaws. They don't usually look too closely when they're robbin' ye."

"So ye gave them worthless coins?" he marveled, simultaneously horrified and impressed.

"Aye."

"But what about them bein' 'misguided men with bad parents'?" he said, quoting her.

"That they might be, but eight o' them against two of us?" She shook her head. "The churls didn't deserve a penny."

He laughed. The woman was fascinating. He'd never met a lass so flexible in her morality. Was she saint or sinner? It was hard to tell.

He nudged his horse forward again. "Be careful where ye spend those coins. There are some who'd hang ye for counterfeitin'."

"I'd ne'er use them on honest men," Aillenn said. "But if 'tis our lodgin' ye're worried about, I have enough real silver to stay for some days."

Adam lifted his brows at that. Did she think she'd have to offer silver to stay with Pitcairn? One glance at Lady

Aillenn, and the laird would be fumbling over his feet to accommodate the beautiful lass.

The road narrowed again, forcing him to ride silently behind her. But that was fine. It seemed the more they spoke, the more information she managed to squeeze out of him. And the more she knew, the less secure he was.

Traveling by horse was much swifter than on foot, even when they stopped to rest the animals. To Aillenn's apparent surprise, Adam pulled a brush out of his satchel to groom the beasts. She seemed impressed, not only by his convenient assortment of tools, but by his attention to detail when it came to guises.

Before long, they drew close to Pitcairn's stronghold. It was set above a lush green glen through which a wee burn meandered. Well-protected by a generous bailey enclosed by tall wooden stakes, the keep rose above the forest like a powerful arm challenging the heavens. Unlike Rivenloch's sprawling, Norman-style stone structure, Pitcairn's castle was comprised of a single tower made of gray-weathered wood. The keep was nonetheless substantial. The azure pennant of Pitcairn, featuring the face of a moon, rippled from the top of the tower. Smoke streamed from the outbuildings within the bailey.

"'Tis magnificent," Aillenn exclaimed, pulling up beside him.

"Ye think so?" he said. "Ye should see..." Shite, he'd almost said *Rivenloch.* "Er, the great hall o' the king in Perth."

She nodded. "O' course, 'tisn't as magnificent as my keep in Ireland, but..."

He wondered. She might be good at hiding her identity. She wasn't so good at hiding her emotions. She did seem rather impressed by the castle.

"Shall we?" he said, reining toward the stronghold.

Adam, weary from the journey, looked forward to

ending their travels. But the closer they got to the bailey, the more anxious he became.

Normally, nothing rattled him. Though he was visiting a laird who knew him as Adam la Nuit of Rivenloch, he'd only met the man a few times, and he'd been a good deal younger. Besides, his own kin couldn't recognize him when he was in disguise.

But he was definitely ill-at-ease about this encounter.

It must be the responsibility of looking after Lady Aillenn and her identity that left him on edge.

What if she accidentally used the wrong name? What if her behavior betrayed her? What if she began blathering about their encounter with the thieves? Or his participation in the melee? Or the debacle at the monastery? The slightest mistake could reveal them both.

He wanted to warn her. To instruct her on all the things she shouldn't say or do. To tell her how important it was not to disclose anything about where they'd been or where they were going.

In the end, he decided she should feign to be mute. He would do all the talking.

But before he could issue his instructions, they were already at the gate, and she was calling out cheerily to the guard.

The key to disguising oneself, Eve had discovered early on, was confidence and devotion to the role. So when she was Lady Aillenn, she was forthright, self-assured, and demanding of respect. Anyone encountering her was completely convinced she was who she said she was, because she overwhelmed them with that self-assurance.

She wasn't so sure about Adam. Aye, he'd memorized the clan information she'd given him. But would he be so confident in a role he'd never played before?

She decided to take the lead. It would probably be better if he remained silent anyway.

"Good even!" she called out to the guard as she dismounted.

"M'lady?"

"We've traveled all the way from Perth," she told him. "Might we seek rest here for the night?"

Adam hopped down from his horse and interjected, "One o' Pitcairn's recent guests recommended we stop here."

Eve blinked. She hoped he was right that it was Pitcairn and not Pitfield. After all, he'd stumbled over the name before.

"Prithee wait here, m'lady, m'lord," he said, noting their finery. He called out to a nearby lad. "Ewen, see to the horses." Then he nodded. "I'll alert the laird and return for ye."

Adam pulled the satchels from the saddles, and Ewen led their horses away.

As soon as they were out of hearing, Eve hissed at Adam, "I'll do the talkin'."

Simultaneously, he whispered, "Let me make the arrangements."

They both frowned.

He argued, "I have more experience in these matters." She had just opened her mouth to contradict him when he added, "After all, ye're a titled lady only recently come o'er from Ireland, aye?"

She couldn't deny the story she'd made up, so she acquiesced with a nod. But she had no intention of letting Adam blunder his way through an awkward explanation when she could wrap a man around her finger with a wink and a grin.

So when the guard returned and led them into the keep, she strode through the great hall ahead of Adam. The servants were setting up trestle tables for supper, draping them with tablecloths. She dodged between them, scouring the hall for the laird.

Near the hearth was a well-dressed man with thick waves of brown hair and lively eyes. The noblemen around him hung on his every word and laughed at his every jest. That must be the laird, she decided.

Picking up her skirts, she surged toward him with a smile of sheer delight, as if he were the only man in the hall.

"M'laird!" she gushed. "What an honor to meet ye!"

Her enthusiasm and her appearance excused her rudeness as she barged into the group, lowered her gaze, and executed a deep curtsy that may have revealed just a bit of her bosom.

When she lifted her eyes again, the men were left speechless.

"And ye are?" he asked, perusing her slowly from head to toe as if measuring her beauty and calculating her charms.

"Oh, muddled me!" she said, feigning fluster. "I am Lady Aillenn o' Bhallach, m'laird."

His eyes danced with pleasure. "An Irish lass?"

The others chuckled in approval.

She cast him a coy glance. "Aye, m'laird." Then she straightened with playful pride. "I'm the daughter o' Tiarna Fursa." It never hurt to impress a man with one's bloodline.

"Is that so?" She had his full attention now. Ignoring the others, he stepped toward her, his hand extended. "The honor is mine, m'lady."

She slipped her hand into his, and he covered it with his own, bestowing upon her a wide smile.

"M'laird," she murmured, leaving her hand in his and looking up at him with liquid eyes, "I've come to ask... May

I count on your hospitality this eve? 'Tis been a long day o' travel from Perth, and I fear my audience with the *king* has quite exhausted me."

There was a soft gasp from the men.

The laird's reply was rough with surprise. "The king? Indeed?" He gave her another long look of appraisal. "O' course ye're welcome here. Stay as long as ye like." He called out to a maidservant. "Tilda, ready the rose chamber."

"Oh, m'laird, how generous!" Eve exclaimed, gracefully slipping her hand away. "We are so grateful."

He blinked. "We?"

"Ah, if I didn't have my head attached..." she said, clucking her tongue. Then she turned toward Adam. "This is Ronan, my—"

"Husband."

CHAPTER 9

Adam hadn't meant to blurt the word out like that. He hadn't meant to say it at all. They'd agreed he would pretend to be Aillenn's brother.

But when he saw the way Pitcairn was looking at the lass, as if he planned to feast on her for supper, he couldn't help himself. He wasn't about to leave her to the wolf. And he figured claiming her as his own was the best way to protect her.

Aillenn clearly didn't approve of that decision. She shot him such a look of horrified outrage that he almost recoiled from the impact.

He knew how she felt. It was aggravating as hell to have an accomplice destroy your best laid plans. But desperate times called for desperate measures. Flexibility. Improvisation. Now that he'd made that bold introduction, she'd have to follow his lead.

He dropped the satchels, stepped forward and offered his hand. "M'laird."

Pitcairn looked as if he'd like to refuse it. But though he was a bit of a knave with the ladies, he was obliged to follow the code of chivalry. Noblemen were expected to be civil to one another. He flashed Adam a quick smirk and briefly squeezed his hand, then didn't give him a second glance. Which was good. If he'd studied Adam as thoroughly as he'd done the lass, he'd surely have recognized him as the warrior of Rivenloch he'd met before.

The laird was probably wondering how long they intended to stay and regretting his carelessly generous offer. Adam decided to ease the man's fears.

"'Twill only be for the night," he said.

Aillenn smiled in agreement. Then, apparently deciding they didn't look enough like a couple, the saucy lass linked her arm through Adam's and gazed up at him with adoring eyes. Adoring eyes with just a gleam of vengeful mischief.

She was going to be trouble. He could see that.

The trouble began the moment Tilda showed them to the rose chamber. A very large, conspicuous bed curtained in rich red velvet monopolized the room. A linen-lined wooden tub sat on a dais in one corner. Two chairs, their cushions embroidered with red blossoms, flanked the tub, as if set there to observe bathers. The white plaster walls were painted with green twining stems and red roses, broken only where the hearth guarded a low-burning fire. Against one wall stood a small table topped by a basin and pitcher, a mirror, a comb, linens, and vials of assorted oils.

"What a lovely chamber," Aillenn exclaimed.

Adam frowned. It was clearly the room Pitcairn used to entertain his mistresses.

"Would m'lady like a warm bath after supper?" Tilda offered.

"That would be delightful," Aillenn gushed.

Adam frowned. That would not be delightful. It would be dangerous.

"Isn't that a kind offer, Ronan?" Aillenn said with a bright smile.

"Kind. Aye."

Tilda continued. "There's enough fuel for the fire to last the night, and I think ye'll find the bed comfortable." She gave Aillenn a wink. "'Tis goose-down."

"Lovely."

"I'll send a maid up to fetch ye for supper," Tilda said. "Meanwhile, if there's anythin' ye need, m'lady, m'laird, I'm a whistle away."

The instant Tilda bobbed her head and closed the door, Aillenn whirled toward Adam. Her smile vanished. She frowned and poked him in the chest.

"Why did ye tell him that?" she hissed. "Why did ye say we were married?"

"I...panicked," Adam lied.

"Ye? The man who feigned to be the emissary o' the Pope?" She crossed her arms over her chest. "I don't believe that. So why then?"

He curled his lip, rubbing at the spot where she'd poked him. "'Twas an accident."

She arched a dubious brow. "An accident is fallin' into the burn. Ye announced it like ye were the town crier."

Damn. Could he hide nothing from the lass?

"Fine," he grumbled. "I didn't like the way Pitcairn was lookin' at ye."

"What do ye mean?"

He scowled, waving his arms in disgust. "Did ye not see? He was lickin' his lips like ye were his next meal. His eyes all full o' hunger. His droolin' chin on the floor. His trews swellin' up like—" He stopped as he saw Aillenn begin to blush, wishing he could stuff the words back into his mouth. Then he lowered his arms and sighed. "I only meant to protect ye from unwanted advances."

"I know how to thwart unwanted advances."

"Do ye?" he accused, unreasonably vexed. "Because the man didn't seem to be the least bit thwarted."

"Why should ye care?"

"Because I..."

He hesitated, staring into her inquisitive eyes. Eyes that shone like dark pools in moonlight. Eyes full of kindness and strength, wit and wisdom.

What? Love you? Want you for myself? Can't stand the thought of anyone else touching you? Holding you? Pressing their lips to...

"I told ye," he decided gruffly, averting his gaze. "I'm a protector."

She sighed. "I understand. Truly I do." She moved forward, taking his right hand between her own and speaking earnestly. "But I swear to ye, Adam, I don't need protectin'. I've been on my own for a while now. I can protect myself. Ye have to trust me."

He'd held his breath from the moment she'd taken his hand. Her skin was soft, warm, comforting. And the way she was gazing at him now—with sympathy and reassurance—made his heart flicker with affection.

"Besides," she added with an enigmatic smile, patting the back of his hand before releasing him, "how do ye know his advances were unwanted?"

Her offhand remark hit him like the blow of Brand's lance, straight in the gut.

Was she attracted to Pitcairn? She'd said she wished to secure a husband before her father could drag her back to Ireland. Did she think Laird Pitcairn might be that husband?

It was troubling.

Pitcairn might be handsome. Rich. Young.

But the laird had a reputation for philandering. A sharp tongue with servants. And a reckless love of gambling.

He was completely wrong for Aillenn.

"'Tisn't true, is it?" he asked her. "Ye don't have feelin's for Pitcairn?"

She shrugged and turned away from him. "What does it matter now? Ye've already told him ye're my husband."

Eve smiled a secret smile as she sauntered toward the table and poured water from the pitcher into the basin.

Adam was jealous. He might be a master of disguise. But when it came to his emotions, he was as transparent as glass.

She soaked a linen rag and began dabbing at her face and neck.

Why his jealousy pleased her, she wasn't sure. Perhaps it was because it felt like it gave her the upper hand. Like she was in control. Even if her heart wasn't so sure of that.

Whatever the reason, it also gave her a wee thrill to know her flirtations with another—even if they were feigned—bothered him. It meant that he might have feelings for her.

It was a foolish hope, she knew. Utterly ridiculous. Completely inappropriate. What good were such feelings when she was a nun?

While she mused in silence, wiping away the dust of the road, she heard the crackle of peat as Adam stirred the fire behind her.

"I'll take the floor here," he murmured.

"What?" She whirled to face him.

"The floor. I'll sleep beside the fire."

"Absolutely not," she decided. "The lodgin' was *your* discovery. Ye should take the bed."

"Don't be absurd. I'm not goin' to sleep on a goose-down pallet while an Irish princess beds down on the floor."

His offer was kind. But it offended her nun's sense of charity, humility, and fairness.

"I can't possibly accept your offer," she said. "Ye protected me from outlaws. Managed to procure us horses and lodgin' for the night. Sacrificed yourself so I wouldn't fall into the burn." She shook her head. "A soft, warm bed to sleep in is the least I can give ye to show my gratitude."

What she really wanted to give him was a soft, warm bed with *her* in it. But that was only her wayward thoughts racing astray like a runaway steed. Besides, she noted he'd carefully omitted the option of sharing the bed. To a man who claimed his chief duty was protection, she supposed such an arrangement was unthinkable.

He grunted in dissatisfaction over her decree and gave the flickering peat on the hearth one last prod before coming to his feet.

"Ye're a stubborn lass, aren't ye?"

"Me?" She didn't think she was stubborn. She merely stood her ground when she knew she was right.

An amused smile blossomed on his face, taking her breath away. "I've heard there's nothin' more stubborn than an Irish lass."

That might be. But she was no Irish lass. "I've heard the same said o' Scotsmen."

"Then I suppose we'll find out who's the—"

There was a knock on the door. "M'lady, m'lord," a maid called out, "I'm here to take ye to supper."

Eve gasped and whispered, "Already?" They were hardly prepared to play husband and wife.

"Good, I'm starvin'," Adam murmured. To the maid he said, "We'll be right out."

He grabbed the wet rag she'd used, rubbing it quickly over his face.

But Eve's heart raced. "There's no time to get our new story straight."

He shrugged and gave his hands a quick scrub as well. "We'll have to make one up as we go."

That was easy for him to say. He seemed to thrive on living dangerously. Making last-minute decisions. Taking risks without batting an eye.

Eve preferred to think things out carefully. To plan. To pay attention to detail. To create a seamless character with a complete history and live in their skin for a while.

It wasn't that she never had to improvise. Sometimes she had to rely on her wits to correct course if she got into trouble.

That worked when you were steering the steed on your own. When another person didn't have to follow your lead and remember the route. But Adam had a mind of his own. He might well seize the reins and steer her in a direction she didn't want to go. Like calling himself her husband when he was supposed to be her brother.

"M'lady," Adam said, offering his arm.

Like that. Already he was doing it. Taking the lead.

With a sigh, she looped her arm through his, donned her most charming smile, and let him lead her to supper.

Eve was glad to be seated beside Pitcairn, with Adam on her other side. That way she could respond quickly to the laird's questions without fretting Adam might blurt out something ridiculous. As Lady Aillenn, she'd enjoyed many suppers with noble strangers. She knew what questions were likely to be asked. And she had answers at the ready.

"So what brings ye to Scotland, m'lady?" Pitcairn asked, stabbing a large chunk of mutton from the pottage and shoving it between his teeth.

She opened her mouth to give her usual reply. She'd fled Ireland because her father had betrothed her to a withered old soldier. She would not return until she secured a husband of her own choosing.

And then she realized that her usual reply wasn't going to work. Not with Adam portraying her husband.

In her instant of panic, Adam rushed in to fill in the story.

"We sought an audience with the king to discuss a possible match for Aillenn's sister, Lady Blinne."

Eve's throat tightened. She was impressed. He'd remembered their sister's name and that Eve had mentioned a meeting with the king. He'd even come up with a believable mission. But would Pitcairn believe it?

Indeed he did. In fact, his sudden interest in the idea gave his eyes a greedy shine.

"Is that so?" he asked, swallowing the bite of mutton. "But o' course she couldn't be as beautiful as Lady Aillenn?"

"No one is as beautiful as Lady Aillenn," Adam said.

The ladies at the table sighed.

Eve knew he was only making flattering conversation. But something about the tone of his voice almost made her believe him.

"My husband is blinded by love," she replied with modesty, placing a hand on his sleeve. "My sisters are far more beautiful than me."

Pitcairn almost spit his wine. "Sisters? Ye have more than one?" The prospect of an alliance with a beautiful Irish bride chosen by the king was likely compelling.

"Aye," Adam replied. "Two o' them. Blinne and Caitilin."

Eve was still on edge, despite the fact he'd recalled their names correctly. She took a sip of wine to calm her senses.

"Tell me about them," the laird urged.

Eve described them as she'd invented them, exaggerating their beauty a wee bit to keep him interested.

"And your father?" Pitcairn asked. "Is he eager to see them wed?"

"Oh, aye." She thought quickly, placing her hand atop Adam's. "Ye see, as the eldest daughter, the next in line for Tiarna will be my husband, Ronan."

How curious to say that. *My husband.* She'd never portrayed a character with a husband. The words rolled with pleasing ease off of her tongue.

"But my father," she continued, "would like to see my sisters wed to Scottish noblemen."

"I see." Pitcairn swirled his wine thoughtfully. Clearly he was weighing his odds of wedding into Irish royalty.

Meanwhile, the ladies, fascinated by Ronan, quizzed him.

"How long have ye been wed?" one of them asked.

"Two..." he said.

"Months," she supplied, though in retrospect, she thought it might have been better to say "years."

"So ye're newlyweds," another exclaimed. "How wonderful."

"Were ye betrothed?" the first lady asked. "Or was it a love match?"

"Betrothed," Eve replied. It was the easiest answer.

Unfortunately, at the same instant, Adam said, "'Twas love at first sight."

Eve's eyes widened. "That is, we *were* betrothed, but—"

"After the betrothal was signed and we met for the first time," Adam interjected, "I knew I had to have her."

The ladies sighed again. So did Eve.

"Where did ye meet?" someone asked.

Eve chose the most logical place. "At my father's keep."

But Adam waxed poetic. "When I first laid eyes on Aillenn, she was standin' beneath a laurel tree...outside her father's keep...watchin' the sun rise. She turned at my approach, and I remember she looked like a saint, her dark hair haloed in golden light, and her beautiful eyes shinin' like gems." He clapped a hand to his chest. "When she smiled at me, I knew I'd ne'er love another."

He looked her straight in the eyes then, and Eve felt her heart catch at the warm affection in his gaze. Everything in her brain told her he was only creating a fiction to maintain their identities. But her soul told her something else.

"And what did ye think o' *him,* m'lady?" another woman wanted to know.

She stared at the lady, struggling for words. Then she decided she could let inspiration answer for her. Moving her gaze to Adam, she spoke the truth.

"I thought he looked like...Adam."

By the furrow in Adam's brow, he feared she meant to expose his real identity.

She rushed to add, "The first man. Made by God in His image. Handsome. Heavenly. Perfect."

There were oohs and ahhs over that.

Adam blinked in surprise. "Did ye really?"

She nodded, which seemed to please him.

Now the ladies wanted to know everything. "Tell us about the weddin' feast."

"How many guests were there?"

"What was served for dinner?"

"Roast venison," he replied, just as she was saying, "Fresh salmon."

He added, "Roast venison *and* fresh salmon."

She said, "'Twas a magnificent feast with dozens o'—"

"Hundreds o' guests," he blurted, then amended, "At least it *seemed* like hundreds."

"Oh aye," she said. "My da spared no expense, so happy was he to see me wed to such an esteemed warrior."

"Warrior?" Pitcairn scowled at Adam, as if his memory had been stirred. "What did ye say your name was?"

"Ronan. But I'm sure ye wouldn't have heard o' me. 'Tis my first visit to Scotland."

His answer seemed to satisfy the laird. "What's your weapon o' choice?"

She answered for him, fearing he might know nothing about Irish weapons. "He's an expert with the axe."

"Indeed? And do ye have your axe with ye, Sir Ronan?"

Eve paled. She hadn't imagined the laird would want to see it.

But Adam knew what to say. "Nay. We came in peace. I

thought it might be unwise to greet the Scottish king with an Irish axe."

"True." Pitcairn chortled. "It could be considered an 'axe o' war'."

It was a terrible jest. But everyone at the table laughed, Adam most of all, who raised his cup to the laird in a salute.

The rest of the evening went smoothly enough. If Eve misspoke, Adam was there to soften her words. When Adam paid her husbandly attention, she was careful to mirror his mood.

After a few cups of wine, the border between fact and fiction began to blur. The adoration Adam expressed felt real. His words of affection made her heart melt. His warm glances made her blush. The touch of his fingers upon her arm stirred her blood. The press of his thigh against hers seemed right...and comforting...and arousing.

How could it not be real?

After their simple meal of mutton pottage, they shared a dish of blancmange.

Adam spooned a bite of the sweet, milky dessert into her mouth, lowering his gaze to her lips.

It might have been moor muck for all the attention Eve paid it. She was far more intrigued by the soft glow of his gaze. His gentle smile of encouragement. The inviting temptation of his mouth.

Swallowing down the blancmange, she returned the favor, taking the spoon and feeding him.

"Mmm."

That wee sound seemed to curl around her ear into her brain, bringing every nerve to life.

There was a tiny drop of blancmange left on his lower lip, and it took every ounce of her restraint not to lean forward to lick it away.

Adam recognized the smoke in Aillenn's gaze. It was raw lust. And it wasn't the blancmange she lusted after.

The smoldering glance she gave him shot a bolt of desire through him. His eyes darkened. His chest swelled. And betwixt his legs, the beast roused.

In one way, that was good. Healthy lust added authenticity to their claim they were newly married.

But they'd both had enough wine to be careless. And if they got distracted, mistakes might be made.

She was staring at his mouth now. She wanted him to kiss her.

He wanted to. God, how he wanted to. And he suspected she wouldn't pull away.

But he couldn't.

Surely it was unseemly to kiss at the table, wasn't it?

On the other hand, perhaps everyone would assume they were simply enthusiastic newlyweds.

Or they could claim it was Irish tradition to kiss after blancmange.

He took a deep preparatory breath.

Then, before he could close the distance and press his lips to hers, the maidservant Tilda poked her head between them.

"If ye're ready," she said, turning her head to speak to each of them, "I'll send the servants to fetch water for your bath now."

Aillenn gave a stunned nod.

Tilda smiled. "Would ye be wantin' assistance?"

"Nay," Adam hurried to say. "We can manage on our own."

He remembered the chairs positioned near the tub. The last thing he needed was Pitcairn deciding to "assist" Aillenn with her bath.

The rest of the dinner discussion was a blur to Adam.

All he could think about was the sultry fire in Aillenn's eyes and the tempting, forbidden fruit of her mouth. The animal raging in his braies refused to be leashed.

Somehow he managed to thank Pitcairn for his hospitality.

Somehow he bid farewell to the other nobles and bowed to the ladies.

Somehow he followed Aillenn and the maidservant up the stairs to the guest chamber.

But all the while he sailed adrift in a languorous haze of longing. Imagining Aillenn slowly removing her gown. Baring her lovely breasts. Sliding her leine over the graceful curve of her hips.

"The servants will be up presently," Tilda told him.

He nodded, not truly hearing her words.

Then she closed the door to give them privacy.

He stared down at the latch, steeling himself to face the woman he desired beyond reason. The woman who seared his blood and confounded his brain. The woman he knew he dared not approach.

No sooner did he turn than she rushed at him, pushing him back against the door.

He sucked in a breath as she pressed hungry lips to his. Tasting him. Savoring him. Devouring him. She clenched her fists in his shirt and moaned softly in her throat.

She tasted of wine and blancmange and longing. And the sensation shredded whatever bit of restraint he had before.

He answered her kiss with a passion that bubbled up from his loins, overflowing reason like pottage overboiling on the fire.

Who was this woman who shifted from shy virgin to masterful temptress in a heartbeat?

A mistress of disguise, to be sure.

But which one was the real Aillenn?

Later. He would find out later. For now, as every fiber of his being was filled with the current of love's lightning, he wanted only this. More of this.

Eve wanted more.

More.

More what?

She didn't know. But her greed felt insatiable. Now that she'd tasted desire, her appetite was whetted for something deeper, more intimate, all-consuming.

She clutched at his shirt, pulling him closer. Yearning. Seeking.

He parted her lips with his own, delving into the warm hollows of her mouth with his tongue.

She gasped. Aye. This was what she craved.

She let her tongue tangle with his. A frisson of lust coursed through her body, awakening every nerve. When he groaned, the sound called to something primitive and feral inside her.

Her breasts swelled against him. Her nipples grazed with sensuous delight against the linen of her leine. Low in her belly, betwixt her thighs, she felt a taut need. A hunger. A demand.

In another moment, she might have explored that demand.

But there was a sudden scratching at the door.

CHAPTER 10

The interruption was as shocking as pouring cold water on molten metal. In a panic, Eve broke free and scuttled backwards.

Glancing at Adam, she saw he looked exactly like she felt. Breathless. Ravenous. Stunned.

Catching her breath, she managed to croak out, "Who is it?"

"Your bath, m'lady," a man replied.

Adam pushed off of the door, but she noticed he reached down to adjust the bulge below his belt.

She blushed, knowing that must be for her. Then she blinked the smoke from her eyes, tossed her head, straightened her gown, and answered the door.

A sour-faced gentleman came in, followed by three beardless youths.

They staggered in, carrying large pails of cold water on yokes across their scrawny shoulders. Copious linens were draped around their necks. They carefully navigated the distance from the door to the tub. Their faces were sweaty. Their brows were pinched in concentration. They were obviously overburdened and weary from climbing the winding stairs.

Eve's first instinct was to help them.

But she was Lady Aillenn now. And a proper lady would

do nothing of the sort. Aillenn was accustomed to having servants at her beck and call, doing her bidding, no matter how difficult.

Meanwhile, the sour-faced man settled a great cauldron of water onto the fire for heating.

The youths dropped the bath linens onto the bed. Then they poured water from the pails into the tub, managing to spill only a drop here and there. All but the last lad. His pail caught on the tub's wooden edge and tipped. Water sloshed outside the tub, down the dais, and spread across the floor.

"Finlay!" the man snarled.

The youth panicked and dropped the pail, spilling more water.

The sour-faced man charged forward in rage and seized Finlay by the front of his leine. While Eve looked on in frozen horror, he threw the poor lad against the wall.

Finlay's head hit the plaster with a loud crack, and he sank to the floor, dazed.

Eve gasped. "He didn't mean... 'Twas an accident."

The man ignored her. "Ye!" he barked at the other two lads. "Clean this up before I knock your heads together!"

Before they could comply, Adam lunged forward. To Eve's astonishment, he grabbed the brute of a master by the scruff of his neck. Dragged him, kicking and bellowing, to the tub. Then plunged the man face-first into the water, holding him under.

Eve held her breath.

The man struggled in Adam's grip, his body twisting, his legs kicking.

What was Adam doing? Did he intend to drown the brute? She looked on in fear as he maintained an iron grip on the man splashing frantically in the water.

Finally, Adam let him up. But he wasn't finished. He coiled his fist in the drenched linen of the man's leine and lifted him up on his toes.

Inches away from the sputtering man's face, he bit out, "Lay so much as a finger on them again, and I'll lop off your hand."

No one could help but be intimidated by the smoldering fury in Adam's eyes and the deadly quiet of his voice.

"Do ye understand?" Adam demanded.

The man gasped, choked, and nodded. He knew he was outmatched. At least he *believed* he was outmatched. Eve imagined he would be less cooperative if he knew Adam was not the son of an Irish lord, but a common outlaw.

Adam released him. "Go. The lads will clean this up. Get out o' my sight e'er I change my mind and decide to drown ye after all."

Once released, the man attempted to hide his fear behind bravado. He straightened his shoulders and walked stiffly toward the door. When he slid across a wet spot and almost lost his balance, Eve tried to not take undue glee in his misfortune. He closed the door behind him with more force than was necessary.

But now, Eve no longer had the heart to pretend indifference. She rushed to Finlay, who sat on the floor.

"Are ye all right?"

He reached behind his head. When his fingers emerged, they were smeared with blood. Nonetheless, he nodded.

"Nay, ye're not all right," Adam said, hunkering down beside the youth. He snatched up a linen bath cloth and pressed it carefully against the gash in the lad's head. "How long has that swine been tormentin' ye lads like this?"

One of the other lads answered as he mopped up the floor with another cloth. "The master has always been heavyhanded, m'laird."

The third youth, whom Eve noticed had a purple bruise under his eye, said, "He says 'tis the only way we'll e'er learn, m'lady."

"Did he give ye that?" she asked, nodding toward his cheek.

The youth lowered his head and confessed, "I was lookin' after my sickly brother yesterday and came late to the castle."

The second lad chimed in, "The master doesn't abide lateness."

Adam growled. "I should have drowned the churl when I had the chance."

But Eve's instincts to help and heal heard something different in the third lad's words. "Ye said your brother is sickly?"

"Aye, m'lady. And my ma was called away to help with the lambin'. I was the only one close at hand to look after him."

Eve made up her mind then and there. "I have some skill with herbs. In the morn, I'll look in on your brother and see if I can help."

Adam made a noise that sounded like he'd swallowed a bug. Then he gave her a brittle smile and said, "Darlin', don't ye remember? We've got to get an early start if we want to get to—"

"This is more important, sweetheart," she said, fluttering her lashes and daring him to contradict her. "'Tis the least we can do when these lads have been so sorely mistreated."

She saw a muscle ticking in his jaw. Of course Adam was upset. He'd just done something to draw attention to himself. 'Twas the last thing a master of disguise wanted. No doubt the news of the laird's Irish guest who'd finally given the cruel master his due by almost drowning him would soon be whispered among the servants. The Irish guest would be lucky if he wasn't compromised.

But she had to admire Adam's courage. His integrity.

His sense of right and wrong. Clearly, wielding justice had been worth the risk to him.

Just as looking after the lad's sickly brother was worth the risk to Eve.

"Bless ye, m'lady," the youth said, gratitude shining in his eyes.

Still, Adam looked displeased. They would have to make sure to take all precautions to avoid drawing even more attention to themselves.

Finlay's head stopped bleeding, though there was a large knot left which he said throbbed with every beat of his heart.

"I have just the thing," she said, digging in her satchel.

Adam frowned when he saw the stoppered vial.

"'Tis only willow bark," she assured him, removing the cork. She pulled a wooden cup out of her satchel and nodded toward the pitcher set on a small table by the bed. "Fetch me a bit o' water, aye?"

When Adam returned with the cup, she sprinkled a bit of the powder into the water. "Drink this down all at once. It tastes terrible, but 'twill take away the pain."

After a bit, Adam elbowed the youth and wiggled his brows at Eve. "'Twas satisfyin' to see the man squirmin' a bit, aye?"

Finlay gave a weak smile and nodded.

A proper nun would have scolded Adam for taking the Lord's vengeance into his own hands. But Eve didn't feel like a proper nun at the moment.

"Indeed."

He gave her a wink that set her heart aflutter.

By the time the mess was cleaned up and Finlay's pain had begun to subside, the cauldron on the fire was steaming.

Finlay asked, "Shall we fetch the lady's maid now to help with your bath?"

"That won't be necessary," Eve said.

She'd forgotten for a moment that she was Lady Aillenn, who had servants for everything. Still, it seemed silly to be bathed by someone else when she was perfectly capable of washing herself.

Then she remembered she wouldn't be by herself. Adam would be in the chamber.

Should she ask for a maidservant after all?

She'd nearly lost her wits, just kissing him. Almost forgotten who she was. What she was. What she was here to do. She'd been completely out of control.

But that kiss had been dizzying. Invigorating. Exhilarating.

In the end, she decided to remain silent and allow destiny to steer her course.

The lads gave their solemn vows to Adam not to say anything about the master's brush with death. Then they left.

She raised a dubious brow. "Ye don't really think they'll be able to keep their word?"

He shook his head. "I wouldn't be."

"Neither would I."

"Which is why I was hopin' to get an early start in the morn, *before* the tales get spread all o'er the keep," he said pointedly.

She sighed. "I couldn't refuse to look after the lad's sick brother, any more than ye could refuse to give that brute his due."

He nodded. Then he stared at his clasped hands. "About...before..."

"Aye?" Her heart was in her throat.

"I should have stopped. I'm sorry."

A tiny fissure cracked her heart. *Nay,* her mind spoke. *Don't be sorry. I'm not sorry. Nay, ye should have gone on and on, driven me mad with desire. 'Tis what I wanted, after all.*

Instead, she said the correct thing. "'Twasn't your fault."

That was true. She'd been the one to launch herself at him against the door.

"We have to keep our wits about us," he said.

"O' course." She supposed he was right. Damn him.

He wrapped his hands in linens to protect them from the heat. Then he fetched the cauldron of simmering water from the hearth and poured a measure into the tub. "More?"

She tested the temperature with her hand. "Oh aye, much more, all of it." Then mischief wagged her tongue. "Otherwise, 'twill be cold by the time ye get your turn."

He arched a brow at her. "Just how long a bath are ye plannin' to take?"

She grinned. "When did ye say we were leavin' on the morrow?"

"Saucy lass," he chided, pouring in the rest of the hot water. "Be out before midnight, or I'm climbin' in beside ye."

Eve choked out a laugh. Her cheeks turned to flame. Adam's words had painted a vivid picture in her mind, and it wasn't an altogether unpleasant image. Unsure what to do or say in reply, she turned away from the bold knave and busied herself rounding up the linens.

"So tell me," Adam said, setting down the cauldron and unwrapping the linen from his hands, "how does an Irish noblewoman know so much about curin' ills?"

She wasn't about to tell him she was a nun with access to an extensive herb garden and medical texts. So she shrugged. "How does an outlaw know so much about sword fightin'?"

His eyes sparkled with amusement. "Point to Lady Aillenn," he acknowledged.

One by one, Eve picked up the vials on the table to sniff at their contents. It seemed cruel to make Adam bathe in water scented by flowers. So she chose one with a warm and spicy scent.

As she poured the oil into the steaming water, Adam let out an audible yawn that was definitely forced.

"I fear my eyes grow weary," he said, sitting on the edge of the bed and pulling off his boots. "Wake me when ye're done, aye?"

She saw through his ruse. He was trying to be chivalrous. Standing guard over her while assuring her he'd keep his eyes closed. It was an honorable gesture.

Why then did she feel a twinge of disappointment?

Why did she half hope he'd steal a glance at her through the velvet curtains?

What was wrong with her?

After all, he'd said it himself. They needed to keep their wits about them.

True to his word, he climbed atop the coverlet, stretched out on the bed, and closed his eyes. One hand reached up to loosen the tie around the curtain, and the velvet folds fell to obscure his view.

With a shuddering sigh, Eve proceeded with her bath. She pulled off her shoes and hose. She removed her gown, draping it carefully over a chair. In the convent, she was expected to bathe in her leine for decency's sake. Here, she wasn't required to be so modest. Still, she took one precautionary glance toward the bed to be sure he wasn't sneaking a peek.

From behind the curtain, she could hear the soft sawing of his breath. He must be deep in slumber.

In one hasty movement, she slipped out of her leine and sank into the tub.

Then she let out a long sigh.

The water was heavenly. Hot. Fragrant. Soothing.

She'd have to be brief, of course. Despite her threats, it would be unfair to leave Adam with a chilled bath.

But for the moment, she rested her head against the padded wooden edge of the tub and closed her eyes, relishing the warm waves that eased her body and calmed her thoughts.

Feigning sleep was nothing new for Adam. He'd done it all the time as a lad when he'd returned late to Rivenloch after a midnight excursion. Later he'd learned it was a good way to either avoid difficult conversations or to listen in on secret conversations.

Now, however, he was having a hard time keeping his breathing slow and steady.

Though it would be easy enough to spy on her from the shadows of the bed, he'd vowed he would not. And he was a man of honor.

But bloody hell. Just the sweet smell of the bath oil, knowing it would cling to her skin and scent her all evening, made his nostrils flare. The sound of her entering the bath—her soft sigh, the light plash of the water as she moved the wet linen over her body...

His mind created a vision so intoxicating it made his breath quicken. His heart pounded. His blood surged. He didn't even want to think about what was happening between his thighs.

Eventually he heard her rise out of the tub. Heard the sluice of the water over her glistening body. He envisioned drops rolling down her smooth shoulders and over her creamy breasts. Trickling toward the rosy tips of her chilled nipples.

His eyes sprung open, staring unseeing at the bed's canopy.

Lord, his loins ached.

And he wondered how he was ever going to cool his blood enough to emerge safely from this velvet refuge.

He didn't have long to wonder.

In spite of her promises, she'd taken a notably brief bath, briefer even than his sister Feiyan, who hated wasting time she could be sparring by soaking in a tub.

That meant he had to stop imagining Aillenn naked. Soon.

The feat was nigh impossible when she neared the bed and he could smell the sweet spice of her damp body.

"Adam," she called softly.

He froze, feigning sleep.

"Adam," she repeated.

He remained still.

Finally she grasped his shoulder in her bath-warmed hand and gave it a shake. "Adam."

He pretended to rouse, looking at her through the narrow slits of his eyes, and murmured, "Is it my turn?"

"Aye."

She was draped in a dark cloak. But underneath she wore only her leine. A few damp tendrils of her hair clung to her neck, and a stray droplet of water trickled across her collar bone to disappear between her breasts.

He gulped.

It was a shame the water hadn't grown cold after all. Perhaps then it would cool his hot blood.

He sat up, raking his hands back through his hair.

"How is the bed?" she asked. "Soft?"

"Aye," he said, pulling the curtain back.

She sat down beside him, looking fresh. Smelling divine. And wreaking havoc.

He fought the overpowering desire to tip her back onto the pallet and bury his face in her fragrant neck.

Instead he gave her a stern frown. "Ye won't peek, will ye?"

She raised her brows. "Did *ye*?"

"O' course not." He snorted, indignant. "I'm a man of honor."

Then he got up, shooed her inside the canopy, and made a point of closing the curtains securely.

"Wait," she said. After a moment, she handed her cloak to him through the curtains.

Dear God, she was wearing just her leine now, wasn't she? Her thin, flimsy, sheer leine.

With a shuddering sigh, he plodded toward the dais, draping her cloak over the chair, next to her gown. He shrugged out of his clothes and sank into the water. It was—against his wiser hopes—deliciously hot.

Only later did he realize the wicked lass had never actually promised she wouldn't peek.

Eve was absolutely going to spy on Adam. It was rare she had an opportunity to glimpse a naked man.

As a nun, she'd stumbled a few times across elderly priests taking advantage of the convent tub. They'd looked plump, pale, and lumpy, like uncooked apple coffyns.

And sometimes the beardless lads of the village swam naked in the nearby loch.

But she'd seen few grown men. So she was naturally curious.

Would God have approved?

Certainly.

After all, hadn't man been made in His image? And given that this man's name was Adam...at least, she *thought* his name was Adam...what could be more fitting?

Standing up carefully on the pallet, she stepped toward the split in the curtain. Taking a hem in each hand, she opened the gap the tiniest bit, just enough to peer through the crack.

He must have been in a hurry. He'd already shed his clothing. The unexpected sight of his naked body made her bite her lip to stifle a gasp.

If this was what God's Adam looked like, it was no wonder Eve had been tempted into sin.

His body was perfectly proportioned, exactly like the drawings she'd once glimpsed of the statues in Rome. His shoulders were wide, with arms that were well-muscled, but not bulky. His legs were sturdy and covered with a light dusting of hair. His buttocks were firm and smooth. And when he turned to enter the bath, she bit harder into her lip, for none of the priests or young lads or drawings of Roman statues had exhibited an appendage in such a state.

She gulped.

Of course, she wasn't naive. She'd seen enough animals to know that the members of males swelled to a larger size when they were preparing to mate.

Why it hadn't occurred to her that it would be much the same with humans, she didn't know. But even so, it made no sense, because Adam wasn't preparing...

He sank into the water before she could steal another glance.

She would have closed the curtains then, but he was facing her. The movement would have drawn his attention. So she clamped her lips together and continued to watch.

He laid his head back against the edge of the tub. His face immediately dissolved into pleasure as he sank lower into the water until just his face was showing between the knobs of his knees. He sank lower still, letting the waves close over his head for an instant.

When he emerged, he slicked back his drenched hair and used a cloth to wash his face and neck. His movements were brusque as he scrubbed his shoulders, arms, and chest. Eve knew if she were performing the task, she'd be far gentler.

The idea made her cheeks grow warm. She closed her eyes, censoring her view, but not her errant thoughts as she listened to every gurgle of water and grazing of wet linen upon his flesh.

When she dared to peek again, he was finished washing. Now he rested his neck and arms upon the rim of the tub and closed his eyes, letting the soothing water lull him into tranquility.

In a shadowy, wayward part of her mind, she wished she could join him. She imagined being snuggled against him, cradled in the crook of his arm. Leaning against his powerful shoulder. Resting her cheek on his chest. Tracing the muscles below the level of the water with curious fingers.

An erotic longing began inside her, filling her nether parts with a kind of hunger. The place between her thighs tingled as if lightning hovered in the air. With her every breath, the friction of linen against her striving nipples filled her with a keen need. Her eyelids grew heavy until she watched him through a haze of yearning.

"I know ye're peekin'," he suddenly intoned.

Startled, she lurched, losing her precarious balance on the bed. She made a grab for the curtain, but it only opened wider. Losing her footing completely, she clung to the fabric with a death grip to keep from falling. But her weight was too much for the frail velvet, and the curtain began to rip with agonizing slowness.

In the time it took her to gasp in a mortified breath, he'd leaped from the tub to come to her rescue.

What exactly happened, she wasn't sure. There was a flash of flesh and then a tangle of slippery limbs and shredded velvet, terrified yelps and determined grunting. They touched each other in a dozen improper ways. But in the end, after a confusion of grasping and twisting, clinging and holding, he managed to keep her from crashing onto the hard planks.

"Are ye all right?" he asked.

She nodded. But it was absolutely not true. Her heart was pounding like a fuller's hammer against her ribs. And it wasn't only from nearly falling off the bed.

He was holding her upright against him, but her feet didn't touch the floor. Tendrils of his hair dripped water onto her bosom as he tipped his head down to hers. His dark eyes looked like boundless pools as he gazed at her in concern. His nostrils flared, and his stubbled jaw clenched as he held her safe in his powerful arms. Her thinly veiled breasts were crushed against his wet chest. And lower, she could feel the bulge of his naked loins pressing against that part of her that had burned with yearning.

He exhaled in relief, and she felt his sigh all the way down her body.

With a half-smile, he murmured, "I wish I could say the same for the cur—"

She didn't take time to think.

She acted on instinct.

Wrapping her arms around his neck, she surged forward to press her lips to his in a kiss of relief and gratitude. At least she *told* herself it was only relief and gratitude.

CHAPTER 11

So astounded was Adam by Aillenn's kiss, at first he didn't respond.

He felt wretched for frightening the poor lass into losing her balance. For causing the destruction of Pitcairn's bedcurtains. For shocking the woman with his nakedness. For manhandling her in his efforts to keep her from falling.

The fact that she was kissing him was at odds with his guilt.

But it didn't take long for that guilt to dissolve in the onslaught of her affection. And it didn't take long for his body to respond. Perhaps too eagerly.

Her lips were supple yet demanding. Engaging yet tentative. She tasted of wine and blancmange and her own unique flavor of desire.

He filled his nostrils with the clean, damp, spicy scent of her, and exhaled a shuddering breath spiced with longing.

She explored his mouth with her tender tongue, exclaiming with soft sounds at each new discovery. Pressing her fingertips into the nape of his neck, she pulled him closer, deepening the kiss, gasping with urgency.

This was dangerous.

They were in a risky situation. Mellowed from the bath. Besotted with wine. Alone. Half-naked.

She was losing control. And he could feel his own restraint slipping away.

Already his cock pulsed with anticipation.

But Adam was not a man to take advantage of a woman's weakness. His Rivenloch sense of honor was strong.

So despite the fire burning in his loins, he broke off the kiss.

"We should not..."

The hurt in her liquid eyes silenced him. "But I want to. I want this."

He lifted a corner of his lip in a rueful smile. "So do I. But at least let me get dressed."

"Nay."

Her reply appeared to shock her as much as it did him. "Nay?"

She gulped as if the word had come out of her mouth unbidden. Then she stared at a spot in the middle of his chest and said, "I want ye. All o' ye."

"All o' me?" His voice came out on a croak. "What do ye mean, all o' me?"

By the shy ducking of her head, he knew very well what she meant. The lass wanted him to swive her.

God, how he wanted to. But they barely knew each other. He wasn't entirely sure who she was. And she certainly didn't know who he was. How could two complete strangers engage in such an intimate act?

Still, need smoldered inside him. They didn't *feel* like strangers. And she was offering herself to him. She was obviously not a novice to love play, no matter what she'd hinted at about it being her first kiss. If she ached for him as much as he did for her, would it not be rude to refuse?

Besides, he knew other ways to satisfy her. To satisfy them both. Ways that wouldn't leave her with consequences, regretting what she'd done in the heat of passion.

"Are ye sure?" he murmured.

She leveled her eyes at the vein he could feel pulsing in his neck. "I want to do this. I wish to feel...everythin'."

He closed his eyes and let out a shuddering breath. Like an enchanted key, her words of consent unlocked the shackles of his reluctance, dissolving his doubts.

"Then ye shall have your wish," he murmured.

He lifted her back onto the bed. She sank into the coverlet with a sigh. For a moment he only looked down at her. Reveled in the longing in her glazed eyes. The hunger of her open mouth. The breathless rise and fall of her bosom.

There was no need to rush.

Aye, his body demanded him to seize the moment. Strike while the iron was hot. Take her swiftly before he could be stopped.

But he was no savage. His erection wasn't going anywhere. Besides, he'd learned the advantages of letting a woman dictate the pace. And, as honor reminded him, taking things slowly would give her the opportunity to change her mind.

Her leine was as sheer as fine mist over her beautiful breasts, which were of modest size, yet far more elegant than he'd envisioned. And lower, the pale linen was shadowy where dark curls guarded her womanhood.

As he loomed over her, she scanned his body as well, dwelling on his shoulders and chest. She tucked her lip under her teeth as if she wished to devour him.

That gesture made him harden with a groan.

Then she lifted her hands tentatively to touch his bare skin. Her fingers felt so delicate upon his ribs. As soft as the sweep of an artist's brush, painting him in colors of desire.

He lowered his eyes to the top of her leine.

"May I?" he whispered.

She nodded.

He slipped his fingers beneath the neck edge of her leine, sliding the fabric down to reveal more and more of her tempting body. The rapid pulse at her throat. The graceful edge of her collar bone. The soft curve of her bosom.

Her eyes drifted close. Her mouth fell open. She shuddered with anticipation as he peeled the leine off of her shoulders.

He gradually bared her breasts, slowly grazing the tips with the linen, making them stand erect before freeing them from the garment.

"Lovely," he breathed.

More lovely than he'd imagined. The pale orbs of her breasts were crested with small nipples the color of tawny pink averin berries.

He used his thumb to measure the throbbing in her neck before gliding his fingers along her collar bone and over her sweet shoulders.

Then he ventured farther, watching her face carefully for signs of distress. Her eyes were still closed. But he could read her reactions in the crease of her brow, the tension in her mouth, the pace of her breathing. Lower and lower he swept his fingers, making sensual circles atop her breasts and dipping down between them to caress the flesh with the back of his knuckles.

Sensing no resistance, he widened the circles to encompass her breasts, and her brow furrowed as she strained toward him, as if willing him to touch her nipples.

He smiled. He knew how to be a tease. But he would torment her—and himself—no longer.

He cupped her breasts from underneath and let his thumbs sweep over the sensitive nubs.

She drew in a sharp breath. Her eyes squeezed tight. But she didn't stop him. Instead, she made a mew of yearning deep in her throat.

That sound fueled his lust. He ached deep in his groin.

"May I kiss ye," he rasped out, brushing his thumbs over her again, "here?"

She trembled uncertainly for a moment. Then she gave him the tiniest of nods.

His mouth felt divine. Eve didn't know what emotion stirred her. Fear? Excitement? Deliriousness? Her heart thundered like a wild storm on the heath. And she didn't want it to stop. Didn't want *him* to stop.

Adam's hair tickled in the most delicious way as he lowered his head. His breath sent shivers of delight down her body. When he kissed the space between her breasts, however, she felt one brief frisson of guilt. That was the spot where her convent cross usually hung.

Dear God, if he'd known she was a nun...

Before she could continue that thought, he pressed his lips again and again with gentle affection upon her breasts. And a warmth spread through her that dissolved all guilt. Erased all care. And enveloped her heart.

When he took her nipple into his mouth, she gasped at the sudden spark that seemed to ignite her body. And when he began to suckle there, using his tongue to bathe her flesh and his lips to draw her in, she arched her head back, lost in a sensual haze.

Finally taking his fill, he moved to the other nipple. She groaned as the burning in her veins grew to unbearable proportions. A prickling deep in her loins demanded to be relieved.

Then he released her. For a moment, she was distraught. She nearly disgraced herself by begging him to continue. But he wasn't finished. And he seemed to know what she wanted.

He tugged on her leine, pulling it down until she could free her arms, then lower to reveal her belly, her navel, and the very top of her curls.

"Ye've made me a map," he murmured.

She opened her eyes just enough to see the glimmer of amusement in his eyes.

He touched the three wee dark dots that formed a straight line down the middle of her belly.

She had to smile. She'd had the tiny spots from birth. Her sisters had told her all manner of things about them. That they were where the faeries had kissed her. Where the Devil had poked her with a spear. Where a wee coney had shat on her. No one had ever called them a map.

"Shall I see where it leads?" he whispered.

She blushed, but her body surged at his words. She felt the tender flesh between her thighs swelling almost to the point of pain.

"Please," was all she could rasp out.

He kissed each spot, traveling lower and lower. And then his hands moved to her hips.

"May I see...all o' ye?"

She swallowed. That was what she'd said to him. She wanted all of him. It wasn't too late to turn back. He was giving her permission to stop him.

But she didn't want to stop him. This was an adventure. She'd likely never get an opportunity like this again. To be touched this way. To be held and kissed and caressed. To feel these feelings.

Instead of answering, she lifted her hips and let him drag the leine from her.

She kept her eyes closed. She felt truly naked. Exposed. Vulnerable.

"Look at me," he urged.

She frowned.

"Please," he said.

She managed to peer at him through the slits of her eyes and the filter of her eyelashes. But what she saw in his face melted away her fears.

His eyes were glazed with the same passion she felt. His lips were parted with soft longing. A light sheen of sweat settled on his brow, which was creased with restraint.

"Are ye certain ye want this?" he said, though she could see in his gaze that it would destroy him if she said nay.

"Aye," she croaked.

He lowered himself to kneel beside the bed. Then he caught her behind the knees, gently dragging her forward until her buttocks were at the edge of the pallet.

With a coaxing touch, he parted her knees a few inches.

She felt her face redden. No one had ever seen this part of her. She was tempted to slam her legs back together.

"So beautiful," he breathed. His breath curled over her, ruffling her hair, warming her flesh.

Soothed by his praise, she closed her eyes and surrendered, letting him spread her legs wide.

Never could she have imagined the pleasure of his fingers parting the petals of her womanhood. The heady thrill of the trust he engendered. The keen anticipation of his touch.

But when he lowered his mouth to her, her delight turned to disbelief. Surely he couldn't mean to...

She gasped and recoiled as his tongue contacted her most sensitive spot. Yet it wasn't a recoil of pain, only surprise. And a sizzling current so powerful it frightened her.

"Ye like that?" he murmured.

She couldn't look at him, so she gave him a nod.

"Do ye want more?"

She nodded again, wondering if she could endure such torment.

He bathed her with his tongue—leaving sensuous designs on her burning skin, tugging at her swollen flesh—until, lost in a fog of carnal awakening, she writhed senselessly on the bed.

When she thought he could torture her no more, her own body began to sharpen responsively. It began at the point where his tongue danced upon her. But it quickly spread its tingling deep within her. Soon she felt like the vibrating string of a harp, plucked to a pitch that resonated in everything around her. Louder and louder the vibration rang. Stronger and stronger the waves of sound grew.

And then the music stilled, as if it could ring no higher. From that fever pitch, erotic shudders shook her body as she cried out in delicious release.

The air was filled with her gasps for a long while afterward as he gently returned her body to her. Then he lifted her legs and laid her back onto the bed.

She was struck with wonder. Never had she felt such ecstasy. Such victory. Such accomplishment.

"Ye're so beautiful," he breathed, staring down at her.

She *felt* beautiful. And relaxed. And cherished.

Now she understood about carnal longing. Once tasted, dalliance like this would be hard to resist. It was difficult even now to think about never feeling this way again. Yet she still hadn't enjoyed the full measure of lovemaking.

She wanted to. *Needed* to. If she intended to be a chaste nun the rest of her life, she wanted to just once experience what it was she was sacrificing.

Of course, she couldn't let him know she was a nun. She'd have to pretend she was a worldly woman who knew what she was doing.

Before she could lose her courage, she looked up at him and whispered, "Will ye couple with me now?"

Adam was prepared to walk away. Even now. While every vein in his body was on fire. His ballocks ached with eagerness. And his cock throbbed in demand.

Adam was a Rivenloch, after all. And Rivenlochs were models of chivalry.

But her whispered entreaty utterly destroyed his willpower.

She wanted this. She wanted him. He'd be a fool to turn her down.

"Please?" she added.

"If ye wish."

He climbed up on the bed beside her. Then he rose on one elbow to study her exquisite form. Her beauty was astonishing. Why she'd been able to fool the monks into thinking she was a bearded old pilgrim, he couldn't imagine. Every supple curve and pliant plane of her body was smooth and shapely, made to tempt a man.

"Ye know, lass, ye're as temptin' as Eve," he told her.

Why that made her start, he didn't know. But her eyes widened for a panicked instant before she gave him a shy smile and replied, "I doubt Eve had a 'map' on her chest."

He doubted Eve had a navel either, but he wasn't about to get into a theological discussion with the woman. He grinned down at her adorable three moles, touching each one in turn with a fingertip.

She reached up, threading her fingers through his wet hair and pulling him toward her.

He obliged her, pressing a tender kiss upon her lips.

Her return kiss was not so tender. She was a fiery lass. She flaunted her passion like a banner. But he had always respected a woman who knew her own desires, who didn't play coy about them.

She feasted on his lips, as if he was her last meal. Her hot breath rasped across his cheek, and she made small moans of pleasure that summoned the ancient beast inside of him.

Continuing to kiss her, he rose above her on his elbows, cradling her head between his arms. Then, using one leg to nudge her thighs apart, he lowered himself until they were chest to chest, hip to hip, skin to skin.

She released a shaky sigh into his mouth.

He held his breath, wondering if he might spend himself before they even had the chance to couple.

Swiftly slipping his hand between them, he stroked her wet folds to smooth the passage. Then, positioning himself carefully, he eased forward bit by bit.

Impatient with his caution, she surged up beneath him, impaling herself. She gasped, and for an instant he wondered if he'd hurt her.

Then she began to move beneath him. Lunging up and falling back in an instinctive rhythm. Surrounding him in a warm, wet chrysalis that would soon change him from an engorged caterpillar into a glorious butterfly.

It had been months since Adam had swived a woman. He wouldn't last long. But by her ragged breathing, neither would she.

Like a stream with banks swollen by a sudden summer storm, a flood of lust rushed through him that he could hardly contain.

Soon her breath caught, and she began to buck in the throes of climax, arching up as if lightning had struck her. He followed at her heels, and it took every ounce of effort to pull out of her to spill his seed harmlessly across her belly.

With a groan of satisfaction, he fell back, spent. For a while, the sawing of their mingled breath was the only sound in the chamber aside from the occasional pop of the fire. He reached out a hand to clasp hers, and it seemed they floated together on a cloud of contentment.

He could have stayed there forever.

Eventually he remembered courtesy.

Gently unclasping her hand, he murmured, "I'll bring a wet cloth."

"Mmm."

When he returned to clean up the mess, she was asleep.

He smiled. Lying there, she looked fresh and young and innocent. Her dark hair spilled haplessly across the linens. Her cheeks were rosy as apples. Her lips were cherubic. Her faint sprinkle of freckles seemed like a dusting of happy stars. She was so perfect, she could have been a saint.

But he knew better now.

Despite appearances, Aillenn was full of life and fire and spirit. A woman of depth and passion. A woman who craved adventure. Who followed her instincts and her heart.

A woman as free and impulsive as he was.

How he'd ever imagined she might be a nun, he couldn't fathom.

How Aillenn had drifted off, she didn't know. She expected the violent explosion of their coupling would keep her awake and alert for hours. But somehow she woke up, tucked under the coverlet, to the sound of Adam snoring beside her in the dark.

As promised, he'd swabbed the mess from her belly.

It had been thoughtful of him to guard against impregnating her. She'd been so distracted by carnal longing that the thought hadn't crossed her mind. Of course, that was exactly what the abbess had warned the sisters about. Eve was lucky Adam was responsible. Without his precaution, she might have ended up in a horrible predicament.

All in all, however, she was highly pleased with what had happened.

Coupling with Adam had been divine. They were Adam and Eve indeed. She felt as if she'd glimpsed Eden. Captured lightning. Grasped the stars. Looked upon the face of God.

It made sense, of course. Creating new life was a miracle. It was only logical that God would make the act that created that new life miraculous as well.

She snuggled closer to the warm, naked, beautiful man who had taken her to heaven.

This was God's will, she decided. The Lord was showing her the way.

CHAPTER 12

When Adam woke at dawn, the first thing he saw was Aillenn perched on the edge of the bed, dressed only in her leine, sewing. He blinked a few times. Even in the dim light, she was more beautiful than yesterday. Beautiful and fascinating and tempting. But he dared not delay their journey further by pursuing that line of thinking.

"What are ye doin'?" he croaked.

"Ah! Ye're awake."

She quickly covered herself with the bedcurtain. He wondered why. He'd seen—and touched and kissed—every bit last night. Every delectable inch of her.

Clearing his throat and his thoughts, he scrubbed at his eyes and sat up. "Is that the curtain?"

"Aye. I'm repairin' it." She glanced at him, unable to hide the pleasure in her eyes at the sight of him. "I'm almost finished." Then she shyly lowered her eyes to where she clutched the curtain to her chest. "I want to thank ye."

"Thank me?"

"Aye, for..." She gazed at the spot where they'd made love.

He couldn't help but grin. "'Twas my pleasure."

She gave him a sly glance. "I think from now on I shall have to insist on goose-down pallets."

"From now on?" The idea of a future with her pleased him immensely.

She pretended she didn't hear that. She went back to her sewing, frowning intently at her work as he pulled on his braies and slipped into his leine.

He was completely dressed by the time she snipped off the final thread and slipped needle, thread, and scissors back into a case in her satchel.

"There," she said. "'Tisn't perfect, but 'twill have to do. I have a task to attend to."

A task? Oh aye, he remembered. Aillenn had promised to look in on Finlay's wee brother.

He hung the curtain while she dressed, doing his best to hide the ragged seam in the folds of the drape. Then they packed up their satchels, grabbed an oatcake and ale in the great hall to break their fast, and bid Pitcairn a grateful farewell.

Finlay brought them their horses. Then the lad led them to his home, a nearby crofter's cottage.

Adam squinted at the thick smoke coming through the roof. It was common wisdom that the ill should be closeted in a warm environment. But the Rivenlochs came from Vikings. They believed in clean water and fresh air.

"What's your brother's name?" Aillenn asked Finlay.

"He hasn't got one yet. He was born but a sennight ago."

Eve's heart sank. Whatever confidence she'd had crumbled. Though she dared not admit it to Finlay or anyone else, there was little hope for a bairn who fell ill so soon after birth.

"Shite," Adam said under his breath.

She gave him a sharp glare. He obviously understood the odds as well. But there was no point in discouraging Finlay.

She meant to do what she could. She would comfort the bairn. She would comfort the family. And, for the love of God, she would open the door to let in the outside air. Why people believed peat smoke was good for sickness, she didn't know.

Mostly what she would do is pray. She was a woman of faith after all. She believed in miracles. And if she prayed with a pure heart, entreating God to save this poor infant, surely He would intervene to save the child's life.

True to her fears, when Finlay opened the door, a cloud of smoke coiled out.

"Leave the door open," she and Adam said simultaneously.

She cocked a surprised brow at him. Perhaps he believed as she did, that sick people thrived on fresh air.

She waved away the smoke as she stepped into the cottage. By the fire was a wan young woman with a pinched face holding a swaddled bairn.

"They're here to help, Ma," Finlay said. "I'd stay, but the laird needs me at the keep."

The woman looked confused. It probably wasn't every day a nobleman and a lady stepped into her cottage. But she was too desperate to question their motives.

"My bairn is so sick, m'lady," she whimpered. "Can ye do anythin'?"

Eve rushed forward to take the bairn from her. The wee lad was pale, struggling to breathe. His lips had a bluish cast, no doubt from lack of breath. "He needs fresh air."

She carried him toward the door while Adam flung open the shutters on the two windows.

The young woman clasped her hands over her mouth. "Are ye sure?"

Eve nodded. That was one thing of which she was certain. Perhaps the *only* thing.

When she carried the bairn into a patch of sunlight

coming through the door, the wee thing didn't flinch once. He hadn't the strength. He barely had the strength to breathe.

"Has he been fed?" she asked.

"He won't take the teat," the young woman said. "I've tried givin' him milk from our cow...honey...a wee bit o' gruel. He won't eat a thing." She dissolved into tears.

Eve placed the back of her hand on his brow. It was hot and dry.

"Water?" Adam suggested.

She nodded. "A clean, wet rag."

While she waited, she closed her eyes and murmured a long and fervent prayer for the child.

Adam brought the wet rag, and she squeezed a dribble of water out of it onto the bairn's lips. But there was no response.

She opened his mouth with her finger and drizzled a little moisture within. But he was too weak for even that. And she dared not pour any more into his mouth, lest he choke on it.

Adam came up beside her and mumbled, "He's not breathin'."

He was right. Her heart leaped into her throat. It was one thing not to eat. It was another not to breathe. Her mind raced. What herb was good to clear breathing?

Mint. "My satchel. Look for the green vial."

Adam nodded. There was no time for ceremony. He dumped the contents of her satchel across the rush-covered floor. Costumes and weapons, books and tools, food and bottles spilled out with a clatter. But though he inspected each label on every vial, he couldn't find a green one.

Then she remembered. She'd used the last of it for Sister Eithne's sore throat.

"Bloody hell," she mumbled in frustration.

"What do ye need?" he asked.

"Mint."

He grimaced doubtfully, but he upended his satchel anyway and began rummaging through the copious contents.

Meanwhile she continued reciting under her breath every prayer she knew, praising God in His mercy, calling on the Lord's forgiveness, beseeching Him to restore the wee bairn to health, giving Him all glory and praise.

To her amazement, Adam returned with a packet of dried mint. Was there anything he didn't have in that satchel?

"Can ye heat a wee bit o' water?" she called over her shoulder to the bairn's mother. "Not too hot, warm to the touch."

The woman nodded.

It would take several moments before the water was warm enough to steep the mint and make an infusion to help the bairn breathe.

Adam apparently thought that was too long. Before Eve could protest, he snatched the bairn from her, pinched its nose closed, and blew a light breath into his mouth.

She was mortified and curious all at once. Would that work?

The air trickled out, but the bairn didn't take another breath in.

Adam repeated the process with the same result.

Five more times he blew into the bairn's mouth, inflating his wee lungs. But nothing helped.

"The water's warm," the mother called out.

Eve took the bairn from Adam and said, "Put the mint in the water, and bring the wet rag."

She prayed once again. This time with more force.

"Almighty God, ye have the strength and the wisdom to perform miracles. Ye know the answer to all questions.

Ye have the power to heal all ills. Prithee do not abandon this child in his innocence, this child who will one day be your faithful servant. Do not torment this devoted family by takin' away the source o' their joy and the lamb o' their comfort. Prithee remove the Devil's hand from the bairn's throat, and breathe the Holy Spirit into him, in the name o' Jesus Christ our Lord. Amen."

Adam brought the small pot of hot water on a thick pad of linen. She flipped the bairn over on his belly along her forearm and draped the wet rag over his head and the steaming pot, trapping the mist beneath for him to breathe.

But she could feel nothing on her forearm. No movement at all.

Tears started in her eyes. And she suddenly realized with horror why it wasn't working. Why God wouldn't answer her prayers.

It was too late. She knew that. Yet in desperation, she offered one last silent entreaty.

Merciful Lord, prithee do not suffer this bairn to die for my sake. Forgive me all the sins that I have done, thought, and said. Send me cleanness of heart and purity of soul. Strengthen me with your might, that I may always withstand evil temptations. If ye will in your infinite mercy save this bairn, I vow I will live virtuously and love ye with all my heart, with all my might, and with all my soul, so that I may never offend ye, but ever follow your pleasure in will, word, thought, and deed, through Jesus Christ Thy Son. Amen.

Adam murmured gently, "M'lady, I think he's gone."

"Nay." The word came out on a sob. "Nay, he can't be."

But she knew he was right.

And now she realized it was her fault.

She had forsaken her calling. Succumbed to earthly temptations.

And this was her punishment.

Tears rolled down her face, past her trembling chin.

Adam spoke softly. "Do ye want me to take him?"

She shook her head. She had one more task to do. Using the warm mint water to baptize the infant, she murmured the familiar words to bless him.

Then she took a moment to swallow down her grief and square her shoulders.

A nun's purpose wasn't only to heal the sick. When that wasn't possible, it was her task to comfort the survivors.

She straightened and tenderly turned the bairn over, cradling him in her arms.

When she turned toward the bairns' mother, the woman's face crumbled with devastating knowledge. She clapped a hand over her mouth to filter the keening wail that erupted from her soul.

It took every bit of strength Eve had to walk toward the woman without collapsing in anguish. She handed the bairn carefully to his mother.

"I'm so sorry."

She was supposed to say something philosophical, like "'twas God's will" or "he's in the Lord's hands now." But she didn't have the heart to cheapen the woman's grief with words that felt empty and inadequate to her pain.

Instead, Eve wrapped an arm around the woman and let her weep upon her shoulder.

Adam, closing the door for their privacy, began packing up the satchels.

After a while, the woman ceased crying enough to whimper, "The poor wee bairn didn't even have a name. He was ne'er baptized. He'll not be goin' to heaven."

"Aye, he will. I baptized him e'er he died with the water ye warmed." She mustered a weak smile of reassurance. "I hope ye like the name Nael. It means 'gift o' God.'"

"Nael," the woman repeated, holding the bairn close against her breast. Then she nodded in approval as a tear trickled down her cheek and onto the infant's swaddling.

After making sure the woman could manage until Finlay returned, Eve and Adam departed in respectful silence. But as they rode along southward path for Strivelin, lost in their sorrow, they couldn't seem to find a way to break that silence. So it continued all morn.

The thoughts in Eve's head, however, clamored like warning bells, punishing her with insistent clanging. Telling her she had lost her way. Saying she was wicked. Wanton. Sinful.

That was the reason God had let the bairn die.

Last night, in one moment of weakness, Eve had fallen from grace. A nun. She'd let herself be tempted by carnal pleasures. Reveled in the garden of the Devil. Like the woman for whom she'd been named, Eve had tasted the forbidden fruit.

It had felt miraculous at the time. A perfect union of souls. A transcendence of body and spirit that felt like something holy. She'd been so convinced it was God's will.

But now she knew better. And His retribution had been swift and brutal.

It had been made much worse by the knowledge that His wrath had hurt not only Eve. It had devastated a woman who didn't deserve such pain. And killed a guileless bairn who hadn't lived long enough to even understand sin.

She had no words for the remorse she felt. And so she continued to ride, weeping quietly, endlessly, not daring to speak, until hours later they crossed the wooden bridge over the River Forth at Strivelin.

Adam was the first to break the silence. Departing the bridge, he rode up even with her.

"'Twasn't your fault, ye know," he murmured. "Ye mustn't blame yourself. Infants are...fragile."

Eve knew what he was trying to do. But in this circumstance, he was wrong. She *was* to blame.

She couldn't tell him why. She didn't want him to think *he* was responsible in any way for her lapse of morality.

After all, he didn't know she was a nun. And a virgin. None of it was his fault. Making love had been *her* idea. She'd asked him to couple with her. Practically begged him.

She couldn't say any of that.

So instead she said, "I know."

"I doubt even a master surgeon could have saved the lad."

She sighed. Perhaps not.

But her prayers could have. If God had deigned to listen.

Of course, He had not. Why would He listen to the supplications of a fallen nun?

"Perhaps the child was too good for this world," Adam said by way of comfort.

She nodded. It was kind of him to say so.

"At least he is with God now," he added. "'Twas thoughtful o' ye to baptize him."

She stiffened. She'd halfway hoped he hadn't noticed. She'd done it out of habit. It sometimes fell to a nun to bless an infant. And a midwife might baptize a newborn they feared was going to die. But it must seem strange to him for an Irish noblewoman to go to the trouble.

She shrugged. "'Twas the least I could do." Then, in a hurry to change the subject, she said, "Do ye know of an inn in Strivelin?"

She'd stayed in Strivelin before at an inn called The Swan. But for what she planned, she needed to find a place where they didn't know her. Where she could slip in unnoticed and escape without a trace.

"The Red Lion?" he suggested. "They have a chamber with a goose-down pallet."

Eve's heart sank. He was so full of hope. So full of affection for her.

But soon she was going to have to deny him. Deny herself.

She couldn't reveal her sorrow now. So she pasted on a fake smile and urged her horse forward before he could glimpse the pain in her face. Pain that stung and filled her eyes to overflowing with tears of regret.

Dear God, how could she leave him?

How could she live without him?

How could she ever be happy again?

By the time they arrived at The Red Lion and let a lad lead their horses to the stable, Eve was only half-feigning the headache she claimed to have.

"Would ye see to the room?" she asked Adam, rubbing her temples. "My head is achin' somethin' fierce."

"O' course. Go on upstairs to the first chamber. I'll pay the innkeeper and bring up the satchels."

She drew her cloak around her and pulled her cowl up over her head. Entering the main room, she crossed directly to the stairs, passing invisibly through the benches of travelers hunched over their pottage. She rushed up the steps and closed herself behind the door.

Glancing at the generous bed draped in blue cotton, she felt a twinge of melancholy. The mattress probably *was* goose-down. But she'd never know, for she meant to sleep where all penitents belonged, on the floor.

Adam considered it a travesty for Aillenn to sleep on the ground when there was a perfectly good pallet—a goose-down pallet—a few yards away.

She'd claimed that being near the warm fire helped her headache. He wasn't sure he believed that.

Perhaps her grief over the bairn was still too sharp for her to be consoled by the comfort of a warm bed.

He offered to sacrifice his comfort for her, to sleep beside her on the floor. But she shook her head.

Something else was wrong. Something was troubling

her. Ever since the infant's death, she'd distanced herself from Adam, hardly speaking, and then only in frosty tones.

Almost as if she thought it was his fault.

Trying to understand the workings of her complicated mind kept him awake, staring up at the brass medallion in the middle of the canopy, while he listened to her drawing in the calm breath of slumber.

When he finally surrendered and dozed off, it was into a heavy sleep.

So heavy he didn't wake until dawn.

So heavy he never heard her leave.

When he saw the empty place by the hearth, he roused as if he'd been slapped awake.

Where was she?

He sprang up, running frantic fingers through his hair and blinking the sleep from his eyes.

Had she left him?

It was a mad thought. She didn't belong to him, after all. Yet the feeling persisted.

Where had she gone?

He tried to calm himself as he dressed in haste. But his heart pounded as if he'd been called to battle. He shoved his arms through his surcoat and buckled his belt with shaking fingers.

Then, as he pulled on his boots, his eye caught on something slouched against the hearth. It was Aillenn's satchel.

Relief hissed out of his lungs. He'd been a panicking fool.

She wouldn't have left without her satchel.

Perhaps she'd only gone to the privy.

Or maybe she was downstairs, breaking her fast.

Catching his breath and trying to smooth his hair and his nerves into some semblance of order, he snatched open the door and resisted the urge to careen down the stairs.

Though he scoured the inn from top to bottom, upstairs and down, Aillenn was nowhere to be found.

The innkeeper knew nothing. And the lodgers gathered before the fire, who hadn't seen the young lady, were only growing more curious and suspicious of him as he continued his relentless questioning.

His pulse began to throb again.

Could she have been abducted? That might explain why she'd left her satchel behind.

But how could that happen under his watchful...

That was just it. He hadn't been watchful. He'd fallen into a deep sleep, not even noticing when she went missing.

Cursing himself for a fool, he returned to the bedchamber.

Time was wasting. He had no idea how long she'd been gone, or even in what direction she was headed. But he'd pursue her to the ends of the earth, if need be.

Shouldering her satchel, he perused the room for his.

It was gone.

Eve set out from The Red Lion on foot in the dim light before dawn, shivering.

Not from fear. Traveling alone was almost always safe in a nun's habit.

Not from cold either. The wool was heavy and warm.

She shivered from the burden of what she was doing.

She'd made a difficult choice, and she still wasn't sure it was the right one.

Prithee do not follow me ~ Lady Aillenn

That's what the missive she'd left for him said.

She felt she owed him more of an explanation than that. But she couldn't say more without revealing her identity. And she needed to make a clean break of it. To forget him if she could.

Her heart was heavy as she plodded along the path.

It had seemed so clear yesterday—as she held the wee bairn in her arms and felt his precious life slip away—that she was being punished. God had shown her the cost of violating her vows. It could be nothing else. She'd sinned, and the price of her sin was a life. Now that life would be her cross to bear.

She should have felt the satisfaction of penance today. She had prayed this morn, renewed her vows, and asked for absolution. Now she'd removed herself from temptation. She planned to return to the convent straightaway to devote herself with new vigor to the church.

Why then did she still feel so uncertain of her decision?

Because being in Adam's arms made her feel like she was in the embrace of an angel. Kissing him had been tasting ambrosia. Touching him, flesh to flesh, had made her spirit sing. Coupling with him, she'd soared to heaven and seen the face of God.

How could such a stirring act of love and devotion not be God's will?

It had felt like a miracle. Now she understood why the abbess spoke against it so vehemently as a distraction from one's Holy Purpose.

It was a distraction. But was that so bad? Now, even worse than creating a lifetime of insatiable thirst for pleasure of the flesh, her heart ached as she realized a terrible truth.

She loved Adam.

Of course she would miss his kiss, his touch, his body.

Eventually, she supposed that longing would fade. She would forget how his smile quickened her pulse. How his glance heated her blood. How the brush of his fingers inflamed her senses.

But his companionship? Without that, she was going to be absolutely bereft.

Without his wit, his laughter, his passion, her life would be dull. Meaningless. Empty.

It had taken only a few days. But it was enough. Her heart belonged to him.

The tears welled in her eyes, blurring the trees lining the path. But she could hear the trickle of a burn ahead where she could get a drink of water and wash her face.

She dared not linger, of course. She knew he would try to follow her. And he would have the advantage of being on horseback.

But he'd been sleeping peacefully when she left. At least she supposed he was at peace. Though she had to wonder how that was possible when he snored like an ox.

Her lips curved into a trembling smile. The fond memory made her eyes fill even more.

She stopped beside the burn, setting aside her satchel. Then she hunkered down to splash her face with the bracing water.

With her eyes squeezed closed, she groped for the satchel, intending to use the linen rag she kept on top to dry her face. It wasn't there. Instead, she felt something made of leather, a bit of knobby fabric, a pair of scissors.

She frowned. Then she remembered Adam had dumped out the contents rather haphazardly yesterday to search for her mint. He'd probably been just as careless returning them to her satchel.

She opened one eyelid to take a better look.

Then both eyes flew open.

It wasn't her satchel.

It was Adam's.

In the dark, she must have picked up the wrong one.

"Shite," she hissed, forgetting for a moment she was dressed as Sister Eve.

Now what would she do?

Patting her face dry on her veil, she considered her options.

She couldn't go back to exchange the satchels. He'd surely be up and about by now.

But what would he think when he found she'd taken his belongings?

She sighed. She didn't mind being thought of as an imposter. But she didn't like being considered a thief.

"Bloody hell."

This would only hasten his pursuit of her, no matter what her note said.

For now she had a few advantages. She'd left hours ago. And he didn't know where she was headed. But he could make up for lost time and guess her direction. She'd have to be looking over her shoulder all the way to her next place of refuge, the convent near Cumbernauld.

Scrambling back onto the road, she easily felt the difference now. His satchel was much larger, heavier, full of things that rattled. How had she not noticed that before?

As she barreled along the path, it occurred to her that without her satchel she was missing the tools of her survival and the tricks of her trade. Without her lady's gown and her archer's garb, her maidservant's rags and her monk's robe, her false beards and her faux blonde hair, who was she?

Apparently, she was stuck as Sister Eve. Nothing more. She found that idea surprisingly distasteful and disappointing.

Then she began to wonder exactly what was in Adam's satchel. There was no time to look now. But he'd told her the contents were a source of fascination among his clan. Her curiosity was definitely piqued.

She passed several travelers along the way, but thankfully, no outlaws. No outlaws except for Eve, who was apparently a genuine thief now.

After a long day of travel, not daring to stop for food, she was relieved to arrive in time for dinner at the convent. She was also relieved to have avoided interception by Adam. At least she told herself she was relieved. Still, there might have been a wee bit of disappointment mixed into her feelings.

That disappointment was sharpened when she retreated to her cell after dinner and opened the satchel.

It smelled like him. Leather. Chain mail. Spice. Soap.

The scent wafted over her like a cloud of yearning.

She reached into the satchel with timid hands, as if she trespassed into his secret world.

She pulled out a garment of pale linen and held it up to her face, inhaling the freshly laundered smell, hoping for a trace of Adam's essence. Then she held it up in the candle-light.

With a startled gasp, she dropped it again.

Braies.

She stared down at the undergarment, lying like a pale flounder on the pallet.

She stifled a giggle.

Was this a spare garment? Or was Adam walking around with no braies? Had he been compelled to ride on a horse without his braies?

This suddenly struck Eve as terribly amusing. And when she thought about what she'd left behind in *her* satchel, it became even more hilarious.

Would he have to resort to wearing her leine? Her stockings? Her gowns?

The image of Adam stuffed into her scarlet velvet made her burst into laughter.

"Are ye all right, Sister?" someone called from the cell next door.

"Oh aye, fine."

But she couldn't get the grin off her face as she imagined his disgust at what she'd left him.

Eve, on the other hand, found his satchel a treasure trove of possibilities. There were useful tools, exotic weapons, leines and robes, belts and pieces of armor, assorted beards and boots, bottles and casks.

She fell asleep with the gleam of adventure in her eyes and the pair of linen braies nestled against her cheek.

CHAPTER 13

illenn had been taken. That was the only logical conclusion Adam could come to.

His heart clanged against his ribs like the harsh strike of a broken bell.

Someone had stolen his satchel. Perhaps Aillenn had awakened and caught the outlaw in the act. Perhaps he'd decided to steal the lady as well.

How could Adam have dozed through it all?

Riddled with guilt, he raced to the stable.

Both horses were there. If Aillenn had fled of her own accord, she would have taken one of them.

There was no other conclusion to be drawn. She'd been abducted.

Adam felt sick.

He saddled up his horse with trembling fingers and slung Aillenn's satchel over the saddle, leaving the second animal as payment for the lodging.

Mounting up, he headed for the road, uncertain which direction to go.

Adam had one purpose. He was a protector. He protected those he loved and those who were too weak to protect themselves.

But this time he'd failed.

Worse, he'd failed the person he was beginning to think

might be, as his romantic cousin Isabel liked to say, The One.

The idea had begun whispering in his ear long before they consummated their affection. Even before that first kiss, he'd had the sense that Aillenn was special. Unique. Exceptional.

He was fascinated by her quicksilver wit and her undaunted spirit. By the way she danced through life, skipping from identity to identity with the ease and grace of an elusive butterfly. He admired her generous soul and her fierce determination. Her easy laughter and her sensitive heart. He even relished her complexity, knowing with Lady Aillenn he would never be bored.

How then could he have let The One be taken from him?

Clenching his jaw and steeling his gaze, he reined the horse onto the main road.

Which direction?

They'd been headed south toward Glasgow. If someone had marked them for theft, it would have been from the north as they passed by. It made sense that the fox would return to his den.

Making up his mind, Adam turned the horse northward and urged it to a clip.

Hours later, he'd found no sign of her. The travelers he questioned along the way had glimpsed no beautiful noblewoman. Nor had anyone at the alehouse where he stopped midday to rest the horse and fill his belly.

Halfway through devouring mutton pottage by the fire, he suddenly remembered he might not have the where-withal to pay the alewife. His possessions were gone.

Shite.

He carried his entire life in his satchel. His costumes, his tools, his coin. How would he manage without them? He hadn't yet sifted through what was in Aillenn's satchel, but he imagined the contents would be fairly useless. Which meant he'd need to waste more time, paying for his supper with his labor.

With a sigh, he retrieved the satchel slouching beside the hearth and opened the top.

There was a missive scribbled with char on a piece of torn parchment.

Prithee do not follow me ~ Lady Aillenn

His mind reeled as he studied the words. What did they mean?

They meant she hadn't been abducted at all.

She'd left of her own accord.

The pottage sank to the pit of his stomach like an anvil in mud.

So "Lady Aillenn" *was* a common outlaw, after all. She must have played a long game—tempting him, luring him in, getting him to trust her, to *care* for her. In the end, like a Judas in a paramour's clothing, she'd betrayed him, stolen his satchel and his coin and left him.

How could she do such a thing?

How could he have been such a gullible fool?

His emotions quickly curdled, from worry to hurt to bitterness. He crumpled the missive in his fist.

Then he wrenched open the satchel.

Had she left him anything? A penny? A weapon? Balm for his broken heart?

She *had* left him something.

Everything.

On top was her scarlet velvet gown. Beneath that were other robes and cloaks, hose and slippers, wigs and caps, a sheathed dagger, a comb and mirror and jewels in a velvet bag, packets and crocks of medicine, her sewing tools, hard cheese, dried herring, oatcakes, and at the very bottom, a purse heavy with coins. A few were lead, but most of them were silver.

He scowled. What did *that* mean?

He considered these new circumstances as he counted out payment for his pottage and ale.

She'd obviously left of her own free will. So perhaps the guilt-riddled lass had left him the coin as payment for her betrayal. He hadn't counted it, but he had to wonder if there were thirty pieces of silver in the purse.

Then she'd written *Do not follow me*?

He'd be damned if he'd heed that advice. He'd absolutely pursue her. There were irreplaceable things in his satchel. The costume he'd used for King Malcolm. Holy vestments. Hairpieces. Weapons. A notebook of cures. Keys to manors all across Scotland. A pick for those places for which he didn't have keys. His spare braies. Most importantly, it held his Rivenloch medallion.

He dared not lose that. It was his identity. If it fell into the wrong hands...

She probably wouldn't believe it was real. At least that was his hope. Indeed, he hoped she'd be disappointed with the cache she'd stolen. It contained little of worth to the average person.

But it was of immense value to him.

Oh aye, he'd follow her.

He wouldn't let her get away with this crime.

He'd insist on justice. Demand the return of his satchel.

And he'd hope, where his chest felt empty and silent, for the return of his heart.

Fueled by pottage and the thirst for retribution, he set out with renewed determination. This time he'd ride south as had been their original plan.

She'd gone on foot. She couldn't get far.

By nightfall, he arrived at the village of Cumbernauld.

Adam had no way of knowing how Aillenn was dressed or what identity she'd taken. She might be visiting a castle as an Empress from the East or sleeping in a stable as Joan the milkmaid.

He found lodging at the local inn as Sir Robert, a nobleman who'd fallen on hard times. He softened the wealth of his lordly garb by covering himself with a ragged cloak from her satchel.

As he sipped ale by the door of the common room, he peered closely at its inhabitants. A beggar hunkered by the fire. An aged crone slurped at her pottage. A mercenary all in black stared at the floor. None of them were Aillenn.

Where could the deceitful wench have gone?

Eve had a rule when she traveled. She rarely wore the same guise two days in a row. That way, anyone following her wouldn't be able to accurately describe her.

The strategy hadn't worked with Adam. He seemed to be able to see through every disguise. But it worked with everyone else.

So when she departed the convent, she made a small detour into the thick of the woods to change her clothing.

Adam's garments were naturally too large for her. She had to be creative. Since there were a number of monasteries where she was headed, she opted for the identity of a monk, Brother Matthew. She wore a loose-fitting cassock bloused over the cord that secured it and an oversized hood that covered her hair and hid her face.

While she searched for the wooden cross she knew he carried, she found another piece. A small silver medallion. It looked very old. She squinted at the engraving.

Amor vincit omnia. Love conquers all.

Then she inhaled sharply.

She recognized the words. It was the motto of the Rivenloch clan.

She was still on a mission for the Rivenlochs. After she returned to the convent, she intended to pay a visit to Hew and Carenza, the couple she'd united, to let them know they were safe from Gellir's wrath, that he'd been wed to another.

But if Adam had engaged recently with the Rivenlochs...

Lucifer's ballocks! Had he stolen the medallion from them?

The idea filled her with a mixture of horror and admiration. She too had tangled with the clan, and it was perilous work. The Rivenlochs were a discerning lot. Not much got past their notice.

Still, to steal from one of them? Adam must have a target on his back now. Perhaps she should count her blessings that they were no longer traveling together.

Still, his absence didn't feel like a blessing.

It felt like a curse.

She didn't realize how lonely the road would feel after enjoying his delightful company.

Her journey toward Glasgow was bursting with the signs of spring. Red squirrels spiraled up trees. Sparrows sang from the branches. Meadowsweet blanketed the sunlit glens, their scent blown on gentle winds. And yet, with no one to share such things, they were only a sad reminder of her solitude.

Had her namesake felt such sorrow after indulging in the forbidden fruit from the Tree of Knowledge? In the Bible, Eve's punishment—to be banished from the Garden of Eden—had been severe.

But had she regretted what she'd done?

Or, given a second chance, would she have done it all again?

It was a difficult question.

A question that tormented Eve on the plodding journey to Glasgow.

A question she couldn't answer, even when the monks welcomed her into the monastery as one of their own and she prayed on it all night long.

If he got away with this, Adam thought, it would indeed be a miracle.

He'd discovered, after taking inventory of her things, that Aillenn had taken her nun's habit with her. That was likely what she was wearing. Which meant she must be staying at convents.

If Adam wished to shadow her, he'd need to have access to those convents.

Unfortunately, he couldn't look less like a nun.

He had to make do with what he found in Aillenn's satchel.

The robe he was using for a habit was far too short, so he had to walk hunched over like an old woman. He fashioned a length of linen into a veil and another he pinned to the veil as a makeshift wimple. There was nothing he could do about his boots or the shadow of a beard on his face. So he provided distraction by way of a knobbed branch he used as a walking stick, waving it about cantankerously, forcing bystanders to keep their distance.

He'd had to sell the horse. There was no way to explain why an elderly nun would ride a fine steed.

Consequently, it took him four times as long as it should have to cover the distance to the nunnery at Glasgow. By the time he arrived at the convent, he ached from miles of hunching, limping, and brandishing the staff. The one blessing was that night had fallen. Thus the abbess took pity on the aged sister and didn't look too closely in the dark at her manly boots or her stubbled chin.

Adam discovered, to his dismay, the nuns ate like birds. It was a good thing he'd availed himself of Aillenn's hard cheese and oatcakes, for supper was a disappointing bowl of thin neep pottage and horsebread.

But what he lacked in nourishment, he made up for in news.

After supper, Adam overheard three sisters in the cloister having a discussion about the king in hushed tones. His ears perked up.

"Did ye hear about Laird Fergus o' Galloway and the king?" one of them murmured. "Rumor has it—"

"Rumor?" a second sister scolded. "Pah!"

"This 'rumor' I heard from the abbot himself."

"Ah, then 'tisn't a rumor," opined a third. "'Tis practically Gospel."

"What did he say?"

"He said the king is preparin' an attack on Galloway."

Adam frowned.

"What? I thought peace was made at Perth."

"Aye," the third agreed. "By an emissary o' the Pope."

Adam had to smile at that.

"'Twas," the first said, "among the other lairds. But Fergus wasn't at Perth."

"I should think the king would be *happy* Fergus didn't lay siege with the others."

"That's just it, "the first nun whispered. "I think the other lairds may be sidin' against Fergus."

"What?" said the second.

"What?" said the third.

"Think about it," the first confided. "Fergus has been a thorn in the side o' the other lairds for years. Wreakin' havoc. Sackin' their villages. I think they convinced the king to attack Fergus first so they can exact their own vengeance."

"Ooh, that's clever."

"Wait. Do ye have proof o' this?"

"Nay, but consider," the first replied. "The king has been in France for a year. Why would he care a whit about Fergus?"

"True."

"The lairds, though, they've had Fergus nippin' at their heels, raidin' their land, stealin' their cattle. They have reason to despise him."

"Well," the second said, "I suppose Fergus *does* need to be taught a lesson then. He can't go on bludgeonin' his neighbors."

"Right," said the third. "The king can't have his lairds bickerin' among themselves o'er every wee thing."

"Do ye think Fergus knows the king is comin'?" the second asked.

The first replied, "He's likely got spies in the king's army."

The other two gasped.

She went on to say, "And if he's got men on the inside..."

"Fergus will know where to waylay the king."

"Right."

There was a long pause while they thought this over.

"Do ye suppose the king will be comin' past Glasgow on his way to Galloway?"

"'Tis likely."

"Ooh. I've ne'er seen the king."

"Nor have I."

"I've heard he's the picture o' chivalry."

"And quite devout."

The conversation continued as the sisters compared reports about the magnificent king they'd never seen, reports that were largely unsubstantiated.

Adam knew Malcolm. While it was true the young king was chivalrous, devout, and somewhat of a romantic, he was weak of body and easily manipulated by flattery. His reason for going to France had been self-indulgent. He could now claim the questionable honor of having been knighted by the English King Henry.

But despite his shortcomings, for centuries the Rivenlochs

had been fiercely loyal to the Crown. If the king meant to attack Fergus at Galloway, the Rivenlochs would be at the forefront of the fighting.

What Adam and the lairds knew—what the king may not be fully aware of—was how much land Fergus had already acquired through his underhanded, tyrannical tactics. Reiving livestock. Burning fields. Raiding cottages.

There had long been rumblings among the Rivenlochs about Fergus's ambitions to create his own empire in the west. Because his loyalty wavered, Fergus might as easily pledge his land to the English king as the Scottish monarch. And that would threaten all of Scotland.

Adam would be damned if he would surrender the centuries-old Rivenloch estate to the English.

It was his responsibility to protect his clan. That meant he had to find a way to give the king the advantage against Fergus.

Adam retired to the cell the nuns had offered him. He lit the sconce and sat on the thin pallet that was definitely not goose-down.

What was the best way to help the king?

He'd go to Galloway, he decided. He'd spy on Laird Fergus. Using a false identity, Adam could become a trusted ally to Fergus and learn what kind of fighting force he had. Who his strongest warriors were. What weaponry they preferred. Where their weaknesses lie.

So busy was Adam concocting his strategy, he forgot for a moment about the woman he was supposed to be following. He was abruptly reminded when he opened the satchel, searching for possibilities for a new disguise.

Aillenn's flowery scent, lingering on the scarlet velvet of her gown, wafted out of the satchel, transporting him immediately to the heavenly night of their tryst.

It would be a long while before that memory would fade.

But for now he had to push it aside.

Sorting through the garments, he decided they were completely inadequate. Too small. Too tight. Too frail. He *had* to find Aillenn and get his satchel back. It was a matter of life and death.

Now that he was on a royal mission, he needed every tool he owned. Not the least of which was his Rivenloch medallion. If things became desperate, his true identity—his tie to the Rivenloch clan—was his defense of last resort.

The coat of mail felt even heavier on Eve's body than it had in the satchel. Perhaps because it added to the guilt already weighing heavily on her shoulders.

It was ludicrously long, hanging past her knees. But she figured she could pass for a young knight who'd inherited his older brother's armor.

Adam also had bits of plate armor in his satchel—epaulets, poleyns, sabatons. But they were difficult to attach without the help of a squire. The mail would have to do.

Adam's boots were huge. But she would make them work. She supposed, as with hounds, it wasn't unusual for a lad's feet to grow first before the rest caught up. Still, she needed to stuff them with linen just to walk without blistering her heels.

She slipped his blue tabard over the mail. Then she affixed his sheathed dagger to his belt and buckled the belt around the tabard, making sure it wouldn't drag on the ground.

She secured her hair with a leather tie and settled his chain mail coif over her head.

This new character would be Sir Peredur from Gwynedd. For simplicity's sake, she decided his mother and father had died of fever. His older brother had been killed in battle, leaving Peredur his armor. He was a mercenary, lending his loyalty and his sword—or in this case, his dagger—to a laird who would see him housed and fed.

She imagined she *did* look like Peredur, the hero in the lore of Cymru, who'd only seen knights from afar and tried to emulate their appearance with the materials at hand. At least she hadn't needed to resort to wearing a bucket on her head or wielding a weapon made of wood.

Of course, Eve didn't plan to fight. She'd simply offer her services for hire to the captain of the guard and leave on the morrow. The disguise was good enough to gain her entrance, a meal, and a place to sleep for the night at Rowallan Castle.

The fact that she had to bed down on the stone floor of the armory, crowded in between the sweaty, smelly, snoring ranks of the Rowallan men-at-arms would have been mortifying to any of her sisters at the convent.

But Eve had never been afraid of new experiences. That, of course, was what often got her into trouble. She never backed down from the challenges God put in her path, whether that meant dining with a king or sleeping in a stable. Rescuing a drowning lamb or saving a servant from a beating. Abducting a Rivenloch bride or exploring her own carnal desires with a handsome outlaw.

She furrowed her brows as she burrowed further under the thin wool coverlet someone had thrown her, using her satchel to distance the warrior next to her who kept trying to cuddle in his sleep.

If only he could be Adam, she thought with a sigh. She hadn't realized how much she would miss him. His warmth. His gentleness. His affection.

She wondered... Could her sensual exploration with Adam have been part of God's plan?

If so, what had been its purpose?

If it was only to teach her not to succumb to worldly temptations, it seemed like an unnecessarily heavy-handed lesson that had come at a cruel price.

And the curious thing was leaving earthly pleasure behind didn't make her feel more devoted to the Lord. Indeed, she'd never felt *less* connected to God. She felt abandoned.

Adam had never made her feel abandoned. He'd insisted on following her everywhere. He'd cared for her. Protected her. Made her feel bright and beautiful. Visible.

And when he'd joined with her in body, in heart, in spirit, she'd never felt closer to the angels or more convinced of God's miracles.

Tears started in her eyes at the memory.

She supposed it was blasphemy to think such a thing. But why would God create such a transcendent experience if only to forbid his most devoted servants from enjoying it?

It was that question that haunted her dreams all night long and prodded her awake before dawn.

She'd meant to leave early anyway, before her fellow soldiers could discover the young mercenary Sir Peredur wasn't all he appeared to be.

She stole out of the armory, picking her way around the dozing warriors, and crept quietly through the great hall. The servants were already awake. They shuttled about, stoking the fire, raking the rushes, and feeding the hounds. They were too busy to take note of the young warrior with a big satchel and oversized armor creeping across the hall.

The scent of fresh-baked oatcakes made Eve's mouth water.

She drew herself up like a brash youth and caught the arm of a passing maidservant. Then she growled out, "Bring me a pair o' buttered oatcakes, will ye, lass?"

The maidservant nodded. "Would ye like ale as well, sir?"

"Aye."

The maid bobbed again and left at once to fetch her breakfast.

Eve sighed at the sad truth. As Sister Eve or Lady Aillenn, she never would have earned such hasty service. But as soon as Eve put on trews and a coat of mail, every maid hopped to do her bidding.

This time it was worth employing the male advantage. The oatcakes were delicious, and the warm butter reminded Eve of the humble pleasures of the convent.

She told herself she was looking forward to her return. After all, there was a simplicity to a nun's life, an order that was always comforting to Eve after she'd had one of her wild adventures. Without her satchel of costumes, she'd be unable to engage in such enterprises anyway, at least until her father sent more coin. But that was probably for the best if she wanted to work on her piety.

Laboring as the convent's dairy maid was one of her favorite pastimes. There was something both peaceful and magical about turning fresh milk into cream and butter, curds and whey. She particularly enjoyed getting her hands in the bowl, working her fingers through the warm milk until it slowly thickened into soft, creamy butter. It felt to Eve like she was imbuing the butter with her essence, her joy, her love.

She popped the last piece of oatcake into her mouth and licked her fingers. She wondered who had imbued this butter with their love.

Finishing off her ale, she slipped out the entrance of the great hall, skirted the keep, and headed toward the main gate.

She'd reach her home in Mauchline before Vespers. One more day's journey, and she'd be safe behind convent walls. There, protected from the object of her carnal temptation, she'd have plenty of time to pray, reflect, and mull over the moral questions that lingered in her soul.

In time, she was sure her longing would fade.

In time, she might even forget the charming pretender.

So she vowed as she set out on the southern road. But her quivering chin and the forest blurring in her vision did not agree.

Adam's hands had never felt so soft. Of course, that was why dairy maids were notoriously desirable mistresses. Kneading milk into butter made their skin creamy and supple. Still, no matter how soft his hands were, no one would have made the mistake of inviting Gunnhild the Dairy Maid to their bed.

Gunnhild was oversized and ugly, with a great wart upon her nose, wrinkled skin, a hairy chin, a raspy voice, and an enormous wool gown that resembled a knight's pavilion.

She had clean hands, however, and that was all that mattered to the overworked cook at Rowallan Castle whose dairy maid had taken ill the previous night. So Gunnhild was immediately put to work, preparing bowls of butter for the morn's oatcakes.

It wasn't an unpleasant task. It was almost magical, the way the milk could be transformed. And being close to the great hall allowed Adam to monitor the activities of the castle denizens.

He'd still seen no sign of Aillenn. He'd been so certain when he'd arrived last night that she must be here. There weren't many options for lodging nearby. No monasteries. No convents. No inns. Rowallan Castle was the obvious choice. It was also populated enough that anyone could slip in easily unnoticed.

As Adam had. He'd wrapped himself in a few plaids from Aillenn's satchel, covered his head with a makeshift wimple and veil, applied raw egg to his face to create wrinkles, and affixed a wart made out of a mushroom to his nose. Thus he'd become Gunnhild.

What Gunnhild's special talents were, he hadn't decided until he heard the cook complaining about a dairy maid that had taken ill. Gaining the cook's confidence was a matter of simply volunteering to fulfill her duties.

Between batches of butter, he was able to make several observations of the castle denizens.

After breakfast, he ranged the keep, searching every face for the one that haunted him.

At midday, he slipped out of the castle in a crowd of merchants to scour the woods and the nearby village.

In the end, Adam had to give up. He rinsed the egg from his face and plucked the wart from his nose. He changed back into his lordly attire. Then, discouraged, he set out on the southbound road.

By dusk, Adam was forced to admit he'd lost his quarry. It had been three days with no sign of her. By now she could be anywhere.

He supposed he shouldn't be surprised. After all, no one had ever been able to track Adam either. And unfortunately, the vixen had as much talent for subterfuge as he did.

He didn't intend to give up. Ever. The woman had betrayed his trust, and he needed some kind of retribution for that. Even if it was only the return of his things.

But for now he had to change his priorities. He had to be about the king's business. How soon Malcolm would attack Fergus, he didn't know. He needed to be prepared.

Still, wherever he went and whatever he did, he'd remain vigilant. He'd look for Aillenn in every face. Study every nun, every archer, every noblewoman, every servant who crossed his path. Keep his ears alert to every murmur, every laugh, every sigh he heard. He had her scent now, deep in his lungs and his soul.

If and when she crossed his path, he'd know.

Lady Aillenn—whoever she really was—might think she'd escaped unscathed. But Adam wasn't done with her. Not by any means.

Three more days passed, and Adam began to wonder if he'd only imagined the beautiful changeling he'd been pursuing. There was absolutely no trace of her. She'd vanished like mist in sunlight.

Though he'd inquired at every alehouse between Rowallan and Ayr, he found nothing. It didn't help that he couldn't describe the person he hunted. And in the end, he had nothing to show for his efforts but an ale-induced headache.

Lying on the threadbare straw-stuffed pallet of the cheap inn he'd found on the outskirts of Ayr, Adam eyed the satchel beside the bed. If Aillenn were here, he'd ask her which of the dozen vials contained a remedy for an aching head. But the unmarked potions were useless to him. For all he knew, he might end up drinking hemlock.

As his temples pulsed, he frowned at the satchel. Its contents were mostly unhelpful. Except for the silver coins. Those he'd used to keep his belly full and a roof over his head. But the rest were only a painful reminder of the woman who had broken his heart.

It would be best if he pretended he'd never met her. He could imagine she'd been one of the fae folk—charming, elusive, and dangerous—who'd left him a cache of silver. Perhaps by her leaving, he'd escaped a close brush with death.

It would be an easier story to believe if he didn't have her possessions weighing him down with the stark proof of her existence.

He reached down and wrenched open the top of the satchel.

There it was again. The red velvet gown. And with it, the cloud of feminine fragrance that wafted forth to fill his nostrils and his heart and his loins with wistful longing.

He needed to get rid of it before it drove him mad.

It was half a day's journey to his sister Feiyan's keep, Castle Darragh. Perhaps he'd go there on the morrow. It would be a relief to be himself for a while. He'd give Feiyan the satchel of clothing and trade it for something more useful. And he could confer with Feiyan and her husband Dougal mac Darragh about rumors of the king's forthcoming attack on Fergus before heading to Galloway himself.

He lifted Aillenn's gown to his face to take one more deep breath. He closed his eyes as desire and pain washed over him. Then he stuffed the garment back into the satchel, wishing he'd never met the beautiful deceiver with the wide, wet, innocent eyes.

CHAPTER 14

"Feiyan!"

Adam waved up at his sister from Darragh's courtyard.

"Adam!" she cried.

She'd been doing her *taijiquan* drills atop the wall walk as usual. He'd been watching her graceful movements for several moments from below, peering between the crenellations. It was a rare person who'd dare interrupt Feiyan's exercises. But Adam knew she'd forgive her brother.

"What are *you* doing here?" she asked, leaning over the parapet to peer down at him. "No one warned me you were coming."

"Am I not welcome in my sister's keep?" He crossed his arms in false outrage.

"Don't be a dalcop," she scolded. "I'll be right down."

She eyed the rampart for a moment, as if she was considering leaping down to the courtyard from there. Then, being heavy with child, she reconsidered and rushed back into the keep to take the stairs.

Adam couldn't help but smile as she waddled briskly across the courtyard. It wouldn't be long before she delivered.

Feiyan, however, was frowning. Instead of the welcome embrace he expected, she gave him a great shove. Even the castlefolk milling about the courtyard seemed taken aback.

"Where have you been?" she demanded. Then, glancing about at the witnesses, she lowered her voice to bite out, "The last time I knew your whereabouts, you were pretending to be the Pope's emissary at Perth, negotiating with the king."

"And?"

"If the king had found out—"

"But he didn't."

"Do you know the risk you took?"

"Risk?" he hissed. "You're a great one to talk about risk. You're an outlaw." He lowered his voice to a whisper. "An assassin."

"Was. Besides, I didn't kill him."

"Nay, you married him."

She rubbed her belly, probably glad she hadn't killed Dougal after all.

She narrowed her eyes to slits. "Anyway, I never tried to kill a king."

"Would anyone know if you had?" Feiyan's stealth was legendary.

She ignored that. "And then you disappeared." She gave him a chiding punch in the shoulder.

"That's not true. I came to the tournament at Perth."

"Nay, you didn't."

He arched a brow at her. "Would anyone know if I had?"

She exhaled in disgust and frustration. It annoyed her immensely that she could never recognize her own brother in disguise.

"So why have you come?" she asked.

He frowned, disappointed. "Do I need a reason?"

"Nay, but there's always a reason."

That much was true. Protecting a large clan like Rivenloch,

spread from coast to coast across Scotland, kept him occupied. It was rare he had time for leisurely visits.

"Well, first, I've brought you something for trade."

He held up the satchel.

Her eyes widened. "Your satchel?"

"'Tis mostly clothing and motley bits I have no use for."

"You're giving up the contents of your infamous satchel? Are you sure there's room in the courtyard to empty it?"

He smirked. "The satchel isn't mine. It belonged to… someone who doesn't need it anymore."

She nodded. "Someone you killed."

"Killed?" he exclaimed. "Why is that the first thing you think, sister? I hardly ever kill people. You, on the other hand…"

Feiyan waved his words away. "So what do you want in trade?"

"A gambeson. A coat of mail. Weapons. Oh, but," he said, digging in the satchel to retrieve the purse of silver. "I'll keep this."

She raised her brows at the clink of coins. "Indeed? *Now* who's the outlaw?"

"I earned this," he assured her.

From across the courtyard came a friendly call. "Is that Adam?"

Adam's brother-in-law Dougal came striding toward him. Since his tenure as Laird of Darragh, Dougal appeared even more self-assured and responsible. He carried their firstborn daughter, and his eyes shone with pride and the spark of imminent fatherhood again.

"Dougal, good day," Adam said. He winked and waggled his fingers at his wee niece, who shyly buried her face in her father's gambeson.

"Sweetheart," Feiyan said by way of greeting her husband, "Adam's decided to go to war."

"What?" Dougal said, putting down the three-year-old, who ran off across the courtyard.

"What?" Adam echoed. "I didn't say that."

"Why else would you ask for weapons and armor?" Feiyan asked.

"'Tisn't that simple," Adam said.

Dougal gripped his shoulder in a brotherly fashion. "If 'tis armor ye need, then armor ye shall have. I remember all ye did for us in the battle for Darragh."

"I appreciate that, but I'm not going to war." Then he furrowed his brows. "At least, I don't think so. And I'm not asking for charity. I've brought something in exchange."

Adam handed the satchel to Dougal.

Dougal narrowed his eyes at the satchel. "This isn't—"

"Nay," Feiyan said. "'Tisn't *the* satchel."

Dougal seemed disappointed. "Where *is* your famous satchel then?"

"'Tis...on loan at the moment."

"On loan?" Feiyan didn't miss a thing. "What does that mean?"

Dougal gave her a chiding smile. "Now, Feiyan, let's not interrogate your poor brother. At least not yet," he said with a wink. "Come in to the hall. We'll have an ale."

As Dougal requested, they kept the conversation light and friendly. Feiyan told Adam about the frustrations of sparring while pregnant. Dougal talked about the challenges of managing a keep. And Adam regaled them with some of his recent adventures. He omitted mentioning the enchanting shape-shifter he'd met on his travels.

Of course, it would come out eventually. Feiyan might not recognize him in disguise. But nothing else missed her notice.

After supper, she invited him to the solar, where she could look through the contents of the satchel. She immediately perceived what he'd neglected to mention.

"These are a woman's things."

He shrugged. "I told you I have no use for them."

"I suppose 'twould do no good to ask how you came by them?"

"I'll tell you...one day."

"Fine. I'll donate the clothing to the local convent."

"Good."

"Now will you tell me why you need battle gear?"

Swearing her to secrecy, he explained what he'd heard about the king planning an attack at Galloway. They both knew the moment the clan found out, all of Rivenloch would rush to defend the king. But Adam felt they needed better information before they charged in blindly.

Feiyan agreed, but he could tell she wanted to get involved. She was frustrated that her condition made it impossible.

Though Adam would never tell her so, he was glad she was incapacitated. Galloway was too close to Darragh for his comfort. The last thing his pregnant sister and her new laird of a husband needed was a war so soon after the battle for their castle.

He told her his plans. He meant to see if what the other lairds at Perth had said was true, that Fergus had been making raids on their lands.

"One more thing," Feiyan said as he rose to bid her goodnight.

He turned at the door.

"I know you never go to tournaments," she said.

That made him smile. He never missed a Rivenloch tournament. It was just that no one ever recognized him, and he always slipped away before they could.

"But we're having one in late summer, here at Darragh," she said, rubbing her round belly again. "Dougal has promised I can spar in the tournament after the bairn is born. And we'd be honored if you would attend."

Adam knew that was Feiyan's way of inviting him to meet his new niece or nephew. He wouldn't miss that for the world. But he couldn't resist teasing her.

He arched a brow. "You think you're going to be fit to compete?"

She scowled, then arched a brow back at him. "You'll have to return and find out."

"I'll *try* to make it."

She sighed. "Fine."

He winked and nodded as he left the solar. "Good night."

Her announcement made this business between the king and Fergus even more pressing. A summer tournament meant the whole Rivenloch clan would be coming to Darragh. If war began at Galloway, they would be the nearest warriors at hand, the first to engage in the fighting.

He had intended to stay longer at Darragh, but with this greater urgency, haste was imperative.

If Fergus had installed spies among the king's men, it was necessary for Adam to be the eyes and ears of the king in Fergus's army.

To infiltrate Fergus's ranks, Adam needed to appear nondescript, ordinary, a simple man-at-arms. He knew a fine warhorse would make him too noticeable. The Fergus holding of Kenmure was two or three days away on foot. So as much as he'd disappoint his sister, he'd have to bid her farewell on the morrow.

Adam couldn't afford to risk having anyone in the Fergus clan recognize him. So from the Darragh armory, he chose discarded armor—battle-scarred plate, mail that was missing a few rivets, a dented helm, a splintery spear, and a sword that had seen better days. Things no self-respecting Rivenloch knight would own.

Feiyan naturally thought her brother was a clodbrain for taking such inferior gear.

He also needed a disguise that would be easy to maintain, yet make him difficult to identify.

Normally he didn't like to make long-lasting changes to his appearance. It made him less flexible in a crisis. But this was a serious mission with a serious purpose. He might need to inhabit this character for a month or more.

So as soon as he left Darragh, he used his dagger to cut his long hair short.

Over several weeks, the thick stubble of his jaw would grow into a proper beard.

Once he drew near to Fergus's holdings in Galloway, he took his time, loitering at inns and alehouses along the way, picking up bits of conversation and casually inquiring about work.

He wasn't disappointed. It seemed Fergus *had* been sending raiders out to trouble the neighboring clans. The activity had escalated in the last several weeks. Most of the clans were recruiting men to guard their towns and herds against attack.

But they weren't the only ones.

When Adam crossed into Galloway and arrived at the keep at Kenmure, it was clear Fergus was building his clan forces as well.

Joining the ranks of Fergus's men-at-arms at Kenmure was easy. His captain was eager to enlist the services of dark-bearded, short-haired Ness MacNeill, a man-at-arms who had all his own equipment, even if it was rusty and dented.

As for learning the laird's ambitions, Adam didn't need to bother becoming a trusted confidante. Fergus was open and boastful about his plans. He regularly visited the armory to discuss strategies with the captain. It was clear he meant to expand his already sizable holding.

Adam wondered if that was the real reason the king wanted to put a stop to Fergus. If the Laird of Galloway hoped to enrich himself with more and more property, he could eventually become a threat to the Crown.

A go-between could play a key role in alerting the king to Fergus's plans. It would require stealth and deception. But those were two of Adam's most valuable assets.

Eve sighed as she poked the final row of peas into the soil of the convent garden.

Ordinarily, she loved being outdoors in the warm spring sunlight. She liked tending to the crops while her sisters toiled nearby in the orchard. She enjoyed the sensation of damp earth crumbling between her fingers. Appreciated the small miracle of creating new food from a single seed.

But she hadn't been happy for weeks.

The abbess had asked no questions upon Eve's return. Eve considered this a mercy, for she was certain her sin was written across her forehead. A sin that seemed even more reprehensible in the peaceful, pious halls of the convent.

She'd wept and prayed.

She'd fasted and taken a vow of silence.

She'd isolated in her cell and foregone the pleasure of bathing.

But none of her acts of penance had brought her relief or forgiveness.

Was this how the rest of her life would be? Nothing but pain and guilt? Longing and shame?

Part of her felt she deserved it. At least she *had* a life, which was more than God had given poor, wee Nael. Perhaps she should accept a lifetime of sorrow with grace and dignity.

Worse, no matter how vehemently she prayed, how much she hungered, how many tears she shed, she couldn't stop the dreams that plagued her in her sleeping hours.

She dreamed of *him.* Of the gallant, generous, exciting man who had swept her off her feet and fed her a sweet feast of forbidden delights from his loving hands. Again and again she dreamed of what they'd done.

Then she dreamed of what they *might* have done. The rapturous trysts ahead of them. Their wedding night. The children they'd have. The blissful life they'd lead. Going on adventures. Battling outlaws. Finding purpose. Doing good.

Every morn she awoke in grief over her loss. Wishing she could forget him. Wishing they had never met.

Every morn her gaze would catch at the satchel propped in the corner. And every morn she swore she would get rid of it. Banish Adam from her mind. From her heart. From her soul.

But she couldn't. She told herself it was because taking the satchel would be stealing. His things had worth, after all. A coat of mail. Armor plate. A dagger. His medallion. They were too valuable to simply discard. Neither did she dare donate them, for fear his identity might be revealed.

In her heart, however, she knew the real reason she couldn't part with them.

It was foolish hope.

Hope that somehow he might return for them.

Hope that when he did, God would decide she'd paid enough.

Hope that her dreams of a bright future might come true.

She straightened at the end of the row, pressing at the stiff small of her back. Shielding her eyes from the sunlight with her hand, she looked over the convent wall toward the far road.

A horse and rider were coming.

Was it...?

Her heart raced even as her brain told her she was wrong.

It wasn't Adam. Adam she would have known anywhere. Still, the rider looked familiar.

That was no common palfrey, but a fine warhorse.

And the person riding it was a woman. A noblewoman.

Eve straightened. She knew who it was.

"Lady Feiyan," she murmured.

The sight of the lady, a Rivenloch, made her heart flip. Eve's first thought was that her crime—stealing Gellir's bride—had been discovered. Somehow Lady Feiyan had found out that Eve was the one responsible.

Then she realized Lady Feiyan had been at Perth. She'd seen Gellir happily married to the maidservant Merraid. Surely Feiyan and the rest of the Rivenlochs were no longer angry about the abduction of Carenza, his first betrothed. After all, things had ended well for Gellir.

Eve knew things had ended well for Carenza as well. She'd brought the bride to this very convent to unite her with her lover, Gellir's cousin Hew. Could that be why Feiyan had come? To press Eve into revealing what had become of Carenza?

Eve wouldn't tell her. She was a woman of honor. She'd sworn to keep Hew's secret. No one but Eve knew the happy couple had been living in a wee remote byre in the woods.

But Lady Feiyan's presence reminded Eve she needed to get word to Hew and Carenza. They were safe now, forgiven for their impulsive elopement. They could come out of hiding.

As she watched Feiyan enter through the cloister gate, she couldn't help feel a thrill of excitement. Eve was starved for the company of women from the outside. Women who weren't literally holier than her. After Eve's fall from grace, she felt as if everyone in the convent was her superior, that she could never make ample amends for her sin.

Completely forgetting her vow of silence, Eve rushed forward to greet her.

"M'lady Feiyan," she said, holding her hand out. "Welcome."

Feiyan took her hand.

Eve's eyes lowered involuntarily to the lady's swollen belly. She grinned and blurted the first thing that came to mind. "Och, ye're takin' your bairn for a ride, are ye?"

Fortunately it didn't offend the lady. She lifted her leg over the saddle and said, "Might as well get the child accustomed to my horse."

Eve helped the lady down. As she did, her gaze settled on the satchel hanging from Feiyan's saddle. Settled on it and recognized it.

It was hers.

Her heart began to pound. Chaos stirred her thoughts as she tried not to stare at it.

Why did Lady Feiyan have Eve's satchel?

Had Adam given it to her?

How had their paths crossed?

Was Feiyan the one from whom Adam had stolen that Rivenloch medallion?

Had Feiyan stolen Eve's satchel in retribution?

"After all, I can't afford to lose my skills," Feiyan confided, "if I'm to participate in the summer tournament."

Eve summoned up a shaky smile, trying to betray none of her panic. Only half listening, she mindlessly echoed, "Summer tournament?"

"Aye, at Darragh, after the bairn is delivered."

When Feiyan's words finally registered, Eve's eyes lit up. Her worry vanished. A tournament. "At Darragh, ye say?"

"Aye."

"Will your whole clan be there?"

"They had better. 'Twill be in celebration of the laird's new grandchild."

Irresistible visions of waving pennants and flashing swords, sparkling armor and clashing blades danced through Eve's mind. What a spectacle it would be. A tournament to rival the king's at Perth.

Eve had to find a way to compete against Jenefer of Rivenloch again.

Her thoughts were interrupted by the abbess, who waddled forward with breathless haste. "May we be of assistance, m'lady?" she sang out.

"Perhaps," Feiyan replied. "You see, I have this satchel of clothing and other items. I thought you might be able to distribute them to those in need."

Outrage sizzled up Eve's spine. Charity? She was giving Eve's goods to charity? And what about the silver? There had been a decent amount of silver in that satchel.

Unless Adam had pocketed it for himself.

Of course he had. He might have no use for Eve's clothing and herbs. But everyone had use for silver.

"We'd be happy to, m'lady," the abbess said, "but next time, prithee send a servant." She clucked her tongue and added, "Ye shouldn't be ridin' about in your condition."

Eve could see by the vexed ticking in Feiyan's eye that she'd grown weary of such helpful warnings.

The abbess continued. "Give the satchel to me, m'lady, and I'll—"

"I'll take it," Eve interjected. "I'll get it into the right hands, m'lady. The abbess shouldn't be travelin' about. Not in her condition." She gave Feiyan a clandestine wink.

Then, while the abbess was sputtering, she unhooked the satchel from the saddle and slung it over her shoulder.

It felt lighter. Of course it felt lighter. The knave had naturally taken all her coin and who knew what else. She only hoped he'd left her something of value.

"I'll leave within the fortnight, m'lady," Eve announced, glad of the excuse to quit the nunnery for a while. "I know a woman not far from here who's in need. She'll be so grateful for your gift."

Indeed, Eve *was* grateful. With any luck, the satchel would contain a fitting disguise. One she could use for the mission she'd put off for too long now. Letting Hew and Carenza of Rivenloch know they were out of danger.

CHAPTER 15

The abbess found excuses to keep Eve at the convent for a full month more. Probably to punish Eve for her impertinence. Or perhaps in the hopes that Eve's impulsive spirit might be tamed with several more weeks of thoughtful reflection.

Of course, Eve could have escaped at any time. She'd done it before. But if she was doomed to live a loveless life as a nun, she supposed she should accustom herself to the discipline and self-restraint the profession required. A few weeks wouldn't make that much difference.

On the last day of her captivity, however, Eve was itching to leave. She bid the abbess a quick farewell and started out on foot just after Prime. She changed into her red gown in the woods and left her satchel with her habit behind a tree.

It was satisfying to have a Greater Purpose again. To be doing something more significant than laundering habits and polishing crucifixes. What she did today would change the course of history. She was helping mend a rift in the powerful Rivenloch clan.

Surely that was God's plan.

And He'd chosen Eve to be a part of that plan.

At the moment, all the Rivenloch clan knew was that one of their own, Sir Hew du Lac, had stolen his cousin

Gellir's bride, Lady Carenza of Dunlop, intending to reunite her with her true love. What they *didn't* know—what only Eve knew—was that Carenza's rescuer *was* her true love.

Naturally, they also didn't know what had become of Hew after his mission. But Eve knew. She occasionally used the secluded byre herself as a safe haven. From the outside, it appeared to be a rotting shed tucked into the deepest part of the forest and covered with vines. But inside it was quite hospitable, clean and dry. It was possible to live comfortably there for months.

Of course, they didn't want to be there for months. But since the abduction had arguably been a crime, they dreaded the shame it would bring upon their clans. And since the marriage had been accomplished without the king's approval, they feared Malcolm's wrath. Worse, they worried the king might dissolve their union.

Eve couldn't help but smile as she sauntered through the woods, imagining their delight when she told them all was repaired and forgiven.

Now she could reveal to the couple what had happened in Perth. She could tell them Gellir had married *his* true love, Merraid. Merraid had been knighted by the king for her bravery, and she'd secured the king's forgiveness of Hew and Carenza for their disobedience.

All would be set aright.

Eve took a deep breath. It was good to be out in the world again, smelling the summer flowers, feeling the warm breeze on her face and the spongy path beneath her feet, hearing the birdsong and...

She stopped.

She'd heard something behind her. The loud snap of a twig.

She turned. No one was there.

She slowly turned back and continued down the path. But this time her ears were attuned to every sound.

There it was again. The crack of a branch, as if a heavy boot stepped on it, followed by a shuffle of leaves.

This time she didn't stop.

Someone was traveling behind her. Not on the path. Just off the road. Moving through the trees.

She kept her pace steady and began humming as she walked.

As she suspected, her air of nonchalance made her pursuer less guarded. His footfalls became careless, and she could tell he was growing closer.

Was he an outlaw?

It was likely. But she knew how to handle outlaws. She didn't have her dagger, but she had her wits, which were almost as sharp.

Several moments passed. She got through seven verses of the song she was humming. Still he made no move to intercept her.

What were his intentions?

There was a large alehouse just around the bend. Smoke rose from the roof. A donkey and two mules were tied outside. She'd be safe inside.

She ducked under the sign of the broom above the alehouse entrance and pushed the door open. The interior was dark, but she could make out the figures of several travelers who were quenching their thirst at tables scattered about the room.

She quickly headed for a bench in the shadows.

A maid emerged from the kitchens. Eve flagged her down to take her order.

"An ale, please."

Before she could receive her cup, the door opened to admit a new visitor.

The man immediately scanned the room. In the dark, his eyes skipped over her. Then he frowned and turned to hang up his cloak.

Was he the one who'd been following her?

She drew in a sharp breath when she saw the insignia on his tabard. It was a red lion rampant on a gold field. The king's crest. This man was a royal guard.

Was he here for her?

Several dire possibilities raced through Eve's mind.

Her part in Carenza's abduction had been revealed.

Someone had discovered the silver she'd given to the outlaws was counterfeit.

She'd been accused of murdering the bairn who'd died in her arms.

The king had found out she possessed the stolen Rivenloch medallion.

Adam had reported her as a fugitive outlaw.

She shrank farther into the corner as the man settled himself at a bench beside the door, a spot where he could survey the whole room.

He looked fierce, just the sort of strong and ruthless bear of a man that a frail ruler like King Malcolm would use to enforce his commands.

"Here ye are, m'lady."

Eve jumped, startled by the maid as she set a mazer of ale down on the table.

The action drew the man's attention. When Eve swiftly lifted the cup to her lips, mostly to hide her face, his gaze followed her movements.

With two fingers, he summoned the maid. He motioned her close and murmured something in her ear. Eve was certain he was inquiring about her. The maid glanced her way and shook her head.

He stopped looking in her direction then. But Eve knew better than to assume he was no longer interested in her. He simply knew he no longer needed to keep his eye on her. She couldn't go anywhere without him noticing. So he could dally over the ale.

What he'd asked the maid, she didn't know. But she could almost always rely upon the sisterhood of women when she needed a quick escape.

She summoned the maid again and rose on shaky legs, feigning illness.

"Miss," she gasped, "I fear I'm goin' to be sick. Do ye have a chamberpot in the kitchens?"

"Och! Come with me then, m'lady."

Eve didn't look at him, but she felt the man at the door stiffen as the maid led her from the common room.

Once she passed into the kitchens, Eve turned to the maid with an urgent plea.

"Miss, that man at the door, the one in the king's colors?" She grasped the maid's sleeve. "He's been followin' me. I fear he's after my virtue. Prithee let me out the back door."

The maid's mouth went round. She blinked in surprise. In that moment, Eve knew they'd found a womanly connection. The maid would usher her out the kitchen door now to escape into the woods.

But then the maid turned her head and screeched, "She's tryin' to get away, sir!"

So much for the sisterhood of women. Left no choice and begging God's forgiveness, Eve bit out a curse and gave the maid a hard shove backwards toward the common room. The lass collided with the king's man.

While they tussled, Eve scrambled for the back door, intentionally knocking a pot of pottage onto the floor behind her. She turned once at the door, just in time to see the guard go sprawling in the slippery mess.

Then she tore away from the alehouse. She sprinted down the main road, getting some distance on her pursuer before ducking into the shelter of the trees.

Fortunately, the byre wasn't far off. But one had to know the way. The king's man from Perth would get lost in the dense woods before he ever found it. Or her.

It was familiar landscape to Eve, however, so she stopped a moment to catch her breath, leaning against the trunk of a pine.

Now that she had time to reflect, she realized how much she'd missed this. Narrow escapes. Subterfuge. Quick thinking.

It made her feel alive.

She couldn't believe that wicked maid at the alehouse had turned her in at the first opportunity. Still Eve had managed to escape. She had to grin. Watching the fierce guard slide through the pottage like an otter on ice had been entertaining.

"Och, Eve," she scolded. "Shame on ye."

That wasn't the way for a nun to behave.

Perhaps she wasn't fit to be a nun.

Still, she wasn't exactly an outlaw. No matter what the king's guard thought.

She wanted to do good. It was just more fun doing good when her heart was beating fast.

When she reached her destination, her interaction with the exiled Rivenloch couple was hurried. With the king's man tracking her, she didn't dare linger.

She was impressed with what they'd done with the byre. Love had turned the hovel into a home. And Hew had turned Carenza into a glowing mother-to-be.

Eve experienced a wee twinge of envy over their contentment as a couple. Painful memories flashed through her mind. Adam's kiss. His gaze. His smile. His touch.

But she didn't let it show. She couldn't let anything—even a royal guard on her trail—diminish their happiness.

She told them what had happened since they'd become fugitives. That King Malcolm had returned to Scotland. That there had been a brief siege by some of the lairds at Perth, but peace had been made.

She gave them the good news that they were forgiven by the clan and shocked them with the fact that the king had knighted the maidservant Merraid and then married her to Gellir.

She said they could go home safely now.

Hew, however, was a Rivenloch through and through. He wouldn't accept anything that wasn't properly executed. So he tasked Eve with getting their wedding document officially signed by the clan lairds of Rivenloch and Dunlop and sealed by the king. Only then, he said, would he feel safe to return.

She agreed, but warned him it might take time.

First, however, she had to make it back to the convent.

Fortunately, Carenza still had the nun's habit Eve had loaned her. She'd kept it since the night they'd fled. So Eve exchanged her red velvet gown for the habit.

The royal guard might be able to outpace the lady fleeing in red. But he wouldn't glance twice at the nun strolling back along the road.

Her return to the convent was happily uneventful. She was still beaming from her victorious exchange with Hew and Carenza and her successful escape from the royal guard.

She arrived to even more encouraging news. Her father's annual stipend had arrived.

That meant she had enough coin to have Adam's gambeson altered by the tailor in the village to fit her and to purchase a new bow and arrows. She could compete in the upcoming Rivenloch tournament at Darragh and win back the silver she'd lost.

"Who did you say you were?"

King Malcolm leaned forward in his chair from the far side of the pavilion and narrowed his eyes at Adam.

Adam's heart pounded.

He resisted the urge to wrench his arms out of the royal guards' vise-like grip.

Never before had he feared someone would unmask him and discover his true identity. His talent for deception had always served him well.

But this—stating clearly he was Sir Adam la Nuit of Rivenloch and not being recognized by his own king—this made his blood simmer.

Considering the king had been out of the country for some time, and the fact that Adam looked nothing as he had before—with cropped hair, a full beard, and battered armor—he supposed it was no surprise that his identity was being challenged. Still, it was humiliating.

He'd been caught in the forest, exactly as he'd intended. He'd managed to stray far enough away from Fergus's clansmen on his own to seek out the camp of the king's army. And he'd allowed the king's men to take him into custody.

"I'm Sir Adam la Nuit of Rivenloch, Your Grace. We've met before."

"Rivenloch?" he replied, giving him a head-to-toe perusal. "You don't look like a Rivenloch."

"I'm...in disguise."

The guards snickered at that.

Adam felt a muscle tick in his jaw.

The king gave him a smug smile, clearly amused. "In disguise? I see. And what proof do you carry that you are a member of the Rivenloch clan? A seal? A ring? A document?"

Adam sighed.

This was Aillenn's fault. It was hard not to be angry with her. If the scheming wench hadn't switched the satchels weeks ago, he'd have the medallion now as proof.

"My clan medallion was stolen, Your Grace."

The guards snickered again.

Adam felt the veins in his neck bulging.

The king steepled his fingers in front of him. "So you have no proof then?"

The guards chuckled aloud.

Adam clenched his jaw. He'd had enough. He'd risked his life, voluntarily embedding himself in the keep of the enemy to spy on the king's behalf.

Proof? The king wanted proof he was a Rivenloch?

Fueled by the cold blood of his Viking forebears and the hot blood of his Scots ancestors, he wrenched his left arm out of the guard's grip, turned to the guard on his right, and gave him a hard punch just above his smirking mouth. A punch that crunched the bones of the man's nose and made him stagger away in pain.

The guard on his left drew his dagger. Adam dodged the quick thrust, seizing the man's wrist and bending it backwards until he dropped to his knees with a yowl. Adam grabbed the weapon before it fell from the guard's limp fingers. Then he faced the two soldiers at the pavilion door. They were armed with swords.

He could still best them. Hell, he could kill them. But that would be a mistake.

Instead, he rushed at one of them, blocking the man's upraised blade with the haft of the dagger before diving toward his shins to bowl him over backwards.

While he disentangled himself from the fallen soldier, he lost the dagger. The second guard had time to take a few swings at him. Adam dodged right. Then he rolled left. At the third strike, he managed to kick the man's hand, altering its course. The blade whistled past Adam's head, missing him by an inch.

Borrowing one of his sister Feiyan's tricks, he leaped to his feet, did a quick spin and, with his heel, kicked the guard full force in the side of the head. The man went down like a puppet with its strings cut.

Adam located and scooped up the dropped dagger, bracing himself for more attacks.

There were none.

Breathing heavily, he glanced at the king.

Malcolm looked suitably frightened. As he should have been. Adam still had a dagger. If he'd been a foe instead of a loyal vassal, he could have killed the king.

Instead, Adam came forward, lowered himself to one knee, and offered Malcolm the weapon, hilt first.

The king didn't bother taking it, saying in awe, "You *are* a Rivenloch."

"Aye, Your Grace."

The king squinted to study him more thoroughly. Adam wasn't sure it helped.

"Ah, of course, we see it now," Malcolm said. "We remember you from...from..."

Malcolm obviously did *not* remember him, though they'd met several times before. But that was fine with Adam. Until now, his invisibility had always been a useful gift.

"Last spring, I came to my cousin Gellir's wedding tournament at Perth, Your Grace," Adam told him. That much was true, even though he'd been in disguise.

"Aye, that's it."

The fallen guards began to rouse. They grumbled, trying to regain their balance and their dignity as they saw Malcolm and Adam conversing peacefully.

The king asked, "Why have you come, Sir...?"

"Adam. Sir Adam la Nuit. I've come to serve Your Grace."

"Serve me? How?"

"I've come to be a royal scout."

"A scout?" He scratched his chin. "You mean a spy?"

"If you wish."

"On whom do you mean to spy?"

Adam glanced at the recovering guards. Could he count on their silence?

The king waved them away. "Leave us."

"But Your Grace..." the man gripping his injured wrist protested.

"This *is* Rivenloch," the king said. "I trust him."

The guards reluctantly left.

When they were alone, the king asked again, "On whom do you mean to spy?"

"Fergus."

"Fergus." The king feigned indifference. "Why would you—"

"I believe Your Grace intends to attack him."

Malcolm blinked. "Where did you hear that?"

"There is no faster conduit for secrets than the church."

Malcolm's brows rose. Then he sighed. "We must learn to take care with our confessions from now on." His brow creased in concern. "Does Fergus know?"

"I don't think so." Surely Fergus would have boasted about fighting the king if he knew he was nearby.

"So what do you propose?"

"I've been living in Fergus's household at Kenmure for weeks now. He's been strengthening his fortresses. Building his army. Hiring mercenaries."

"Mercenaries...like you?"

"Like me."

"Mm." The king steepled his fingers. "Surely he doesn't think he can defeat the whole of the Scots army."

"Fergus's numbers are growing. Parcel by parcel, he's taken much land already, expanded his influence." Adam didn't mention that the Scots' loyalty to their king had been in question since Malcolm had become so friendly with the English king. "He doesn't wage war like a lion, Your Grace. He attacks like a pack of hyenas biting the lion."

"And how would you fight those hyenas?"

"If you find out when and where they intend to bite..."

The king nodded. "I see. And you plan to provide that information?"

"If I can, Your Grace."

"This would be invaluable," Malcolm agreed. "But if you're caught..."

Adam was confident he wouldn't be caught. Ness MacNeill had already managed to fade into the background at Kenmure. He was a soldier of average skill and even temper. He held no opinions. He spoke little. He kept to himself. No one would notice him missing.

"I wouldn't expect to be rescued," he assured the king.

"Spoken like a true Rivenloch," the king remarked.

CHAPTER 16

Like a true Rivenloch, Adam also meant to keep his word to Feiyan about attending the tournament at Darragh, even if she wouldn't realize he was there.

He could spare a few days away from spying for the king. Fergus had no immediate plans. And it had been too long since Adam had taken account of his clansmen.

He need not worry he'd be recognized. Not only did he look nothing like the long-haired, clean-shaven Adam the clan knew and loved. There were also so many contestants camped on the hillside, teeming in the courtyard, spilling onto the lists, he could have easily gotten lost in the crowd, even without a disguise.

The one precaution Feiyan had been careful to take was *not* inviting Fergus. For that, Adam was grateful. He'd lived long enough among the clan as the mercenary Ness MacNeill that he might not be so easily overlooked, even in his current attire.

Just to make very sure he wasn't recognized, he decided to participate only in the archery. Today his name, appropriately enough, was John Schott. His costume was drab and unremarkable. Over a faded saffron leine, he wore a long, thickly padded brown gambeson that added weight to his frame. Beneath that he wore dark brown hose and brown boots. He covered his head with a flat linen coif topped by a brown cowl. His beard was now full enough to hide the contours of his jaw.

The most difficult thing to hide was his excitement at catching a glimpse of his sister holding Adam's new nephew, Logan. He saw the surge of pride in Dougal's eyes as he presented their son to the Rivenloch clan.

And then he felt a sharp pang of envy. Envy and loss. This was the kind of family he'd imagined making with Aillenn. One where he gazed at her with utter adoration. She gazed at him with complete devotion. And together they celebrated the bairn they'd made out of the sweetness of their love.

But it was not to be. Perhaps it would never be so for Adam. He had trouble imagining another woman with whom he could feel so honest, so enchanted, so free.

His throat thickened, and his eyes filmed over.

That wouldn't do. He couldn't aim a bow with watery eyes. And nothing would attract more unwanted attention than a weeping contestant.

Brusquely wiping his eyes with his thumb, he turned away from the touching sight. He flexed his bow to test its bend and examined the fletching of his arrows to prepare for the archery contest.

He paid little heed to the dozens of lesser contestants. It was rare anyone could best his cousin Jenefer. It was her he most wished to face. He doubted he could win. But he definitely wanted to try.

Many foreign archers were announced. Alfonso de Borja. Otto of Cologne. Abu ibn Yusuf. Falco de Malisio. Adam recognized none of their names. He only glanced up briefly when they were called.

Most of his attention was on the contented couple sitting beneath the canopy in the stands, his smiling sister and her proud husband, who were more interested in their children than the archery contest.

Again, his heart sank.

He wanted that. He wanted their happiness.

Never before had Adam longed for that sort of existence. He'd always assumed it wasn't meant to be.

His was no kind of life for a wife, much less a child. He knew that.

Adam was too reckless. Too restless. Too invisible. An unpredictable shape-shifter like him could hardly expect to be known, much less loved, by anyone.

And yet Lady Aillenn had made him feel loved.

She'd appreciated his spontaneity. She'd admired his disguises.

With her, he'd almost been able to envision a blissful future.

"John Schott!" came a call in the distance from the archery field.

With her, he could imagine lazy morns... adventurous afternoons...

"John Schott!"

Passionate nights...

"John Schott!"

Adam started.

Shite. That was him.

"Aye!" he confirmed, "Here!"

He began to trot up through the line of archers. But so rattled was he at his wandering mind and his lapse in character, he tripped over his own feet and fell to one knee.

The archers around him snickered as his quiver slipped off his shoulder and the arrows slid out, scattering on the ground.

Bloody hell. The last thing Adam wanted to do was draw attention to himself.

He scooped up the arrows as quickly as he could.

One of the archers took pity on him, dropping down beside him to help.

"My thanks," he mumbled.

"Of course," was the reply.

He inhaled sharply. That voice.

He whipped his head around.

It was her.

Aillenn.

To anyone else, she appeared to be an olive-skinned Italian youth in a jaunty feathered cap and parti-colored tunic and trews. She even had a slight foreign accent to her husky voice.

But Adam wasn't fooled. Not for an instant.

She looked as shocked as he felt. Her eyes widened. Her mouth parted. She froze.

He held his breath, ignoring the rush of joy that filled his veins. He knew one careless glance or word could mean discovery for both of them.

She seemed to understand as well. She gave him the last arrow and looked immediately away, leaving without another word.

But now he was a wreck.

What was she doing here?

Was it coincidence, or had his sister Feiyan invited her?

Did Aillenn know he'd be here? How could she? He'd told no one.

And how the devil had she recognized him when his own clan didn't?

Part of him was still vexed with Aillenn. After all, she'd left without a word. And she still had possession of his satchel. His armor. His medallion. His heart.

But he couldn't stop the waves of ridiculous cheer coursing through his brain.

He thought he'd never see her again. Yet here she was, looking more beautiful in a cap and trews than any woman he'd ever seen in his life.

He approached the shooting line. His breathing was ragged as he pulled an arrow from his quiver. Nocking it into the bow, he belatedly realized he'd forgotten to don his bracer to protect his forearm.

He let out a snort of annoyance.

It didn't matter. He was going to shoot badly. He couldn't concentrate on anything now. Not with the woman who'd broken his heart looking on.

He loosed the arrow. The string scraped his forearm. The shaft wobbled and landed in the outermost ring of the target.

He growled and turned away.

"Falco de Malisio!" called the herald.

Adam watched Aillenn approach the line. He rubbed at his jaw in disbelief. How anyone was fooled, he couldn't fathom. Especially when she'd chosen a gaudy, eye-catching costume of bright blue and yellow.

But fooled they were.

From the corner of his eye, he saw his cousin Jenefer watching her. Surely Jenefer would recall young Jehan of Rouen, the archer she'd shot against before. Surely she'd recognize that Falco de Malisio was the same person, despite the darkened skin.

But she didn't. For one thing, Falco didn't shoot nearly as well as Jehan. Falco's first arrow hit just outside the target. It seemed Adam wasn't the only one suffering from agitation.

Eight others shot. Their skills were impressive. But Jenefer was the only one to hit dead center.

Adam planted himself on the line for his second attempt. He had to do better this time. He'd fastened on his bracer. He licked a finger, and tested the wind.

Then he made the mistake of glancing at Aillenn.

By the Saints, he wanted her, even in that garish outfit. He could imagine slitting the laces of her tunic and baring her lovely breasts. Sliding the trews down her silky thighs and burying his head between her...

He gave his head a shake to clear it and squinted down the course.

But when he raised his bow, all he could see was how much the target with its rosy bullseye looked like a breast.

His shot went wide. This time it landed in the straw outside the target.

Adam bit out a curse under his breath. A few disgruntled onlookers booed.

He was likely out of the competition now. That damned lass had utterly distracted him.

But two could play at that game.

She shot next. Standing close by, he crossed his arms over his chest and stared at her.

Unless part of Falco's character was that he was a terrible archer, Aillenn seemed just as rattled by Adam's presence. Before she could even aim, her fingers slipped on the bowstring, and the arrow fluttered to the ground at her feet.

She was allowed to try again. But she might as well as have skipped her turn. The arrow landed in the outer ring. The crowd muttered in disappointment.

He supposed the other archers shot well. He paid little heed to them. All he could think about was Aillenn. Here at Darragh. His sister's keep. Standing less than five yards away.

Now that they'd been reunited, would she try to explain herself?

Was she only a clever outlaw? Or had she had a good reason for abandoning him?

Did she feel guilty for leaving without a word?

Or would she avoid him and steal away as she had before?

He had to make sure that didn't happen. She owed him his medallion. And an explanation.

Eve's hopes of winning an archery prize at the tournament were dashed.

But that was the least of her worries.

What was Adam doing here? Had he managed to follow her after all? Had he been waiting all this time to confront her in the most public place possible?

Her heart told her nay. When they first locked eyes, he had looked just as astounded as she felt.

But what were the odds, in all of Scotland, that they should turn up at the same place at the same time?

The way her heart had flipped over when she recognized him—despite his cropped hair and his full beard—had shaken her to her core.

She thought she'd exorcised him from her brain. Tucked him into a dim corner of her mind as a distant memory. Relegated him to the past as one would a fond old friend.

But seeing him in the flesh, with his dark and piercing eyes, his flaring nostrils, his firm yet supple mouth, had left her breathless.

Like a beast waiting in the shadows to leap, her feelings for him came roaring back to life.

Her heart thrummed. Her blood warmed. Her nerves sizzled.

Every solemn vow she'd made at the convent—to forget him, to forget his kiss, to forget his love—burned into vapor as readily as silk over a flame.

She had imagined she could close her eyes and ears to love. Ignore affection as one did hunger or thirst until it was tamed. Or pray to forget the earthly feeling and replace it with holy devotion.

It was clear now that none of that was possible. Once tasted, the fruit of temptation could not be put back on the Tree of Knowledge.

But what was she to do with that knowledge?

She didn't even know his disposition.

Was he angry with her? Disappointed? Hurt?

There was no way to tell. At the moment, they were John and Falco. They couldn't exactly converse in any meaningful way.

Should she try to meet with him later in secret?

Or would it be best to pretend they'd never seen each other?

It was his turn again at the archery. This was his last shot. And hers.

She looked at him with all the yearning deep in her soul as he eyed up the target. Then he trained his eyes on her, and she caught her breath at the intensity of his gaze.

This time when he shot, he didn't even glance at the target. He was still staring at her when his arrow went wide of the straw bale and landed in the sod beyond.

There were grumbles from the crowd.

He'd intentionally thrown away his shot. He didn't want to compete in another round. That meant he either intended to speak with her as soon as possible, or he wanted to flee before she had the chance to catch him.

But two could use that tactic.

She was no longer interested in shooting against Jenefer anyway. That chance was long gone. It didn't matter how well or badly she did.

She turned sideways to the target. As she drew her bow, not bothering to aim, she briefly met his gaze and let the arrow fly.

It stuck in the ground, shy of the bale.

The crowd growled. Now they were both out of the competition.

They still dared not interact for fear of revealing their identities. But leaving the archery range, Adam passed her, murmuring, "Let us meet down by the sea."

She gulped. The sea? Did he mean to drown her? Surely he couldn't be that vexed. By switching satchels with him, he might have been inconvenienced. But she'd left him a fortune in coin.

Besides, she'd always meant to return his things to him. *He* might be a thief. But Eve didn't want that sin upon her soul. And it was clear God had given her this opportunity to make things right.

If Adam meant to find privacy, the seashore *was* a good choice. Everyone else would be within the walls of Darragh, preoccupied with the tournament.

Getting there meant a rugged walk that gradually scaled down the steep cliff behind the keep. The breeze sweeping up the rise lifted her tunic and almost whipped off her feathered cap. She clapped a hand on her head and struggled to manage his satchel as she descended the sandy slope studded with tufts of beach grass.

It was a beautiful morn. The sun twinkled off the firth. Gulls screed and swooped through the currents of wind. The water sighed and foamed along the shore, rolling pebbles and tumbling shells.

This was the site of the great battle where the Rivenlochs had regained Castle Darragh for Laird Dougal and Lady Feiyan. It was hard to believe, looking at the smooth gray expanse, that the landscape had once been littered with the dead and dying, the sand stained with blood.

The beach looked deserted. Adam must have been delayed.

That was fine. She had to settle her thoughts, slow her pulse, calm her nerves.

What would she say to him? Confess her true identity?

Tell him that swapping satchels had been an accident? Apologize for leaving him so abruptly?

Or should she go on the offensive and question him? Ask him how her satchel had ended up in the hands of Lady Feiyan? Charge him to explain why he possessed a Rivenloch medallion? Demand to know what he was doing at the Darragh tournament?

The aggressive approach was frankly more appealing. Eve had done nothing wrong, after all. She didn't need to share her secrets. It was Adam who had much to answer for.

Empowered by renewed confidence, she strode across the shore, close to the cliff's base, heading toward the towering rock that supported the castle.

There was a secret entrance carved into the foot of the cliff. The Rivenlochs had used it to infiltrate the castle on the day of that infamous battle, climbing up the stone steps that led to the keep. It had once been used as a gaol of sorts, the entrance covered by a locked iron gate set into the rock. Eve had never seen the place. But it was the stuff of legends now.

She skirted the wall, alternately looking for the bars of the gate, casting her gaze out over the sparkling firth, and glancing back the way she'd come to see if she was being followed.

"Aillenn," came a sound so faint, she almost thought it was only the hissing of the sea.

When she turned, Adam was just ahead. His dusky clothing had made him almost invisible until he pushed off of the dun-colored cliff wall.

At the tournament, she'd only stolen glances at him. Now her eyes could feast. On his broad shoulders. His dark hair. His piercing eyes. She'd forgotten how alluring he was. She suddenly felt like a starving beggar seated at the king's table.

"Adam." Her voice came out on a sigh.

She didn't mean it to. She meant to harden her heart against him. She dared not let him melt her resolve. No matter how her will wavered, she must follow God's path, return to the convent, be a nun. And Adam must return to his life of crime. She couldn't fool herself into thinking it could be otherwise.

But now that they were face to face, now that she saw him—not as a faded memory, but a living, breathing, tempting human being—all her best intentions threatened to vanish as quickly as sea foam on the shore.

"Ye look..." she said. Handsome? Magnificent? Breathtaking? "Different."

He quirked up a corner of his mouth. "Not different enough, apparently."

A smile tugged at her lips. They'd always been able to see through each others' disguises.

"Ye look..." he quipped with a frown, running his gaze down the length of her, "the same."

She gave him a chiding scoff. She absolutely did not look the same. Not in this ludicrous attire with the silly feathered cap and walnut-darkened skin.

Then he grew serious and nodded at the satchel. "I believe that's mine?"

"Oh. Aye." She held it up like a shield between them. "Foolish me. I must have picked up the wrong one when—"

"And 'tis all there?"

She blinked. "Aye. O' course." Did he honestly think she would steal his things?

Apparently he did. He took the satchel from her, set it on the sand, and then hunkered down to rummage through the contents.

"'Tis all there," she said. "I swear."

He grunted.

She supposed she couldn't blame him for having

doubts. For a while, he'd believed she was an outlaw like him.

"'Twas a mistake," she reiterated. "'Twas dark when... when I..."

"When ye what?" His darting glance pierced her like an arrow. "When ye abandoned me?"

She swallowed hard. He made it sound so harsh. So cruel. So personal. "'Tisn't what ye think."

"And what do I think?"

"That I ran away."

"Ye *did* run away."

"Not from ye," she told him.

He barked out a grim laugh. "Aye, ye did. Ye even left me a note. Ye told me not to follow."

"But not because..." she said. "Not because..."

She couldn't find the right words for her reasons or the memories that swept through her head. Memories of his soul-searing kiss. His eyes glazed with passion. His limbs entwined with hers. His groans of ecstasy shivering in her ear as his flesh rubbed in delicious bliss against hers.

"Not because o' ye," she said. It was only half a lie.

"Shite," he said under his breath. He stopped rummaging through the satchel. His shoulders dropped as he stared at the ground, shaking his head. "See, that's just it. I keep askin' myself, 'Why? Why did ye leave?'" His voice was roughened by the weeks of torment she'd caused him. "Was it because ye wanted the spoils all to yourself?"

"Nay," she said, horrified at the thought.

"Nay," he agreed. "After all, ye left your coin behind. So then I thought maybe ye were after this." He held up the Rivenloch medallion.

"Nay."

"Nay," he echoed, "because I see ye've returned it." He tossed it back in the satchel.

"As should ye," she murmured as an aside. "'Tis a dangerous piece to be carryin' around. Ye don't want to tangle with that clan."

He gave her a brief, bleak smile as he slowly rose to his feet. Then his eyes grew shadowed and full of hurt. "So all I can think is ye left because ye don't care for me. Ye regret what we did. And ye ne'er want to see me again."

"Nay." The word came out like a sob. "I mean... Aye. I mean..." Never want to see him again? That wasn't true at all. She wanted to see him every day for the rest of her life. And the last thing she wanted to do was to wound him. "Ye don't understand. Ye *can't* understand."

"I understand," he said sadly. "I thought we were kindred spirits. I thought ye cared for me."

"I *do* care for ye."

"I thought I was more to ye than a tryst on a goose-down pallet."

"Ye *are*. Ye *are*, Adam. And that's just the problem. Can't ye see?" The damning words were out of her before she could stop them. "I love ye. I *love* ye."

Adam couldn't have been more stunned if he'd been knocked in the head by a club.

Apparently, she'd caught herself by surprise as well. She clapped her hands over her mouth as if her words had accidentally escaped.

Now what?

Adam had met her here with one purpose in mind. To secure the return of his medallion.

If, in the course of retrieving it, he happened to confront her with the cruelty of her abandoning him, that closure would be honey on his oatcake.

But then he'd made the mistake of admitting she'd wounded him. He'd bared his damaged soul to her. Given her every opportunity to gloat over the wreckage she'd left of his heart.

Never in his wildest dreams had he imagined she'd reply with a confession of love.

He frowned, deciding, "That makes no sense."

"That I love ye? Perhaps not. But I *do.*"

"Nay. It makes no sense that if ye love me, ye would leave me."

"I... I..." Her face crumpled into an expression that appeared to be either longing or dismay.

He could only stand there and wait for her to decide which it was.

She lowered her gaze then to stare at her twisting fingers. "I'm not who ye think I am."

He couldn't help but snort at that. "I'm not certain either of us know who we are anymore."

"I'm serious," she said. "I lied to ye. I'm not Lady Aillenn. I'm not e'en from Ireland."

He considered that and then nodded. She'd been convincing. But he'd always had his doubts.

"Ye're not surprised?" she asked.

He shrugged. "Should I be? I'm not the Pope's emissary from Rome either."

"But ye're not disappointed?"

"That ye're not an Irish noblewoman?" He shook his head. "Nay."

"But I deceived ye," she said.

"We both did a bit o' deceivin'." Hell, he was *still* deceiving her. "But 'tisn't the Irish noblewoman I fell in love with."

His words made her blink. "Ye're...in love with *me?*"

He was a halfwit to admit it. To hand her his broken heart, giving her the opportunity to break it again.

Still, as she stood before him with hope in her wide eyes, he knew he was helpless to resist her.

"Fool that I am," he murmured, "aye, I'm in love with ye."

Her brow creased. "But ye can't be. If ye knew..."

"Knew what? Who ye are?" He shook his head. "The heart feels what it feels, whether ye're a queen or a milkmaid..."

"But I'm not—"

"An archer from Rouen or Malisio..."

"But—"

"Or the most notorious outlaw in all o' Scotland."

He lowered his gaze to her half-open mouth. He could resist her no more. Those were the lips he'd been dreaming of for weeks.

And when he closed the distance, she didn't resist. Instead, she lifted her face and closed her eyes in anticipation.

CHAPTER 17

The kiss was even more stirring than Adam expected. Their mouths met at first with tender restraint, then with ardent enthusiasm, and finally with starved passion.

He lifted his hands to caress her jaw.

She pressed her fingertips into the fabric of his gambeson.

She moaned against his mouth, and the sound sang through his veins. Igniting desire. Filling him with desperate longing.

He wanted her. Now.

And he could tell she wanted him as well.

The hidden entrance to the castle was a few yards away. The gate would be locked, but there was enough of a recess in the rock to afford the privacy of shadows.

He broke away from the kiss and swept her off her feet.

She gasped and cleaved to him. Her eyes were smoky. Her lips were wet with yearning.

He ducked into the hidden break in the rock, carrying her into the dim passage. Then he set her gently down.

He meant to woo her sweetly. Slowly. Patiently. He'd frightened her off before. He wouldn't make that mistake again.

But patient she was not.

She flung away her cap and kicked off her boots. She shoved down her trews under her leine, dropping them to pool at her feet. Then she tried to tear off his gambeson with her bare hands.

Her eagerness drove his own. He wrenched down his trews, tossing them aside with his boots.

Unable to delay longer, he turned and hefted her up against the iron bars of the gate. Cushioning her back with one arm, he used the other to lift her hips.

She clung to him, wrapping her legs around his buttocks. Scarcely did he find the hot, wet center of her desire than she thrust forward, sheathing him in a heavenly warmth that took his breath away.

He wanted it to last for hours. Not only because the divine friction of her flesh upon his was thrilling. Not only because trysting with a woman who loved you was more intoxicating than mere physical sensation. But because he wished to leave no question this time that they belonged together. He wanted to leave his scent so indelibly upon her she'd never want to leave him again.

But after only a few dozen thrusts, she began to gasp out his name, tensing in growing agitation. It was all he could do to hold them both upright as his cock drove inside her and his ballocks tightened with need.

Then she cried out and arched against him, bucking like a wild colt, and he could no longer contain his fervor.

He tried to withdraw from her. It was the honorable thing to do. The safe thing. But she clung to him too tightly. With a final desperate hope that she knew what she was doing—that she wanted this—he let out a helpless bellow and pumped his seed into her.

Their gasps mingled with the soughing of the sea as they slowly descended from the lofty heights of ecstasy. He gradually withdrew from her and set her gently on her feet on the sandy rock.

He meant to apologize for his haste. But she reached up to grasp his face in her hands, entreating him with a look to tell her the truth.

"This *is* meant to be, isn't it?" she asked. "We *are* meant to be together?"

Relief coursed through his veins. A tiny part of him had been uncertain. Even now. Even while they were sharing their bodies. Their hearts. Their souls. He'd fallen hard for her. And he feared that she might not feel the same way. That she might abandon him again.

"Aye," he said, meaning it. "I'm sure of it."

Eve knew it had to be true. Otherwise, why would it feel so right?

It wasn't as if she was turning her back on God, was it? After all, a person could serve God in other ways. One didn't have to be a nun.

Perhaps she would reform Adam. Turn him from an outlaw into an upright member of her clan. That would be a godly purpose.

Or together they could go out into the world to right injustices, like holy mercenaries of His will.

Or maybe they would make lots of children who would grow to serve the church.

She grinned at the thought. It seemed an absurdly simple task, for she thought she could easily couple with Adam every day for the rest of her life.

They sank onto the soft ground. She snuggled against Adam's chest and twined her bare legs around his. For a long while they nestled together in silence against the rock, peering out at the firth washing against the shore.

Eventually they'd need to leave. But for now, she thought she could happily exist in the arms of this wayward rogue until the sun crossed the sky and the stars lit up the eve.

She smiled, murmuring, "Eve."

"What?"

"My real name."

"Your real name is Eve?"

"Aye."

There was silence. And then she was rocked by the movement of his low laughter.

She turned on him, annoyed. "What?"

"Then we're definitely meant to be together."

"Oh." She'd forgotten about that. "Adam and Eve. Aye, I suppose we are."

She wouldn't tell him the other part. That she was not just Eve. She was *Sister* Eve. Now that she'd decided to change her fate, perhaps that revelation was unnecessary. Perhaps she could quietly leave the convent and never again mention her former calling. Keep her past a secret and avoid a lot of awkward exchanges.

Her father, of course, would be disappointed when he learned she was no longer a nun. He liked having a representative of his clan in a holy order. Though he oft complained that Eve didn't have a suitable temperament for the convent, he figured marriage to the church was more attainable for her than finding a bridegroom who would put up with her wild and impulsive nature.

But she'd show him. She'd found Adam. He was everything she could hope for in a husband. Honorable. Kind. Strong. Brave. Generous. And, except for the minor detail of his profession, everything her father would find acceptable in a son.

In time, she knew, the two of them would have to meet.

The fact that they'd expressed their devotion and consummated their love meant they were as good as wed. But even as the youngest daughter, Eve felt compelled to seek her father's permission for marriage.

Eventually she'd have to reveal her true identity to Adam. She'd tell him she was the daughter of a wealthy merchant. That would probably come as a troubling shock. He'd likely prefer she were his equal. A commoner. And an outlaw like him.

"Shall we dress," Adam said, nudging her from her thoughts, "before rumors arise about the pair of terrible archers trystin' outside the gaol?"

She snickered.

As they slipped back into their clothes, she wondered again how her satchel had come into the possession of Lady Feiyan.

"What did ye do with *my* satchel?" She already knew the answer, but she wondered what he'd tell her.

He shook his head. "Gone. To be fair, I didn't think I'd see ye again." There was a touch of melancholy in his voice. A melancholy she well understood.

"What about my coin?"

"Spent."

"Spent?" That startled her. That much coin was meant to last at least half a year. "All of it?"

"Ye left me with next to naught to wear," he said defensively. "I couldn't exactly fit into any o' your gowns. I had to purchase new armor."

"And a new beard, I see," she said, eyeing the thick growth on his chin. "Or did ye make that out o' the hair ye chopped off your head?"

He scoffed. "I grew this beard myself, ye wicked vixen."

She giggled. He was an easy target for her teasing. "And what about my gowns?" she asked casually. "What did ye do with them?" She lowered her eyes, hoping he wouldn't lie to her.

"Gave them away to those less fortunate."

His answer was cursory, but accurate enough. Lady Feiyan *had* donated the garments to the convent.

After they dressed, he scrutinized her costume, straightening her cap. Then he shouldered the satchel.

"I'll go first," he said. "Ye follow at a distance."

"Wait." She'd only just reunited with him. She couldn't bear the thought of parting so soon. "When will we..." She caught her lip under her teeth and dipped her eyes in suggestion. "Meet...again?"

He returned her smoky look.

She could read his thoughts in his smoldering gaze. He wanted to hold her again. Caress her again. Ride the waves of surrender with her again. She blushed.

But after a moment his brow creased. "We can't be caught together at the tournament. 'Tis too risky."

She sighed and nodded. He was probably right. "After the tournament then?"

He furrowed his brows even more deeply. "I hate to do this to ye," he said with a grimace. "But there's somethin' I have to attend to first. It may take a fortnight or so."

"A fortnight?" A frisson of alarm shivered up her spine. *Something to attend to?* That sounded awfully vague. And dismissive.

Did he mean to leave her? Was this revenge? Now that he had his precious satchel, would he give her a taste of her own betrayal and abandon her?

With her heart in her throat, she reiterated, "Somethin' to attend to?"

"Aye."

"And what's that?" If he was telling the truth, he could be more specific.

"I can't tell ye."

"Can't tell me or won't?"

"Won't," he admitted.

Eve's heart dropped. She'd always heard there should be no secrets between husband and wife. The abbess said keeping hold of secrets was harder than keeping hold of leeches, and once your grip on them was lost, they could suck the life out of you.

"Why not?" she asked. "Do ye not trust me?"

"I do, but..." He winced. "This is a matter o' grave secrecy and great importance."

"If 'tis so important, maybe I can be o' help."

"Nay. Not this time."

She blinked in surprise. They'd seemed like such companionable cohorts before. Perfect partners in crime. And now that they'd agreed they belonged together, she expected to share their adventures. The fact he was choosing to exclude her was hurtful.

"Fine," She raised her chin in defiance. "'Tis just as well. Ye're not the only one with somethin' important to attend to."

Actually, that was true. She still had that mission to accomplish for Hew and Carenza. Getting the king's seal on their marriage document. Traveling to Perth and back would take at least a fortnight, probably more.

"Indeed?" he said with a disbelieving snort. "And what would that be?"

She arched a brow. "I'm not at liberty to say."

He smirked. "Fair enough." But after a moment, he cocked a concerned eye at her. "I hope 'tisn't too dangerous."

"Oh, 'tis *very* dangerous," she taunted.

"Now ye're tryin' to worry me."

"Are ye worried?"

"O' course I'm worried."

She smiled in satisfaction.

Until he added, "Without Lady Aillenn on my arm, innkeepers won't be givin' me goose-down pallets anymore."

She gave him a chiding cuff on the shoulder.

He laughed.

It was a beautiful sound. A sound she wanted to hear

every day for the rest of her life. Every day, she supposed, after he returned…if he returned.

She sighed. "A fortnight or so? That seems an eternity. Where will we meet again?"

"We seem to have a way o' findin' each other."

That was true. But she didn't like leaving things to chance.

"What about Mauchline?" she suggested. Hew and Carenza had been wed in Mauchline. "'Tis a quiet village not far from here."

He nodded. "Good. I know the place."

His approval of Mauchline was a good sign. Perhaps he wasn't leaving the area…or her.

Then he gave her a lusty look that erased all her doubt.

"*Twill* be an eternity, my love," he said, cupping her chin and rubbing his thumb across her cheek. "I'll be countin' the hours."

He leaned forward, giving her a kiss that was somehow both sweet and fiery. A long, lingering kiss of honey and flame.

She was still dizzy with desire when he reluctantly ended the kiss and pressed her away.

"I have to go," he murmured.

She watched him go. As he walked across the shore, she admired his long stride and the way the wind tugged at his trews, displaying the flex of his muscles with every step.

She fought back the tempting tingle of arousal. The urge to follow him at a run. To collide with him, throw him down on the damp shore, tear off his clothes, and have her way with him again.

She bit her lip. It seemed being a respectable wife might require even more restraint than being a nun. She'd have to work on her impulsive nature. At least in public places.

Adam could feel her gaze all the way across the shore. He hoped the brisk climb up the slope to the castle would temper his lust. At the moment, his cock felt like a pavilion pole straining at his trews, and he couldn't get the ridiculous grin off his face.

He had what he wanted now. His Rivenloch medallion. And an acceptable, if incomplete, explanation for Aillenn's departure. Eve, he corrected. Eve to his Adam. The most magnificent Eve to grace an Adam's arm.

Once he sorted out this royal matter with Fergus, he'd be free to tell Eve the truth. Who he was. What he was.

She'd no doubt be thrilled. She'd evidently heard of his clan. She'd called the Rivenlochs *dangerous*. What had she told him? *Ye don't want to tangle with that clan.*

Certainly not as an enemy. But as a Rivenloch bride, she'd be welcomed with open arms.

Of course, he'd still secure permission from Laird Deirdre for the official match. But as far as a common lass like Eve knew, their agreement and consummation meant they were already wed. And that was fine with him.

Adam's identity might change from day to day. His face and clothing and stature were as variable as the moon.

But she would learn his heart was steadfast. And now that he'd found a woman who saw him for who he truly was, he would be forever loyal.

As far as whatever mission she claimed to be on, he doubted it was dangerous at all, if indeed such a mission even existed. She'd probably invented it out of spite, to repay him for his callousness. The fact that she wished to meet at nearby Mauchline indicated she didn't intend to stray far.

He was glad of that.

Though she was capable of defending herself, he feared for her safety.

Though she was quick and bright and clever, he worried about her impetuousness.

Though she was inventive and creative, he fretted over her vulnerability.

And though he was loath to admit it, no matter how capable, quick, or inventive she was, he knew he'd agonize over her every moment they were apart.

By the time he crested the cliff, Eve was but a wee blue and yellow speck walking beside the lapping firth. But he dared not linger. There was much to do. A laird's rebellion to put down. A king to aid. And the sooner Adam began his work, the sooner he could return to the woman he meant to make his bride.

No longer interested in the tournament, Eve decided to leave Darragh at once. The quicker she could secure the king's seal and tie up the Rivenloch affair, the quicker she could resume more pleasant pastimes with Adam. So she packed up her bow and arrows and set out for the convent.

Most of the tournament participants had already arrived at Darrah and wouldn't be leaving for another two days. So she had the path through the woods to herself.

She wasn't sure if it was the favorable weather or the heavenly afterglow of lovemaking, but she felt curiously alive as she ambled along the road.

Bees hummed through the summer-heavy air. Butterflies sipped from nodding blossoms. The sun dribbled down through patches of new green leaves like butter melting onto the path.

Despite the distracting delights of the forest, she knew danger might lurk around every corner. A wee part of her was always wary. And that part of her started feeling... watched.

Watched and followed.

Whoever was trailing her was careful. They didn't draw too near. They didn't make much noise.

If she were asked how she knew someone was there, she wasn't even sure she could say. She just *felt* them.

As long as they didn't approach, there was no need for concern. She'd be back at the convent before long.

Still, it diminished a bit of her pleasure as she strode along the path. She could no longer casually muse about her future with Adam. She couldn't enjoy the songs of birds calling through the branches. Or the lazy afternoon treks of squirrels in the oak canopy. And she was compelled to find a very thick stand of concealing brush when she could no longer go without relieving herself.

She was almost all the way to the convent when she stopped by a stream to take a drink. She used the opportunity to steal a surreptitious glance in their direction from beneath her feathered cap. The last thing she needed was to bring trouble home to her sisters.

She caught only a quick glimpse before they hastily retreated the way they had come. But it was enough.

There were two of them. And they wore the colors of the king.

CHAPTER 18

Sometimes Adam had to marvel at just how invisible he was.

Fergus's men didn't seem to notice he'd been gone for the better part of two days, competing in the tournament at Darragh.

At least once a sennight, he wandered afield to report to the king, yet no one missed him.

And now the two commanders muttering together in Fergus's armory paid no heed to the fact that Adam sat nearby, absently polishing his sword while hanging on their every word.

They debated in hushed tones of fear and anger and frustration.

"We're outnumbered, I tell ye. The king will slaughter the whole clan."

"For a wee bit o' raidin'? Ballocks."

"'Tis more than raidin', and ye know it. Fergus has... ambitions."

"He only wants to take back what's rightfully ours."

"Reivin' cattle is one thing. But why is he besiegin' holdin's that ne'er belonged to us? And why is he collectin' oaths o' fealty from other clans?"

"To keep the peace."

"He doesn't want peace. He wants power."

"Is that so bad? It seems the king would rather dally in France than rule at home."

"He's not in France now. He came home to Scotland, and now he's at our threshold. He's already laid two villages to waste."

Adam blinked. Was that true? Spying on Fergus's movements for the king, he hadn't paid much heed to the king's movements.

"All the more reason to defend ourselves and fight back."

"Against the entire royal army?"

There was a long silence before the second man admitted in a very quiet voice, "Some are sayin' Fergus has been drinkin' mead and sharin' a table with the English."

"Which proves my point. Fergus doesn't mean to stop with clan land. He's formin' an alliance with our enemy. He's got his eye set on rulin' the whole west o' Scotland."

"Aye? So? What's wrong with that? With the English fightin' beside us..."

"Ye trust the English? Once they've got their claws into Fergus land, ye think they'll hand it o'er to the laird with a wink and a smile?"

The other man sighed.

"And then where will we be?" He didn't wait for an answer. "Trapped between the Scottish king and the bloody English with nowhere to go."

"Hell."

"Right. We're already losin' too many. And Malcolm's troops aren't only attackin' the men-at-arms. He's goin' after the villages. Our women. And children."

"So what do we do?"

"God knows."

They suddenly noticed Adam and started.

"Shite! How long have ye been there?"

Adam shrugged.

They frowned at him, but must have decided he looked too simple to understand what they were discussing.

"Come on," one of them said to the other, nodding toward the door. "The walls have ears."

They left while Adam appeared to continue obliviously polishing his sword.

Mad thoughts, however, churned through his brain.

Could what they said be true?

The king had been less than forthcoming about his advances.

Was it as the men claimed? Had Malcolm attacked Fergus women and children? Burned crops? Decimated villages?

The thought left a sour taste in his mouth. While the Rivenlochs had always been loyal to the king, they had never condoned unchivalrous warfare. And Adam knew they wouldn't condone it now.

He was torn.

He couldn't live with himself if those villages had been destroyed because of information he'd shared with Malcolm.

And yet he couldn't commit treason against the Crown by withholding information from the king that might get his troops killed.

He needed to talk to Malcolm, face to face. Get him to disclose his next plan of attack. And report back to Fergus with an early alert.

With forewarning, at least someone would be there for defense. There might be a brief skirmish, but fewer casualties, and there would time to evacuate innocents.

Adam hoped the two sides could ultimately settle things without a battle. The Rivenloch clan was always happy to defend Scotland against foreign invaders. But they hated to get involved in clan wars.

Unfortunately, it sounded as if Fergus's commanders

had had no success in curbing their laird's appetite for land.

Perhaps Adam could convince the king it was a mistake to make an enemy of England, particularly in light of his recent friendship with King Henry. And then he might be able to persuade Fergus to relinquish the idea of expanding his holdings and instead be grateful for the full return of his ancestral clan lands.

The negotiation would be a complex undertaking. But Adam was sure he was the best Rivenloch for the task.

In the shelter of the trees just outside the convent, Eve quickly changed out of her archery garb and into her habit.

She figured her encounter with the royal guard who'd followed her to the alehouse might have been by chance. But now she'd seen two more. That could only mean the king himself was near.

Was he looking for her? Surely not. He had far more important things to do. And yet...

As she strode through the gates of the convent, Sister Eithne rushed across the cloister.

"Och, Sister Eve!" she said by way of greeting. "Have ye heard?"

"Heard what?"

"The news," she said, eagerly wiggling her thick brows.

Eve didn't have the patience for this. Not today. The only thing Sister Eithne liked to cook up more than her famous pottage was scandal. "News or rumor?"

"News." She drew close to confide, "The abbess got it from Sister Mary, who got it from Friar John, who got it from the nuns at the convent near Glasgow, who heard it from an abbot—"

"Fine," Eve said, biting back impatience. "The news?"

The cloister was empty except for the two of them.

Nonetheless, Sister Eithne paused to survey the space, making sure no one was listening.

"'Tis the king," she whispered.

Now she had Eve's attention. "The king?"

Sister Eithne nodded. "He's comin'."

Eve's heart pounded. Maybe he *was* looking for her. She glanced around the cloister. "Comin' where? To the convent?"

"Nay, nay." She waved away Eve's confusion with a laugh. "Wouldn't that be somethin', the king comin' here? Nay, he's goin' to Galloway."

"Galloway." If that was true, then the presence of the royal guards must have nothing to do with her. Perhaps they were scouting the area to ensure the king's safe arrival in Galloway. "Why?"

"They say he's goin' to attack Laird Fergus."

"Fergus? Why?"

"No one knows."

That was troubling. Galloway wasn't far from the convent. If war broke out...

Sister Eithne's eyes twinkled as she elbowed Eve. "Maybe we'll get to see the king."

Eve had already met the king. She hadn't been that impressed. But she pretended to share the sister's excitement. "Wouldn't that be somethin'?"

Sister Eithne giggled and then hurried the rest of the way across the cloisters toward the kitchens. It was almost time for supper. She no doubt had preparations to make.

So did Eve.

As long as the king wasn't looking for her, this seemed like a blessing. Now she wouldn't have to travel to Perth to get the king's seal. Malcolm had come to her.

She'd simply dress like a noblewoman, find the royal encampment, and request an audience with the king.

Since she'd left her red velvet gown at the byre, she'd need to procure a new disguise. Thankfully, she had enough coin left from her father to commission a fine gown in azure brocade from the village tailor, as well as purchasing a white silk wimple and veil, a simple girdle of silver chain, and a pair of tall wooden pattens to attach to her boots.

The gown wouldn't be finished for several days. Meanwhile, she ventured forth doing charitable works as Sister Eve. All the while, she collected bits of information from alewives, crofters, beggars, and bakers, trying to determine the whereabouts of the king, but learning little.

She also performed one not so charitable act. She needed to make certain she looked very different from any other versions of Eve the king had seen. So when she happened to spy a fine white horse stabled at a roadside inn, she took the liberty of harvesting its tail hair to make a pair of braids.

After a fortnight, her gown was ready. But she still hadn't located the king. Then, as fate would have it, on the way back from the village to the convent, she came up behind a pair of slow-traveling monks chattering on about the grand encampment they'd just passed in the forest.

It had to be the king's.

When the monks noticed her, they stopped talking, which only enforced her belief it was indeed Malcolm's retinue they'd seen in the woods.

There was no time to waste. She knew roughly where the king was now. But he could move his troops at any time.

Just after Prime the next morn, Sister Eve stole out the convent gates into the woods and transformed into Lady Hilda of Dunlop, the invented cousin of Lady Carenza. She slipped into the azure brocade gown, girdling it with the silver chain. She secured the horse tail braids to either side of her head, tucking them under the wimple and veil.

Because Lady Hilda despised mud, she buckled the protective wooden pattens onto the bottom of her boots, conveniently adding four inches to her height. Then she powdered her face with a light layer of chalk and painted her lips with red-stained beeswax.

Lady Hilda, Eve decided, was the farthest thing from a nun. She was a proud and sultry woman with distinct power over men. Her noble bearing and strength, as well as her height and snowy tresses came from Viking blood on her mother's side. Most important, she had a smoky gaze and a throaty voice that could charm and cajole and convince even a king to do her bidding.

She checked to be sure she had the marriage document in her satchel. Then she took a few cautious, teetering steps to get used to the pattens, which were a full two inches taller than any she'd worn before. Making her way slowly along the path, lest she twist an ankle, she retraced her steps back to the spot where she'd heard the monks talking about the encampment.

The monks must have taken a smaller side path that diverted from the road into the woods. She watched for that branching trail.

The first side trail dead ended at a large boulder fifty yards in. The second trail dwindled to nothing after a few turns. But the third trail appeared to be well traveled, and after about a half-mile, Eve could glimpse red-and-gold-striped pavilions through the trees.

The camp was already awake. The air was filled with the clinking of pots, the stomp of boots, the low mumbles of men, and the acrid scent of smoke.

She'd come early to catch the king when he was least occupied and most vulnerable. If she approached him before he was fully awake, she'd be more likely to get his cooperation.

"Who are ye?" came a sudden gruff voice behind her.

Alarmed, Eve whipped around.

But Lady Hilda wouldn't be alarmed. So Eve drew herself up to her full height—plus four inches—and looked the guardsman in the eye with a sultry smile.

"Lady Hilda of Dunlop, here to see the king." Then she drew her gaze slowly down the front of the man's tabard, as if sizing him up for a tryst. "Who are *ye?*"

Her frank appraisal rattled the guard. "I...I'm M-...M-... Martin. Martin o'—"

"Mmm, Martin," she purred. "What a magnificent name."

"M'lady?"

She wrinkled her nose at him. "Maybe later we'll meet again?"

He gulped.

She released a sigh of regret. "But at the moment, I'm here for the king."

If the guard mistook her to be a consort, that was his own fault. It would help her get an audience with the king all that much faster.

He led her through the camp, where she understandably received a lot of astonished glances. Women who weren't cooks or laundresses were rare in a soldier's encampment.

Once they arrived at the royal pavilion, the guardsman spoke to a fellow guard, who entered the king's quarters. After a moment, she was allowed in.

She tried not to appear shocked when she saw the king half-reclining on his pallet in only his sheer leine with the coverlet pulled up to his waist.

He gave her an appreciative smile.

"To what do we owe this lovely surprise?" he asked. "We didn't order a consort."

She gave him a silky reply. "Why, Your Grace, I'm flattered, but I fear ye misunderstand my presence here. I'm Lady Hilda o' Dunlop."

Malcolm was understandably flustered. He stammered and then glared at his guards.

She swept in to soothe him. "But I'm so very grateful for your attention, and I apologize for the earliness o' the hour. This should take but a few moments."

The king seemed mollified by her words, though he modestly pulled the coverlet up to his neck.

"I'm the niece o' the Laird o' Dunlop and cousin to Lady Carenza," she told him with a nod of deference.

"Lady Carenza," the king echoed.

Naturally he'd heard of Carenza, even if he hadn't been back in Scotland long. Her beauty and sweetness were legendary.

"I've been sent to request royal approval o' Lady Carenza's betrothal."

She reached into her satchel and pulled out the rolled parchment. She hoped he wouldn't notice that, according to the document, the marriage had already been accomplished.

As she expected, the king was uncomfortable enough with his misjudgment of the situation to wish to be done with her as soon as possible.

"Scribe!" he called.

"I think ye'll be well pleased with the match, Your Grace."

Her words made him reconsider. After all, Lady Carenza was a valuable asset when it came to clan alliances. "Who is the bridegroom?"

"Sir Hew du Lac o' Rivenloch."

"Rivenloch?" He stroked his chin, seeming to consider the match. But he couldn't hide the satisfaction in his eyes. To be able to reward his most loyal clan with such a prize was propitious indeed. "Aye, that would please us."

Thankfully, the king paid more heed to the flourish of his signature and the proximity of the hot sealing wax to his leine-clad chest than to the words on the document.

As promised, their exchange took but a few moments. He seemed relieved to be rid of her and done with the whole embarrassing ordeal.

With the first and most difficult part of her mission accomplished, Eve could rest easier. She thanked the king, curtseyed, and exited the pavilion.

Just outside, she took a moment to collect her nerves. She carefully rolled the dried, sealed parchment and tucked it into her satchel. Then she crouched to tighten the buckles on her pattens.

She rather liked the height these pattens gave her, she decided. They made her feel imposing. And powerful. Perhaps she would wear them more often.

She suddenly heard the king call out a greeting from inside his pavilion.

She blinked. She would have sworn he'd said "Adam."

Then she chided herself. He could have as easily said Edmund or Baldwin...or Madam. Even if he had said Adam, there were probably a dozen Adams in the king's service.

Still, it troubled her. Eyeing the guards behind her and the soldiers milling about, she slipped back around the shadowy side of the pavilion and leaned close to listen through the canvas wall.

The king was speaking.

"We hear congratulations are in order for your clan."

The response was muffled. She placed her ear against the fabric, not an easy feat with a thick horsetail braid.

The king continued, "Your cousin Hew's betrothal?"

"Ah. Aye, Your Grace."

Eve froze. It was hard to be certain. The accent was more noble, less rustic. But his voice...

He asked, "Did my aunt Deirdre send word?"

It *was* him. It *was* Adam.

But "cousin Hew"? "My aunt"? Was he feigning to be a Rivenloch? Was that why he needed that medallion?

"Nay, not Deirdre," the king said. "Lady Carenza's cousin was just here. Did ye not cross paths?"

Eve's heart stopped. Shite. What if Lady Carenza didn't *have* a cousin? What if Adam knew that?

"Her cousin was just here?" Adam replied. "I didn't see him."

"Her," the king corrected.

"Her?" Adam echoed. "Hmm. Is that so? I don't believe we've met."

Eve's heart began pounding like a fuller's mill. She could hear it in his voice. He knew. She couldn't imagine how, but he knew.

The king continued, "So what news do you bring from the enemy camp?"

Enemy camp? Was Adam a spy?

"It's worse now, Your Grace. He's besieging keeps of other clans, demanding fealty from the survivors."

"Fealty?"

"Aye. There are some who believe he wishes to form an alliance with the English against Your Grace."

"What the devil? This is serious indeed."

Eve scowled. Who were they talking about?

"We shall muster the troops this eve," the king decided. "We'll attack at dawn."

"At dawn?"

"Aye. Knock down the rebellion ere breakfast."

Eve chewed at her lip. She had to make herself scarce. Not only because she'd overheard something she shouldn't have. But because she suddenly realized the truth.

Adam wasn't feigning to be a Rivenloch. He *was* a Rivenloch.

And even if the king wasn't perceptive enough to realize he'd once played the Pope's emissary, he apparently knew Adam of Rivenloch well enough to trust him as a royal spy.

Her brain suddenly spun in a maelstrom of shock and

fear, surprise and dismay, disillusionment and horror.

How could she not have known?

The fact that he could carry off an air of nobility so well should have been an obvious sign.

Just like the rest of his clan, he was strong, handsome, and bright. Now that she thought of it, he even bore a resemblance to the other Rivenloch men she'd seen. He had the same broad shoulders. The same square jaw. The same fierce eyes.

No wonder he'd been so eager for the return of his medallion. The piece was legitimately his.

But she'd been blinded by her affections. And he'd taken advantage of that blindness. He'd made her fall in love with him.

Her eyes welled. Her throat closed. How could she have left herself so vulnerable?

Then she gave her head a firm shake. She couldn't dwell on her failure.

She had to figure out what to do now.

As much as it crushed her, as much as it made her heart crack in two, she had to face the truth.

Adam had never been serious about marrying her. The idea was absurd. He thought she was an outlaw. A Rivenloch bachelor was a valuable pawn. The king would never allow him to wed a female thief.

But of course Adam had known that all along.

So Eve must have been part of his cover as a spy. A foil to afford him anonymity. A traveling companion to help him embed himself into whatever clan he had under surveillance.

He'd deceived her—kissing her, holding her, swiving her—all the while letting her believe he was a common outlaw like her.

Tears of heartbreak threatened at the corners of her eyes.

It was as if she'd slept with with a stranger.

She'd been so full of affection and desire and hope. He'd awakened things inside of her she'd never known were there.

Now she mourned the life she might have led. The husband she might have adored. The mother she might have become.

Her chest felt as if an anvil had been set on top of it. Her heart ached with loss and longing.

Yet more than just her heart was at stake.

There was no time for grief. She had to protect her mission.

Adam knew about the marriage document now. He would be furious if he found out it was Eve who had manipulated the king into signing it. He might try to seize it. To destroy it.

She couldn't let that happen. She'd sworn to Hew and Carenza that she would see their union sealed. She owed them a debt of honor.

She had to flee.

As she turned and wove her determined way through the campfires, she spied persistent M-M-Martin hovering at the edge of the camp. He took a tentative, hopeful step toward her as she neared. But she gave him a quick shake of her head, instantly quelling his advances. Then she hurtled past the last pavilion and through the forest, eager to get back to the safety of the convent.

A few hundred yards down the path, she realized while her pattens gave her desirable stature, the wobbly things were slowing her. She stopped for a moment, crouching down to unbuckle them and shove them into her satchel.

Then she rose again and lunged forward, abruptly colliding with a thick wool gambeson.

CHAPTER 19

From the first moment the king mentioned a visit from Lady Carenza of Dunlop's cousin, Adam's suspicions were aroused. Why would the king hear about the marriage between Carenza and Hew from a mere cousin of the bride and not from the Laird of Rivenloch? It didn't make sense.

Apparently, this cousin, a woman, had the marriage document in her possession. She even convinced the king to put his seal on it.

Just who was this mystery cousin?

Adam was fairly certain Carenza had no cousins.

But inventing a cousin sounded like the sort of audacious scheme someone like Adam—or Eve—might attempt.

Was it possible? Could Eve have contrived such a thing? For what purpose?

His suspicions were quickly confirmed. As soon as he exited the king's pavilion, he spied a well-dressed noblewoman teetering out of the camp on ridiculously tall pattens. Shoes no sensible lady would wear.

And while he didn't recognize the shoes or the limping gait, he'd know that luscious body anywhere.

He followed her. Once they reached the forest, catching up with her wasn't difficult. She could hardly hobble at a decent pace, balancing on the infernal wooden blocks.

When she stopped to remove them, he slipped silently past her through the trees. Then all he had to do was wait for her to resume her flight.

Still, he was surprised when she literally crashed into his arms.

Even more surprised when she scrabbled at him in panic.

"'Tis me. Adam," he told her, placing hands of reassurance on her shoulders. "What's wrong?"

The fear in her eyes dimmed, but she flashed him a too bright smile. "Adam." Her voice sounded shrill and strained. "What are ye doin' here?"

"I could ask ye the same thing."

She wasn't fooling him. Guilt was written all over her face.

"I mean, 'tis a lovely surprise," she gushed, avoiding the question. She pressed her cheek against his chest and gave him a squeeze, but it felt forced. "It seems ye were right. We do have a way o' findin' each other."

He pulled her back to take a look at her painted face. "I don't believe I've met *this* lady before."

Faint alarm shot through her eyes like subtle lightning, so brief another man might not notice. But he could see it.

"Caterine," she said with a French accent, clearly improvising on the spot. "I am Caterine of Paris."

That wasn't what she'd told the king.

"I see." He lifted one of her coarse pale braids with a finger. "Horse hair?"

She nodded.

He brushed a finger across her cheek. "Chalk? And beeswax for your lips?"

"A lady likes to look her best." Her tone was smug, but there was a tremor in her voice.

"The pattens are a nice touch."

"They were...unwise," she admitted. "But what about ye?"

she said, going on the offensive. "Who is this man with the rusted mail and the patched gambeson? Is he part o' your 'somethin' important to attend to'?"

Adam hadn't expected her to turn the tables on him. He was so concerned with finding out Eve's business with the king, he'd forgotten about his own secret mission. He couldn't have her prying into his affairs. He couldn't tell her who he was portraying either.

But just like her, he could invent characters from whole cloth.

He affected a gruff new accent. "Sir Walther, German mercenary."

"And are ye here to fight for the king?"

"The king?" he said, feigning surprise. "Which king?"

Eve froze for an instant, obviously realizing her misstep. How would she know the king was here?

Recovering quickly, she shrugged. "Doesn't every mercenary fight for the king?"

He chuckled in response. Eve *was* a fast thinker.

Still, she was getting too close to the truth for comfort. The fact she'd managed to talk her way into the king's pavilion was bad enough. That she was feigning to be a person working on behalf of the Rivenlochs, a person who could easily be proven not to exist, was worse. But if she found out Adam was a spy, she would likely want to help him, and that would be perilous.

"Listen, Eve," he said. "We need to leave. As soon as possible."

"Leave? Why?"

"The woods are thick with...mercenaries. This is a dangerous place to be."

"Is that what I heard in the forest as I passed?" Eve said, feigning ignorance about the king's pavilion. "I thought 'twas a company o' pilgrims. Are ye travelin' with them?"

He avoided answering her directly. "Do I look like a pilgrim?" Before she could reply, he decided, "We'll go to Castle Darragh."

"The site o' the tournament?"

He nodded. "I know the place well. 'Twill be safe there."

No doubt he knew the place, Eve thought. His Rivenloch clanswoman lived there.

Now she knew how her satchel had ended up in Lady Feiyan's hands.

Though she'd agreed to go with him, journeying to Darragh seemed dangerous. She couldn't take on a third identity. It was too risky. What if Feiyan recognized her, either as the colorful young archer who'd thrown the match at her tournament or the nun who'd offered to distribute her donation of clothing to the poor?

Did Adam intend to reveal his secret to Eve when they arrived, that he was a Rivenloch? When he introduced her to Lady Feiyan, would it be as an outlaw he'd met while traveling or his beloved betrothed?

Sadly, Eve knew the answer to that. And neither option was good.

"We should travel as clergy," she decided. "'Tis safest that way."

She could simply be Sister Eve. Feiyan knew her as a nun already, and Adam would assume Eve was playing a part.

He nodded in agreement. "Good."

He began pulling monk's robes out of his satchel. She dug in hers for her habit and a rag to wipe the powder from her face.

Then she stopped. If he was in such a hurry to spirit her away... "Wait. If there are mercenaries about, doesn't that mean war is imminent? Where do ye suppose the fightin' will be?"

He tensed his jaw, but made no comment. Of course that was what it meant. But if Adam was spying for Malcolm, he'd tell no one the king's battle plans.

He frowned sternly. "We'll be safe at Darragh."

She knitted her brows in concern. "'Tis only that there's a convent not far from Galloway, near Mauchline. I have...acquaintances there. I need to know they'll be safe."

"They'd ne'er attack a convent," he said. "'Tisn't honorable."

She hoped he was right. She'd heard the king. He intended to attack Galloway ere breakfast. That seemed rather dishonorable for a king so devoted to chivalry.

Eve prayed she hadn't given away too much, mentioning the convent. She planned to never have to reveal that part of her life to Adam. It would be much easier for both of them if he never knew he'd swived a nun.

To be fair, she supposed she shouldn't be angry with Adam for hiding the fact he was a Rivenloch. His minor transgression paled in light of Eve's glaring and ongoing deceit.

Their church garments afforded them some protection as Adam led her along the path. But loose soldiers roaming the forest could be as unpredictable as a pack of wolves. So they made their way toward Darragh in silence.

A few hours into their journey, Adam stopped in front of her.

She collided with him. Then she went quiet.

There was a sound coming from the trees up ahead. Sobbing.

Ignoring Adam's cautious "shh," she passed him on the trail to follow the sound.

He bit out one annoyed, "Eve!" and then followed her.

A young woman lurched toward them on the trail. She wore only a torn leine, which hung off one shoulder. One of her boots was missing. Her hair hung down over her face.

There was blood smeared on her hands and across her front. Her eyes were glazed, as if she'd seen unspeakable horrors. And the sound of her sobbing struck at the core of Eve's heart.

Eve rushed toward her.

The woman glanced up. Her eyes widened at the sight of a priest and a nun.

"Help!" she cried. "Thank God, ye've come to help!" She fell on her knees and clasped her hands before her. "I prayed for the Lord's help, and He sent ye."

Sister Eve's compulsion to be of assistance drove her to enfold the woman's bloody hands in her own.

"What's happened?"

"'Tis my husband," she gulped out. "He's sore wounded."

Eve frowned. Her husband? It was the woman who looked like she'd tangled with wolves. "But what about ye?"

"I'm...fine," she lied, her voice shaky. "But my husband was injured tryin' to protect me."

"Protect ye from whom?" Adam's voice dripped with a vengeful hunger Eve had never heard in him before.

The woman shook her head. "Two men. I don't know..."

"What's your name?" Eve asked.

"Fonia."

"Fonia, take us to your husband."

Fonia nodded, wincing in pain as she got to her feet. Then she motioned them to follow her.

Adam caught Eve's arm and spoke under his breath. "Are ye certain this is wise?"

Eve whispered back, "We have to help her."

He grimaced.

"I know ye're in a hurry," she murmured, "but if we can be of assistance—"

"'Tisn't that. 'Tis only...we're not physicians."

It was clear he was remembering the infant they'd lost.

And to be honest, she too was haunted by the prospect of failure.

But she had to ignore that self-doubt. She couldn't let it hamper her ability to help.

"Maybe not," she agreed. "But I have to do what I can. I won't be frozen by fear."

"Nor will I. But...ye said there was a convent nearby. With *real* nuns. Nuns with a knowledge o' healin'. And, if they can't save him, they can at least save his soul. We can take him there."

Eve's breath caught. She couldn't go there with him. Not to her own convent.

Then Adam would know the truth. That she was a nun. That he'd trysted with a nun.

Thankfully, she was saved from coming up with an excuse not to go when Fonia suddenly let out a horrified shriek.

"The alehouse! Simon!"

Not far down the path, Eve spotted smoke billowing from the roof of a roadside alehouse.

It was on fire. And by Fonia's cry, her husband was inside.

Just as Eve caught the woman to keep her from running into the burning building, Adam bolted past them both.

Without hesitation, he wrenched open the door, pulling it off its hinges. Smoke boiled out, and he raised an arm to shield his face. Then he disappeared inside.

Eve stilled in shock. Her heart leaped into her throat.

Why had he done that?

It was impulsive. Reckless. Dangerous.

What if he couldn't find Simon?

What if he didn't come out?

Eve held her breath, fearing the worst, while Fonia whimpered beside her. Time churned like an oxcart through mud as she watched the doorway with tearing eyes. The acrid odor of burning thatch stung her nose as flames licked up through the smoky roof. Still he didn't emerge.

When she finally glimpsed Adam's broad back, he was dragging a man out through the door and away from the conflagration. Her breath escaped in a relieved whoosh.

Fonia raced toward them, skidding to her knees beside the limp body. "Simon!"

Adam covered a racking cough with his sleeve. His face was sweaty and soot-stained.

Eve spared one glance at Simon. Then her gaze returned to Adam.

The hem of his robe was on fire.

"Adam!" she cried. "Your cassock!"

She charged forward. Together they beat the flames into smoldering submission.

By now, the entire roof was ablaze, roaring with fury. It was too late to save the structure.

Was it too late to save Simon?

Eve crouched beside him and felt his neck for a pulse. He was alive, but unconscious.

His chest was covered in blood from a nasty dagger that protruded from his side.

Eve felt a sudden twinge of uncertainty. She could cure headaches. She could bandage cuts and scrapes. She knew what herbs to use for stomach ailments and bruises and the pain of monthly courses.

But she'd never had to deal with mortal battlefield wounds like this.

Perhaps Adam was right.

Perhaps she'd taken on something that was beyond her skills.

But there was no time to take him to the convent. He'd already lost a lot of blood. And at the very least, if she had to give him last rites, she was qualified to do it.

It would mean revealing the truth to Adam, that she had the authority to deliver last rites. But when it meant saving a man's soul, it was worth the price.

Fortunately, Adam had seen wounds like this before. When you lived in a clan full of warriors, someone was always getting wounded.

He hunkered down beside Simon to examine the injury.

"'Tisn't too deep," he said, blinking the ash from his eyes. "It looks like it missed his heart. If we can stop the bleeding..."

"I have linen for bandages," Eve said, opening her satchel.

A dagger puncture would require more than just a bandage. The cut would need to be stitched closed first.

"Do ye have a needle and thread?" he asked.

"Aye."

"And Fonia, do ye have..."

The poor woman was clutching her husband's hand, trying to massage it back to life.

"Och, Simon," she wailed. "Don't leave me."

Fonia was too upset to be of much help. But Eve was steady as a rock.

"Ye'll need verjuice and honey as well," she said, finding them in her satchel.

"Good. I'm goin' to pull out the dagger," he told her. "But we'll need somethin' to stop the bleedin'."

"Use this," she said, pulling out the blue brocade gown she'd worn as Lady Hilda. "'Tis thick and sturdy."

"Are ye certain?" That gown must have cost a fortune.

"Aye. Savin' a life is its best use."

Pride swelled his chest. Eve might be small and plain and invisible to most. But to Adam, she was a heroine. Strong. Beautiful. Brave. Magnificent.

While Eve bunched the fabric into a compress, she told

Fonia, "Ye need to pray for him now. Harder than ye've e'er prayed. Ask God to save him."

Fonia obliged, letting go of Simon, closing her eyes, and clasping her hands in fervent prayer.

Whether Eve believed prayer would work or if it was only a way to keep Fonia calm and distracted, Adam wasn't sure. But it was a wise suggestion.

"When I pull the dagger free," he told her, "ye'll need to press very firmly against the wound. Can ye do that?"

She nodded, though he saw she'd gone a bit pale. He could cross surgeon off the list of her possible true identities. Whoever Eve was—outlaw, nun, noblewoman, or tournament champion—she probably wasn't used to seeing so much blood.

"Ready?" he asked, wrapping his fingers around the haft of the dagger.

She nodded.

The blade slipped free more easily than he expected. That was a good sign. Simon made a soft groan, still only half-conscious. But blood oozed out, and Eve's blue brocade bloomed dark scarlet as she closed her eyes tight against the grisly sight.

He set aside the bloody dagger and, taking mercy on her, gently replaced her hands with his own.

"I've got this," he said. "Can ye thread the needle and soak it with verjuice?"

She nodded, no doubt glad to be relieved of the gruesome duty.

While he kept pressure on the wound, he eyed the discarded dagger.

It was a standard weapon. It could have belonged to anyone. But when his glance caught on the metal seal embedded in the haft, his blood ran cold.

It was the Scottish royal insignia. Simon had been stabbed by one of the king's men.

An unthinkable possibility reared its ugly head.

"Fonia," he whispered out of Eve's hearing. "Whose clan do ye belong to?"

"Fergus," she murmured back. "Why?"

The terrible truth hit him like a quintain in the gut. But he forced a smile of reassurance to his lips. "Ye have clanfolk to care for ye then?"

"Aye."

Adam ground his teeth. Bloody hell. The king needed a firmer rein on his men-at-arms.

It wasn't difficult to figure out what had happened. Rogue royal soldiers had stopped at the alehouse, drank too much, and decided to avail themselves of the charms of the Fergus clan alewife. Her husband had intervened to protect her and been stabbed for his efforts. And to destroy the evidence, the men had set fire to the alehouse.

He felt sick. War was supposed to be noble. Armed warriors fighting armed warriors. Not innocent innkeepers and wives murdered in their dwellings. Not defenseless crofters and children slain in cold blood. Not unarmed clanfolk suffering burned fields, butchered cattle, and decimated villages.

Both sides, it seemed, were guilty of dishonorable battle tactics.

He'd witnessed the lawless raids from the Fergus clan.

Now he saw evidence of rampant violence on behalf of the king.

Adam was trapped in the midst of the corruption. By oath, he must be loyal to King Malcolm. But in his soul, he knew what the king allowed was wrong.

The only way out of the turmoil was to subdue both sides. To somehow convince them that war wasn't the answer. But he wondered if that was a hopeless endeavor, considering how much men loved to wield weapons.

He'd subdued an uprising before, at Perth, between the

king and his rebelling lairds. For that, he'd used the power of the church. He doubted it would work in this situation. But perhaps, being a spy on both sides of the war, he could whisper in the ears of the two leaders and persuade them to come to a peaceful compromise.

Eve, averting her eyes, presented him with the threaded needle.

He carefully removed the blood-soaked gown. The cut was still there, but the bleeding had subsided for the moment. Still, he had to work fast.

"I'm goin' to need both o' ye to help hold him down."

Though he worked quickly, stitching up the wound was an unpleasant task. Simon jerked awake and moaned with each jab of the needle. And Fonia sobbed with each of his moans of pain.

Finally it was done.

"A dollop o' honey, a clean bandage," he announced, "and Simon should be good as new."

Eve wasn't so sure about that.

Simon had roused with a yelp when Adam made the first stitch to close his wound. He was obviously glad to see his wife unharmed and the knife out of his side. But the pain of the needle was fierce. And sometimes infection set in after such a wound. On top of his physical suffering, the sight of his smoldering alehouse was doubtless dispiriting.

With Fonia's encouragement, he survived the rest of the stitches.

As for Eve, she hadn't been able to watch. She couldn't imagine how Adam could endure it. On the other hand, she supposed a Rivenloch warrior had to be accustomed to inflicting and repairing wounds.

She handed him the pot of honey and linen for bandages.

While he worked, her gaze lit upon the dagger lying nearby. She narrowed her eyes at the button set into the haft. When she recognized the king's insignia, she stifled a gasp.

Had Simon been stabbed by a royal soldier? Were Fonia's attackers in the king's army? Was this the kind of war against the Fergus clan Malcolm's men-at-arms were waging?

It seemed too horrible to consider. And yet the evidence was undeniable.

She had to tell Adam.

He might be the king's man. But surely he'd never approve of such senseless violence against innocent clanfolk.

She had to make things right. More than ever, she sensed that God had called her here. Led her to this place to redress those wrongs. She would find the men who had assaulted Fonia, stabbed Simon, and set fire to their alehouse. And she would see they paid for their sins.

While Fonia and Adam were distracted, Eve wiped the bloody dagger on the grass and slipped it into her satchel.

Eventually, a group of neighboring clanfolk came to seek the source of the smoke. By then the fire was mostly out, leaving the alehouse smoldering. Exclaiming in dismay and empathy, they comforted Fonia and Simon. They thanked the kindly monk and nun profusely. And they offered the homeless couple lodging and food until they could recover.

Eve and Adam bid them farewell, knowing they were safe in the bosom of their clan.

But as soon as they returned to the path, Eve confronted Adam.

"We can't go to Darragh yet," she said.

"Why? They'll be fine," he assured her. "Their clanfolk will care for them."

She pulled the dagger from her satchel. "This is why." She showed him the royal insignia. "King Malcolm's men did this. We need to make this right."

He stared down at the dagger for a long while. Then he sighed.

She was prepared for him to be resistant. After all, though she wasn't supposed to know who he was, she knew he'd sworn allegiance to Malcolm. She expected he'd try to make some improbable excuse for the soldiers' actions.

He'd say the dagger wasn't proof. It could have been stolen by someone else.

Or the stabbing had been an unfortunate accident, despite all appearances otherwise.

Or perhaps Simon had attacked Fonia, and the soldiers had only been defending her.

The last thing she expected was for him to agree with her.

CHAPTER 20

Adam had hoped the dagger was missing. If Fergus found hard evidence the king was perpetrating violence upon his clan, it would only add fuel to the fire and make peace more difficult to achieve.

But he couldn't explain that to Eve. She knew nothing about his identity, his fealty, his purpose.

She only knew that, like her, he believed in justice, fairness, and honor.

So what else could he do but agree?

"Aye, ye're right. This shouldn't go unpunished. But I fear findin' them will be like findin' a drop of ink in a loch."

Of course, she knew exactly where they were. She'd spoken with the king herself. But she couldn't reveal that or she'd have to explain what she'd been doing and why she had in her possession a document of marriage for Hew of Rivenloch.

"They must have come with the king," she pretended to reason. "'Tisn't an easy feat to hide a royal retinue."

"And yet," he argued, "have ye seen a royal retinue in your travels?"

"In the last fortnight, I've crossed paths with more than one royal guard in the woods. One followed me into an alehouse before I lost him. And another pair pursued me through the forest ere I gave them the slip."

That troubled him on two counts. One, he didn't want to think about other men trying to get their hands on Eve. And two, for someone intent on a stealthy attack, the king was giving his soldiers too long a leash. He needed to warn Malcolm he was playing a dangerous game.

"So where do ye think—"

"Adam!" She interrupted him with a gasp of feigned surprise. "Maybe those weren't pilgrims I heard in the woods."

"They weren't?" He had to admit, she was a convincing liar. He almost believed her naivete, even though he knew better.

"What if *they* were the royal retinue?" she asked, her eyes wide.

Damn the lass. She was foiling him at every turn.

He nodded sagely. "Ye may be right."

He did plan to return to the encampment. But he didn't want Eve with him. He wanted her safely behind Darragh's strong castle walls.

Still, he knew once she got an idea in her head, she would not be talked out of it. That was how they'd ended up in bed together. While he admired her fortitude and perseverance, in this instance, it was inconvenient.

If he refused to go with her, she'd only find a way to go around him, even if it meant escaping from Darragh and making her way back to the king alone.

He couldn't let her do that. The king's men had already pursued her twice. What was to stop them from catching and assaulting her the way they had Fonia?

The thought left a bitter taste in his mouth.

Eve was strong and capable. Clever and independent. Wise and quick-witted.

But she was not a Rivenloch.

She might speak and dress and act like a warrior. But she grew faint at the sight of blood.

She had no idea how hazardous it was to tangle with royals. To get embroiled in a clan war. To be a woman alone among soldiers full of fever and bloodlust.

The idea shook him to the core.

Nay, the only way to keep her out of peril was to stay by her side, to accompany her on whatever thorny mission she was on.

Then, when the time came to shield her from real danger, he'd have to waylay her. It would require deceit. Betrayal of her trust.

In the end, it would be worth it to keep her safe. But would their love be strong enough to endure such betrayal?

He wondered.

Her eyes lit up. "We'll go back then? And search for the king?"

"On one condition," he told her. "If by some miracle, we find him, and we're granted an audience..."

"Aye?"

"We'll ask him to marry us."

This time Eve's gasp of shock sounded genuine. She blinked, baffled. "Ye mean it?"

He nodded.

"But...ye don't e'en know who I am."

He gave her a tender smile. "I know who ye are," he said, reaching out to place his fingertips over her heart, "in here."

Eve's throat thickened as she returned a trembling smile.

Did he mean that? Did he truly not care who she was? Or was Adam such a loyal vassal to the king that Malcolm would allow him to wed whomever he willed?

She supposed it wasn't out of the question. After all, the king had approved the marriage between Sir Gellir and a maidservant. But as far as Adam knew, Eve was an outlaw. Certainly a line had to be drawn somewhere.

And if he was so sure of their love, why wouldn't he tell her who he was?

Of course, she realized. She already knew the answer to that.

Adam was spying for the king.

He couldn't tell her who he was, because knowing might endanger both their lives.

She followed him down the path with newfound understanding and respect. He was a man of his word, and he'd sworn not to disclose his mission. It followed then that he would keep his word when it came to his promise to her.

Eve daydreamed as they walked through the woods. She imagined the beautiful wedding they'd have. At her father's humble keep with all her friends and clan? Or at the magnificent castle of Rivenloch with glorious warrior maids and knights in polished armor?

She didn't care, as long as Adam was by her side.

She would wear her beautiful scarlet gown.

Nay, she remembered, she'd left it at the byre with Carenza. There might not be an opportunity to fetch it.

Lady Hilda's azure brocade gown would have been stunning. But it was soaked with blood.

Maybe her father would be so glad to see her wed to a Rivenloch, he'd commission new wedding attire for her. Of course, it would have to be tasteful and meaningful.

Perhaps one in emerald silk embroidered with the flowers and birds and woodland creatures the two of them had encountered in their travels.

Or a modest fawn-colored linen to reflect Eve's years of pious good works.

Brilliant lapis lazuli skirts sewn with gemstones to impress her new clan.

Or something in soft peach-colored velvet to tempt her bridegroom.

She imagined the happy years ahead of them.

Side by side, they would pursue their Greater Purpose. Doing good deeds. Helping those in need. Saving troubled souls. Teaching honor and respect, chivalry and charity to others.

She was imagining the exciting adventures they would embark upon when the road passed by a narrow deer trail.

"There's a burn not far from here along this trail," Adam said. "We can eat and drink. And I'd like to wash off the ashes."

The burbling burn cut deep into the sod, rolling playfully along in the sunlight. Bright birches stood tall along the shore, and willows hung over the water.

Eve found her plaid and spread it on the soft bank. She prepared food from their satchels—hard cheese, oatcakes, butter, dried apples, and a jack of ale.

She was about to tell Adam it was ready when she heard a plash of water.

He'd stripped off his cassock and was wading into the middle of the burn.

Her breath caught.

The shimmering reflection of the sunlit waves danced upon his naked skin, illuminating every curve and muscle. His back looked like the strong trunk of an oak, and below, his buttocks tensed as he made his slow descent into the water—to his calves, his knees, his thighs.

The sight of him was doing curious things to her body. Her heart thrummed against her ribs. Her face suffused with heat. Her breath grew rapid and shallow. Her nether regions began to rouse like a flower after a spring rain.

As he sank lower in the water, his broad shoulders rose, and he shuddered once at the cold.

Then he plunged under all at once.

She gasped at his boldness. That water had to be icy. Now she was sure the Rivenlochs were descended from Vikings.

He shot back up again almost at once and made quick work of scrubbing the ash from his wet hair, his face, his beard. Then he sluiced the water up over his shoulders and chest.

Eve couldn't keep her eyes off of him. He'd been well named, for he looked as perfect as God's Adam to her.

Then she remembered she'd held that perfect body against hers. Kissed his delicious mouth. Caressed his supple muscles.

And now he'd vowed to tryst only with her for the rest of his life.

She was the luckiest lass in the world.

The thought of the heaven she'd found in his arms propelled her desire even higher.

Her tongue slipped out to lick her lip in speculation.

She wondered...

She spared a cursory glance around the trees to make sure they were alone. Then, while he rubbed his hands briskly over his ash-coated skin, she quickly removed her coif and veil and slipped out of her habit.

For Sister Eve, it was a brazen thing to do. But for Eve the adventurer, it was just another impulsive undertaking that thrilled her senses and excited her spirit.

She considered joining him in the burn. But she didn't have his Viking blood.

Instead, she settled herself like a sunning selkie in the middle of the plaid and waited for him to notice.

He emerged, dripping and clean, shaking the water off and slicking back his hair with both hands. Then his gaze lit upon her, and he froze mid-step.

She watched as his chest rose and fell and smoky lust

filled his eyes. Never had she felt so exposed and yet so desired.

His eyes grazed her slowly, lingering on each part of her, setting her afire inch by inch.

He approached cautiously, as if he feared he might frighten her off.

When he stepped from the water, she peered up at him with a sultry question. "Are ye hungry?"

One side of his mouth curved up into a devilish smile. "Oh aye, lass."

He needed no more invitation. Shoving the food aside, he joined her on the plaid.

With an impish grin, he pulled her to him.

She shrieked in protest at his cold, wet skin as he held her close.

"Shh," he warned. "Someone may hear us."

"Ye're wicked," she whispered with a shiver.

"Ye invited me, selkie."

"That I did."

Already she was beginning to warm in his embrace. And when he cradled her chin and kissed her, she forgot about everything but the lovely feast he offered.

"Mmm," he murmured against her mouth, "this is delicious fare." He nibbled at her lips, pretending to taste her. "Cherries." He sampled the top of her cheek. "Peaches." He moved his hand down the side of her neck, rounded her shoulder, and lowered his palm to capture her breast. "Mmm, manchet." He bent down to nip gently at her flesh, as if taking a bite of bread.

Her head was spinning. But her appetite was whetted. And she wanted to take him on this sensual journey as well.

She eased her hand down his backside and clasped his firm buttock. "I see ye've brought bacon."

He chuckled low against her ear. "I've a sausage as well."

She could feel it. Pulsing. Warming. Hardening against her.

He turned his hand and glided his palm over her belly into her nest of curls.

"But I think this to start," he murmured, sliding his fingers to separate her wet, womanly folds.

He lowered his head, moving between her thighs to tease her flesh with his tongue. She arched in ecstasy to meet him, reveling in the contrast of cool water and warm sun and the divine sensations he painted upon her. Again and again, he bathed her, until she thought she could bear no more.

Then he withdrew.

For one distressing moment, she thought he was finished with her. But in the next moment, he eased into her with his firm staff, and she moaned as her desperate wish was fulfilled.

With measured grace, he made love to her on the warm woolen plaid under the dappled sunlight while the babbling burn played a peaceful song.

At first they moved in a soothing rhythm. Theirs was a dance of nature and quiet and calm.

But soon their tender striving intensified, growing more and more frenzied. Eve writhed against the heat. Her fingers clawed at the plaid. And Adam's eager groans drove the music to a faster pace. The forest around them disappeared, and Eve saw only Adam in this beautiful Garden of Eden.

With a sharp cry of discovery, she soared high above the trees. He followed in her wake, and they flew like a pair of swans across the sky.

Then they shuddered down together. But it was a long while, wrapped in each other's arms, before Eve began to notice again the murmuring burn and the filtered sunlight and the slight scratch of the wool beneath her.

"Strange," Adam mumbled. "I'm even hungrier than before."

She grinned. "That's a pity, because ye may have kicked the butter into the burn. But I'll see what I can salvage."

They dressed, and then she rounded up the scattered food. They only lost a few oatcakes to the mud, and she managed to blow off the bit of dirt that stuck to the hard cheese.

But when they packed up to leave, Eve felt refreshed and rejuvenated, renewed and reassured, secure in the knowledge that Adam had their future well in hand.

Adam wanted to kick himself. He never should have swived Eve.

Not the first time. And definitely not now.

The trust in her eyes tormented him. The joy in her face pained his heart.

He'd distracted her enough for the sleight of hand he required. But that distraction had taken on a life of its own.

He'd never dreamed she would want to lie with him. Not here, in the wilds of the woods. Not now, when she was so determined to meet with the king.

He could have, *should* have refused her.

Aye, she'd been nigh irresistible, reclining there like an alluring selkie. Her body glowed in the patch of sun. Her dark hair spilled down over her pale shoulders to caress her delicate breasts. Her sultry gaze melted him like butter.

But he had more willpower than that. He was a man of honor. Certainly he could have resisted her. He could have turned and dived back into the burn, letting the cold water shrink away all desire.

Instead, he'd succumbed to temptation, just like Adam in the Bible, accepting the forbidden fruit from Eve. It had been sweet and delicious and satisfying.

But now, having her look up at him with such adoration as they neared the encampment, knowing what he had to do, he felt like the worst traitor since Judas.

"Do ye think we're close?" he asked.

"Just up ahead," she told him. "Not far from where we met."

He let her lead the way, praying for courage.

At sight of the first red-and-gold pavilions, she turned to him with a knowing nod, telling him wordlessly that it was indeed the royal encampment.

They moved through the pavilions, garnering little attention, for they appeared to be harmless clergy. But Adam was still amazed that they'd been here only a few hours ago, and no one seemed to recognize either of them.

Adam they might overlook. Men didn't give him a second glance.

But Eve was breathtaking, whether she was clad in a lady's gown or a nun's habit. That no one saw that was unfathomable.

At the far end of the camp, the king emerged from his pavilion.

"Let me speak with him," Eve murmured.

Adam knew that was a bad idea. The men-at-arms might not realize that Sister Eve was the same woman who'd teetered by on pattens just this morn. But surely the king would.

Still, that might be for the best.

"All right," he said, drawing the cowl close around his face. "I'll be right behind ye."

She hurried forward, calling out softly, "Your Grace!"

The king looked up.

"May we have a word, Your Grace?"

"Sister?"

Apparently, the king was as blind as every other man. Without her makeup, her horsetail hair, her lavish gown, and her ridiculous footwear, Eve was apparently unrecognizable to him.

"I'm Sister Eve, Your Grace," she said, "and this is Brother…" Too late, she realized they hadn't given him a name.

"Adam, Your Grace," he supplied. There was no need to lie to the king. All would be revealed in a moment. "May we speak privately?"

The king looked slightly annoyed. No doubt he was tired of speaking and eager for war.

Out of Eve's sight, Adam pulled off his cowl to show the king his face.

Now Malcolm recognized him. His brows lifted, and he waved them forward into the pavilion.

Adam had promised to let Eve speak, so despite the king looking to him for a report, Adam allowed her to break the news. Let her tighten the noose around her own neck.

"Your Grace," she said, "'tis with great regret we must inform ye of a terrible sin committed by two o' your men today."

"A sin?" Malcolm sighed. "What sin?" He no doubt imagined the terrible sin was going to be skipping Mass or imbibing too much mead.

"They entered an alehouse in the woods, Your Grace, owned by the Fergus clan. Violated the alewife. Attacked the alewife's husband. And then burned down the alehouse."

The king made a grimace of distaste, but he didn't seem particularly shocked. "And you have proof our men did this?"

"Aye, Your Grace."

She took the satchel off of her shoulder, opened it, and began rummaging through the contents.

"I have the dagger used to stab the man," she said. "It bears the royal insignia."

"I see. And what do you have to say about this, Rivenloch?"

Adam stiffened. The king had called him by his clan name. Now Eve would know. Now she would realize who he was.

Eve's blood grew cold.

The king had called him Rivenloch. Not Brother Adam. Malcolm must have recognized him from their earlier conversation, despite the monk's costume.

She told herself none of that mattered. Adam might be upset that Eve knew who he was. But he could explain himself later. All that mattered at the moment was showing the king the incriminating dagger. Getting restitution for the alewife and her husband. Stopping the atrocities being carried out by his men.

Shite. Where was that damned dagger?

Adam cleared his voice and said cryptically, "I have my own suspicions, Your Grace."

"Aye?"

"The woman is lying."

Adam's accusation was so unexpected, it took Eve a moment to comprehend it.

In the brief silence, the king chuckled as if Adam had made a jest. "Lying? A nun?"

"She's not a nun, Your Grace, any more than I'm a monk," Adam said. "She's a spy like me."

Adam's confession was calculated. Icy. Heartless.

For a moment Eve couldn't move. Couldn't breathe. What was he saying? Why would he tell the king such a thing?

She tried to imagine a useful reason for Adam to pretend she was a spy.

She could think of none.

"Nay, Your Grace," she gasped out, digging feverishly for the dagger. "I have the proof here."

Unable to find it, she upended the satchel and shook it, spilling its contents onto the ground. Desperate, she scrabbled through the clothing and tools and foodstuffs.

The dagger was nowhere to be found.

"Look there, Your Grace," Adam said, pointing to something strewn among the litter.

He lifted up the fine silver piece to show the king. The Rivenloch medallion.

"She stole it from me," Adam said.

The blood left Eve's face.

He had done this. *Adam* had taken the dagger out of her satchel and planted his medallion there.

Why?

She looked at him, bewildered.

For the first time in her life, she was unable to think of a single thing to say. It felt as if he'd plunged her into a bog. And the drowning mire was closing over her head.

She entreated Adam with furrowed brows, seeking some explanation for his treachery.

But he wouldn't spare her a glance. He only stared at the king. His eyes were grim. His face was as hard as stone.

"She's a spy for Fergus," Adam said.

The king gasped, echoing Eve's shock.

He continued. "She probably planned to capture me and demand ransom from Your Grace."

Eve blinked in disbelief. Was this the man who had vowed to marry her? Who had promised to ask the king to perform their wedding?

The king growled.

Adam continued. "Does Your Grace remember the woman who came to you this morn with the Rivenloch marriage document?"

Eve could barely breathe as the king narrowed his eyes at her.

"It can't be," he said.

"'Tis." Adam nodded to the twin horsetail braids and the pair of high wood pattens on the ground. "There is her costume. And here," he said, sweeping up the rolled parchment, "is the document Your Grace signed."

"Nay," she managed to croak out, reaching toward him as if she could snatch it from his hand.

He handed it to the king.

Her throat ached with the pain of treachery. Tears burned behind her eyes. Why was he betraying her?

"Adam?" she begged.

He made no reply.

"Adam," she sobbed.

"Guards!" the king called out.

Two royal guards rushed through the pavilion flap, their hands at the ready, clapped on their sheathed swords.

"Take her," the king instructed.

Finally, Eve's instincts for survival overcame her wounded heart. Adam might have crushed her with his cruelty. But she would not go quietly.

She tore off her coif and veil. Sweeping up the hard cheese that had spilled from her satchel, she withdrew the wee eating dagger she'd stabbed into it earlier. Then, kicking aside the skirts of her habit, she faced the two guards with fight in her blood and fire in her eyes.

They drew their swords.

She gulped.

The blades were long. Sharp. Gleaming. Her puny knife was no match for them.

Still, she blew out a forceful breath, steadying herself.

"Wait!"

It was Adam.

The king raised his hand, halting his men.

"By rights as a Rivenloch, Your Grace," Adam said, "I claim this captive."

The gears clicked in Eve's head. Was he trying to rescue her after all? Did he mean to spirit her away from the king? But why hadn't he just let her explain to Malcolm about his men and their crime? Why had he changed the plan?

"I may have a use for her," he continued.

"Indeed?" the king said.

"She's a beautiful woman and a talented trickster," Adam said. "She's likely valuable to Fergus. She may be a useful pawn against him."

What the Devil was he trying to do?

"What do you suggest?" the king asked.

"Belay the attack on the morrow," Adam said. "I'll go to Fergus and tell him his spy was captured. I'll say Your Grace is willing to negotiate her safe return, but only if there are no clan raids in the next fortnight."

"A truce?" The king scoffed. "Our men are eager for battle. The rebellion cannot continue. Fergus is wreaking havoc. The war must be won as soon as possible."

"But would it not be more chivalrous, Your Grace, to make a bloodless end to the rebellion? Earn the loyalty and admiration of your subjects by not...killing them?"

Eve understood what he was trying to do. It was the same thing he'd done at Perth. Avoid battle and bloodshed through diplomacy.

It was a worthwhile endeavor. An honorable effort. Maybe peacemaking was Adam's Greater Purpose.

The king chortled. "A Rivenloch advocating for peace?"

Eve tensed. The king was right to doubt him. The Rivenlochs were a warring clan. Negotiation was the last thing a warrior of Rivenloch would suggest.

"We may be a clan of warriors, Your Grace," Adam replied, "but our motto is *Amor vincit omnia.*"

"Love conquers all," the king translated, amused.

Adam gave a further assurance. "If Fergus breaks the truce, Your Grace, summon my clan. They can be here by the new month, and together we can lay siege."

Eve wondered how he was going to pull that off. And how did she figure into his scheme? Was she just meant to be, as he'd said, a "useful pawn"? Did Adam intend to sacrifice her to protect the king?

If he deserted her, leaving her with Malcolm, she was doomed. A ransom from Fergus for her safe return would never come. Fergus didn't know her, much less value her. The king would eventually execute her as a spy.

Eve stared at Adam, unable to decipher his intentions. It seemed he was willing to dismiss her as a sacrificial lamb. He refused to look at her, and she could read nothing in his expressionless eyes.

"Very well," Malcolm said. "The Rivenlochs have served us faithfully for generations. We will entrust this matter to you. We will wait till after All Souls Day...as long as Fergus abides by the truce."

Adam bowed his head in thanks. "Your Grace will keep the lass safe and unharmed?"

Eve's heart lightened with hope. If he was concerned for her welfare, perhaps he did care for her.

Then he added, "Her value must be retained. Otherwise, leverage will be useless."

Her value? Leverage? Was that all she was?

Eve began trembling then. Whether it was from hurt or fear or fury, she wasn't sure.

Adam still wouldn't look at her. She knew why now. Guilt had made a coward of him. He meant to abandon her and couldn't look her in the eye to do it.

"We'll keep her safe," the king said, "if she'll put away her weapon."

Eve had forgotten she was gripping the eating knife in her fist. At the moment, she wanted to hurl it at Adam. But that would gain nothing.

Instead, she dropped it to the ground.

"Take her to the physician's pavilion," the king commanded.

"She's a wily wench," Adam warned. "Your Grace would be wise to put her in chains."

Eve's trembling was definitely rage now. *Chains?*

"Do so," the king ordered.

The guards sheathed their swords and grabbed her by the arms.

"Wait," Adam said. "I'll need proof for Fergus."

He picked up her dropped knife, seized a lock of her hair, and cut it off.

Then, before she could glare and spit out an epithet at the man who had condemned her to imprisonment for the next fortnight, they marched her roughly out of the pavilion.

Thank God she was too furious to feel the pain of her broken heart.

CHAPTER 21

Adam rubbed his fingers again over the silky lock of hair he'd tucked into the top of his hauberk, against his heart.

He was miserable.

He trudged toward the Fergus stronghold, wondering if he'd done the right thing.

He may have ruined his chances to live happily ever after with the woman of his dreams.

She might never forgive him for betraying her.

Yet what other choice did he have?

What Eve didn't understand, what her innocence wouldn't allow her to believe, was that reporting the bad behavior of the royal soldiers would have fallen on deaf ears. Men-at-arms always committed horrific acts—rape, murder, destruction—in the course of war. And kings always looked the other way. Even kings like Malcolm who prided themselves on chivalry.

That was the real reason Adam devoted his life to keeping his warrior clan out of as many wars as he could.

The warriors of Rivenloch had always behaved honorably. To do otherwise would have earned them expulsion from the clan. That legacy had been passed down through generations.

But kings came and went. They varied in their sense of

gallantry and were likely to waver once they sat on the throne and grew drunk with power. As for mercenaries and simple soldiers, they weren't expected to possess a moral compass. Most presumed that waging war included taking spoils.

In truth, it impressed Adam that an outlaw like Eve possessed such a strong sense of justice. She was intent on seeking fair recompense for the alewife. He admired her for that. If it were possible, he would have fought for atonement as well.

But in this instance, in wartime, it wasn't possible. Such actions would be perceived as giving aid to the enemy. Eve would be branded a traitor.

Still, he knew the lass couldn't be convinced to let go of that expectation of justice. So he'd initially decided, if he wanted her to be safe from the fighting, he'd have to drag her, by force if necessary, to Darragh.

Of course, that was an ugly proposition and not a good way to start a marriage. If he brought his bride-to-be kicking and screaming to his sister's castle, he'd never hear the end of it from his clan. And that was only if she didn't manage to trick her way *out* of the keep. He could easily imagine her manipulating Feiyan's men with her winsome ways and catapulting herself back into the midst of danger.

Which would drag *him* back to a place of turmoil as well. Worried about Eve's safety. Concerned she would try to confront the king. Afraid that, left to fend for herself, the same fate that had befallen the alewife might await his precious bride.

The idea sickened him.

Nay, the only way to deal with the stubborn lass was to go along with her. To lull her into complacency and then close the shackles of safety around her wrists when she least expected it. Which was exactly what he'd done.

She'd been hurt. Of *course* she'd been hurt.

He couldn't bear to look in her eyes and see the pain he'd inflicted upon her. But it was clear in the tremor of her voice.

Once she understood he'd tricked her and meant to imprison her, she'd gotten past the heartache, and her hurt had turned to anger. But he wondered if she would ever be able to forgive him.

His intentions, of course, were absolutely honorable. He meant to keep her out of harm's way. And he could think of no safer place for her than as a royal hostage.

If Malcolm believed Eve was somehow valuable to Fergus, that he could use her as leverage, the king would ensure she was well protected by his best men. That protection would be backed by the full force of the royal army. And Adam couldn't wish for more proficient guards.

Nonetheless, they were only men. They would be vulnerable to Eve's machinations. The clever lass could mince and cajole, flirt and weep like a skilled player upon a stage. If they somehow let her persuade them into giving her an inch of freedom, she would take a yard, and he'd probably never see her again.

Which was why he recommended the shackles.

She despised him now. He was certain of that. But he would rather endure her hate than be tied up in knots over her safety.

As far as Fergus, Adam knew it was the man's hunger for power that drove him. He ruled by strength and threat and cared little what consequences his people suffered, as long as he profited.

His own clanfolk weren't interested in expanding their holding or destroying the homes of their neighboring clans. They didn't care about allying with the English or rallying against Malcolm. That was why Fergus needed to hire mercenaries to do his fighting.

His clanfolk simply wanted to live their lives. Harvesting crops. Raising children. Falling in love. Dancing. Singing. Praying. Celebrating birth and marriage and holy days.

They were people like the alewife and her husband, living in peace and being good neighbors.

They had no interest in risking life and limb for a bigger plot of land. They were satisfied with what they had.

But men like Fergus could never have enough. They wanted more and more and more. And when their appetites were that voracious, they consumed everything in their path.

Adam knew Fergus had to be stopped. He'd made too many aggressions into neighboring territories, threatening to divide Scotland and rule over the west as king.

But he didn't agree with Malcolm that all-out war was required to rein in Fergus's ambitions.

Fergus was still just one man with a few allies.

Like a bad tooth, he could be removed with no harm coming to the rest.

And Adam could be the one to do it.

When he arrived at the Fergus stronghold, Adam demanded to see the laird immediately. Unfortunately, having made himself invisible for weeks as the mercenary Ness MacNeill had its drawbacks. It took several threats and coercion of a guard at the tip of a blade to be granted an audience.

When Fergus greeted him with a frown, Adam told him he'd seen the king's troops.

"I doubt that," Fergus grumbled. "If ye had, ye wouldn't have come back. Not in one piece anyway."

"I tossed a comely lass in their path," Adam said, giving him a knowing wink. "They were too busy takin' turns on her to pay heed to me."

Fergus chortled at that.

"I have information that may be o' value to ye," he continued.

"Information?" Fergus raised a dubious brow. "And what sort o' value are ye hopin' to extract from me?"

Adam shrugged. "Not much. I'm reasonable. Maybe an extra cup of ale at suppers."

"And how do I know this information is worth an extra cup of ale?"

"I give ye my word."

Fergus snorted. "The word of a mercenary?"

"I'll tell ye the information. 'Tis up to ye whether ye believe it or not."

"Fine. Tell me your information."

"I heard tell the king is plannin' a siege."

Fergus's eyes widened. "On the Fergus stronghold?"

"Aye."

"When?"

"After All Souls Day."

"All Souls Day is..." He stopped to calculate. "A fortnight hence."

"There's more."

"What more?"

Adam hesitated. He needed to play to Fergus's expectations of him as a mercenary. "That will cost ye an extra oatcake each morn."

Fergus looked disgruntled. "Done."

"He's got the Rivenloch warriors with him."

Fergus paled.

"And he's waitin' for the English troops to arrive."

"English troops?" Fergus barked. "What English troops?"

"Malcolm has forged an alliance with Henry. They've joined forces against ye."

That was a lie. But it served to rile Fergus. His face contorted with rage.

"What?"

No doubt the news would upset Fergus. He was counting on Henry siding with him against Malcolm.

Fergus snagged Adam by the front of his hauberk and drew him up short. "Ye'd better be tellin' me the truth."

Adam resisted the urge to shove the laird away. Instead, he gave him a grim smile. "Why would I lie? Ye're payin' me fairly. And now, with the extra provisions of ale and oatcakes..."

"If I find ye've led me astray..." Fergus threatened.

Adam shrugged. "M'laird, they already outnumber us by half, e'en without the English. If we attack on the morrow as planned? With the Rivenlochs in their ranks, we'll lose half our men."

"Lucifer's ballocks!" Fergus let go of him and began to pace, rubbing an angry hand over his beard.

"I do have an idea," Adam offered.

"What?" he spat, unimpressed with the guidance of a common mercenary. "What idea could ye possibly have?"

"Ye have one clear advantage," Adam told him. "Ye know he's comin'. Ye know where and when. And ye know we're outnumbered. If we lay low for the next fortnight, we'll lose no more troops. And there will be time to gather up the provender to withstand a siege."

"And then what?" Fergus exploded. "The Fergus clan will singlehandedly hold off the entire armies of England and Scotland?"

"Ye won't have to, m'laird. Once they've besieged the keep, ye'll summon the neighbor lairds who've sworn fealty to ye. They'll come up from behind and surround the kings' armies. Ye'll be in a position to attack from both sides."

Fergus scowled, considering this.

Adam added, "And since the attack will be upon the Fergus stronghold, 'twill be seen by everyone in Scotland as an act of aggression by the king."

Fergus nodded. "How many men do they have?"

Adam had to strike a balance with his reply. Too few men, and Fergus might imagine he could defeat them in a surprise attack. Too many, and he might consider retreat an option, which would only extend the battle.

"Five dozen at least. Seven with the Rivenlochs." To be honest, Adam wasn't sure there were two dozen Rivenloch warriors of fighting age. Even if there were, some always stayed behind to defend their own keeps. And some like Adam were roving in parts unknown. But the number sounded impressive.

"Shite." Fergus's brows came together. He punched his fist into his palm, grinding it as if squashing a bug. "After All Souls Day?"

Adam nodded.

"I want ye by my side," Fergus told him.

Adam knew his remark had nothing to do with loyalty and everything to do with mistrust. Fergus wanted him close at hand. If things went awry, Adam would be there to receive the brunt of his rage.

Adam would deal with that when the time came. At least for now, he had prevented a surprise attack on the king and kept Eve safe from harm.

Eve had no intention of remaining a prisoner. Not even a privileged prisoner of the king.

She had things to do. A Greater Purpose to achieve.

Adam may have thought he could use her as a means to an end, a pawn he could sacrifice to bring him closer to King Malcolm.

But he'd underestimated her determination and her skill.

She was no helpless hostage, waiting faithfully in the hopes Adam would return to free her. Indeed, she doubted he'd return at all. Why would he? He'd get no ransom from Fergus.

What then was he planning?

She couldn't guess.

But she wasn't going to sit idly by until her fate was decided for her.

She couldn't escape at once, of course. Building trust took time. But abiding in the pavilion of the physician had its advantages.

She found, even shackled, she could be of some use. First of all, she'd cooperated with her captors. They were probably so relieved to have a willing prisoner, they didn't question her choice when she offered her hands to be shackled in front of her rather than behind.

The physician in whose pavilion she was imprisoned wouldn't speak to her. At least not at first. He'd likely been warned by the king that she was a spy, that he should beware her lying tongue.

But she quickly discovered, as with most of those in the healing profession, he was a gentle man with a kind nature, driven to help others. All she needed to do was convince him they were kindred spirits.

She began by reciting her prayers at frequent intervals. The king had told the physician she wasn't really a nun. She would prove him wrong.

She made the usual entreaties, of course. Grant me Your grace. Give me time for repentance. Your will be done. But she added her own personal prayers. For the health and safety of the soldiers on both sides. For the forgiveness of those who had wronged her, wittingly or unwittingly. For God to guide the physician's hands. And for the improving welfare of all those he treated.

The physician couldn't help but be influenced by her good will.

Soon a royal guard came in with the complaint of an aching belly.

"Ye as well?" the physician said with a sigh. "The cook

must have served rotten meat. Ye're the fourth today. I'm out o' ginger, but I have oil o' rosemary. 'Tis the best I can do."

"Good sir," Eve said softly, "I have ginger." She nodded toward the corner of the pavilion, where the guards had left her things. "In my satchel."

He looked at her with suspicion, as if she were offering him poison.

The guard groaned and clutched his abdomen.

The physician frowned and reluctantly reached for her satchel.

He pulled out the vials, reading the markings until he came to the one with ginger. He uncorked it and sniffed at the contents. Then he dribbled a wee bit on his palm and tasted it. Satisfied, he spilled a few drops upon the guard's tongue.

The guard grimaced in disgust and tried to spit it out. "'Tis poison! Ye've poisoned me!"

"Nay!" he barked, closing the man's jaw with his hand. "'Tis only a strong flavor. Ye'll be fine."

As the guard began to wheeze, likely making the effect of the ginger worse, the physician shook his head and shared a smile of amusement with Eve.

"Go on then," he told the guard. "Lie down for a while, and 'twill pass."

The man's eyes were watering when he left, but he nodded.

When he'd gone, the physician corked the vial and slipped it back into her satchel. "I'm ne'er sure whether ginger is a healin' herb or a clever distraction."

She gave him a conspiratorial smile. "I suppose 'tis good medicine, as long as it works."

"That 'tis. Thank ye, lass." He shook his head. "I'll have to speak with the cook. I've used up all my ginger just this morn."

"Ye're welcome to mine," she said. "Take as much as ye need."

"Ye've got quite a treasury o' herbs," he remarked.

"We practice some medicine at the convent."

"The king said ye were a spy."

"I fear His Grace was misinformed." She lowered her gaze. "O' course, as a woman o' God, 'tis my duty to forgive."

"Ye *are* a nun then?"

"Aye. I'm Sister Eve from the convent near Mauchline."

"Peter Macgeil," he said with a nod of his head.

"I'm glad to meet ye, Peter Macgeil. And please help yourself to any herbs ye require. I have just one request."

"Aye?"

"Would ye be so kind as to bring me a chamberpot and linens?"

As she predicted, Peter looked horrified that the king had forgotten such a simple necessity. He glanced at her shackles in concern.

"I can manage," she assured him.

He brought her the chamberpot and abruptly left to give her some privacy.

Using it was not an easy feat, but having her hands bound before her made it possible. And the fact she made no attempt to escape in his absence made Peter trust her that much more.

A few more soldiers and a maidservant came in with stomach complaints, and Eve prayed aloud for them while Peter administered the ginger drops.

Finally a warrior arrived with a serious gash in his forearm, one he'd earned from what was supposed to have been a practice match. Judging by the scars that roped his arms, it wasn't the first time he'd been injured.

Peter examined it, winced, and clucked his tongue.

"We may have to cauterize it."

Eve blanched. Cauterizing was an extreme measure, she knew. Not only was it excruciatingly painful. It was only successful some of the time. Often infection set in, causing the loss of the limb.

"Nay," she blurted out. Then, before she realized what she was offering, she said, "I can do it. I can stitch it up."

"Aye, stitch it up," the injured man urged, none too eager to have a hot brand pressed against his flesh.

Peter looked as if he was entertaining the possibility. Then he grimaced with regret. "I can't unlock your shackles, lass."

The warrior frowned down at her, confused. "Ye're in irons?"

"I don't need them unlocked," she said.

Even as the words spilled out, she regretted them. What the Devil was she offering? She'd never sewn a man's flesh in her life. The one time she'd seen Adam do it, she'd nearly fainted.

Yet somehow she knew she could do it. She could steel herself for the gruesome task, remember her Greater Purpose, pray for strength, and save this man's arm.

Peter stared down at the wound and pursed his mouth in indecision.

The warrior had no time for his hesitancy. "Give me opium wine. Let her stitch me up."

"All right."

He pulled a bottle out of his great chest of medicines and handed it to the warrior, who began guzzling it down.

"Not too much," Peter warned as he kept pressure on the wounded arm.

With his free hand, he reached into a velvet-padded section of the chest and retrieved a length of fine catgut and a silver needle.

"Can you hold this?" he asked Eve, indicating the blood-soaked linen pad over the wound.

She bit her lip and gave him a curt nod. Then she set her hands to the task, stanching the flow.

Peter snatched the opium wine from the warrior, who would have drunk himself to death, and drizzled it over the needle and catgut. Then he quickly threaded the needle.

"I'll keep him still and hold the wound closed," he said. "Ye stitch, aye?"

She nodded, still aghast that she'd offered her services. But it was too late to back out now. The warrior was depending on her. The physician was depending on her.

At his first bellow of pain, Eve had to resist the urge to drop the needle, cover her ears, and cower into a shivering heap.

But if he could endure this, so could she. And if Adam could save a man's life with his bare hands, she was hardly going to let him best her.

So, drowning out his groans by murmuring prayers for strength, she continued to stitch until the opium finally took him to a place of peace. By then she was able to regard her handiwork with less horror and more of an artistic eye. She made sure to keep the stitches small so they would heal neatly.

"Ye've done this before," Peter said, snipping the catgut with a small pair of shears when she was done.

"Nay," she admitted. "'Twas God who guided my hand."

It felt like the truth. Indeed, she began to wonder if perhaps she was meant to be a healer.

Fortunately, she wasn't so distracted by the idea of her new calling that she forgot to take measures for her eventual escape. As Peter bandaged the wound and cleaned up the bloody linens, she secreted the shears in her skirts.

She set to work at nightfall, after the campfires were banked.

Picking the lock of the shackles was fairly easy using one narrow blade of the shears. While Peter snored from his pallet, she freed herself and retrieved her satchel.

Before she left, she cast one last look toward the physician. He was a decent man. She hated to deceive him. She hoped the king wouldn't make him suffer for her escape.

Slipping the vial of ginger out of the satchel, she placed it atop his chest of medicines and stole out into the night, headed for the convent.

CHAPTER 22

"**E**scaped, Your Grace?" Adam couldn't exactly say he was surprised. Even with shackles. But he thought it would take Eve a little longer to enchant the guards into letting her go. He'd hoped to return before she slipped her bonds and got herself into worse trouble.

According to the king, she'd managed to break free of her chains in less than a day. Even more impressive, she hadn't used the power of her charm at all. According to what remained of her shackles, she'd picked the lock with the physician's shears.

Adam had to hide his disappointment and dread.

It would do no good to accuse the physician of carelessness. The king had probably already given him a tongue-lashing he'd never forget. Besides, the man seemed almost as distraught over her disappearance as Adam.

It would avail Adam nothing to blame the king. He just had to come up with a new strategy that didn't involve rescuing Eve...yet. Now that the lass was loose among bloodthirsty warmongers, the best thing for all concerned was to subdue the hostility on both sides.

"I think we can go ahead with the siege the day after All Souls, Your Grace," he said.

"But we've lost our leverage," the king said.

"Fergus doesn't know that."

"He will once the hostage returns to him."

"I don't think she *will* return," Adam said.

"Nor do I," the physician chimed in. Then, immediately mortified at his own boldness and glared into submission by the king, he silenced.

Adam added, "She was abducted while under Fergus's protection, Your Grace. She won't trust him to protect her a second time."

"Where do you think she's gone?" asked the king.

Adam glanced at the physician. He knew something. But he wasn't going to say it.

"It doesn't matter," Adam lied. He'd question the physician later. "As far as Fergus is concerned, Your Grace still holds her captive."

"Fergus agreed to the truce?"

"Aye. He won't attack."

"Fine." The king sighed. "I suppose 'twill give us time to build a trebuchet."

Adam bowed and took his leave.

He hoped he could keep the stories he'd told straight.

The king believed Fergus was keeping the peace because he held Eve hostage.

Fergus believed the king was keeping the peace because he was waiting to amass a bigger army.

They both believed the siege would happen on the day after All Souls Day, which it would, but only because Adam had made it so.

He sighed. After this was over, he'd need to go on a very long pilgrimage to atone for all his half-truths.

Eve's trek through the forest at night was blessed by the full moon. It shone like a light to guide her home, reinforcing her sense she was doing the right thing in returning to the convent.

Twice betrayed by a Judas, it was time for her to accept her fate. Life as a nun. Doing God's work. Sworn to lifelong chastity.

But if this was her chosen path, why did the stars of her destiny blur overhead as she followed it?

Why did her heart ache with loss for what would never be?

Why did she weep all the way through the woods?

By the time she reached the convent, dawn was breaking, and she was all out of tears.

But her silence was only a temporary surrender. Her peace was only a facade. Deep in her soul, she knew she'd bear the scars of grief forever.

She managed to steal into the convent and to her cell without being noticed. That was another gift from God. For if any of the sisters had taken note of her missing wimple and veil and seen her blood-stained habit, there would have been questions.

She sat on her pallet and eyed her spare set of clothing hung on a hook. She'd have to burn the bloody habit. She wasn't sure if her wimple and veil were in her satchel. The guards must have stuffed her belongings into it after she'd emptied it on the floor of the king's pavilion, looking for the royal dagger.

She dumped the contents onto the pallet.

Her veil and wimple were there. Her herbs. Her provender. And her costumes.

Those she would need no longer. She would go adventuring no more.

She choked on a knot of sorrow.

Then one other item caught her eye.

The marriage document.

Her breath stopped.

She assumed either the king or Adam had confiscated it. But nay. There it was. Intact.

For the first time in three days, her heart lightened. She had one last mission. Something significant to do. Something meaningful. Something to occupy her and keep her from dwelling on her lost love.

There wasn't much time. The siege Adam had talked about would happen after All Souls Day. Once war began, she'd trust neither the Fergus clan nor the royal troops. She needed to be home in time to protect her convent sisters from harm.

First, however, she'd warn the abbess. Insist the nuns keep to the convent for the next fortnight. Tell her there were rumors of war. Warn them to remain inside on Samhain and several days following, just to be safe.

Naturally, on the day of her leaving, the abbess vehemently protested. She argued it was unsafe for Eve to wander if war was afoot. She said Eve's father would never forgive her if something happened to Eve. She even tried to make Eve feel guilty for abandoning her convent sisters.

But Eve knew this was important. So she confided in the abbess. She told her she was going to Rivenloch. She told her it was a secret mission of utmost importance for the clan. She vowed that when she returned, she would not venture forth on such a mission again. She'd train as a physician and serve the community. This would be her final adventure.

If Eve's voice choked up at that confession, the abbess didn't notice. She was too delighted by the idea that Eve was going to be a messenger for the famous Rivenloch clan.

Filling her satchel with provender and borrowing the convent mule, Eve began the long ride to Rivenloch. She maintained her identity as Sister Eve and stayed at convents along the way. It was more boring than traveling as Lady Ailenn or Jehan of Rouen. But the prospect of seeing the illustrious castle of Rivenloch at the end of her journey buoyed her spirits.

The trek took longer than she intended. The mule was old and tired easily. But eventually, after six days, she arrived. And while her imagination had filled in the details of what she'd heard described, nothing could have prepared her for the magnificence of Rivenloch. Set on a rise overlooking vast crofters' fields and a pair of twin lochs, it was stately and well constructed for defense, with a double concentric wall surrounding the keep. Clearly, it was intended to serve as a strong fortification for the clan.

But attention had been paid to the comforts of living and beauty as well. Sheep and coos dotted the verdant hillside. Gardens and orchards bordered the vast courtyard. There was a great stable, a dovecot, and a mews for falcons. Structures built along the inner wall included workshops for an armorer, a baker, a jeweler, a leatherworker, and sundry other services.

Dust rose from the practice field adjoining the keep as warriors fiercely clashed and battled as if they waged real war. The thunder of hooves announced great chargers as mounted knights tilted at a quintain.

Inside, the imposing walls of the great hall, filled with the shields and banners of conquered foes, were softened by the lively activity of the castle denizens. The lovely smells of bread and cinnamon and roasting meat mingled with the scent of fresh rushes and smoke from the blazing fire.

Maidservants and kitchen lads hurried across the room, bearing baskets and platters, setting up trestle tables, chattering away. By the fire, three sweaty warriors in chain mail drank ale and laughed together. In one corner, a pack of hounds napped. In another, a pair of toddlers played with wooden knights. To Eve's right, a young fair-haired lad of about fifteen years sat on a stool, laboring over some intricate wooden structure, while a lass a few years older examined his handiwork.

It was hard to believe that this was the home of the most feared and ferocious clan in all of Scotland.

Then Laird Deirdre herself entered the hall.

She was splendid. Tall and wide-shouldered, with long braids the color of winter wheat. She wore a leather hauberk over a sky blue surcoat that perfectly matched her eyes. Upon her breast rested a silver Thor's hammer, and a long sword was sheathed at her hip.

As brave as Eve usually was, Deirdre intimidated her. She gulped. How would the laird receive the news that her nephew had wed without her permission?

The king had approved the marriage. That should be enough.

Still, Eve bit her lip, and her fingers fumbled with the scroll.

The fair-haired lad looked up from his work, noticing the rolled parchment. "What's that?"

"Ian," the lass beside him chided, "don't be rude."

"I'm not rude. I'm curious."

The lass detected Eve's hesitation. "Is that for the laird?"

Eve nodded.

"Ma!" Ian called out.

Eve was mortified, especially when Deirdre's gaze turned her way.

The lass shushed Ian, then turned to Eve and murmured, "I'm Isabel, the laird's daughter. Come. I'll introduce you."

Eve followed the lass, who had all her mother's beauty, but was as sweet as the laird was fierce.

Isabel whispered, "What's your name?"

"Eve."

"Laird Deirdre, may I present Sister Eve."

Deirdre's appraisal was swift but thorough. She was obviously used to sizing up her adversaries with a single glance. "Sister."

Eve could tell Deirdre was not impressed with her. And though she understood why, it rankled at her. This was not who Eve truly was. A cowering nun who jumped at her own shadow. A shrinking sister who turned the other cheek at any affront. A humble agent of God whose only purpose was to serve.

She was Eve MacAnndra. Merchant's daughter. Outlaw. Irish noblewoman. Archery champion. She straightened her spine. "M'laird."

"The sister seems to have some business with you, Ma," Isabel said.

"Is that so?"

"Aye, m'laird," Eve said, presenting the scroll.

Deirdre looked at it, but was in no hurry to take it. "What is it?"

"'Tis a marriage document."

Beside her, Isabel let out a gushing sigh. "I knew it! I knew it had to be something romantic!"

Ian growled and rolled his eyes. He clearly didn't share his sister's love of romance.

Deirdre was more practical. "A marriage document between whom?"

Eve took a deep breath and forced herself to hold the laird's gaze. "'Tis an agreement between Lady Carenza o' Dunlop and...Sir Hew du Lac o' Rivenloch."

Isabel let out a squeal of delight.

Deirdre's face turned to ice. "Agreed to by whom? By *them?*"

The laird had likely had enough of her offspring marrying whomever they willed. After all, even her own marriage had been arranged.

Of course, Eve knew the story. Everyone did. Lady

Deirdre had tricked the bridegroom into wedding her instead of her sister. So in a way, she'd chosen her own husband as well.

Isabel intervened. "Would that be so bad, Ma? You let Gellir marry his ladylove."

"Let?" Deirdre bit out. "Gellir was betrothed to Carenza."

"But she didn't love him, Ma," Isabel said. "You know that. And he had no feelings for her."

Deirdre's response was a low growl that sounded a lot like Ian's.

"'Tis a perfect match," Isabel said. "Everyone loves Carenza, and she'll ne'er break Hew's heart."

In light of Deirdre's continued glower, Eve decided to disclose, "King Malcolm has already approved the marriage, m'laird. It requires only your mark and that o' the Laird o' Dunlop."

Isabel clapped her hands together rapidly with excitement. "Another wedding!"

"Let me see," Deirdre said, taking the scroll and scanning it.

Isabel grabbed Eve's arm and squeezed it, biting her lip as she awaited the good news.

Finally Deirdre sighed. "Fine. It seems to be in order. I'll sign it. But first, I want to know how *you* ended up being the bearer of such news."

Eve was afraid of that. Now she would have to disclose the whole story and hope her nun's habit would protect her from the laird's wrath.

While Deirdre listened in stony silence, punctuated by Isabel's gasps of wonder, Eve said she was a close friend of Hew's. Hew and Carenza had fallen in love and were both heartsick when Carenza was betrothed to Gellir. Hew requested that Eve escort Carenza away from her wedding to meet with Hew.

"Escort?" Deirdre asked with a raised brow. "Or abduct?"

Eve blushed.

Deirdre continued, "Was she taken against her will?"

Louder than she intended, Eve replied, "Nay! I would ne'er do such a thing."

"And where are they now?"

"I can't say," Eve said, lowering her eyes. "I vowed I would not."

Deirdre didn't like that answer. She looked daggers at Eve. "Are they safe?"

"Aye," Eve was quick to assure her. "They haven't been apart. Hew has watched o'er her since that day."

Deirdre scowled. "That was months ago."

Eve nodded.

But what she thought was reassurance triggered something very different in Deirdre. "She's likely with child now then."

Eve gulped.

Deirdre cursed under her breath. Then she muttered, "What kind of nun gets embroiled in this sort of mischief?"

Isabel cooed, as if this was exactly the kind of entertaining exchange she enjoyed.

Eve, however, was getting more and more agitated. It seemed the laird was missing the point. What did it matter how the deed was accomplished? She had the document in her hands, and it was approved by the king.

Deirdre narrowed her eyes. "Are you even a real nun?"

"O' course I'm a real nun," Eve snapped in a tone that wasn't the least bit nun-like.

Isabel drew in an exaggerated gasp. "You aren't *that* nun, are you?"

Ian looked up to interject, "What nun?"

"The nun Hew tried to court," Isabel told him.

Eve's cheeks flushed hot.

"You *are*," Isabel confirmed with delight. "She *is*."

"That was an honest mistake," Eve muttered. "I wasn't wearin' my habit at the time."

Deirdre's brows rose at that.

"Nay," Eve quickly corrected, "I mean, I wasn't wearin' my habit, because I was wearin' a gown."

"So are you a nun or not?" Deirdre asked.

Eve grimaced. "Sometimes."

Deirdre's brow darkened.

Isabel giggled. "Och! She's a master o' disguise, isn't she? Just like Adam."

"What?" Eve felt all the air empty her lungs. Surely she'd heard wrong. "What did ye say?"

"My cousin Adam. One day he's a monk. The next he's a warrior. Once, at Darragh, he feigned to be a rat-catcher. He's such a talent. He can make himself nigh invisible."

Eve's head was spinning. She'd somehow hoped Adam was some obscure and distant Rivenloch relative the laird barely knew.

"Are you all right?" Deirdre asked in concern. "Ian, give her your stool."

He brought the stool, and Deirdre helped her to sit. "And bring her a cup of water. Isabel, stay here with her. I'm going to fetch the scribe."

When Deirdre was gone, Eve dared to ask Isabel, "Adam is the laird's nephew?"

"Aye."

"And do ye know where is he now?" She hoped he hadn't returned to Rivenloch.

"No one e'er knows," she said, "though the real question is *who* is he now?"

Ian brought the cup of water, and she took a long drink.

Isabel asked, "Why are you so interested in Adam?"

Eve choked on the water.

Before she could answer, Isabel made her own guess. "Och! Have you met him? If you know Hew, maybe you've crossed paths with Adam?"

The water made a long, cold path into the pit of Eve's stomach.

Isabel continued. "With him being a sometimes monk, and you being a sometimes nun…"

Isabel stared at her now, and Eve got the feeling she had some gift of sight that let her peer into a person's soul.

"You *do* know him, don't you?" she marveled. "You know him. And you *care* for him."

Eve blanched. Was it written so plainly on her face?

Ian scoffed. "Not everyone is in love, Isabel."

"But *she* is," Isabel. "Aren't you?"

"I'm a nun," she said stiffly. "I cannot love any man."

"And yet you do." Isabel's voice was full of a sympathy so wistful, it nearly brought Eve to tears.

Deirdre rushed up, followed by a scribe.

"Feeling better?" she asked.

Eve nodded. But she wasn't feeling better. She was more miserable than ever.

Deirdre nodded. "Then you may return to…" She waved her hand. "Whatever convent allows its nuns to do such mischief. I plan to deliver this myself. I only pray I'm not too late."

It hadn't occurred to Eve that the marriage needed to be secured before a bairn was born. But of course it made sense. The laird couldn't have a Rivenloch heir considered illegitimate.

She trusted Laird Deirdre would do the right thing and secure Dunlop's seal.

Now all she wanted was to hurry home. The siege was imminent. And safe behind convent walls, maybe she could forget all the foolish things she'd said and done in front of Adam.

She was sure his clan would never forget her. This would make her the laughingstock of Rivenloch.

She'd accidentally beguiled Hew of Rivenloch.

Stolen Gellir of Rivenloch's bride.

And swived Adam of Rivenloch.

Now that her task was finished, she prayed she'd never see a Rivenloch again.

CHAPTER 23

Adam looked up at the clear, star-spattered sky from the wall walk of the Fergus keep. Two nights ago, the moon had been new, the relentless darkness broken only by the ritual bonfires of Samhain.

Now, on the night of All Souls, the fires were gone. The moon was a thin sliver, dim enough to lend cover for the royal army's march on Galloway.

Stealth wasn't necessary, of course. There would be no surprise attack. As far as King Malcolm was concerned, the arrival at night was to prevent the Fergus clan from collecting resources to withstand a siege. He expected Fergus to be unprepared and at his mercy.

Of course, Fergus had been warned. He was ready. Adam himself had helped the laird to prepare the castle for siege. The clan had already gathered enough livestock and food to last through the winter.

If things went Adam's way, however, the siege would never actually happen. The conflict would be resolved before dawn.

Fergus didn't completely trust Adam. He insisted Adam wait beside him atop the wall walk to watch for the king's arrival. If the royal army didn't come as he'd predicted, that would make it easier for Fergus to toss Adam from the parapets.

Fortunately, the king's men did show up. And they had a trebuchet.

Thankfully, it was too dark for Fergus to notice their ranks included neither the Rivenloch warriors nor the English troops Adam had promised. But Fergus was satisfied his spy had told him the truth. King Malcolm had indeed arrived on All Souls Day.

That extra level of trust endeared Adam to Fergus. Once it appeared the king's men had bedded down for the night and didn't plan to attack, Adam suggested they go together to the great hall for an ale and to brief the clan on what would happen on the morrow.

An ale turned into three for Fergus.

Once he'd thoroughly wet his whistle and was sufficiently emboldened by drink, Fergus addressed the clan with his typical pomposity. He boasted about his cleverness, bragging that he'd foiled the king, who thought he could catch Fergus with his trews down. He declared he would be victorious against Malcolm and send him whimpering home with his tail betwixt his legs.

After his vainglorious speech, he sent the clanfolk to an early bed so they would be bright-eyed and battle-ready at dawn.

The laird, however, was not in the habit of going to bed without being deeper in his cups. He gathered four of his closest advisors to join him in drunken revelry. They worked up their courage for the siege by berating the king, calling him an infant, a maiden, a kiss-arse.

Adam quietly slipped into their ranks.

Seeing the trebuchet had given him an idea.

"M'laird," he said, "ye know, we could do some real damage before the siege."

"Damage? What sort o' damage?"

"A wee group of us could steal out o' the keep and into their camp. The moon is barely a crescent, and they've banked their fires. No one would see us."

"A wee group of us?" one of the men barked.

"Are ye mad?" another said. "We'd get caught."

"And killed," chimed in a third.

Adam explained. "We won't go near the pavilions. And we won't attack anyone. But we *could* set their trebuchet afire."

Their brows shot up at that idea. Then the men began chortling with glee.

"Aye!" Fergus shouted, clapping Adam on the back. "Brilliant."

"Who's with me then?" Adam asked.

The enthused men were less enthusiastic about pulling off the deed themselves.

"Come on, lads," Fergus urged. "'Twill be as easy as reivin' coos."

They still balked, muttering excuses.

Fergus snorted. "Hell. I'll go myself if ye're a bunch o' milksops."

"Nay, m'laird."

"'Tis too risky."

"Don't be a halfwit," one man said, taking hold of Fergus's arm. "Ye can't go, m'laird."

"Who are ye callin' a halfwit?" Fergus roared, pulling his arm away. "I can and I will."

"I'll go," Adam volunteered. "And I'll keep the laird safe."

His men were drunk, but not that drunk. They understood the risk of venturing into enemy territory, where they were outnumbered. They also weren't about to leave their laird in the hands of a mercenary they barely knew.

Two of them reluctantly agreed to go. The other two said they'd watch from the wall walk with bows and arrows at the ready.

Adam wasn't worried about the two atop the wall walk.

It was too dark for archery, even if they hadn't been too drunk to aim.

He was most concerned about the two guards who'd agreed to accompany him. They were the least drunk of the four. They would be the hardest to manage.

Fortunately, Adam was a Rivenloch by birth. Though he'd chosen a different path from his kin, he'd been raised a warrior. He knew how to handle guards.

It was full dark when the four agitators slipped out of the keep. They couldn't risk bringing a lit brand to start the fire. So the two guards were armed with flint, steel, and straw.

They were also armed with swords.

Adam carried a dagger. Inside his hauberk he'd tucked a large square of white linen.

A quarter of the way toward the king's camp, Adam made his move with fluid stealth.

In one graceful movement, he unsheathed his dagger and set it at Fergus's throat while with his other hand, he drew Fergus's sword and tossed it away. He turned to the two guards before Fergus even had a chance to gasp in surprise.

The guards instinctively drew their swords.

Adam shook his head. They could see he had Fergus at his mercy. One wee slip of the dagger, and the laird's life would end.

"Traitor," one of the guards bit out. "We should ne'er have trusted ye."

The other quietly fumed.

"Toss your weapons away," Adam whispered.

They only tightened their grips.

"Toss them away," he repeated with deadly calm, "or I'll slay your laird."

Fergus tensed. "Drop your weapons," he begged in a voice strangled by fear. "Do it."

They reluctantly complied.

"Now return to the keep," Adam murmured, "unless you want to be slaughtered by the royal guard."

They hesitated.

"Go," Fergus said through clenched teeth.

Adam watched them leave. When he was confident they wouldn't return, he continued toward the king's encampment with his hostage.

"He'll kill me, ye know," Fergus muttered.

Adam told him the truth. "Ye're too valuable to kill."

"I should have known ye were a traitor."

He probably *should* have at least suspected it. Hiring mercenaries was risky.

As they drew closer, Fergus tried to bargain. "What is it ye want? Coin? Land? A title?"

"Peace," Adam told him. "I want peace."

He stopped near the first pavilion. Reaching into his hauberk with his free hand, he withdrew the linen square and waved it high.

Then he called out, "Your Grace, Laird Fergus of Galloway wishes to surrender."

Fergus sputtered at that, but he dared do no more, not with a blade at his throat.

Royal guards immediately emerged from the pavilions. The king was summoned from bed to greet his adversary.

Fergus denied having surrendered. He refused to swear loyalty to Malcolm. With false bravado, he said his whole clan would rather burn inside the keep than bow before a maiden king.

Fortunately, Malcolm took the insult in stride. He could see Fergus was in his cups. He was magnanimous in return. He told Fergus none of his clansmen would be harmed, and his keep would remain intact.

Adam suspected the royal army was less than happy about that. They probably wished to fire their new trebuchet at least once.

In the end, the king was pleased. He'd won a bloodless battle. Behaved chivalrously. Lost no men. And the thorn in his side, Fergus of Galloway, had been extracted.

Indeed, Malcolm was so grateful for Adam's help that the next morn he offered him a purse of silver for his trouble.

Adam's first instinct was to refuse. He didn't like the idea of blood money.

But then he remembered the alewife, her husband, their alehouse, and how distraught Eve had been over the injustice. So he accepted the coin and pledged to seek out the impoverished couple. They would get the recompense they deserved.

He only wished he could tell Eve. But there was no way to determine where she'd gone. And by now, the trail was cold.

Unless…

He marched to the pavilion of the king's physician and whipped open the flap. The physician was there, bandaging a soldier's hand. Glancing up and seeing Adam's glare, he finished up and sent the man on his way.

"You," Adam said. "What do you know about the hostage?"

The physician washed his hands in a basin of water. "The nun?"

"Aye."

The physician eyed Adam as if he wondered whether he could trust him. Then he murmured, "I don't think she was a spy."

"Is that so?"

"Aye. I think she *was* a nun."

Adam didn't give his opinion much credit. "Spies are skilled at mimicry. She was very good."

"What she did was beyond mimicry."

"What do you mean?"

"She saved a man's life."

Adam frowned. "Through...prayer?" In his experience, it was rare for a man of science to put much faith in miracles.

"Nay. She stitched up a knife wound. A wound I was goin' to cauterize. I've ne'er seen such skill, such beautiful work."

Adam was struck speechless. Surely that wasn't true. He'd seen Eve at the alehouse. She'd nearly fainted at the sight of blood.

The physician shook his head in wonder. "She knew what herbs to use. And how to wrap bandages. She may not be a physician, but she's had a lot o' practice, healin'. I believe she *is* a nun."

"What difference does it make now?"

"Because I don't think ye want a woman o' God to come to harm...from either side."

That was true.

Adam stated what he now suspected. "You know where she's gone."

The physician nodded. "I think she's fled back to her convent."

If the physician had known Eve like Adam did, he'd never dream she belonged to a convent.

Still, the man had a point. It made sense Eve would find a safe place to go. The convent she'd mentioned before, where she had friends among the sisters, was near Mauchline. He'd told her the king wouldn't attack nuns. It seemed a convenient and likely place of refuge.

"Thank you," Adam said.

The physician caught his arm. "Ye'll keep her safe, aye?"

"On my honor as a Rivenloch."

He'd keep her safe. If she was willing to allow it. At the moment, his was probably the last face she wanted to see.

The best way to infiltrate a nunnery was as a visiting monk. Convent sisters always showed deference to their holy brothers. And it didn't hurt that, disguising himself as a man of God, it would be harder for Eve to publicly vent her rage upon him.

As he trudged through the forest toward Mauchline, he practiced his explanation in a contrite murmur.

"I apologize, Eve. But 'twas a necessary deception I had to employ in the course of avoiding a war."

That sounded good. It would impress her.

"You should be proud, Eve. You played an instrumental part in resolving the conflict between Laird Fergus and the king."

That was good as well. Eve would have a story to tell for generations to come.

"I asked the king to keep you hostage, Eve, because I care for you, and I knew it was the place you would be the most safe."

Aye, that was the one. That would soften her heart.

"It may make you glad to hear the king rewarded me with silver for my negotiations, Eve, and I delivered the coin as restitution to the alewife."

Even better. Eve would be relieved to know he'd sought justice so selflessly.

Then he sighed.

All of them were true. Yet the words sounded like feeble excuses for his wretched behavior, even to his own ears.

He feared her heart would never heal from the damage he'd done to it. And if that happened, he didn't think he'd find happiness again.

He was still brooding over what he would say when he arrived at the convent. It looked old, but well-kept, standing in a broad clearing of the wood. A stone wall surrounded the close, with bare-limbed fruit trees peering over the top.

When he passed through the gates, he saw several nuns toiling in the yard. Some were pruning the trees. Others tilled small patches of soil by hand. He perused their faces. None of them were Eve.

A pair of novices pulling neeps from the garden spotted him first, whispered together, and then ran off, probably to fetch the abbess.

A moment later, a rosy-cheeked, matronly nun greeted him from across the close.

"Brother, welcome!"

Behind her scurried the two novices, and the laborers stopped their work to watch. Life in a nunnery was dull. A stranger was cause for excitement.

The abbess clasped her hands before her. "What brings ye to our fair convent, Brother..."

"Adam, Reverend Mother."

"Adam," she repeated.

Behind her, the novices giggled into their hands.

"Sisters!" the abbess hissed. Then she addressed him. "Forgive their rudeness, Brother. We get few visitors."

The abbess shooed the novices along and ushered him into the refectory. There, two more nuns brought him oatcakes and ale.

Neither of them were Eve.

"What brings ye to our fair convent?" the abbess asked.

"I'm searchin' for an acquaintance o' mine."

"An acquaintance?"

"A nun."

"Ah. And her name?"

He wished the abbess could simply line up all the nuns in the convent and let him take a good look at them. He had no idea what name Eve was using now.

"I'm not certain," he admitted. "She may have changed her name."

More nuns entered the refectory. Giving him sidelong glances, they busied themselves in close proximity, as interested in them as they were in him. They carried empty trays back and forth. Wiped imaginary dirt from the tops of the tables. Rearranged the rushes on the floor. Some brushed so close behind him, he could feel the breeze of their passing.

He studied them carefully. None of them were Eve.

"Oh aye," the abbess said. "Oftentimes a lass will change her name when she enters a holy order. What was her name before?"

"Eve," he said. "Sister Eve."

He might as well have uttered a foul oath.

All the nuns in the refectory gasped and began whispering furiously among themselves.

He frowned.

The abbess's eyes went wide. "Sister Eve?" Then she scowled at the melee around them. "Sisters! Silence!"

They knew something about Eve. What it was, he wasn't sure.

When it quieted, he asked, "Is she here?"

"We did have a Sister Eve here," the abbess said carefully.

He supposed there could be more than one Sister Eve. "What did she look like?"

She shrugged. "Ordinary. Brown-haired. Brown-eyed."

He furrowed his brows. Eve was far from ordinary.

She continued, "A bit...undisciplined."

His breath caught. That had to be Eve.

"Ye said ye *did* have a Sister Eve," he said. "What happened to her?"

Before the abbess could answer, the nuns began chiming in with excitement.

"She's gone on an adventure," one of them said.

"All the way to Rivenloch," added another.

"Carryin' a mysterious scroll."

"A special missive."

"I heard 'twas on the king's business."

The abbess's face purpled. "Sisters!"

They silenced.

"Out!" the abbess shouted.

They filed out, shamefaced.

But he'd heard enough to know it was his Eve. The wily lass had managed to give him the slip. She was finishing her clandestine task with that marriage document.

To be fair, he wasn't opposed to her undertaking. He'd made sure the document got into her satchel. Considering the trouble they'd gone to, Hew and Carenza must be truly in love and deserved to be married. He only hoped Eve could convince his clever aunt, the Laird of Rivenloch, that the king's signature had been lawfully obtained.

"When did Sister Eve leave?" he asked.

"More than a sennight ago," the abbess said.

"On foot?"

"By mule."

He sighed. He was too late. She must have already delivered the document to Laird Deirdre.

He hoped things turned out well for Hew.

As for Adam, he feared it was too much to hope for. In Eve's eyes, he'd betrayed and abandoned her. Failed at protecting her. And turned his back on justice for the alewife. As far as she knew, he was a liar. A thief. A Judas. A serpent. The lowest, most despicable sort of outlaw.

Even if he were given the chance to explain himself, it would be nigh impossible to find her now. From Rivenloch, she could have gone anywhere.

"She should return anon," the abbess said.

His heart skipped a beat. "Return?"

"Aye. She said she'd be back in time for Martinmas."

"She's returnin'?"

"Aye. So if ye'd like to stay, we have a cell for guests. To be honest, we could use a braw man to do a few tasks around the convent."

"O' course."

"We break our fast at dawn," she said, "then have Prime, followed by readin's in the chapter house…"

She continued blathering on with the convent schedule. But Adam heard none of it. His mind was spinning.

Why would Eve go all the way to Rivenloch and all the way back again to this particular convent? Why wouldn't she continue her carefree life of roaming the countryside as he did? Take opportunities as they came? Let Fate steer the course?

A chilling possibility entered his mind.

"…and after Compline, we make an early night of it. When the sun retires, so do we," the abbess finished.

"'Tis a wise practice," he said with a smile of approval. "Tell me, Reverend Mother, how often is Sister Eve here?"

The abbess arched a judgmental brow. "Not as often as she should be."

"When did she first start comin' to the convent?"

"Sister Eve? She's been here since she was ten years of age, so…" the abbess did the sum in her head. "Ten years?"

Ten? His chest sank. He thought she only visited the convent. But now he realized this was her home. She was a nun.

God help him. He'd swived a nun.

His voice came out on a sickly groan. "Someone left her here when she was ten years old?"

The abbess looked puzzled. "I suppose ye could say that."

"She was a foundlin' or a by-blow?"

"Heavens, no!" the startled abbess exclaimed, clapping a hand to her breast. "Her father sent her here. He's a respectable merchant with five daughters."

He blinked, stunned. He'd swived a nun who was the daughter of a respectable merchant.

So many questions raced through his head, he couldn't think of which one to ask first.

The abbess continued in a hushed voice. "She isn't in trouble, is she, Brother? Is that why ye're here?"

"Nay." The word came out on a croak. He was still reeling.

"Because, between ye and me," she confided, "her father is quite a generous donor, and if his daughter is removed from the convent for any reason..."

He nodded. He understood. "No need to fret, Reverend Mother. That's not why I've come. And as far as her father..." His voice cracked on the word. "I won't breathe a word to anyone."

Adam couldn't have been more sincere.

The ugly truth—that he had trysted with a nun—would follow him to his grave.

CHAPTER 24

Eve had promised the abbess she would return before Martinmas. She was going to keep her promise, but only by the skin of her teeth. For the last half of her journey home, she'd had to let the useless mule walk beside her unencumbered while she carted her satchel across her back. She feared this would be the poor old beast's last journey.

She finally reached the convent on the afternoon of Martinmas. After stabling the mule, she passed through the cloisters. She hadn't realized how hungry she was until she smelled the delectable Martinmas feast wafting from the kitchens.

Hurrying to her cell, she dropped her satchel beside her pallet and used the basin to wash for dinner. Her habit was dusty from travel, but since she'd burned her spare garments, it would have to do. Her stomach was growling as she scurried to dinner.

The rest of the sisters were already seated at the trestle tables, murmuring as they waited to be served by the novices.

She smiled. It was good to be back to the familiar faces and sounds and smells of home. And after a lean several days of travel, she was ready for a holy feast.

The nuns looked up when she entered. But instead of greeting her with welcoming smiles, they stopped chattering and swiveled their heads toward the abbess in expectation.

The abbess stood up from the table. "Welcome home, Sister Eve. Ye made it by Martinmas, as ye promised." Then she opened her arm to the place of honor on her right. "Ye have a guest who's been waitin' to see ye."

Eve's smile froze in horror as she followed the abbess's gesture.

Rising from his seat was Adam, dressed as a monk.

The abbess politely inquired, "I believe ye know Brother Adam?"

Eve resisted the urge to spin on her heel and make a hasty exit. Flee to Ireland. Or France. Or even bloody England. As far away from Rivenlochs as she could get.

"Sister Eve." His voice was low, grim, filled with accusation.

It was the accusation in his voice that gave her the strength to stay where she was.

How dared he take that tone with her? As if this was all *her* fault?

He was the one who'd passed himself off as an outlaw when he was a damned Rivenloch.

He was the one who'd betrayed her...twice.

He was the one who'd stolen her heart...and her virtue. Who'd promised to marry her...and then abandoned her.

Her eyes watered now, with grief *and* rage.

But she wouldn't let him win. This was her home. This was her destiny. He was in her house now. She wouldn't let him ruin her entire future. Not again.

"Brother Adam," she said in a level voice.

The nuns were watching both of them expectantly.

She forced a smile. "I hope I haven't kept ye waitin' too long." Before he could reply, she pivoted to the abbess.

"I fear the mule is on his last legs, Reverend Mother. He couldn't even carry me home."

"Well," the abbess said in the awkward silence while Adam stared at Eve. "I suppose I shall have to see about acquirin' a new beast."

Finally, Adam spoke. "The Reverend Mother tells me ye traveled to Rivenloch."

Eve reminded herself never to confide in the abbess again. The Reverend Mother couldn't keep a secret longer than she could hold her breath. And from the lack of impressed gasps from the rest of the nuns, everyone already knew.

But that was a rather bold comment from Adam, knowing who he was.

"Indeed," she said. "I hear ye're quite familiar with Rivenloch yourself, Brother."

A crease formed between his eyes as he realized she might know his secret.

"I've been a few times, aye." His voice faltered slightly when he asked, "Did ye meet with the laird?"

"Oh aye," she assured him.

But from his sickly expression, he was not assured.

"Come sit between us, Sister," the abbess instructed, indicating the space to her right. "Ye must be starvin'. Dinner will be served anon." Adam sat back on the bench, leaving room for Eve, and the abbess leaned toward him to confide, "'Tis quite a feast we serve on Martinmas."

Eve had no appetite whatsoever. Her stomach was roiling with a volatile wave of emotions. Anger. Hurt. Outrage. Sorrow. Shame. Fury.

Nonetheless, she sat quietly beside the abbess as she said a prayer of thanks for the bounty and the novices began to serve dinner.

The first offering was Sister Eithne's famous leek pottage, served with barley rolls and butter.

The conversation around them resumed, but Eve was too angry for words. She stabbed her eating knife into her roll with a little too much force, making Adam flinch.

"Butter?" he asked, offering her the bowl.

To her humiliation, her knife had gone through the roll and linen tablecloth and stuck in the table. She tried to pry it out, to no avail.

"Allow me," he said, enclosing her hand within his on the handle to rock it loose.

She trembled with rage. How dared he touch her with such familiarity in front of her holy sisters?

When the knife was free, she grabbed her hand back so fast, she sliced his finger with the blade.

She hadn't meant to.

Fortunately, no one else noticed.

But he winced and covered the cut quickly with his napkin. Then he leaned close to whisper, "There's no need for violence. We can settle this like *equals*."

His point was clear. Someone had revealed to him she was a merchant's daughter. Bloody hell. What else had they told him?

She was too upset to speak calmly. She slathered butter on the roll and stuffed it in her mouth to stifle a curse of rage.

Meanwhile, novices brought dish after dish. A salat of parsley, sage, mint, and leeks dressed with almond oil and verjuice. A dish of roasted neeps and parsnips. Pastry coffyns stuffed with apples and onions. A great roast of beef presented on a board and decorated with sprigs of rosemary. Pears poached in wine. And darioles of milk, eggs, and cream, cooked into a tart crust.

Hard cider accompanied the meal. It was one novice's task to refill the cups as needed. Eve decided she would keep the lass busy, for she intended to drink away her agitation.

She downed her first cup all at once and slammed the cup on the table, earning a scowl from the abbess.

"'Twas a long journey," she explained.

"So how long were ye at Rivenloch?" Adam asked, pushing his neeps around on his trencher and trying to make the question sound casual.

"Long enough," she told him cryptically.

She popped a large wad of salat into her mouth and instantly choked on the strong verjuice.

As she started coughing, Adam clapped her on the back, which didn't help at all.

She slapped his hand away and stole his cup of hard cider to wash down the sour dressing.

"Are ye all right, Sister?" the abbess asked in concern.

"Fine, Reverend Mother," Eve lied.

Her eyes were watering, her throat burned, and her nerves were stretched to the limit over this awkward interaction with Adam. The last thing she wanted was to draw attention to their skirmish.

Adam's hand tightened on his eating knife as he stared at the slice of roast on his trencher. "Did ye speak to anyone besides the laird?" he muttered.

"Oh aye," she revealed with a measure of admittedly unhealthy satisfaction. "I spoke to a lovely lass named Isabel. Perhaps ye've met her."

Of course he'd met her. She was his cousin.

"The name sounds familiar," he hedged, smiling for the abbess, who'd taken a sudden interest in their conversation.

"She seems to know everythin' about everyone," Eve told him.

He turned as pale as the parsnips.

The novice returned to refill both their cups. They simultaneously took bracing gulps of cider.

After a moment, Adam murmured, "So ye know."

"What?" she whispered back at him. "That ye're a Rivenloch?"

Startled at her mention of his name, he let his knife slip, sending the roast slice out of the trencher and into her lap with a plop.

She squeaked in surprise and came to her feet.

The abbess scowled at her. "Sister Eve! Sit down. Behave yourself."

Eve blushed. She didn't bother explaining what had happened. But she made a particularly fierce glare at Adam.

And in an unladylike fit of revenge, she surreptitiously pushed the neeps to the edge of her trencher and flipped them into his lap.

He made a loud gasp that stopped the conversation around him.

"Is somethin' amiss?" the abbess asked.

"Nay, Reverend Mother," he said. "The neeps are just so delicious."

The abbess smiled. She didn't see the evil glint that appeared in his eyes when she looked away.

But Eve did. So she was only half-surprised when he subtly scooped a piece of wine-soaked pear into his palm and applied it under the table to Eve's thigh, mashing it against her habit for good measure.

She gritted her teeth, eyeing the weapons at her disposal.

She'd eaten half of her apple and onion coffyn. So she picked it up. Gazing off nonchalantly toward the far table, she turned it upside down and let the filling slowly drip down his shoulder.

"Ah!" he cried, jumping up as the slimy mess made its way down his sleeve.

Everyone in the Refectory froze.

Eve tried and failed to contain her laughter.

The abbess gave her a sharp look. "Have ye lost your wits, Sister?"

Mid-laugh, Eve felt something on her arm. Adam had smashed the rest of his coffyn on her sleeve.

Her jaw dropped. She couldn't believe he would do something so out of character in front of all these witnesses. Surely the abbess would realize he was not a monk now.

But if that was the war this scoundrel of a Rivenloch wanted to wage, Eve was there for it.

She picked up her dariole, scooped out the custard with her fingers, and smeared it on his face.

The abbess was beside herself. "Sister Eve! What the Devil?"

But Eve was too vexed to stop now. "How could ye let me believe ye were an outlaw?" she demanded.

Gasps of shock echoed in the hall.

"How could ye let me believe *ye* were an outlaw?" He wiped the custard from his face and smeared it on hers.

"An outlaw?" the abbess exclaimed. "What are ye talkin' about?"

Eve growled in fury. She wiped the custard off her cheek with her thumb and licked it off. It was actually very tasty. But she was more interested in dishing out just deserts.

She grabbed the bowl of butter and plopped it upside down onto his shoulder, twisting it for good measure.

"I couldn't very well tell ye I was a nun," she said. "Not after..." She stopped. She didn't dare confess her terrible sin.

He scooped up the butter and slathered it on the top of her wimple. "Don't ye think ye should have told me *before* we..." He too was unwilling to finish the sentence.

"Ye knew ye were ne'er goin' to marry me, ye bein' who ye are," she said. Now her voice was breaking, and she was miserable. She grabbed her slice of roast and dropped it down the front of his cassock.

"Marry?" the abbess blurted. "Who's talkin' about marryin'?"

Adam groaned with disgust as the roast slid down his chest and caught just above the cincture at his waist.

Eve continued. "Ye should ne'er have let me..." She shook her head, remembering their first tryst.

"Let ye? That's not how I remember it."

That wasn't how she remembered it either. She'd practically thrown herself at him. Still, it was unforgivable of him to bring it up in front of everyone.

All she could do in her defense was splash her cider in his face.

He sputtered in surprise and tossed his head, shaking the cider droplets from his beard. Then, with a narrow and determined gaze, he picked up his cup to return the favor.

Eve ducked out of the path just in time. The wave of cider sloshed past her and smacked into the face of the abbess.

For one terrible moment, time stopped. The abbess's face was frozen in a grimace of alarm and disgust. The nuns were petrified. The only sound in the room was the faint drip of ale rolling off the abbess's quivering chin onto the table.

Eve held her breath.

She expected the abbess would rise with injured dignity and speak in an imperial voice, commanding Adam to be gone and Eve to return to her cell.

Never in a million years did she expect the abbess to seek vengeance.

The indignant old woman swept up her own cup of ale in one angry claw and tossed its contents toward Adam.

Unfortunately, her aim was not very accurate. A small

portion splashed his brow. The rest splattered onto the nun beyond him.

The sister across the table from her broke into peals of laughter, which caused the affronted nun to throw half a buttered roll at her. The roll bounced off of her and landed on the bosom of the sister beside her. That sister shrieked in outrage, casting one parsnip at the tosser and another at the giggler for good measure.

Then the battle was on. One offended sister took revenge on the next. Smearing custard on veils. Pouring cider over wimples. Wiping verjuice on habits.

Soon the air was filled with flying neeps and sailing salat. Bounding rolls and hurled coffyns. Parsnips and pears flung like missiles from a catapult. The Refectory echoed with shrill screams of insult punctuated by raucous shouts of triumph.

All the while, even though for all intents and purposes, she'd started the melee, the abbess yelled, "Stop! Stop it, I say!"

It was no use. Chaos reigned. And Eve still had matters to settle.

"Ye deserted me," she shouted over the crowd, prodding Adam in the chest. "Ye let me believe ye wanted to marry me, and then ye left to spy for the king."

He grabbed her finger to stop her pokes. "Ye let me believe ye wanted to marry *me*. But once ye were given the chance, ye went straight back to the convent."

She snatched her finger away. "Ye betrayed me. Ye told me ye were goin' to help me find justice for the alewife. But ye ne'er intended to help at all, did ye?"

"I did help her," he said, snapping up a napkin to dry his beard. "I gave the alewife my reward."

"Your reward for what?" she said, dodging a half-eaten roll someone threw. "Capturin' me and tellin' the king I was Fergus's 'spy'?"

A stray splat of custard hit his shoulder. "For endin' the war."

She grew still. "Ye ended the war?"

"Aye. Why do ye think I'm here now?"

"The siege is o'er?" That was admittedly impressive.

"Aye." A pear flew past his head.

"How did ye do it?"

He sniffed. "I tricked Fergus into surrenderin' ere the king laid siege."

That made sense. But not all of it did.

She picked up her napkin and swabbed at the sticky custard on her cheek. Then she narrowed her eyes. "Why did ye let the king take me prisoner? And put me in shackles?"

"I was tryin' to keep ye safe, out o' harm's way. I knew the king wouldn't harm ye." His face took on a sad demeanor then. "And how did ye thank me? By breakin' free and fleein' across Scotland, completely out o' my protection."

They were at an impasse.

It seemed they'd both meant well.

But how could they get past the deception they'd used on each other? The falsehoods they'd told? How could they forgive the betrayals?

One couldn't have a relationship built on lies.

She had to take off her mask and tell him the truth.

The food skirmish was coming to a close now. Not because the nuns had come to their senses and realized the childishness of their behavior. And not because the abbess had demanded a ceasefire. But because they were running out of munitions.

Still, as Eve perused the Refectory, she saw breathless, bright-eyed, pink-cheeked nuns who hadn't had so much fun in months. And that made her realize this really had never been her world. Why else had she spent so much time escaping it?

"This is your doin', Sister Eve," the abbess accused, gesturing to the mess of neeps and pears, meat and rolls, custard and cider strewn about the tables and floor. "What do ye have to say for yourself?"

Eve had much to say. But it was meant for Adam. She faced him, placed a hand on his chest, and gazed into his deep, warm, inviting eyes.

"After I met ye, Adam, I decided to give up the veil," she confessed.

The other nuns whispered in wonder.

She continued, speaking her truth from the heart. "Once I felt what 'twas like to love and be loved, to not be...invisible, I knew I could no longer hide behind convent walls, pretendin' I had no worldly desires." The room silenced. "I meant to break the news to my father, come what may, and make a life with the man with whom I'd fallen in love."

Adam's eyes melted, and he clasped his hand over hers, against his heart.

"And I planned to make a life with you, Eve, damn my clan's demands," he told her. "Once I met you and found a kindred spirit...a woman who brought me joy and life and love...a woman who *saw* me for the first time—not as a Rivenloch, but as a man—I wasn't about to let anything stand in the way."

The nuns gasped at the revelation he was a Rivenloch and then sighed at his romantic words.

She smiled up at him, her eyes watering. "I don't blame ye for takin' my virtue. I volunteered it. But ye convinced me ye wanted to marry me."

He nodded. "I shouldn't ne'er have trysted with ye. But I did want to marry ye. I still do."

Her heart was pounding so loudly with the rush of love flowing through her veins, she didn't realize how deathly quiet the hall had gone.

In the silence, the abbess addressed the nuns, who were shocked speechless by the confession.

"And so ends our Martinmas morality play," the abbess intoned, giving Eve a stern sideways glance before initiating a round of applause. "So ye see, novitiates, this is why ye must always battle diligently against the Devil and carnal desire."

EPILOGUE

Castle Rivenloch
Winter

Adam had told Eve there was nothing like a Rivenloch wedding feast, and he was right. It didn't matter that it was the dead of winter. The great hall was full of candles and music and merrymaking, crowded with clanfolk, friends, and neighbors.

All of the local and many of the distant Rivenloch clan attended the wedding.

Adam's sister Feiyan brought her new bairn all the way from Darragh. She recognized Eve as the nun from the convent, but couldn't believe she was also the archer from the tournament.

Adam's cousin Jenefer couldn't tell Eve was the same person as the French lad she'd shot against at Perth.

His other cousin Hallie thought Feiyan and Jenefer were fools to mistake lovely Eve for a male archer, but she didn't remember her as the nun who'd been at Perth.

It still confounded Adam how his clan could be so gulled by someone he considered uniquely beautiful. But Eve was grateful that, for him, she was never invisible.

Isabel, the romantic young lass Eve had met before,

delighted in showing off the decorations she'd arranged. Beeswax candles lit up every corner. Fragrant herbs were strewn atop the rushes on the floor. Swags of holly and ivy decked the walls. Even the hounds wore sprigs of holly on their collars.

Isabel's clever brother Ian had devised a special final dish in honor of the newlyweds. It was a sugar subtletie sculpted in the form of a castle that he claimed was—just like Adam and Eve—"not all it appeared to be." When he gave Eve a tiny silver axe to crack the delicate exterior, the sugar castle broke apart, revealing a golden dragon made of almond paste and dyed with saffron.

Everyone cheered. No one was more impressed than Eve.

The Rivenloch warriors—male and female—were anything but shy. They regaled each other with tales of adventure and full-throated boasts, each one more improbable than the next.

The hounds barked in excitement over the smells of roasting meat and slavered at the sight of stripped bones that would soon be theirs.

The musicians played over the conversations, plucking a lute, blowing a sackbut, beating a tabor, and finally resorting to the raucous bagpipes in order to be heard.

Now the feast was nearly over. The trestle tables in the great hall looked like a battlefield. Bones littered the trenchers. Splatters of red wine and brown sauce stained the tablecloth. Knives were tossed carelessly onto the platters. Finally, after hours of course after course, the white linen napkins had been thrown down like banners of surrender.

But Eve felt uneasy. There was one thing more to come. And she dreaded it.

From Adam's cousins, she knew all about the traditions the Rivenlochs had carried down from their Viking ancestors. Training women for battle. Using longboats as funeral pyres. Bathing every day. Telling stories about gods and goddesses, fantastic beasts and mythical hammers. Young Ian had spoken eagerly about the sunwheel he was building to roll down the hill in celebration of Yule.

According to wedding custom, the ladies always undressed the bride for bed. The men carried the groom up to her and put him in bed with her. Then they waited outside for proof of the consummation—bloody linens.

The last thing Eve wanted to do was disappoint her new clan by refusing one of their traditional rituals. But it seemed barbaric. Humiliating. And, unfortunately, too revealing of the truth.

Adam seemed to sense her disquiet.

"What's wrong?" he murmured.

"Everyone knows I was raised in a convent," she whispered back.

"Aye?"

She glanced involuntarily toward the steps leading to the bedchamber Isabel had shown her. The bedchamber that had been prepared with fresh linens decked with flower petals for the newly married couple.

"Mmm," he said. "Are you worried about the wedding night rites?"

She winced in apology. "I don't want to ruin anythin'. Your clan has been so kind to me. And I know how important tradition is to them. But the linens won't be bloody, Adam. They'll know I didn't come to this marriage a virgin."

Adam gave her a wise and sober nod.

But inside he was grinning.

He doubted many Rivenloch brides had come to their marriages as virgins. His clan wouldn't dare demand anyone go through such archaic rites. As Laird Deirdre had long ago decreed, such traditions were an abomination, an insult to women, and the ruin of perfectly good linens.

His clan *would*, however, mercilessly harass the newly-weds. And he didn't want to give them the pleasure. Not on his wedding night. Not when his bride sat beside him, looking up at him with dewy apprehension in her eyes.

He wanted her all to himself.

"Damn tradition," he told her. "I have an idea."

Adam figured it would be the clan's own fault if they let the bride and groom out of their sight and they happened to disappear.

Perhaps if his cousin Brand hadn't been helping himself to so many portions of beef, if Logan hadn't been bellowing out his heroic tales, if Hew hadn't been fondling his new wife under the table, and if Aunt Helena hadn't been quarreling with Uncle Colin, they might have noticed when Adam stole upstairs and Eve slipped out of the great hall.

Stuffing the goose-down pallet through the high bedchamber window was not an easy feat, especially with Eve watching from below. But Adam managed to get it past the shutters and heave it onto the sill. Then he pushed it over until it toppled onto the sod.

Eve waved up at him, letting him know it was undamaged.

Then he grabbed a pair of plaids and came downstairs. Creeping back through the crowd, he exited into the courtyard.

Together, he and Eve wrested the pallet across the courtyard to the stables. He'd seen the stable lad at the feast, so the outbuildings would be deserted and relatively warm.

At one end of the stables was a pile of clean straw. He dragged the pallet on top of it. There were horses at the other end. But they were calm, likely used to visitors having midnight trysts.

Once he closed the door, it was as black as a cave.

They wasted no time, divesting of their wedding attire in the dark and stripping down to their leines.

"I can't see anythin'," Eve complained.

"Well then, my love, I suppose we'll have to go by touch," he replied, reaching out to sweep his hand across her jaw and into her hair.

"Will we?" she murmured.

With one hand, she patted at his chest, feeling her way up to his shoulder and then inward to his neck.

But while he was distracted by that hand, she clapped her other hand boldly over his braies.

He sucked in a breath of pleased surprise.

"What's this?" she teased. "I can see naught in this darkness."

He didn't have the wit to reply at the moment. Instead, he closed his eyes with a groan and caught the back of her neck, pulling her close for a kiss.

She tasted of wine and sugar, almonds and desire, an intoxicating combination that made him harden at once.

She sighed into his mouth, and he let the fingers of his free hand drift down her body, sowing heat through her thin leine. He brushed over her supple breasts. Gently squeezed her nipples. Then ventured farther to caress the lovely planes of her abdomen.

But her hand was doing amazing things to the questing beast between his thighs. It ached with need, pulsing beneath her palm, eager to be free of its linen confines. He needed to couple with her...now...before he recklessly spilled his seed.

So, disengaging from the kiss, he swept her off her feet, laid her out on the pallet, and peeled off her leine. Using one of the plaids to keep her warm, he settled himself between her knees and burrowed underneath.

Of all the succulent dishes at their wedding feast, this one was the most appetizing.

His new bride, Lady Eve la Nuit of Rivenloch, was a dish both tempting and filling. Earthy and ambrosial. Wholesome and decadent. Teasing open the delicate shell of her keep to expose the roaring dragon of her climax was delicious and satisfying.

As she shuddered with release beneath him, he felt need swell his loins. And though he wished he could make the night last forever, he knew relief would come for him quickly as well.

Eve wanted him. Now.

She reached for him, sinking her fingertips into his shoulders to urge him upwards.

"Wait," he said on a chuckle. "I'm still clothed."

"Hurry, husband."

"As you wish, wife."

She heard him wrench down his braies and tear off his leine. Then she felt the heat of him as he hovered above her.

His fingers sought out her womanly folds. She clasped his firm, velvety staff in her hand, guiding him.

He groaned as he entered her, and she arched as he filled her with exhilarating warmth. Their union felt so right. So destined. So perfect.

Because she was blind to his beautiful face in the dark, her other senses compensated, drinking in all the smells, sensations, flavors, and sounds around her.

She smelled the fresh hay and earthy horseflesh of the stables, as well as Adam's own masculine scent—a subtle blend of steel and sweat, leather and cinnamon, smoke and woodruff.

His breath rasped against her ear, and his sensual groans brought out the animal instincts in her body as she thrust against him in carnal pleasure.

He kissed her, opening her mouth to feast with abandon. He tasted sweet and intoxicating, like the mead they'd drunk to celebrate their vows.

Every nerve in her body felt alive, awakened by the searing contact with his flesh as he drove smoothly into her, like a dagger into a sheath. Her blood pulsed. Her skin flushed. Her head swam in a dreamy cloud of longing.

Together they scaled the walls of passion. Climbed a mountain of desire. Flew among the stars of heaven.

When they arrived at desire's destination, they cried out in triumph and ecstasy. And as Eve gazed blindly in the dark—into the face no one else ever recognized, the face she had memorized as well as her own—she realized she would indeed find her Greater Purpose. With Adam.

Afterwards, spent, he slumped off of her, and she collapsed back onto the pallet, breathing heavily and grinning like a fool.

He pulled the plaids over them and tucked her in. "Will you forgive me for bringing you to the stables for our wedding night?"

She laughed. "I'll tryst with ye in the stables *every* night if ye'll keep a goose-down pallet in here."

His laughter was as pleasing as a lute to her ears. She could no longer feel the chill winter air. Wrapped in their plaids and nestled together in the straw of the stables, she glowed from the warmth of their lovemaking.

But surely his clan would find them soon.

"Are ye sure Laird Deirdre won't be angry we left?" she asked.

"I'm sure."

"If the clan wants proof I came to ye a virgin..."

He chuckled. "There's no need to fret." Then he whispered, "To be honest, I bet I can count the number of virgin brides in my clan on one hand."

"Adam la Nuit," she scolded.

"'Tis true. The Rivenloch women are a hot-blooded tribe. My own mother—"

He stopped abruptly.

She'd heard it too. A sound coming from outside the stables. A person.

Panicked, she clutched the plaid to her chest.

He put a finger to her lips, indicating silence.

They were invisible in the dark. They were safe. So far.

But if whoever lurked outside came in, and if they carried a candle...

The door creaked open. Eve held her breath.

There was no candle. They couldn't see her. She couldn't see them.

Whoever it was entered and headed for the horses. When they walked, she could hear the squeak of leather and the clink of chain mail. The intruder was clad for battle.

While Eve breathed soundlessly, one of the horses whickered softly, and she could hear the stranger putting a saddle on the beast.

"Easy, lass," the intruder said. "You and I, we're going on a long journey."

Eve didn't recognize the young man's voice.

Adam did. "Just where are you going, Brand?"

"Bloody shite!" his cousin cried, recoiling so suddenly it startled the horse. "Adam? Is that you? What the hell are you doing here?"

"I could ask you the same," Adam said.

"Don't you have a wedding to attend to?" he challenged, calming the horse. "Or are you hiding out from your bride?"

"I'm here," Eve said, startling him again.

"Holy Mother of...!"

"Sorry," Eve mumbled.

"God's teeth, Adam," Brand said in disgust. "Is this your

idea of a wedding night? The stables? There's a perfectly good goose-down pallet in the wedding bedchamber."

"Not anymore," Adam said.

Eve couldn't help but chuckle at that.

Brand made a sound of exasperation. "You know, the laird has the whole clan searching for the two of you."

"Is that why you're saddling up in full armor and going on a long journey?" Adam asked. "To look for us?"

Brand's hesitation was damning.

Adam realized Brand hadn't come to the stables looking for his missing cousin. He had his own motives.

"All this chaos makes it rather convenient for you, doesn't it?" Adam said.

"What do you mean?"

"'Tis much easier for you to leave Rivenloch and ride away in the dead of night if the clan is busy looking for me."

Brand didn't reply.

"So where are you going?" Adam asked.

"'Tisn't your affair."

"Of course, 'tis my affair. You're my kin," Adam said. "I've always looked after you."

"Not this time," he replied.

Adam suddenly heard his cousin with different ears. Brand might be two years younger than him, but somehow he'd become a man in his own right.

Still, Adam couldn't let Brand just disappear.

"I don't intend to let you wander off without letting anyone know where you're going or when you'll return."

"You mean like *you* do?"

That struck him as powerfully as the lance blow to the chest Brand had given him in the tournament. But he wasn't wrong.

Adam sighed. "Well played, cousin."

"So you'll let me go?"

"On two conditions."

Brand blew out a vexed breath. "What?"

"You tell *me* where you're going. And you won't breathe a word about...this."

He hoped to spare Eve the embarrassment of an awkward wedding night. Bedding his new wife in the stables was not something he wanted bandied about the castle.

"Why would I agree to that?" Brand smirked. "What's in it for *me*?"

"I won't run to your mother and tell her you've gone."

Brand took a moment to think it over. "Maybe *you* won't. What about *her*?"

Eve replied. "I won't breathe a word either."

"Why should I believe you?" Brand asked.

Adam's blood boiled at the insult to his bride. But then he recalled it wasn't long ago that Brand had deemed lasses utterly useless and undeserving of his notice.

Before Adam could reply, Eve answered. "I was a nun. Nuns don't lie."

Adam knew that wasn't true. Not at all. Eve had told dozens of lies. Including this one.

But it was more useful to back her up. "Bloody hell, Brand. You'd question the word of a woman of God?"

Brand let out a long-suffering sigh. "Fine," he conceded. "I'm going to Berwick."

"Berwick?" Berwick was a town on the border between England and Scotland. A war-torn place that was always changing loyalties. With a castle currently used to imprison the king's enemies. "Why?"

"The king has awarded me my first command as a knight," he said proudly.

Adam raised his brows, impressed. "And you didn't want the laird to know?"

"She knows. She commanded me not to go," he grumbled. "She said she'd work out a replacement."

"Why would she do that?"

Eve guessed, "Is it too dangerous?"

"Dangerous," Brand scoffed, taking offense at her words. "Danger is my battle cry."

Adam suspected Eve was rolling her eyes at that.

He told Brand, "There's usually a good reason behind the laird's commands."

"Good reason. Pah!"

"Did she say why?"

"Because I'm second in line, Adam," he bit out. "I'm meant to be laird if anything happens to Gellir. She expects me to stay safe and warm and coddled at Rivenloch while Gellir goes on adventure everywhere."

Adam understood. Brand was bitter. Rightly so.

"Faith!" Eve exclaimed. "That's not fair."

"Right?" Brand said. "Why did I bother becoming a great warrior if my talents are going to be wasted, rotting away in a moldering keep?"

Rivenloch could hardly be called a moldering keep. But Adam got his point.

"Ye have a Greater Purpose," Eve said.

"Aye, a Greater Purpose," Brand echoed. "Which is why I need to go. And why I'm forced to steal off in the middle of the night."

"I'll let you go," Adam decided. "But promise me something."

"What's that?"

"You'll send word to the clan once you arrive safely."

Eve chimed in, "And when ye return, ye'll share your adventures."

"Fine. Good." Adam led the horse toward the stable door. "I have to leave. Now. They may be distracted, searching for you, but they'll come to the stables eventually."

"Do ye have everythin' ye need for the journey?" Eve asked.

"Aye." Then he chuckled. "I don't have Adam's bottomless satchel. But I did steal extra portions at supper."

"Good luck, cousin."

They wished Brand well and saw him safely on his way.

When he was gone, Adam said, "My cousin is right. We should make haste. They'll be here any moment."

As they quickly donned their clothes, Eve asked, "Do you think he'll be all right?"

"Brand? He'll fare better against the English than he will against his mother."

"We're still goin' to follow him, though, aye?"

"Of course."

"Good. Berwick sounds like the perfect place for a honeymoon," she gushed. "Full of romance. Adventure. Danger."

"That *is* Brand's battle cry."

"And maybe our Greater Purpose?"

"No doubt," he said. "Come on. We'll have to pack for the journey."

"Right." Eve wondered, "I don't suppose that famous satchel o' yours is big enough to carry a goose-down pallet?"

The End

THANK YOU FOR READING MY BOOK!

Did you enjoy it? If so, I hope you'll post a review to let others know! There's no greater gift you can give an author than spreading your love of her books.

It's truly a pleasure and a privilege to be able to share my stories with you. Knowing that my words have made you laugh, sigh, or touched a secret place in your heart is what keeps the wind beneath my wings. I hope you enjoyed our brief journey together, and may ALL of your adventures have happy endings!

If you'd like to keep in touch, feel free to sign up for my monthly e-newsletter at www.glynnis.net, and you'll be the first to find out about my new releases, special discounts, prizes, promotions, and more!

If you want to keep up with my daily escapades:

Friend me at facebook.com/GlynnisCampbell

Like my Page at bit.ly/GlynnisCampbellFBPage

Follow me on Bluesky @GlynnisCampbell

Follow me on Instagram @glynniscampbell

Follow me on Goodreads @glynnis_campbell

Follow me on Bookbub @glynnis-campbell

And if you're a super fan, join

facebook.com/GCReadersClan

ABOUT THE AUTHOR

I'm a *USA Today* bestselling author of swashbuckling action-adventure historical romances, mostly set in Scotland, with more than 25 award-winning books published in six languages.

But before my role as a medieval matchmaker, I sang in *The Pinups,* an all-girl band on CBS Records, and provided voices for the MTV animated series *The Maxx,* Blizzard's *Diablo* and *Starcraft* video games, and *Star Wars* audiobooks.

I'm the wife of a rock star (if you want to know which one, contact me) and the mother of two young adults. I do my best writing on cruise ships, in Scottish castles, on my husband's tour bus, and at home in my sunny southern California garden.

I love transporting readers to a place where the bold heroes have endearing flaws, the women are stronger than they look, the land is lush and untamed, and chivalry is alive and well!

I'm always delighted to hear from my readers, so please feel free to email me at glynnis@glynnis.net. And if you're a super-fan who would like to join my inner circle, sign up at http://www.facebook.com/GCReadersClan, where you'll get glimpses behind the scenes, sneak peeks of works-in-progress, and extra special surprises.